“If you like a fun tale set in a
up the Destroyermen series and kick back and enjoy.”
—SFRevu

Praise for the Destroyermen Series

Iron Gray Sea

“With each novel, this new world comes into sharper focus. . . . Readers who enjoy S. M. Stirling, Jules Verne, and Harry Turtledove will find this series enjoyable.” —SFRevu

“*Iron Gray Sea* is a great gift for fans of alternate history, sort-of World War II action, and time-slip/parallel worlds science fiction.” —Kings River Life Magazine

Firestorm

“The action . . . rarely slackens. . . . Intriguing what-ifs and convolutions by the boatload combine with churning, bloodthirsty warfare.” —*Kirkus Reviews*

“The fact that Anderson has a gift for complex plot and dialogue and a fabulous sense of humor makes reading his work a fun and guilt-free pleasure.”
—*North County Times* (CA)

Rising Tides

“Anderson continues to broaden the scope of the story, but never lets the philosophy drown out the action.”
—*Publishers Weekly*

Distant Thunders

“The fun of watching eager aviators take to the air in carved wooden aircraft leavens the nostalgic sense of worlds being left behind and cultures forced by war to undergo unpleasant changes. Anderson raises questions about the morality of chemical warfare, genocide, and summary execution in wartime while holding out the possibility of diplomacy with relentless killers.” —*Publishers Weekly*

“Action sci-fi doesn't get significantly better than this. . . . Anderson launches a new Destroyermen trilogy . . . with this complex but fine and fast-paced tale.” —*Booklist*

continued . . .

"An action-packed entry with strong, relevant moral questions about the rules of combat engagement running throughout the adrenaline-pumping story line. Taylor Anderson is one of the best at military science fiction, as his plots combine cerebral, thought-provoking issues within a great adventure tale; the alternate realm of the Destroyermen saga is worth the journey." —Alternative Worlds

"Simply put, this is great stuff. . . . Anderson does a spectacular job in keeping the history, flair, and can-do attitude of the aptly named 'greatest generation' integrated with an alien world full of unknown pitfalls and dangers. The characters are well developed and easy to identify with and care about, and the story stays fresh and exciting. . . . Read it—you won't be disappointed." —Fresh Fiction

Maelstrom

"Anderson's trilogy of cross-time naval action, Destroyermen, maintains its high quality to the end of this thundering concluding volume. . . . The climactic battle is long, bloody, and suspenseful almost to the last. The ending here doesn't quash hopes that we may see Anderson's displaced World War II Destroyermen again." —*Booklist*

"The pace was fast and kept me wanting to read just a couple more pages. . . . The ensemble cast has a little something for everyone. From a heroic leader and a tortured enemy to power-crazed enemies and [a] wisecracking crew. If you like a fun tale set in a well-developed world, pick up the Destroyermen series and kick back and enjoy." —SFRevu

"With its blending of historical fact, thrilling battle scenes, and science fiction, *Maelstrom* is a novel that anyone who loves reading both military and alternative history SF books will want to add to their libraries." —BookSpot Central

"Experienced military SF readers will enjoy the attention to technical and historical detail." —*Publishers Weekly*

Crusade

"Even better than the excellent *Into the Storm* . . . intelligent action, more skillful handling of a very large cast, and an obstinately maintained refusal to slow the pace."
—*Booklist* (starred review)

"Anderson throws in tense land battles against overwhelming odds, a massive typhoon, and a phenomenal aerial duel, but despite the pyrotechnics, at heart this novel is about how honor and ideals can bend or break under the stressful, life-and-death conditions of total war." —*Publishers Weekly*

"*Crusade* continues an entertaining story arc and exploration of war, honor, and evolution on a world similar to our own. Taylor Anderson is emerging, with two novels in quick succession only months apart, as a solid and imaginative storyteller." —SFFWorld

Into the Storm

"Taylor Anderson has brought a fresh new perspective to the tale of cross-time shipwreck. The action is gripping and riveting . . . the characters are sharply drawn and very human—or inhuman, for two interesting species of nonhuman sapiens are included—and the description vivid. I dipped my toe into *Destroyermen: Into the Storm* and when I looked up, it was two in the morning and a working day had vanished! Anderson is a new talent to watch, and I look forward to the unfolding of this series and his subsequent work."
—S. M. Stirling, author of *Lord of Mountains*

"Taylor Anderson and his patched-up four-stackers have steamed to the forefront of alternative history. All aboard for a cracking great read!"
—E. E. Knight, author of *Appalachian Overthrow*

"Anderson's outstanding first novel combines alternate history and seafaring in a way that recalls S. M. Stirling's splendid Island in the Sea of Time trilogy. . . . Nonstop action . . . works out in the context of extremely high-level achievement at both world building and characterization."
—*Booklist*

"Anderson's alternate history debut combines a love for military history with a keen eye for natural science. Reddy is a likable protagonist, epitomizing the best of the wartime American military." —*Library Journal*

"Paying homage to such tales as *A Connecticut Yankee in King Arthur's Court*, *Robinson Crusoe*, and William R. Forstchen and Greg Morrison's *Crystal Warriors*, Anderson expands on familiar concepts with high-tension nautical battles and skillful descriptions of period attitudes and dialogue." —*Publishers Weekly*

The Destroyermen Series

Into the Storm
Crusade
Maelstrom
Distant Thunders
Rising Tides
Firestorm
Iron Gray Sea
Storm Surge

DESTROYERMEN

IRON GRAY SEA

TAYLOR ANDERSON

A ROC BOOK

ROC
Published by the Penguin Group
Penguin Group (USA) Inc., 375 Hudson Street,
New York, New York 10014, USA

USA | Canada | UK | Ireland | Australia | New Zealand | India | South Africa | China

Penguin Books Ltd., Registered Offices: 80 Strand, London WC2R 0RL, England
For more information about the Penguin Group visit penguin.com.

Published by Roc, an imprint of New American Library, a division of Penguin Group (USA) Inc. Previously published in a Roc hardcover edition.

First Roc Mass Market Printing, July 2013
10 9 8 7 6 5 4 3 2 1

ISBN 978-0-451-41423-6

Printed in the United States of America

To: My much-loved and admired uncles, Raymond and Richard, so recently gone.

Uncle Raymond always said, in his gentle, smiling way, that Navy food did him far more harm than the enemy. Whether that was true or not, we always knew that Uncle Richard had a harder war in many ways. He didn't smile nearly as much—for a very long time.

ACKNOWLEDGMENTS

As always, thanks to my friend and agent, Russell Galen. Thanks also to Ginjer Buchanan and all the delightful folks at Roc. My dad, Dr. Don Anderson, tries to keep me from shocking myself with "electrical contrivances," and Jeanette Anderson (better known as "Mom"), still churns through my first, roughest drafts. (Hugo Award winner!) Kate Baker selflessly manages my Web site in spite of her harrowing schedule. Col. (select) Dave Leedom, USAFR, CO of the 93rd bomb squadron, remains my primary light-aircraft instructor (ironic, considering what he flies for his "day job"). I happily welcome Capt. Dan Dwyer, USN, a career naval officer and naval aviator with over 1,100 carrier landings, to my bull pen of advisors. Pete Hodges is "the Chemist." Eben Bradstreet, Wayne Hawkins, Chief Kent, John Schmuke, and many others help me keep the "beasties" fresh on my Web site, and (Bad) Dennis, Mark, Mike, Lynn, Robin, Carey, Andy—and Jim, of course—along with others I've mentioned before, keep me awash in character-inspiring antics. I know Jim is very short, and therefore generally farther away from flying targets, but someone really should have told him that Henry rifles were not specifically designed for wing shooting. But hey, if it works . . .

There are *so many* people I want to thank for their friendship and support, people I likely never would have known if I hadn't chosen to write this *particular* tale. Active and former military heroes from every branch of the service—and numerous countries—have volunteered their comments, experiences, and technical expertise, and I honor and appreciate them more than I can say. A worrisome number of them remain in harm's way on a regular basis, or still suffer from their wounds. My family and I are ever mindful of this, and though I can't possibly list them all, I'm confident they know who they are. In that vein, I would like to bring attention to the U.S. Veterans Museum in Granbury, Texas. Tom, Cordell, Lawrence, and (until he recently rejoined his lost shipmates) Al Getchel have done their best to honor each of America's veterans, of all her wars, every day.

CAST OF CHARACTERS

Members of the Grand Alliance

Aboard USS *Walker*, (DD-163), Wickes (Little) Class "four-stacker" destroyer. Twin screw, steam turbines, 1,200 tons, 314' L—30' W. 3 x 4"-50 + 1 x 4.7" dual purpose. 4 x 25 mm Type-96 AA. 4 x .30 cal MG + 2 x .50 cal MG. Top speed (as designed) 35 knots. 112 officers and enlisted (current), including Lemurians (L).

(L)—*Lemurians, or Mi-Anaaka, are bipedal, somewhat felinoid people who inhabit the region in and around the Malay Barrier. It has been proposed that they are descended from the giant lemurs of Madagascar.*

Lt. Cmdr. Matthew Patrick Reddy, USNR—Commanding. CINCAF—(Commander in Chief of All Allied Forces).

Cmdr. Brad "Spanky" McFarlane—Exec. Minister of Naval Engineering.

Nurse Lt. Sandra Tucker—Minister of Medicine.

Chack-Sab At (L)—Bosun's Mate (Marine Major).

Lt. Tab-At (L)—Engineering Officer.

Lt. Norman Kutas—First Officer.

Lt. Sonny Campeti—Gunnery Officer.

Lt. Ed Palmer—Signals.

Chief Bosun Fitzhugh Gray—Bosun of the Navy or Super Bosun. Highest-ranking NCO in the

Alliance and commander of Captain's Guard. Currently Assistant Damage Control Officer.

Chief Bosun's Mate Carl Bashear.

Chief Quartermaster Patrick "Paddy" Rosen.

Chief Gunner's Mate Paul Stites.

Gunner's Mate Pak-Ras-Ar "Pack Rat" (L).

Jeek (L)—Flight Crew Chief, Special Air Division.

Earl Lanier—Cook.

Johnny Parks—Machinist's Mate.

Juan Marcos—Officer's Steward.

Diania—Steward's Assistant.

Taarba-Kaar "Tabasco" (L)—Mess Attendant.

Wallace Fairchild—Sonarman.

Min-Sakir "Minnie" (L)—Bridge Talker.

First Fleet (Assigned to the Western Theater, or "Grik Front")

Admiral Keje-Fris-Ar (L)—(CINCWEST)

Aboard USNR *Salissa (Big Sal)* (CV-1), aircraft carrier/tender, converted from seagoing Lemurian Home.

1st Naval Air Wing: 1st, 2nd, 3rd Bomb Squadrons; 1st, 2nd Pursuit Squadrons.

5th and 8th Bomb Squadrons, and 6th Pursuit Squadron from *Humfra-Dar* (remains of 2nd Naval Air Wing) attached.

Atlaan-Fas (L)—Commanding.

Lt. Sandy Newman—Exec.

Surgeon Cmdr. Kathy McCoy.

Captain Jis-Tikkar "Tikker" (L)—COFO (Commander of Flight Operations).

Lt. Mark Leedom—Assistant COFO.

"**Tacos**" (L)—Leedom's backseater.

Aboard USNR *Arracca* (CV-3) aircraft carrier/tender converted from seagoing Lemurian Home. (Specifications similar to *Salissa* except for armament, which includes 50 x 50 pdrs + 4 x 100 pdrs only.)

5th Naval Air Wing

Tassana-Ay-Arracca (L)—High Chief. Commanding.

Frigates (DDs) attached to First Fleet

USS *Dowden**

Captain James "Jim" Ellis—Des-Div 4 Commodore. Commanding.

Lt. Niaal-Ras-Kavaat (L)—Exec.

USS *Nakja-Mur**

Captain Jarrik-Fas (L)—Commanding.

USS *Kas-Ra-Ar***

Captain Mescus-Ricum (L)—Commanding.

USS *Davis****

USS *Ramic-Sa-Ar**

USS *Felts***

USS *Haakar-Faask***

USS *Naga****

USS *Bowles****

USS *Saak-Fas****

USS *Clark***

*Dowden Class—(Square rig steamer, 1,500 tons, 185' L—34' W, 20 x 32 pdrs, 218 officers and enlisted).
**Haakar-Faask Class—(Square rig steamer, 1,600 tons, 200' L—36' W, 20 x 32 pdrs, 226 officers and enlisted).
***Scott Class—(Square rig steamer, 1,800 tons, 210' L—40' W, 20 x 50 pdrs, 260 officers and enlisted).

First Fleet Expeditionary Force (as reorganized):

To promote simplicity, all Lemurian and, ultimately, Allied armies are organized as follows: two hundred to five hundred troops form a battalion. Two battalions form a regiment. Two or more regiments *can* constitute a division. Two or more divisions may constitute a corps.

Pete Alden—General of the Army and Marines. Commanding.

I Corps

General Lord Muln-Rolak (L)—Corps commander.

Hij-Geerki—Rolak's "pet" Grik, captured at Rangoon.

1ST "GALLA" DIVISION

General Taa-leen (L)—Commanding.

Colonel Enaak (L) (5th Maa-ni-la Cavalry)—Exec.

1st Marines; 5th, 6th, 7th, 10th Baalkpan.

2ND DIVISION

General Rin-Taaka-Ar (L)—Commanding.

Major Simon "Simy" Gutfeld (3rd Marines)—Exec.

1st, 2nd Maa-ni-la; 4th, 6th, 7th Aryaal.

II Corps

General-Queen Protector Safir Maraan (L)—Commanding.

3RD DIVISION

General Daanis (L)—Commanding.

Colonel Mersaak (L)—"The 600" (B'mbaado Regiment composed of Silver and Black Battalions), Exec.

3rd Baalkpan; 3rd , 10th B'mbaado; 5th Sular.

5TH DIVISION

General Faan-Ma-Mar (L)—Commanding.

Colonel William "Billy" Flynn—1st Amalgamated (Flynn's Rangers), Exec.

1st Battalion, 2nd Marines, **Captain Bekiaa-Sab-At** (L).

6th Maa-ni-la Cavalry, **Captain Saachic** (L) 1st Sular.

6TH DIVISION

General Grisa—Commanding.

5th, 6th B'mbaado; 1st, 2nd, 9th Aryaal; 3rd Sular*; 3rd Maa-ni-la Cavalry.

III Corps

9TH AND 11TH DIVISIONS

Including: 2nd, 3rd Maa-ni-la; 8th Baalkpan; 7th, 8th Maa-ni-la; 10th Aryaal.

At Andaman Island

USS *Donaghey* (Square rig, 1,200 tons, 168' L—33' W, 24 x 18 pdrs, 200 officers and enlisted). Sole survivor of first new construction. Undergoing major overhaul and reconstruction as of December 25, 1943.

Cmdr. Greg Garrett—Commanding.

Lt. Saama-Kera "Sammy" (L)—Exec. (formerly of *Tolson*).

Lt. (jg) Wendel "Smitty" Smith—Gunnery Officer.

USS ***Tassat********* (Undergoing repairs after zep attack.)

Cmdr. Muraak-Saanga (L)—Commanding (former *Donaghey* exec. and sailing master).

USS ***Scott********** (Undergoing repairs after zep attack.)

Cmdr. Cablaas-Rag-Laan (L)—Commanding.

In Baalkpan

Adar (L)—High Chief and Sky Priest of Baalkpan; COTGA (Chairman of the Grand Alliance).

Cmdr. Alan Letts—Chief of Staff; Minister of Industry; Chief of Division of Strategic Logistics.

Cmdr. Perry Brister—Minister of Defensive and Industrial Works.

Cmdr. Steve "Sparks" Riggs—Minister of Communications and Electrical Contrivances.

Lt. Cmdr. Bernard Sandison—Acting Minister of Ordnance.

Captain Risa-Sab-At (L) (Chack's sister)—Building Marine commando unit.

Cmdr. Russ Chapelle—Awaiting new ship.

Chief Electrician Rolando "Ronson" Rodriguez.

Sister Audry—Benedictine nun.

Surgeon Cmdr. Karen Theimer Letts—Assistant Minister of Medicine.

Surgeon Lieutenant Pam Cross.

Jeff Brooks—Sonarman, Anti-Mountain Fish Countermeasures (AMF-DIC).

Pepper (L)—Black-and-white Lemurian keeper of the Castaway Cook (Busted Screw).

Isak Rueben—One of the Mice assigned to refit of *Santa Catalina*.

Cmdr. Simon Herring—Formerly ONI; to be assigned.

Leading Seaman Henry Stokes, HMAS *Perth*—To be assigned.

Gunnery Sergeant Arnold Horn—Formerly in 2nd of the 4th Marines; to be assigned.

Lance Corporal Ian Miles—Formerly in 2nd of the 4th Marines; to be assigned.

Lieutenant Conrad Diebel—To be assigned.

***Fristar* Home**—nominally, if reluctantly, allied cannon-armed Home.

Anai-Sa (L)—High Chief.

Army and Naval Air Corps Training Center, Kaufman Field, Baalkpan

4th, 7th Bomb Squadrons; 3rd, 4th, 5th Pursuit in extra training.

Colonel Ben Mallory—Commanding.

Lt. (jg) Suaak-Pas-Ra "Soupy" (L).

2nd Lt. Niaa-Saa "Shirley" (L).

S. Sergeant Cecil Dixon.

USS *Santa Catalina* (general cargo). Triple expansion steam, oil fired, 6,000 tons, 420' x 53', 14 knots. Undergoing repair and reconstruction as CA(P) Protected Cruiser. (Projected) 8,000 tons, 10 knots, 240 officers and enlisted.

Lt. Michael "Mikey" Monk—Commanding.

Lt. (jg) Dean Laney—proposed Engineering Officer.

Stanley "Dobbin" Dobson—Shipfitter.

S-19

Lt. Irvin Laumer—Commanding.

"Midshipman" Nathaniel Hardee.

Danny Porter—Shipfitter.

Motor Machinist's Mate Sandy Whitcomb.

Slated for the proposed Corps of Discovery:

Ensign Abel Cook—Commanding.

Chief Gunner's Mate Dennis Silva.

Lawrence "Larry the Lizard," orange-and-brown tiger-striped fur, Grik-like ex-Tagranesi Sa'aaran.

Imperial Midshipman Stuart Brassey.

"Sgt." Moe (L)—The Hunter.

Fil-pin Lands

Saan-Kakja (L)—High Chief of Maa-ni-la and all the Fil-pin Lands.

Meksnaak (L)—High Sky Priest of Maa-ni-la.

Chinakru—Ex-Tagranesi, now colonial governor on Samaar.

General Ansik-Talaa (L)—Fil-pin Scouts.

Colonel Busaa (L)—Coastal Artillery; commanding Advanced Training Center (ATC).

Lord Bolton Forester—Imperial Ambassador.

Lt. Bachman—Forester's aide.

Major Jindal—Imperial Marine.

Mizuki Maru (general cargo). Single-screw steamer, 5,050 tons, 405' x 50', 10 knots. Former Japanese "hell ship" fitted with minimal protection, and 4 x 5.5", + 4 x Type 96 25 mm AA.

Lord Cmdr. Sato Okada—Commanding.

Lt. Hiro—Exec.

Second Fleet (Assigned to the Eastern Theater, or "Dom Front")

High Admiral Harvey Jenks—Commander in Chief—East (CINCEAST).
Task Force ES-2 (Eastern Sea-2)

Aboard USS *Maaka-Kakja* (CV-4). The first purpose-built aircraft carrier/tender, with specifications similar to *Salissa* but slightly smaller, faster (up to 13 knots), and better designed for air operations. 50 x 50 pdrs, 2 x 4.7" dual purpose, 2 x 5.5"/50s.

3rd Naval Air Wing includes the 9th, 11th, 12th Bomb Squadrons and 7th, 10th Pursuit Squadrons. (Thirty planes assembled and thirty unassembled.)

Admiral Lelaa-Tal-Cleraan (L)—Commanding.

Lieutenant Tex "Sparks" Sheider—Exec.

2nd Lt. Orrin Reddy—Acting Lieutenant Commander.

Gilbert Yeager—Engineer (one of the Mice).

Spook (L)—Gunner's Mate.

Sgt. Kuaar-Ran-Taak "Seepy" (L)—Reddy's backseater.

Second Fleet DDs

USS *Mertz*** (Fil-pin-built).

USS *Tindal*** (Fil-pin-built).

HIMS *Achilles* (Square rig side-wheel steamer, 160' L—38' W, 1,300 tons, 26 x 20 pdrs).
Lt. Grimsley—Commanding.

HIMS *Icarus* (Imperial light frigate).
Lt. Parr—Commanding.

USS *Pecos* (Fleet Oiler).

USS *Pucot* (Fleet Oiler).

Second Fleet Expeditionary Force. 4 regiments (2 Divisions) Lemurian infantry, 3 regiments Imperial Marines with artillery train.

Brevet General Tamatsu Shinya—Commanding.

Colonel James Blair—Imperial Marines.

Nurse Lt. Selass-Fris-Ar "Doc'selass" (L)—Daughter of CINCWEST Keje-Fris-Ar.

Capt. Blas-Ma-Ar "Blossom" (L)—2nd of the 2nd Marines.

Staas-Fin "Finny" (L)—Detached from USS *Walker.*

Faal-Pel "Stumpy" (L)—Ordnance striker. Detached from USS *Walker.*

Enchanted Isles

Sir Thomas Humphries—Imperial Governor of Albermarl.

Allied Prisoners of the Dominion

Lt. Fred Reynolds—Special Air Division, USS *Walker*.

Ensign Kari-Faask (L)—Reynolds's friend and backseater.

Respite Island

Governor Radcliff.

Emelia Radcliff.

Lt. Busbee—Cutter pilot.

Bishop Akin Todd.

USS *Finir-Pel****
Lt. Haan-Sor Plaar (L)—Commanding.

USS *Pinaa-Tubo* (ammunition ship)
Lt. Radaa-Nin (L)—Commanding.

Imperial Forces/Vicinity New Britain Isles

Governor-Emperor Gerald McDonald.

Ruth McDonald.

Rebecca Anne "Princess Becky" McDonald.

Sean "O'Casey" Bates—Prime Factor and Chief of Staff for G-E.

Lt. Ezekial Krish—Imperial Liaison to Courtney Bradford.

Lord High Admiral James Silas McLain the Third—Relieved.

HIMS *Ulysses, Euripides, Tacitus*—completing repairs.

Allied Assets in New Britain Isles

Courtney Bradford—Australian naturalist and engineer; Minister of Science for the Grand Alliance and Plenipotentiary at Large.
"Lord" Sgt. Koratin (L)—Marine assistant to Bradford. Recuperating from wounds.

USS *Simms****—Fil-pin-built; under repair.
Lt. Rulk-Sor-Raa (L)—Commanding.

USNR—*Salaama-Na* Home (unaltered, other than batteries of 50 pdrs; sailing Home.)—formerly TF "Oil Can."
Commodore (High Chief) Sor-Lomaak (L)—Commanding.

Enemies

General of the Sea Hisashi Kurokawa—Formerly of Japanese Imperial Navy battle cruiser *Amagi*.

General Orochi Niwa—advising **Grik General Halik.**

General of the Sky Hideki Muriname.

Signal Lt. Fukui.

Cmdr. Riku—Ordnance.

Hidoiame (Kagero Class). Japanese Imperial Navy Destroyer, 2,500 tons, 388' L—35' W, 35 knots, 240 officers and men. 6 x Type-3, 127 mm guns. 28 x Type-96 25 mm AA guns, 4 x 24" torpedo tubes.

Captain Kurita—Commanding.

Tatsuta—Kurokawa's double-ended paddle/steam yacht.

Grik (Ghaarrichk'k)

Celestial Mother—Absolute, godlike ruler of all the Grik, regardless of the relationships between the various Regencies.

Tsalka—Imperial Regent-Consort and Sire of all India.

N'galsh—Vice Regent of India and Ceylon.

The Chooser—Highest member of his order at the Court of the Celestial Mother. Prior to current policy, "choosers" selected those destined for life or the cook pots, as well as those eligible for "elevation" to Hij status.

General Esshk—First General of all the Grik.

General Halik—"Elevated" Uul sport fighter.

General Ugla, General Shlook—Promising Grik leaders under Halik's command.

Giorsh—Flagship of the Celestial Realm.

Holy Dominion

His Supreme Holiness, Messiah of Mexico, and, by the Grace of God, Emperor of the World—Dom Pope and absolute ruler.

Don Hernan DeDivino Dicha—Blood Cardinal and former Dominion Ambassador to the Empire of the New Britain Isles.

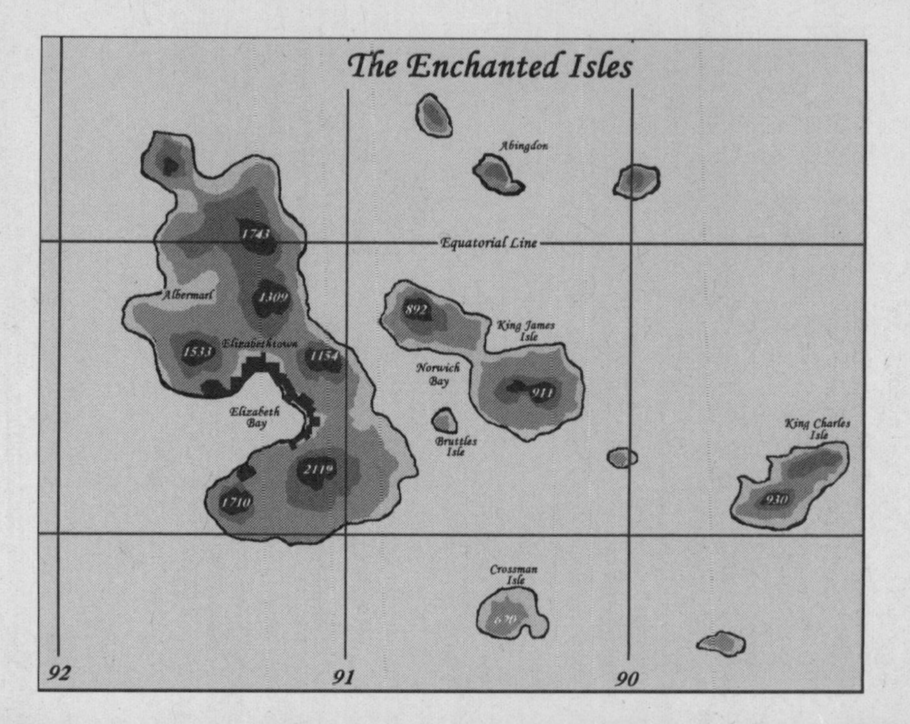
The Enchanted Isles
Abingdon
Equatorial Line
Albermarl
1743
1309
1533
Elizabethtown
1154
Elizabeth
Bay
2119
1710
892
King James
Isle
Norwich
Bay
911
Bruttles
Isle
King Charles
Isle
930
Crossman
Isle
92
91
90

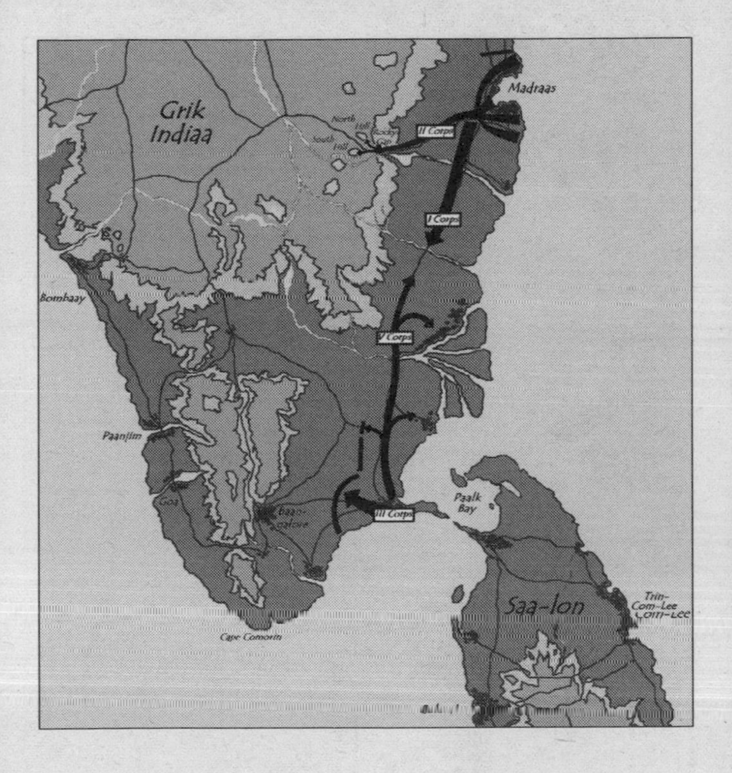

Grik Indiaa
Madraas
II Corps
I Corps
V Corps
Bombaay
Paanjim
Goa
III Corps
Paalk Bay
Saa-lon
Trin-Com-Lee
Cape Comorin

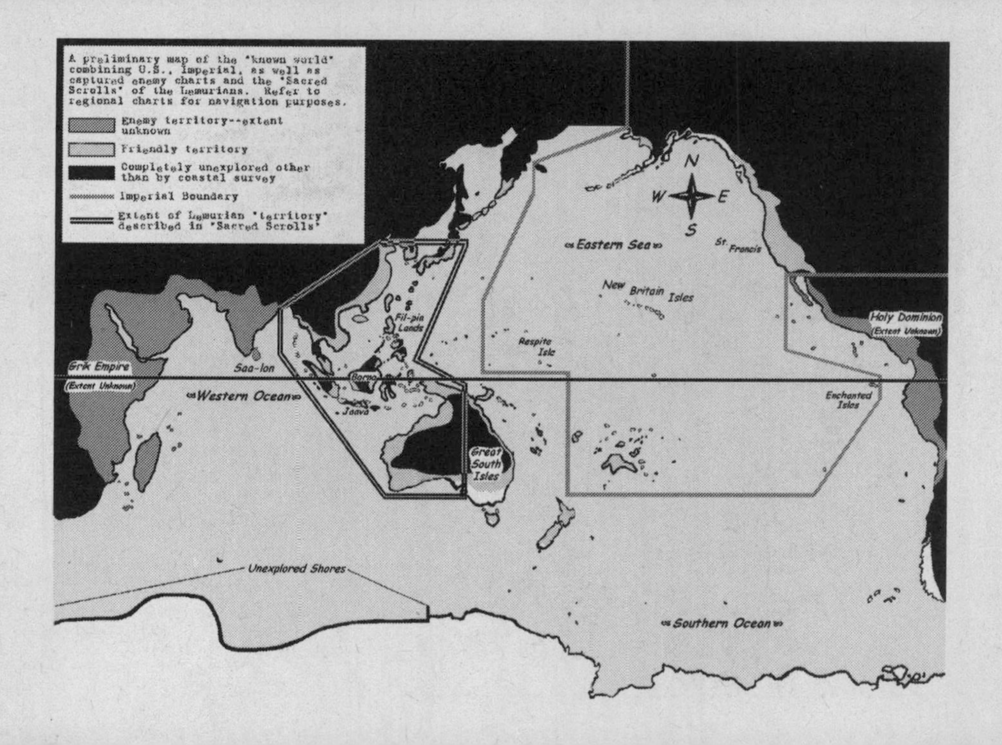
A preliminary map of the 'known world' combining U.S., Imperial, as well as captured enemy charts and the 'Sacred Scrolls' of the Lemurians. Refer to regional charts for navigation purposes.
Enemy territory--extent unknown
Friendly territory
Completely unexplored other than by coastal survey
Imperial Boundary
Extent of Lemurian 'territory' described in 'Sacred Scrolls'
N
W
E
S
Eastern Sea
St. Francis
New Britain Isles
Holy Dominion
(Extent Unknown)
Respite Isle
Fil-pin Lands
Grik Empire
(Extent Unknown)
Saa-lon
Borno
Western Ocean
Jaava
Enchanted Isles
Great South Isles
Unexplored Shores
Southern Ocean

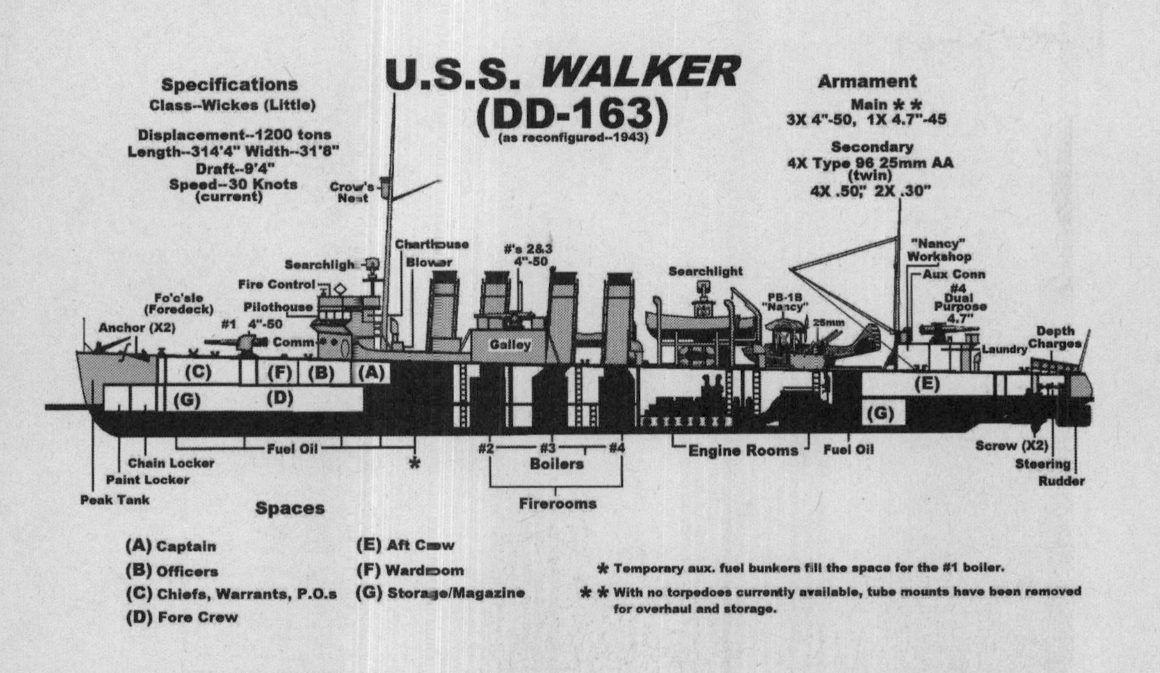

U.S.S. *WALKER*
(DD-163)
(as reconfigured--1943)
Specifications
Class--Wickes (Little)
Displacement--1200 tons
Length--314'4" Width--31'8"
Draft--9'4"
Speed--30 Knots
(current)
Armament
Main * *
3X 4"-50, 1X 4.7"-45
Secondary
4X Type 96 25mm AA
(twin)
4X .50," 2X .30"
Crow's Nest
Charthouse
Blower
Searchlight
Fire Control
Pilothouse
Fo'c'sle
(Foredeck)
Anchor (X2)
#1 4"-50
Comm
#'s 2&3
4"-50
Galley
Searchlight
PB-1B
"Nancy"
25mm
"Nancy"
Workshop
Aux Conn
#4
Dual
Purpose
4.7"
Laundry
Depth
Charges
(C)
(F)
(B)
(A)
(G)
(D)
(E)
(G)
Fuel Oil
*
Chain Locker
Paint Locker
Peak Tank
#2
#3
#4
Boilers
Firerooms
Engine Rooms
Fuel Oil
Screw (X2)
Steering
Rudder
Spaces
(A) Captain
(B) Officers
(C) Chiefs, Warrants, P.O.s
(D) Fore Crew
(E) Aft Crew
(F) Wardroom
(G) Storage/Magazine
* Temporary aux. fuel bunkers fill the space for the #1 boiler.
* * With no torpedoes currently available, tube mounts have been removed for overhaul and storage.

"I must note how odd it strikes me that a region of strife should be referred to as a 'theater.' Perhaps that peculiar little Machiavellian Prussian Clausewitz (what a bizarre combination!) is to blame for the militant association. I always related the term with entertainment—before it began to haunt me with its even broader implications concerning our overall situation. Of course, were not 'theaters,' as we know them, originally created to showcase tragedy?"

—Courtney Bradford, *The Worlds I've Wondered*
University of New Glasgow Press, 1956

PROLOGUE

The Sea of Jaapan
February 2, 1944

The sky was corroded lead, cold and gray with splotches of white. It was lighter in the east, where the sun lingered behind the heavy blanket of cloud, but there was no chance it would make an appearance that day. Beneath the sky the sea roiled, a darker, more tempestuous reflection, and alone upon it—in all the world, it seemed—*Mizuki Maru* shouldered her way through the unkind swells. She was an old ship, smallish, and battered by a lifetime of toil. She'd done honorable service and carried honest freight for most of her many years, but her past few voyages had been of a different sort. She'd been engaged in carrying men—worn, beaten, wretched men—to the last place on earth they could possibly want to go.

If she'd had a soul, it would have broken and fled her to escape the suffering and misery confined within her sad, rusty hull. Particularly after the last voyage. It had been the worst of all. Only a few dozen of the more than five hundred prisoners of war she'd carried—Malays, Aussies, Dutch, Brits, and Americans—had ultimately survived, and it wasn't because they were supposed to. At some point she'd vanished from the world where her Japanese masters made her carry such dreadful cargo and arrived on a world very much the same but entirely, fundamentally different. It was no less savage, however, and her crew—and the crew of the destroyer *Hidoiame*, which escorted her and a war-weary oiler—had murdered as many of her "cargo" as they possibly could. They'd then abandoned *Mizuki Maru*, damaged and sinking. Or so they thought.

That might've been the end of *Mizuki Maru* if that was all they'd done, but during the bloodthirsty massacre of her prisoners they'd taken ashore, the confused, possibly even frightened Japanese sailors also slaughtered the . . . people . . . of a small nearby village. They hadn't been human, but they *had* been people, and, more important for *Mizuki Maru*, they'd been under the protection of a human Japanese man who'd finally realized that regardless of flags and emperors, his honor would no longer allow him to sit idly by.

Prodded by this atrocity against people who'd become his own, "Lord" Commander Sato Okada, formerly of the Japanese Imperial Navy and the mighty battle cruiser *Amagi*, and now Seii Taishogun of the newly established Shogunate of Yokohama, Jaapan, finally joined the human/Lemurian alliance that had destroyed his old ship. Now he lived for little more than revenge against those who'd murdered his "new" people, and to achieve it, he had to destroy others of his own race, his nation—but not his people anymore. For this, finally, he was prepared. At long last, there was no conflict, no sense of frustrated loyalty. His purpose was clear once more, as simple and pure as the cherry blossoms he would never see again. He and his mixed crew, Japanese and Lemurian "samurai" and the scattering of "American" Navy Lemurians, were dedicated to the common purpose of destroying *Hidoiame* and her oiler, and killing or bringing justice to everyone aboard them.

If *Mizuki Maru* had a soul, and it could find her where she'd gone across whatever gulf separated her from the world she knew, it would be at peace.

"Con-taact!" shouted the Lemurian bridge talker standing behind Okada, near the aft bulkhead. The striped, furry 'Cat wore headphones fitted awkwardly to his head, and a wiring harness trailed behind him. "Range, one fi' seero seero!"

A chill swept down Sato Okada's spine. *That close? It can't be the enemy!* "Bearing!" he snapped.

"Two two seero!"

Okada took a calming breath. There was no way his keen-eyed Lemurian lookouts would let them pass *Hidoiame* that close aboard. He strode to the port bridgewing and raised his binoculars, facing aft. *Fish!* he concluded at last as a long, dark object rose into view, then vanished behind a swell. *Another of the giant . . . wrongful fish of this world,* he thought. A spume of atomized spray burst skyward, joined by others, and he focused more carefully. A pack—pod?—of monstrous, air-breathing fish like none he'd seen before moved through the sea just like whales would have done—if there *were* whales. These had some kind of bony-finned, translucent sail protruding from their backs like epic swordfish, and he wondered briefly what it was for. He grunted. So many wonders he would love to explore someday, but they couldn't distract him now. First, he had to attend to the far bigger business of revenge.

"We will reduce speed in case there are more of those creatures about," he said brusquely. "We are already ahead of schedule. We will not be late for our 'reunion,'" he added grimly.

"Ay, Lord," cried the Lemurian helmsman. He was a "Jap 'Cat" to the "Amer-i-caan," or "proper" Navy 'Cats aboard, who were happy to address Okada as Cap-i-taan, but the Japanese humans and Lemurians called him Lord. The engine room telegraph rang up two-thirds, and more bells rang as the dial swung in reply to the handle, while Okada slowly paced the bridge.

He'd arranged a meeting with the enemy destroyer, and, more specifically, her murderous Captain Kurita. Okada's radio operator had been broadcasting in panicky distress ever since they entered these seas, claiming his ship was *Junyo Maru*—yet another vessel transported to this place. Kurita had finally risen to the bait and ordered them to cease their bleating. Once communications were established, they'd lured Kurita to a rendezvous with promises of food, supplies, parts, and ammunition. *Mizuki Maru* already resembled *Junyo Maru* in most respects, but her "mad cook," who alone had defected with his ship, had recently seen *Junyo Maru*. His suggestions regarding color and the like were employed during *Mizuki Maru*'s refit in the Maa-ni-la shipyards.

In addition to altering her appearance, she'd been armed with some of *Amagi*'s salvaged secondary armaments that had been quickly shipped in from Baalkpan. A few of the guns showed, which was not unusual and should further allay any suspicions about her identity. But other weapons were hidden, and Okada hoped they'd come as a *very* unexpected surprise to the far more capable ship he considered his prey.

He contemplated *Hidoiame* for a moment. She was the twentieth—and last—of the *Kagero* class, commissioned in early 1941 as a Type A "Fleet" destroyer. He was familiar with her original specifications and had seen the ship herself before the Old War began. She was about 390 feet long, 35 feet wide, and displaced almost exactly twice as much as the overage USS *Walker*, the flagship of the "American" fleet on this world. She also carried twice the crew, and could probably make thirty-five knots. Again according to the almost pathetically reticent cook, however, *Hidoiame* had undergone alterations as the nature of the Old War evolved. She still carried twin-mounted 127 mm dual-purpose guns in turrets fore and aft, but he insisted that one aft-mounted turret had been replaced by another twin, 25 mm mount to augment her antiaircraft batteries, which brought the total number of twenty-fives to twenty-eight. As far as he knew, she didn't have radar, but also admitted he didn't really know what radar was. He was a cook.

She still carried a four-tube torpedo mount amidships, with four reloads, but her antisubmarine warfare (ASW) suite had been updated with the addition of improved sonar and more depth charges. Apparently, she'd sacrificed a third of her main surface battery to become more formidable against air and undersea targets, but those same antiair weapons would be devastating at the range Okada needed to achieve. He considered his main battery *Hidoiame*'s equal, but radar or not, he had no integrated fire control of any sort, so he had to get close—and he had only four 25 mm mounts to a side. The way he saw it, he had to get his ship within knife-fighting range, and savage *Hidoiame* in the opening moments while he had the element of surprise. If at any time during his approach Kurita decided *Mizuki Maru* was anything other than what she claimed—or, worse, somehow recognized her—she and all aboard her were doomed.

Sato Okada was prepared for that possibility. He was approaching his rendezvous in radio silence—as ordered by *Hidoiame*—but he had a short list of letter codes that could be sent out immediately by his signalman, along with a constantly updated position. Back in Maa-ni-la, they would know what the various letter prefixes meant. A translated as "Action commenced." B meant "Action commenced, surprise achieved." Other letters represented various permutations, but the letter code had been devised primarily in case things went sour in a hurry—and he fervently hoped he wouldn't have to send the letter G, which translated as, "We are destroyed by enemy action. Possibility of survivors is remote." G also signified "Good-bye."

"Con-taact!" cried the talker again. This time Okada barely tensed, assuming the lookout had spotted another . . . school? . . . of the strange fish/reptiles. The things rarely attacked anything larger than a small boat, but they were still a menace. He'd heard *Walker* once did minor damage to her bow when she'd struck one.

"Range and bearing," Okada said patiently. His crew wasn't very experienced, and the excitable 'Cats often forgot proper procedures.

"No range! Is on horizon. Gray on gray is hard to see, say lookout. Bearing tree fi' seero! Tree seero degrees off lef—port bow!"

Okada grimaced. Unless the lookout had seen a mountain fish—unlikely in these waters—they had discovered *Hidoiame* at last. He raised his binoculars and stared through the slightly wavy glass of the bridge windows, but saw nothing but the heaving sea. It didn't matter. The enemy would come to him. *Mizuki Maru* was making enough smoke that they would easily see her even without Lemurian lookouts.

"Should we go to general quarters?" his Japanese exec, Lieutenant Hiro, asked anxiously.

"No. Not yet. But please do ask that mad cook to make something—sandwiches, I suppose—for the crew." He gestured at the cold sea and spray beyond the glass. Slick, black ice was forming on deck. "I wish we had time for him to feed them a hot meal, but unless he has something such ready now, sandwiches will have to do."

"Of course, Lord."

The distant contact slowly resolved itself into a sleek, low-slung shape visible even from the bridge, and familiar to Okada, at least. It *was Hidoiame*. There was no mistaking the broad, overlarge-appearing gun turret on the foredeck, the high bridge, and two swept-back funnels. The ship was pitching fairly dramatically in the swells, and he caught occasional glimpses of the bottom paint at her sharply raked bow.

The wasp comes to the spider, he thought with growing excitement. Theoretically, they'd been in range of *Hidoiame*'s guns as soon as they sighted her, but the destroyer was growing closer to what Okada considered his own maximum range in these seas. *Hidoiame* would always have the advantage in accuracy, with her sophisticated fire control, but his own well-drilled gun's crews should manage a higher rate of fire in local control. Everything would depend on the quality of their individual marksmanship.

"Sound general quarters," Okada said. "But ensure that our Lemurians move carefully to their posts, and that they try to stay out of sight," he suddenly warned. He'd grown so used to his furry people that the notion had just occurred to him, and if he could almost make out the distant Japanese sailors through his binoculars . . . "Then go to the signal lamp yourself and ask if they are who we think they are." He chuckled grimly. "Let us maintain the fiction that we are lost and afraid!"

"At once, Lord," Hiro said, activating the long-anticipated alarm bell and passing the word for all the Lemurian crew of *Mizuki Maru* to stay down behind the bulwarks near their action stations. Only then did he step through the door into the freezing wind on the port bridgewing and began flashing a signal on the Morse lamp.

"Range?" Okada called.

"Tree fi' seero seero," came the talker's reply.

"Very well." He was worried about his enemy's ability to mass so much 25 mm fire on his ship's bridge or guns. It was bad enough what the "light" weapons could do to any other part of his ship. He wanted a range that would make him a difficult target for them, while still giving the crews of his own four 5.5-inchers the best opportunity. He watched while distant signal flashes responded to his own, and he studied the wind and sea. "When the range reaches two thousand, we will turn to zero five zero," he told his helmsman. "That should give us a slightly gentler ride when we unmask our guns and commence firing!"

The gap between *Hidoiame* and *Mizuki Maru* continued to narrow, and after Kurita's terse reply to Hiro's signal, the lieutenant reentered the bridge, his thin mustache and chin whiskers crusted with ice. A 'Cat servant met him and helped him and Lord Commander Okada don their leather and copper battle armor, complete with the traditional weapons of the samurai.

"Take your place aft at the auxiliary conn, Lieutenant Hiro," Okada said formally. "Only remember: whatever happens to me, the ship, to any of us—*Hidoiame* must not survive this day!"

"*Hai*, my lord," Hiro snapped, and jerked a respectful bow before racing aft.

"Two tow-saand!" the talker cried nervously.

"Very well," Okada said, again staring at *Hidoiame*, his tone almost unnaturally calm. "Come to zero five zero." He turned to the talker. "Inform Gunnery Officer Muraa-Laak that he may man his guns and commence firing as they bear."

Mizuki Maru's first rippling salvo was wild and mostly short, but it took *Hidoiame* completely by surprise. Even before the destroyer managed to sound general quarters, a second, better-aimed quartet of shells were on their way, and 25 mm projectiles, chased by bright tracers, groped for her. Three shells landed close aboard but one exploded with a red flash beneath *Hidoiame*'s port hawse and she veered quickly to starboard, throwing a sheet of water high in the air. For a few brief moments, she lay there, her screws slashing a trough, coiling for a sprint, her whole length exposed to Okada's guns. His warriors—his samurai!—made the most of it.

The windows shook and the deck plates quivered as *Mizuki Maru*'s fire grew more sporadic, but also more accurate. Okada watched the two gun's crews forward. Those of the number one gun on the fo'c'sle were Navy professionals loaned by Saan-Kakja, and they performed their evolutions with a competent grace, even though the fur left exposed by their peacoats was white with ice. They sent a 5.5-inch shell arcing into *Hidoiame* right between her forward stack and superstructure. They were rewarded by a swirling black gout of smoke and a billow of yellow fire. The number two gun, exposed over the forward cargo hatch now that the sides of a crate had been taken down, was crewed by survivors of the village their enemies had razed. Their drill was not as crisp as the Amer-i-caan 'Cats, but they served their gun with a vengeful passion and also achieved a hit—this one on the enemy fo'c'sle, just beneath her forward turret.

Okada's pulse thundered with exultation as he saw the rounds strike home, but his mind remained icy and analytical. So far, they'd had everything their way, but their target was beginning to accelerate rapidly now, and *swarms* of 25 mm tracers were starting to reach back for them. *Mizuki Maru* shuddered under their sudden, slamming blows. Smoke streamed away from *Hidoiame*'s aft turret, and a cataract of foam rose alongside and drenched the crew of number two, even as Okada felt a mighty blow somewhere aft stagger his ship. The stutter of impacting twenty-fives became a storm, and glass shattered and flew as some found the bridge.

"Full ahead!" Okada commanded. "Left ten degrees rudder!" A 'Cat slammed the telegraph lever forward amid a clash of bells, and another spun the wheel.

"Full ahead, lef' ten de-gees, ay!"

Another shell crashed into the ship, and Okada heard muted screams and felt the pressure of the blast and the convulsion of tortured steel. The rest of the bridge crew had something to hold on to, but Okada nearly fell. The talker held the headset against his furry ear and shouted over the tumult.

"Number tree gun aft iz out of aaction, an half the twenty-five mounts is wrecked!"

Guns one and two barked and jolted back. Acrid smoke filled the pilothouse through the broken panes, and Okada couldn't see if they had any effect. He lurched toward the door to the bridgewing, but the wood was shattered and he jerked the remains from the hinges and stepped outside. Smoke swirled, and instead of the cold wind, he felt the heat of flames. Looking aft, he saw his ship was burning amidships, and the portside lifeboat was scattered around the base of the funnel near a gaping hole that belched exhaust gas. He clutched the rail with one hand and stared through his binoculars.

Hidoiame was hurt! She had her own small fire forward of the bridge, and the forward turret had never turned toward them. It must be damaged. The aft stack was leaking smoke, low, and more smoke gushed from a pair of large holes aft. Whatever damage she'd taken didn't seem to have harmed her engines, though, and she was still accelerating.

"Left full rudder!" Okada roared over his shoulder. He had to keep as many guns in action as possible, and prevent his enemy from coming around behind him, where only one remained. He'd been right to fear the twenty-fives, he realized. The damn things were tearing his ship apart, and it looked like he had only one similar mount remaining with which to reply. Even now the twin guns kept up a withering fire that probed and detonated around *Hidoiame*'s bridge like bursting fireflies. His number four gun was still firing; he could hear it, even if he couldn't see through the smoke. A blinding flash bloomed directly in front of his own bridge, sending the remaining glass flying among a chorus of cries. He wiped at blood that suddenly blurred his vision and saw corpses strewn around number two, leaving only a single, stunned 'Cat standing there. Number one barked again, and he spun to see the result.

There was a small flare of light, wrapped in a white cloud that looked like steam, amidships of *Hidoiame*. For an instant, he felt triumphant—until there was another flash just like the first and he saw the long, concave splashes that cracked the swell at the destroyer's side, one after another. Sato Okada's blood turned to ice and he thought he felt his heart shatter in his chest. The flashes hadn't been fire and steam—they'd been torpedo impulse charges!

"Full astern!" he screamed. "Right full rudder!" Even as he gave the order, he knew it wouldn't matter. The range was now just a little more than a thousand yards, and the two Type 93 torpedoes—weapons of devastating power and reliability that he was all too familiar with—would arrive in half a minute. It would take longer than that just to reverse the engine. If the range was greater, slowing the ship might spoil the solution, but now only the turn could possibly help—but they'd already been turning to port . . . "Correction!" he shouted, more controlled. "Rudder amidships! Continue full ahead!" All he could do was pray *Mizuki Maru* would pass the point *Hidoiame*'s torpedo men had calculated for their weapons to intersect her path. With so little time, the chances of that were slim.

Another impact forward sent the crew of the number one gun sprawling, but most of them rose and returned to their posts, quickly sending another shell toward their tormentor. Okada lurched back into the pilothouse, where the talker was shouting a steady stream of damage reports, punctuated by the constant drumming and staccato explosions of those wicked twenty-fives. A gout of hot steam gushed through the doorway as something ruptured amidships, and *Mizuki Maru* staggered sickeningly and began losing way. For just an instant, there was near-total silence on the bridge, and Okada's eyes swept the gazes that met him.

"I have failed," he said simply, brutally. "My oath is spent and hollow. Wasted." He paused. "Brace yourselves, my samurai," he breathed softly. He turned to the talker. "Have the signalman transmit code letter G with our current position . . . and my apologies, if he has the time."

The Type 93, twenty-four-inch torpedo was, hands down, the best weapon of its type in service with any navy in the world when Sato Okada crossed the mysterious gulf aboard *Amagi* nearly two years before. Almost 30 feet long, weighing close to 3 tons, and blessed with a speed close to 60 knots and a 1080-pound warhead, it was designed to rupture the thick armor and break the backs of *battleships*. Probably only desperation, or possibly panic, had induced Kurita to waste two such precious, irreplaceable weapons against *Mizuki Maru*, so in that sense, Okada felt a sudden, perverse surge of pride that his ship and crew had forced him to resort to such a drastic measure. But the disproportionate expenditure was on a scale with shooting a beer can with a high-velocity rifle.

Ultimately, the sudden course change, the heavy sea, or the haste with which the torpedoes were launched caused the first weapon to miss its target, speeding invisibly past, mere yards behind *Mizuki Maru*'s rudder. That was irrelevant, because seconds later the next torpedo slammed into her side and detonated with a stupendous dark geyser that dwarfed the ship—and blew the entire stern, aft of the engine room, completely off. Steam and black soot vomited skyward from the stack and gushing fuel oil ignited with a snarling rush.

Mizuki Maru stalled as if her legs had been torn from her hips—which might as well have been the case. Her stern, propeller shaft, and most of her machinery was already nothing but mangled wreckage plummeting to the bottom of the sea. A widening field of burning oil coated the waves around her and lapped at the boat deck, already dipping low.

Sato Okada heaved himself from the deck, practically climbing the aft bulkhead. His left leg didn't feel right at all and he wondered if the concussion had cracked it. The helmsman slid backward and impacted the bulkhead with a cry as the murdered ship settled quickly aft, and her dripping bow left the tumultuous sea and reached for the sky. A naked, oil-soaked 'Cat crawled in through the shattered doorway, wide, bright eyes questing in dazed confusion amid black, matted fur.

The dying roar of *Mizuki Maru* was terrific. Tortured steel groaned and tore with dismal shrieks of agony, and the wooden deck cracked and splintered like rifle fire. Heavy machinery tumbled loose and crashed down deep in her bowels as the bow continued to rise until it was virtually perpendicular. Dimly, Sato Okada saw the number one gun, some of its crew still clinging to it, rip loose and fall against the forward bulkhead of the pilothouse. The bulkhead smashed inward under the impact, and girders pierced and pinned him.

I failed! He railed silently at himself through the waves of agony. So long he'd shunned the friendship of the Alliance, and then only when he personally was affected did he act. Shinya had been right all along. *The day* did *come that my honor demanded more of me—but my pride held me back until it was too late, and my arrogance made me promise what I could not achieve. I failed not only the Alliance that deserved my allegiance, but my crew—my* people*—who deserved my protection!*

Suddenly, a bloody, blackened face appeared before his eyes. It was the mad cook! Okada realized with searing shame that he'd failed him too—perhaps more than anyone—and he didn't even know the man's name!

"Come, my lord," the cook said in a soft, gruff voice. "I must get you free!"

Just then, the boiling, flaming torrent of water and oil burst into the pilothouse, and *Mizuki Maru* quickly slid, blowing and booming, beneath the frigid, tossing waves of the iron gray sea.

CHAPTER 1

***USS* Walker**
Central Pacific
February 22, 1944

The sea was brisk beneath a bright blue sky, marred only by cotton-candy streamers of white. No land was visible in any direction, and the one thing that might catch the eye of some far-ranging, broad-winged lizard bird was a lonely wake that stretched behind a battered, rust gray shape pitching tiredly across the long, deep swells. Such a creature might turn to join several others of its kind, seemingly effortlessly coasting along, pacing the strange ship. The flyers stayed off either beam, avoiding the hint of foul-smelling smoke blurring the tops of two of the four funnels standing high above the narrow hull. Occasionally, one of the lizard birds dropped back and snatched a morsel from the foaming wake, but most maintained almost unerring stations as if shepherding the exhausted ship along.

It had been a tough couple of wars for the old U.S. Asiatic Fleet four-stacker destroyer USS *Walker* (DD-163). The first one nearly killed her. This one, a far different war on a wildly different earth, *had* destroyed her—for all intents and purposes—once already. Refloated and rebuilt after the desperate Battle of Baalkpan, where she defended the Lemurians against the hated, semireptilian Grik and the mighty Japanese battle cruiser *Amagi* in a place that should have been Borneo, *Walker* had steamed straight back into action against new enemies across the vast Pacific, or Eastern Sea. Again, she and her mixed human and Lemurian—American—crew had accomplished more than anyone had a right to expect, but it had cost her dearly in bruises and blood. Now she was nearing the Imperial island appropriately called Respite, where she'd lick her wounds and catch her breath before heading "home" to Baalkpan and a much-needed overhaul.

"Ten-SHUN!" rumbled the hulking Chief Gunner's Mate Dennis Silva, practically guarding the fancy Lemurian-embroidered curtain that separated the passageway from the wardroom. Chairs and stools squeaked and clattered against the . . . less-pleasant shade of cracked green linoleum on the deck, as those in the crowded wardroom stood. (Stools still seemed out of place, but chairs were uncomfortable for Lemurian tails.)

"As you were," Lieutenant Commander (Captain) Matthew Reddy responded mildly, escorting several others into the compartment. He was tall, with premature gray threading his brown hair at the temples. The pace of operations had also cost him considerable weight, giving his finely tailored Lemurian-made khakis a slightly disheveled appearance. His intense green eyes and quick smile undermined any possible impression that he was overwhelmed by his responsibility, however. Captain Reddy commanded *Walker*, but he also bore a great many other burdens on this strange world. Not only was he "High Chief" of the "Amer-i-caan clan," which now encompassed virtually all Lemurian Marine and Naval personnel, but he was also Commander in Chief of All Allied Forces (CINCAF), by acclamation, of all the powers united beneath (or beside) the Banner of the Trees. The wars had been as hard on him as they'd been on his ship, but, like her, like nearly everyone, he'd risen to the challenge.

Those gathered in the wardroom quickly resumed their seats, making way for Matt, Nurse Lieutenant Sandra Tucker, and His Excellency Lord Bolton Forester, the new ambassador from the Empire of the New Britain Isles, to find theirs at the battered table in the center of the compartment.

"Good afternoon, gentlemen . . . and ladies," Matt amended for Sandra's benefit, and for that of Lieutenant Tab-At, or Tabby, the newly appointed engineering officer. Tabby was modestly dressed in a T-shirt and kilt (wearing a top was something she did more often now that she was an officer), but the clothing did little to hide the fact that she was female. The silky gray fur on her arms and face was still blotchy in places where it hadn't quite covered all her steam scars, and Sandra winced slightly at the sight. Her expression turned into a satisfied smile at the thought that Matt—and every other human in the Navy—was going to have to start getting used to the idea of female officers of *all* sorts. She almost laughed out loud when Matt frowned at her.

There'd been female 'Cats aboard ever since *Walker* started supplementing her dwindling human crew with Lemurian cadets. That was the Lemurian way, and if Matt wanted sailors, he had to take both genders. All were "Americans" now, having sworn the same enlistment oath as *Walker*'s original crew. The Marines and the Lemurian Armies were also entirely integrated. Many of *Walker*'s losses in the recent campaign had been made up with former Imperial *women*, however, and incorporating *human* females into the Navy and Marines made almost everyone uncomfortable except said females—and the Lemurians, of course, who didn't know what the big deal was.

Sandra had initiated the integration aboard the new Lemurian purpose-built carrier USS *Maaka-Kakja* (CV-4), originally recruiting women from Respite who were escaping the then-all-pervasive institution of indentured servitude that most women in the empire endured. Matt was furious when he found out, but by then it was a fait accompli. The Imperials were (publicly) furious too over the equality the move implied, not to mention the almost unavoidable precedent it set for their own navy.

When his rage passed, Matt secretly suspected Sandra's move was a stroke of genius that had solved a lot of problems, both for him and for Governor-Emperor Gerald McDonald, who was doing his best to eliminate the age-old

"Company"-inspired institution of virtual female slavery throughout the Empire. Having uncorked it, Sandra had made it practically impossible to put the genie back in the bottle.

Regardless, there were now human females, sea... women running around *Walker*, to the amusement of half the crew—and horror of the rest. Matt understood it, accepted it, even welcomed it for various reasons, but he didn't like it.

"I'm sure you've all met His Excellency, Ambassador Lord Forester," he began, looking across the table at the tall, somewhat heavyset man. Matt didn't know Forester well, but the man was a personal friend of the Governor-Emperor and that spoke well for him. He waited briefly while most politely nodded. "Good." Matt smiled. "Try to be nice to him. It's in all our interests, his people's and ours, that we get along." There were chuckles, and even Forester's face broke into a smile. There had been, and doubtless would continue to be, tensions between the Western allies and the Empire. The Empire had spawned the criminal Billingsley, after all, who'd managed to cause so much trouble. Even now, in its death throes, the legacy of the Honorable New Britain Company was still cause for concern. The societies were very different, and some enmity remained.

"I will do my part," Forester said, absently twisting the graying ends of his massive, stereotypical Imperial mustache. "I'm rather new at this; the Empire has had no diplomatic department, per se, and no real tradition of negotiation. And though we allowed the Dominion to maintain an embassy in the New Britain Isles—which they apparently used primarily to intrigue against us—there has been no ambassador to the Doms for a decade." He grimaced. "Hopefully, there won't be one until the evil that rules there is destroyed." He spread his hands with a small smile at Matt. "Then, of course, we had no one else to talk to until you came along."

Matt refrained from pointing out that the Lemurians had always been there—and the Empire knew it.

The ambassador straightened. "It is no secret that I feel inadequate and wholly unprepared for my new, consequential post, but though I may not be a polished envoy, I understand that I must learn all I can about the military and political structure of your elements of our Alliance. Just watching and listening helps me with that." He smiled more broadly. "I assure you, even listening to the . . . English-Lemurian patois you have developed is most helpful."

There was more laughter. "I think we're even, then, Your Excellency," Matt said. "Courtney Bradford is the best we can come up with for your counterpart, and he's not very polished either." Bradford was an amazingly valuable but . . . odd individual. He'd been an Australian petroleum engineer in the East Indies, but considered himself first and foremost a naturalist. Sometimes Matt wondered if everything that had happened to them since they passed through the Squall that brought *Walker* and her people to this world wasn't some divine attempt to overwhelm Courtney's curiosity. "I think the Governor-Emperor knew our people would react better to someone like you than to someone more 'polished.' As for listening to the gab, knock yourself out. I don't think we have, or should have, any secrets you shouldn't hear. Make yourself comfortable. . . ." He grinned, considering the lively gyrations of his ship. *Walker* rolled horribly in any kind of sea, and was currently pitching rather briskly as well. "If you can."

Matt looked at the others in the wardroom and the grin disappeared. *Time to get down to business*. "Okay, here's the deal. As you're all aware, *Walker* needs a major refit and she's on the binnacle list for now. For some time, particularly since we turned for home, it's been bugging me that a fair percentage of the personnel most needed to accomplish various projects have been cooped up here aboard *Walker*. In the past, I'd have swallowed that frustration, of necessity. But the wonders of this modern world we're building are throwing changes at us so fast that they're hard to keep up with." He shook his head. "Sometimes I feel like the guy living in the house with oil lamps, who never twisted the light switch because he *knew* there was no electricity and all the bulbs were burned out—then somebody just waltzes in and turns on the lights." He grinned sheepishly.

"The point is, before departing New Scotland, I sent a message asking the guys back home to put their heads together and figure out a way to get some of you malingerers off this ship and back to work. In retrospect—I don't know why; I didn't expect much. I knew we could fly you out of Manila, but by then you'd only have a few days on us." He nodded at Ed Palmer, the communications officer. "We just received, via Respite Station, confirmation that two four-engine seaplanes the Air Corps cobbled up—I think they're calling them 'Manila Clippers'—should arrive at Respite at about the same time we do. They're supposed to be bigger, more powerful versions of the three-engine 'Buzzards,' and I've been assured they're reasonably safe and reliable." He paused. "A number of you will board those planes and proceed ahead of us to Maa-ni-la. Some of you will continue on to Baalkpan, via other appropriate fueling stops. Once you reach your respective destinations, you'll commence a variety of assignments that you are, in some cases, uniquely qualified for."

"What kind of assignments?" blurted Silva. The big, heavily tanned, one-eyed man still stood, leaning against the aft bulkhead. His mighty arms were crossed, and the spray of scars on his face testified further that *Walker*'s people had suffered as much as she had. Beside him, much shorter, stood an orangish, tiger-striped creature named Lawrence, or Larry the Lizard. Lawrence's physical similarity to the Grik, with his furry-feathery reptilian form, sharp teeth, and wicked claws, was still a little disconcerting to some, but all knew he was fiercely loyal.

"What kind of assignment, *SIR*, damn your insubordinate soul!" growled Chief Bosun Fitzhugh Gray. Gray was more than twice Silva's age but nearly as big. His decades-old China Station flab was long gone, and if he might not quite be a physical match for Silva, he had infinitely greater moral authority.

"Sir," Silva amended agreeably, and Gray rolled his eyes.

"Let's hear what the Skipper has to say before flapping our gums," Brad "Spanky" McFarlane commanded. Spanky was a skinny little guy, and had once been *Walker*'s engineering officer. Somehow, despite his size, people always remembered him as much bigger than he actually was, and now he was Matt's exec.

"Please," agreed Sandra Tucker. She was even smaller

than Spanky, but her new job in the Alliance was Minister of Medicine, and petite and pretty as she was, she had a will of iron and couldn't be lightly ignored (or resisted) by anyone. She was also, incidentally, Captain Reddy's fiancée. There was a brief, uncomfortable silence. No one resented her hard-earned authority, but some inevitably reflected on the most recent result of it.

Juan Marcos, Matt's self-appointed personal steward to the CINCAF, appeared with a carafe and noisily stomped through the suddenly quiet wardroom on a remarkably complicated peg fashioned for him on New Scotland. He'd lost his left leg during a sneak attack by the Holy Dominion. No one spoke while the little Filipino filled cups with an air of supreme satisfaction. *Well, at least the "monkey joe" is back to normal,* Captain Reddy reflected, staring bleakly at the not-quite-green foam rimming the brew in his captain's cup. Juan had finally returned to duty, relieving Taarba-Kar (Tabasco), his Lemurian replacement. The first thing he'd done was insist on making the local, ersatz coffee the way Matt "liked" it, and since Matt—or anyone—had never summoned the courage to tell the Filipino they *hated* his coffee, they were back to drinking what some described as "bilgewater and boiler soot" in the wardroom. At least they had Imperial tea now, and Juan was content to let Tabasco handle that.

Matt felt his square jaw while Juan finished his rounds. Juan was much better at shaving him than Tabasco had ever been. After finally relenting and letting the Filipino perform that delicate duty, he couldn't very well prevent Tabasco from doing the same after Juan was wounded, and the young 'Cat's hand wasn't nearly as steady. Matt shuddered.

"Uh, thanks," he managed when Juan triumphantly and with surprising agility, swooped back by and topped off his cup, replacing the single, obligatory sip he'd taken. Matt set the cup on the green linoleum-topped table and gazed at the others in the compartment, almost daring them to grin or snicker. Suddenly, he was reminded of other, often desperate, times when he and *Walker*'s officers had met like this. There was a more relaxed atmosphere today, but there were important matters to discuss; matters that would affect the prosecution of the war on its various fronts, and that would require scattering these people—his friends—to remote places once again.

He looked at Marine Major (or Bosun's Mate, if he was at sea) Chack-Sab-At and smiled. The young Lemurian had become one of the rocks of the Alliance, and his brindled tail was swishing slightly in anticipation. They'd discussed his assignment before, and not only was he excited by it, but he also knew that ultimately it would take him nearer his beloved Safir Maraan, General-Queen Protector of B'mbaado. The stunning Safir was a corps commander now in the First Fleet Expeditionary Element.

"Chack, you'll be stopping in Manila, where you'll be joined by Major Jindal and his regiment of Imperial Marines aboard those Dom steam transports captured at New Ireland. They sailed before we did, and took a straighter shot. They should arrive there shortly, and this way, maybe you'll be there to meet them."

"Aye, aye, Cap-i-taan," Chack said.

"There's more. Twenty of the forty-odd POW survivors of *Mizuki Maru*—Army, some China Marines, others too, I'm told—are fit enough and willing to join the cause." He frowned. "Not much else for 'em, poor guys. They're in the same boat we are now."

"Still better than the boat they were in, from what I hear," Spanky practically snarled. "Goddamn Japs!"

"Maybe so," Matt agreed.

"What about the others?" Sandra asked.

"Some are nuts," Matt said simply. "No wonder. Others are physical wrecks." He shrugged. "Some say their war's over, and I can't say I blame them." His jaw worked. "Much as we may need their expertise, we all have to do our best to make sure *nobody* blames them if they choose to sit this one out. Those guys fought like hell, and now we know they were *ordered* to surrender. After that . . . My God, the Japs treated 'em more like you'd expect the Grik would have than . . . people ever would." He glanced at Sandra, then stared back at his cup.

"What will they do?" Sandra asked softly.

"With all the war industry in Baalkpan, Maa-ni-la, and,

well, just about everywhere, I bet they can write their own ticket. There's no shortage of work. Even if they can't fight anymore, they can still help. Hey, let's skip it for now. . . . But don't forget it!" Matt looked back at Chack. "That leaves the others who do want to join us. Somebody, one of them, probably, talked High Chief Saan-Kakja into forming some kind of Brit-style commando outfit." He arched his brows bemusedly. "Maybe they can use some more of Chinakru's lizards for advisors or an opposition force to train against. Anyway, there's that. Ultimately, you'll take those forces and a new Manila regiment and go to Baalkpan, where you'll incorporate a regiment of 'Cat Marines your sister Risa is raising into a division." Matt paused. "You'll command."

Chack blinked and bowed. "Thank you, Cap-i-taan Reddy."

"Who's going straight to Baalkpan, sir?" Lieutenant Irvin Laumer asked politely but intently. He had a very personal reason to be curious. Like most submariners, Laumer wasn't tall or physically remarkable in any way, but Matt had learned he had an extra helping of guts. He'd successfully led the effort to salvage his old submarine, S-19, off a Talaud Island beach—a beach that no longer existed, since the whole island had blown itself apart in a volcanic fit reminiscent of Krakatoa on the "old earth." More recently, he'd been acting exec of *Maaka-Kakja*, a prestigious post, but one he'd relinquished so he could go back to his old sub. He seemed to feel, despite all he'd accomplished, that he still had something to prove, and he could only really do that with S-19.

Matt reflected that Laumer's fixation on the old boat could be good . . . or bad . . . and he had no idea which it would ultimately be. He'd been advised that S-19 could never be a submarine again. Most wanted to just scrap her—but that wasn't right either. Not only would Laumer and all the men and 'Cats who'd worked so hard to save her be crushed, but the boat *did* float and had two running (or repairable) diesels and a four-inch-fifty gun. Matt decided to give the determined submariner his head and ordered Laumer to rebuild S-19 into . . . something else. Even if nobody really knew what that would be yet, Laumer didn't care. Whatever S-19 was fated to become, she would still be his.

"You are," Matt answered, "along with Lawrence, and"—he arched an eyebrow at Silva's looming form, expecting one of the man's . . . imaginative arguments—"Chief Silva." To Matt's surprise, Dennis Silva didn't do anything other than arch his own eyebrows and form that disconcerting, gap-toothed grin of his. "You'll resume command of S-19," he continued to Laumer, "and figure out what to do with her. You may consider that a reward for your efforts, if you like, but I think it's going to be a bigger chore than you imagine. My only advice is not to get any fixed ideas before you start. Talk to your people who stayed aboard; get with Bernie Sandison, Perry Brister, anybody who might have a notion. Draw pictures. Whatever you do with her though, remember: we need practical warships, not pie in the sky."

"Or a pigboat in a poke," Silva murmured down at Lawrence, and Laumer fired a scathing look at him before replying, "Aye, sir. Thank you, sir."

Matt nodded.

"You ain't gonna stick me on that big, leakin' weenie, are you, Skipper?" Silva spoke up. It wasn't really a question.

"No. That would be a waste of your few real talents, and you'd be *much* worse than useless to Lieutenant Laumer. That said, though you are going to Baalkpan, you're *not* on the loose. When not directly involved in the assignment you're about to receive, you *belong* to Bernie Sandison in Ordnance. As far as he's concerned, you're still AWOL. If you don't do exactly what he says, he can hang you, for all I care."

"I swear," Silva mumbled, barely audible. "How come folks are always shakin' ropes at me?"

"What was that?" Spanky demanded.

"Nothin', sir," Silva said, suddenly making a caricature of the position of attention. "Aye, aye, sir! I'll stick to Bernie like malaria! Why, he won't be able to scrape me off with assi-tone—but I'll be back with *Walker* when her refit's done . . . Won't I?"

"We'll see," Matt said seriously, stifling a chuckle. "In the meantime, Adar still wants that expedition into the interior of Borno, to make contact with those 'jungle lizards' you discovered. I think it's past time myself, now that we know not everybody who looks Grik *is* Grik." He grinned at Lawrence, then looked back at Dennis. "We also know for a fact that *looking* Grik doesn't save them from the Grik either, so they have a stake in this war whether they want it—or know it—or not." Matt's eyebrows rose. "According to General Alden, we need jungle fighters, for scouts if nothing else, and we might use them as commandos too. Adar's already begun accumulating supplies and personnel for the expedition. The 'Cat hunter, Moe, a couple of Chinakru's Sa'aarans, and even some of the Grik we captured at Aryaal have committed to participate."

There was a murmur in the wardroom over that. When they left Baalkpan, little progress had been made toward communicating with the creatures.

"So, I guess I've also committed to participate?" Silva asked, arousing chuckles.

"Yes, you have," Matt replied seriously. "You and Lawrence will ensure the safety of the expedition, and do whatever you can to make it a success."

"Who's gonna be in charge?"

"Abel Cook has been commissioned an ensign, and he'll be your superior officer. With Courtney in the east, Mr. Cook is the best-qualified man to lead this . . ." Matt looked thoughtful for a moment, then smiled. "This Corps of Discovery. I know he's awful young, but as you know, he's got a level head—and I'm sure he'll listen to you. I know he's learned to value your . . . opinions . . . in dangerous situations."

Cook had been one of a number of civilian refugees from Java, mostly children of diplomats and other big shots, aboard S-19. Since his rescue, he'd been Courtney Bradford's protégé in the natural sciences. He'd also been abducted and ultimately marooned along with Sandra, Silva, Princess Rebecca, Lawrence, Imperial Midshipman Stuart Brassey, Lelaa-Tal-Cleraan, Sister Audry . . . and others not as lucky. He'd packed considerable adventure into his barely sixteen years, and the gangly teen had generally comported himself well by all accounts.

"Cook's a good kid," Silva said thoughtfully. "And he's probably been livin' in a igloo made outta Courtney's books since he got back to Baalkpan. He's a good choice." He chuckled. "I figger his biggest problem'll be givin' me orders!"

"You may have to teach him how," Matt agreed, "and I feel a little guilty inflicting you on him, but he'll need you. Tell him to feel free to accept a few more volunteers, if he wants." Matt knew Abel's friend, Midshipman Brassey, would be begging Ambassador Forester to let him go as soon as the meeting adjourned.

"Sounds like a hoot, and me and Larry'll do our best for the kid . . ." Silva's twisted grin spread. "I mean, for *Mister* Cook." He poked Lawrence with his elbow. "Won't we?"

"So, who else is leavin' the ship?" Spanky grumbled. "Not too many more, I hope. We've got a lot of work to do when we make Respite, just so we can get the rest of the way home and get to work!" *Walker*'s machinery needed considerable attention after her long voyage and hard fighting; more than they'd been able to give her in the Imperial shipyards. Even more critical than that, however, she needed a dry dock, and the closest one was in Maa-ni-la. She had some damage below her waterline, but what had come to worry Spanky most were the rivets they'd rebuilt her with in Baalkpan. He considered that his fault. They'd formed her new plating from good steel salvaged from *Amagi*, but the rivets were local "iron." It wasn't really iron but some of the first steel they'd attempted, and Spanky had thought it would suffice and made the call. Unfortunately, the rivets had proven remarkably brittle. They resisted shearing, so they weren't apt to fail with the normal working of the ship, but even some of the light roundshot strikes they'd taken had opened seams and launched shattered rivets like bullets. They'd repaired *Walker*'s worst topside damage with good-quality "Impie" rivets at Scapa Flow, but Spanky was increasingly worried they'd pop a bottom seam if they ran into another big storm, or Strakka, like the one they encountered on the voyage out. The ship survived that blow with no hull damage, but real or not, Spanky felt the growing stress on the bottom rivets as if the same ones had been used to hold his guts together.

In response to Spanky's question, Matt glanced at the Bosun, indecisive. Carl Bashear was *Walker*'s Chief Bosun's Mate now, and Chief Gray really was needed in Baalkpan. The Alliance had sprouted a lot of "chiefs," but few had any real leadership experience, especially in combat. Matt envisioned at least a temporary school for Naval NCOs, to deepen that pool of experience and knowledge, and Chief Gray, the Super Bosun, was the natural choice to supervise it. Chief Gunner's Mate Paul Stites could handle the Captain's Guard, and Bashear was fully capable of handling all the deck divisions. Matt really ought to send Gray home, but he was reluctant for several reasons. For one thing, he was Matt's friend and primary—discreet—confidant when it came to matters concerning the crew. Also, like Silva in one respect, Gray thrived under adversity. Despite occasionally proclaiming that he wouldn't mind settling down for a while, he'd hinted that if Matt shuffled him off to be a "schoolmarm," or put him out to pasture, he shouldn't expect him to excel behind a desk or in the classroom. Matt thought the Bosun could and would do the job, but he also knew his heart wouldn't be in it. *Walker* was his home. Whether or not he remained essential to the old destroyer's day-to-day operation, supervising and monitoring her well-being was critical to Gray. He needed her just as badly as she'd needed him in the past, and Matt couldn't shake the feeling—the premonition, almost—that his ship might desperately need her Super Bosun again.

"No. That's all, Mr. MacFarlane. Except the ambassador and his party—if they don't mind flying." Matt regarded Ambassador Forester. "Saan-Kakja, High Chief of All the Fil-pin Lands, and Chairman Adar are both anxious to meet you. In Saan-Kakja's case, she wants to go back to Baalkpan, as she promised her troops she would—but now she's got troops fighting Doms in the other direction, helping defend the Empire." He paused. "Honestly, Ambassador Forester, Saan-Kakja doesn't like the Empire very much, and you really need to make a good impression on her."

"You think I should ride a . . . flying machine?" Forester asked, eyes widening. His aide, Lieutenant Bachman, began to form a protest, but Forester gently silenced him.

"Yes, Your Excellency. I do."

"Well. Indeed . . ." Forester considered. "Tell me, Captain Reddy: has an Imperial citizen ever ridden one of your flying machines?"

"Not to my knowledge, Your Excellency. I believe you'd be the first."

"Splendid. In that case, I simply must, I suppose."

With the meeting adjourned, the wardroom quickly emptied. It was hot in the compartment, even with the portholes open, and the wind direction prevented much air from coming in. The smell of sweat was so all pervasive, no one noticed it anymore. The musty-smelling 'Cats shed all the time, however, and Spanky rocketed up the companionway at the end of the short passage in the middle of a sneezing fit. Even Juan left, herding ahead of him a pair of mess attendants laden with trays of cups. All that remained were Matt and Sandra, smiling comfortably at one another across the wardroom table.

"We're alone," Sandra murmured.

"Scandalous," Matt replied with a grin. "I left standing orders that we're *never* to be left unsupervised, for the slightest instant."

"I guess the whole gang's on report now," Sandra said, standing, and walking slowly around the table toward him.

"Trust me," Matt warned, mock serious, "they'll be severely punished."

Sandra slid onto the chair beside him and gave him an only mildly inflammatory kiss as his arms went around her.

"We better get back to work," he mumbled. "This is exactly why I said we should split up from now on. Can't have us carrying on like a couple of teenagers all the time."

Sandra giggled. "Hey, buster, this is *my* office!" The wardroom served as a surgery in battle.

"Then quick: throw me out, woman! Before the crew gets the wrong idea!"

Sandra giggled again, and Matt smiled. He knew she thought she sounded ridiculous when she did that, but he loved the sound. Finally, she sighed.

"Gets *wise,* you mean. Of course, in spite of us trying to

fool them, they knew about us before *we* did." She snuggled against him. "I *feel* like a teenager," she admitted. "I guess you're right, though," she added wistfully. "Once we're married, we'll see even less of each other than we do now. Even if your silly regulations didn't prevent mates from serving aboard the same ship, I don't think that shoebox you call a stateroom would be big enough for both of us." She kissed him again. "And after we *are* married, nothing will ever keep us apart again."

"When we're not apart," Matt added glumly. She knew what he meant.

"I think you'll have plenty to look forward to," she whispered wickedly. "The sailor home from the sea will always be a happy man."

He chuckled, but then looked at her. "I'm happy now. Only . . ."

"Only what?"

"Well . . . are you absolutely sure you want to go through with it? I mean, it'll be tough sometimes. Maybe . . . Maybe we should wait until the war's over, you know."

Sandra's face grew stormy. "Now, you listen to me, Matthew Reddy! You may be king of the sea, but as soon as you asked me to marry you, and even said *when*, that put me in charge of the whole operation, see?" She smiled, but her eyes were moist. "If you wanted it different, a chance to weasel out later, you shouldn't have asked me right in front of the Governor-Emperor, half our allies, and all the crew!"

"I don't want to weasel out!" he protested.

"You'd better not. Not only would it make me sore—it might wreck the Alliance! The Governor-Emperor wanted to marry us in New Britain, in the cathedral, with more bells and whistles than any wedding I ever heard of! Even Adar was a little put out that we wouldn't wait until we got back to Baalkpan. He wanted to throw a big party, even though 'Cats aren't big on formal weddings. But you promised me a honeymoon! On Respite! The governor there, Radcliff, is already gearing up for a pretty big deal, probably almost as big a wedding as His Majesty would have managed. You are *not* going to leave me at the altar like a dope. . . ." Tears threatened to spill, but she shook her head and dashed a sleeve across her eyes. "Not after all this time, after all we've been through!" Her voice took on a hint of bitterness.

"This war is *never* going to end, Matthew. Don't you see? Someday, we'll beat the Grik and the Doms and whatever else comes along. I don't doubt that anymore. . . . But I know you. You're not just fighting *them*. You'll fight the whole damn world until it's a safe place for the people you care about to live in peace and freedom!" She dried her eyes. "Okay. That's the way it is. That's who you are, and as much as I hate it sometimes, that's also why I love you so much. I DO love you, but you've made me wait an awful long time. I'm thirty, now, Matthew," she said, "and yes, maybe I want kids. Mainly though, I want you, for however often . . . or however long I can have you."

"Okay!" Matt defended lightly, deliberately misunderstanding her mood. "It's your operation, like you said. I wasn't trying to weasel out."

CHAPTER 2

Baalkpan, Borno
Headquarters "Home" of the Grand Alliance
February 22, 1944

Commander Alan Letts carefully negotiated the muddy ruts along the Baalkpan pathways. Deep trenches marked the passage of heavily laden "brontasarry"-drawn trucks that transported the increasingly sophisticated machinery built in the heavy-industry park. The trucks churned along at a regular, previously undreamed-of pace, bound for the burgeoning shipyard that continuously gouged at the dense jungle frontier north of the city. Baalkpan had always been a port city, but now the shipyard sprawled like a fattening amoeba wherever the land touched the bay.

"Watch your step, for God's sake!" croaked Commander Perry Brister, picking his way alongside Alan. "You get in the middle of that, you'll be done." The former *Mahan* engineering officer's voice didn't match his young face and dark hair. It had been ruined when he commanded the defense of Fort Atkinson during the desperate battle against the Grik that once nearly consumed the city. He pointed at a bawling, long-necked beast about the size of an Asian elephant dragging another wheeled cart in their direction. "Smushed or buried," he grated darkly.

"No sweat," Letts said, but slowed his pace. *Someday,* he

thought, *if the demands of war ever give us a chance, we'll have to do something about these damn roads.* They were "repaved" constantly by the almost daily rains—and brontasarry-drawn graders—but the ruts weren't as bad as the goopy slurry between them churned up by the massive, stupid beasts. A man—or Lemurian—could get stuck and maybe *die* in that.

There could be no break in the pace of operations and wartime production, however. Baalkpan—and the young Alliance it led—was only just beginning to hit a stride that might keep up with the demands of an increasingly global war. There could be no slacking off for any reason for the foreseeable future.

The irony's almost funny, Letts thought. Once, on another world, he'd been supply officer aboard USS *Walker,* and even by his own definition he'd been the poster boy for all slackers. One could have argued at the time that the world of the U.S. Asiatic Fleet was already quite different from the rest of the Navy, but that held absolutely zero relevance now. Here, Alan Letts had reinvented himself and was proud of what he'd become and accomplished. He was Chief of Staff to Captain Matthew Reddy and, by extension, a remarkable Lemurian named Adar, who was High Chief and Sky Priest of Baalkpan, and "Chairman" of the Grand Alliance of all Allied powers united beneath (or beside) the Banner of the Trees. Also, even more ironically, Alan had become Minister of Industry for the entire Alliance.

With the recent, more independent additions to that alliance, he wasn't quite sure how *that* post would shake out, but he'd keep doing the job here regardless. He'd recently returned from a stint at the "pointy end," where he'd served as chief of logistics for First Fleet. Initially, he'd gone because he felt guilty. His new sense of responsibility, likely heightened by the birth of his daughter, made him feel as if he'd skipped out on his shipmates and their Lemurian friends by staying in such a cushy berth so long. He realized now what an idiot he'd been. He'd seen firsthand what this war—at least on the "Grik Front"—had become, and he hadn't chickened out. But he'd realized with blinding clarity that the reason he'd actually made a real contribution in theater was because he was a bean counter, not a warrior, and what the various expeditionary forces needed as badly as warriors were more bean counters.

He'd raced back to Baalkpan at the end of the Ceylon Campaign to recruit as many 'Cats—and, frankly, ex-pat female "Impies" escaping their indentured lives—as he could, to establish a Division of Strategic Logistics within the Ministry of Industry. There wasn't an awful lot of extra labor just loafing around the city, and though hundreds had arrived, he'd had to move fast on the Imperial women because the institutions they'd fled were already breaking down and the "supply" might dry up. The women that arrived in Baalkpan were almost universally illiterate, but though the quality varied, they already spoke a variety of English. A common language that used many of the "right" words for things was key to getting the division up and running *now*. Alan and his shipmates had awkwardly learned to get by in Lemurian, but Adar had decreed that *his* People, at least those from his city in the War Industry, learn English. They had to. There'd never *been* Lemurian words for most of what they made. Understandably, that was taking time—and most 'Cats who spoke English already *had* jobs. The destroyermen who'd wound up on this world had already faced one kind of "dame famine." Alan feared another sort.

And now this!

"Hey," Letts said, as he and Perry tried to keep themselves—and, just as important, their new shoes—from sinking in the mud. "You're Minister of Defensive Works and all that stuff. Roads are part of that, right?"

"Sure, and I'll get right on it, soon as you give my engineers a few days to do the job," Perry groused. Both knew there was nothing Brister could do, but the banter was obligatory—and neither had anything else to say. They were headed for the Castaway Cook, a sort of café started by *Walker*'s irascible cook, Earl Lanier, that had evolved into the more or less official Navy and Marine club for what promised to be an . . . interesting meeting.

Two P-40s—*P-40s!*—thundered by overhead, almost wingtip to wingtip, the sound of their Allison engines rivaled by the cheering of Lemurian laborers in the shops and beneath the awnings bordering the muddy pathway. Letts grinned, watching the predatory aircraft climb, banking west out over the bay. As much as he'd accomplished, he couldn't take much credit for the "Warhawks"; their rescue from the old *Santa Catalina*, beached in a Tjilatjap (Chill-Chaap) swamp, was primarily due to the herculean efforts of others, most notably a former Army Air Corps lieutenant named Benjamin Mallory. Like them all, Ben had stepped up to fight an unimaginably terrible war on this opium-dream earth. He was a colonel now, in charge of the whole Army and Navy Air Corps of the entire Alliance.

"Is Ben going to meet us there?" Brister asked.

"Not at the Screw. He's supposed to meet us all at the Parade Ground," Alan confirmed. "Unless he was in one of those things"—he gestured at the diminishing shapes in the sky—"and that was his idea of putting in an appearance." Both men chuckled, but they couldn't hide their uneasiness from each other.

"I wish the Skipper was here," Brister blurted at last, voicing what both were thinking. But Captain Reddy was hopelessly far away, and as Chief of Staff this really was Alan's job . . . but nobody had ever expected he'd have to deal with anything like this. "Or even Adar. How come Adar isn't coming?"

"I tried to get him to," Alan sighed, "but we both figured, finally, that this is something I better try to sort out before he gets involved." He shrugged. "It's not really his problem . . . yet. He'll do what he has to, though, if we can't square it away."

"How are we going to do that?" Brister asked flatly. There it was. And Alan had no idea.

"The same way we've handled everything," he said more firmly. "We wing it."

Brister snorted uneasily. "So that's why Ben's coming, huh?"

The Busted Screw—the decidedly unofficial but more common name for the Castaway Cook—was usually a busy place, and it was jumping when Letts and Brister arrived in time for the midday rush. Traditionally, 'Cats ate only twice a day, but the human destroyermen had arrived among them accustomed to three meals (of some sort) each day, at about the same time. That was a tradition the hardworking 'Cats in the defense industry and military were quickly adopting. Cafés like the Screw were all over the city now, catering to the various Army regiments, but only Naval and Marine personnel (with some notable exceptions) were "permitted" to sit at the benches around the tables or sidle up to the bar beneath the broad roof of the Screw. It was a raucous place, particularly at times like this. Besides the noisy patrons (allowed only the admittedly superior chow during daylight duty hours), no matter how exclusive a joint it was considered, there were no walls and all the noises of the busy bayside activities could be watched and heard.

Letts and Brister went to the centrally located bar and tried to spot their target through the bustle. Despite the sensitive situation, Letts was beginning to think he should have just sent a detail of Marines to escort the newcomers to the War Room in Adar's Great Hall, and to hell with the consequences. He was very busy and irritated that they hadn't reported there when they first arrived, as expected . . . but, then, they didn't *legally* have to, did they?

"Where are they, Pepper?" Brister shouted at the slender 'Cat with white-spotted black fur behind the bar. Pepper was the proprietor of the Screw, at least while Lanier was deployed, and he probably knew more about the state of the Alliance than any living being in Baalkpan. It was ridiculous to presume that he, at least, didn't already know who they were here to see. He probably knew why too, whether the newcomers had blabbed or not.

"Over there," Pepper shouted, motioning with his ears at the farthest table, barely protected by the roof.

Yeah, Letts decided. *He knows something's cockeyed.* He'd seen the Lemurian's concerned blinking. "Thanks."

"You wanna eat?" Pepper asked, coming around the bar and following a few steps while Letts and Brister made their way between the tables.

"Later," Letts said. He wasn't very hungry just then, and needed to get the new arrivals away from the Screw as soon as he could. *There.* He saw them now. Five men sitting alone at a table surrounded by 'Cats who looked at them occasionally, blinking curiosity. "Damn," he said aside to Brister. "They look like hell."

"They all do, those that survived. The Japs really put them through it," Brister replied.

Letts said nothing. The condition of the men could make this even harder. He took a breath and crossed the remaining distance to the table, where he stopped and waited until the men noticed his presence.

"Which of you is Commander Herring?" he asked as courteously as he could. They all wore dungarees they'd been issued in Maa-ni-la before Saan-Kakja tossed the very hot potato they represented at Alan, but none wore any rank designations.

With a grimace of pain, likely from aching joints, one of the skinny men stood. "I'm Commander Herring," he said softly. "Commander Simon Herring, United States Navy."

Letts looked at him. The two were about the same height, but Herring's graying hair established him as at least a dozen years older than Alan's twenty-five, though it was hard to tell. The ordeal he'd endured had doubtless aged him.

"Pleased to meet you, sir," Alan replied. "I'm Commander—or Lieutenant, jg, if that's how you prefer to look at it—Alan Letts. And this is Commander—Lieutenant—Perry Brister. Might I ask that you and your companions follow me? Maybe we can find someplace a little quieter to talk."

"That's fine, Lieutenant," Herring said, "as long as you don't mean 'more private.' Right now, I don't want to go anywhere my friends and I might just . . . disappear."

"Sir, I strongly resent the insinuation. . . ."

"Resent all you want," Herring said. "But maybe you can forgive me if, after what we've been through and under the circumstances, I'm a little careful."

"The parade ground surrounding the Great Hall is as public as it gets," Brister ground out, "but it's quiet. It's a military cemetery now, see?"

The Parade Ground Cemetery that occupied the space around Adar's Great Hall and the mighty Galla tree around which it was built seemed sparsely populated at first glance.

Only about four hundred actual graves occupied a relatively small portion of the vast area at the center of the city. Looks were deceiving. Lemurians much preferred cremation to burial, but a surprising number, Navy 'Cats mostly and a few Marines, lay beneath simple markers alongside their human comrades. They'd ended up more devoted to their shipmates than to tradition. Less than half the humans lost from *Walker*, *Mahan,* and S-19 actually rested there either; many had been lost at sea or died too far away to be brought to this place. For now. Many hundreds of names had been engraved into a great bronze plaque, however, and like the cemetery itself, there was plenty of room for additions. Another, separate plaque, with *thousands* of names representing the people and crew of *Humfra-Dar*, a Lemurian Home that had joined the American Navy and been altered into a carrier (CV-2), had recently been emplaced. The bronze was still shiny, the names still bright.

The cemetery was a quiet place for reflection in the middle of the bustling city, and there were benches here and there in the shade of bordering trees. Ben Mallory was waiting for them when they arrived, gazing grimly at *Humfra-Dar*'s plaque. The scenes and memories that haunted his eyes and hardened his features warred with his otherwise boyish face. He'd known every flyer on *Humfra-Dar* and personally trained many of them. He turned at their approach.

"That never should've happened," he snapped, gesturing at the plaque. "One damn bomb, and Captain Tikker said she went up like a volcano! 'Cats are fanatics about fire safety on their Homes, but we've got them carrying fuel oil, high-octane gas, bombs, and loose gunpowder for the cannons, for cryin' out loud! When you think about it like that, it was inevitable . . . and it'll happen again!"

"I know, Ben," Alan said softly. "Keje's working on new procedures, better magazine and bunker protection. . . ." He shrugged. "None of us were ever on a flat-top. There's so much we're still making up as we go—and nobody was expecting Grik *zeppelins*!"

"Procedures!" Ben grumped, then sighed. "Look, Alan," he said, glancing at his watch. "I'm kind of busy today. We've got those evals on the new radial this afternoon, and I'm still trying to wrap up the nuts and bolts of deploying half my modern birds." He shook his head. "I know I agreed, but there's a lot more to it than just flying the damn things off to the front! Asking me to believe the fuel and airstrips are ready without seeing 'em is kind of like expecting me to believe in the tooth fairy—and I *know* we haven't got parts prepositioned all the way to Andaman yet. We can't afford to lose any ships and pilots on the way, and even if all the ships make it, half are liable to be down, waiting for spares."

"Relax, Ben," Alan said. "This is important. Besides, you just worry about getting the squadron ready. We'll sort out the logistics on my end. It'll still be a few weeks before you get the go date. We're organizing the supply-ship schedule, so if any of your guys have to go in the water, there'll be somebody nearby to fish 'em out in a hurry."

"For what good *that'll* do," Ben replied. Considering the prolific and voracious nature of the aquatic life on this world, particularly within the Malay Barrier, any rescue ship would have to be close indeed.

Letts flashed a pained expression. "We all do the best we can," he said. He truly sympathized with Ben. The P-40s had been a glorious gift, and he knew the airman considered them—and their rapidly improving, mostly 'Cat pilots—almost like children. Alan himself was half tempted to keep them all here. The planes had come in very handy when Grik zeppelins suddenly appeared over Baalkpan itself several weeks before and began dropping bombs. Three Warhawks took to the sky and destroyed the crude dirigibles before they could do much damage, but they'd been the only things available that could have done it at the time. Now they'd armed a few of the home-grown PB-1B "Nancys" for air defense, but the P-40s alone could savage any Grik invasion attempt like the one that had so nearly cost them the city and ended it all. The thing was, they could also savage any similar force that came against First Fleet—and it was better to do it there than here. It was an old argument, but ultimately they all agreed that any weapon, no matter how irreplaceable, was useless . . . if you weren't willing to use it.

"Okay," Ben said, changing the subject. "So, what's up? These the new guys?"

Alan fidgeted. "Sort of." He glanced at the men. "This is Commander Herring." He paused. "I haven't been introduced to the others yet."

"Excuse me," said Simon Herring in a reserved tone. "I'm afraid I've forgotten some of the niceties of civilized behavior." His voice moderated slightly. "Let me present my companions. That stocky fellow there with no neck and the black jungle of a beard on his face is Gunnery Sergeant Arnold Horn. The one that looks like his taller twin *with* a neck is Lance Corporal Ian Miles. Both are from the Second Battalion, Fourth Marines. I shipped out of Shanghai with them to the Philippines, and they've been watching out for me ever since." The men nodded but didn't salute.

"The skinny blond Dutchman there—we're all kind of skinny, I'm afraid—is Lieutenant Conrad Diebel of the Royal Netherlands East Indies Army Air Force. I'm sure he would have appreciated one of the P-40s we saw earlier. He was battling the Japanese—very near here, as a matter of fact—in Brewster Buffaloes until they were all shot out from under him."

"I was shot down twice," the man confirmed in accented English, "but I got four Japs."

The last man didn't wait for Herring to introduce him, but actually stepped forward. "You were on *Walker*?" he asked Letts with a clear Aussie twang. "I'm Leadin' Seaman Henry Stokes, HMAS *Perth*. We was in the Java Sea together."

"You were sunk."

"Aye, with *Houston*, later that night in the Sunda Strait. *That* was a helluva fight! Me an' some o' me mates swam ashore an' dodged the Nips for a few days, but they nabbed us. Set us to breakin' sodding rocks." He shook his head sadly. "Me mates died there or in the ship with these blokes, an' I never seen any o' me other shipmates again."

Perry Brister, still silent, advanced and extended his hand. Hesitantly, the Australian took it.

"You've got quite a collection here, Commander Herring," Letts said. "All with the same . . . reluctant views?"

Herring frowned. "Let me explain. It's not our intention to cause trouble or disrupt your operation here, but you must understand our situation . . . our concerns. Those of us who were in the Philippines were *ordered* to surrender, and we were treated like animals by our captors. Lieutenant Diebel and Mr. Stokes may have had it even worse, but I can only speak to our own ordeal. The misery and despair Horn, Miles, and I witnessed and endured is hard to describe. Discipline broke down completely and men no longer obeyed their officers. It was dog-eat-dog. Sadly, many officers abandoned their responsibility to their men as a result, and the Japs encouraged that state of affairs to make the men easier to handle, I suppose. Ultimately, men just sat there and watched each other die." Real, almost physical pain clouded Herring's eyes. "And all that was long before they stuffed us in that damn ship, where we met these other fellows"—he gestured at the Australian and the Dutchman—"already aboard. The enemy was taking us to die in the coal mines of Japan."

"But you were an officer," Alan said softly. "What did you do?

"Very little, I'm sad to admit," Herring confessed, then hesitated. "You see, as far as the Japs knew, I *wasn't* an officer, and my Marine friends here helped me maintain that fiction."

"But . . . why?"

"Not that it matters here . . . now. I'm—was in—ONI. The Office of Naval Intelligence," Herring replied.

"Sometimes he tried to do stuff," Gunnery Sergeant Horn defended, his voice surprisingly clear and firm, considering his appearance. "We *all* did what we could, and things got a little better as time went on, from a discipline standpoint. But we couldn't let the Japs know Herring was an officer."

Letts looked back at Herring and the man nodded.

"I had connections to the Kuomintang, and I was trying to establish the same with Philippine resistance leaders when the surrender took place. We tried to get out, but we were caught. To preserve the identities of people I was in contact with, we decided I should masquerade as an enlisted man." Herring straightened. "To the Japs, all enlisted men are peasants, Mr. Letts, and therefore incapable of producing any useful information if questioned."

"I . . . see."

"In any event, that was then. Perhaps you can understand why we are hesitant to place ourselves under what seems to be a very . . . irregularly constituted authority. I'm given to understand we won't be forced to serve, and that gives us some relief, but the fact is I *am* a Naval Officer, and the most senior present on this . . . world, by legal reckoning. That leaves me feeling somewhat awkward, and I have a responsibility to these men who have helped me. We won't simply jump aboard this . . . odd alliance without further understanding the situation."

"I can understand that, Commander, and respect it. But why didn't you just talk to Saan-Kakja in Manila? She's a swell dame, and smart as a whip. She could've sorted it out for you."

"I'm . . . not sure the, ah, authorities in Manila fully understood that I needed to speak with the senior *Naval* Officer," Herring said stiffly.

"That's Captain Reddy," Letts stated firmly, "and he won't be here for some time. In fact, you were closer to him in Maa-ni-la."

"That was explained, but . . ."

"He means he—all of us—wanted to talk to *people*," Corporal Miles interrupted sullenly, and Herring glared at him. "There weren't any in Manila besides us and the other survivors of that damn *Maru* . . . well, and a bunch of half-naked broads out of the East someplace."

"Miles!" Gunny Horn snarled, seeing the faces of their hosts redden.

"Well, it's true!"

"That's enough, Corporal!" Herring said, but looked at Letts. "I apologize for the unseemly interruption, but Corporal Miles has voiced a point that still needs clarification. I've heard of this Lieutenant Commander Reddy and what he's done. What all of you have accomplished is impressive, to say the least. But before I submit myself and these others to the authority of a man who is actually junior to me, I need to know just exactly who is in charge here," Herring stated.

"Let me tell you something, Commander—" Ben Mallory began.

"Wait a minute, Colonel," Letts said, stressing Ben's new rank like he hadn't done for his own. "Remember how we felt when we first met the Lemurians? It took us a while to figure things out." He looked hard at Herring. "But that's because we didn't have anyone to tell us that 'Cats *are* people. Well, I'm telling you now, Commander, and don't ever forget it! They may look strange until you get used to them, but we look just as weird to them."

The Dutchman stirred. "But you have placed them in positions of authority! Even your 'supreme commander,' your Captain Reddy, follows their orders! This seems like on our world, you obey the Javanese or . . . Chinese coolies, yes?"

For just a moment, Letts was stunned. It had been so long since something as ridiculous as race had occurred to anyone that it caught him completely by surprise. He knew there were similar issues in the east, that Second Fleet had faced some Imperial bigotry, but from what he understood that was more cultural than racial and the Alliance had largely settled that by saving the Empire's ass.

Ben appeared ready to explode, but Alan cut him off when he spoke in a wintry tone. "Have you seen a Grik, Lieutenant Diebel? We've managed to secure a small number of captive specimens. A couple are practically tame now, and we've finally begun to communicate with them and learn something about them. Most are still kind of wild though, and you ought to go down to the holding pens and have a good, long look. After you get a dose of their claws and teeth and . . . overall terrifying lethality, remember this: *Really* wild Grik can't be taken alive. Only after they've been separated from the pack for a while do they seem to get a notion that they'd rather live than die killing you.

"After that, try to imagine *hundreds of thousands* of them armed with swords, spears, arrows, cannon, and firearms of a sort now too, all coming not just to conquer your territory but to wipe you out! These Lemurians you seem to feel so superior to stopped them and have started to roll them back." Alan shrugged. "We helped. Maybe we helped a lot. But we couldn't have done it without them." He grunted. "Hell, ask the Imperial rebels or Doms in the East how 'Cats stack up against *humans* in combat!"

"I think you misunderstand," Herring said with a warning glance at Diebel. "I'm sure your Lemurians are fine folk, but it has been disconcerting to see them, their Naval personnel in particular, parading around in a semblance of our Navy's uniform, flying the American flag from their ships, and, indeed, considering themselves to *be* Americans! That's odd enough. But then to find this . . . 'American' . . . force subject to the command of . . . foreign . . . leaders!"

"Oh, I get it," Brister suddenly interrupted, speaking for the first time, his rough voice even harsher than usual. "You're wondering why we didn't just take over and how come we don't treat the 'Cats like some people treated colored folks back home. Well, if any of us ever thought that way, we don't anymore. Navy 'Cats *are* Americans, far as I'm concerned. They've taken the same oath you did, and they mean it. Captain Reddy could have taken over, I guess, and made himself king. From what I heard, they practically asked him to. But these people are our friends, Commander, and even if the Skipper had wanted to be king, he knew the Alliance would never hold up and Baalkpan would still be all alone against the Grik. As for being under the command of 'foreign leaders,' well, we are and we aren't. It's complicated." He shrugged, then glared at the Dutch flyer. "But even if we *were* bound to follow their every whim—which we're not—I guess us Asiatic Fleet guys were already used to *that* back home, after Tommy Hart got the shove. . . ."

"You were treated rough by the Japs, Commander," interrupted Letts more softly, before Perry could make an enemy of Conrad Diebel. "And you've wound up in a situation you don't understand. You're being careful and trying to watch out for these other guys. I get that. But in a way, we're still fighting the same war here that we left behind. Sure, we've got a few good Japs on our side, and Shinya, at least, is a swell guy. Another Jap named Okada took the ship that brought you here up against the tin can that was with her." He lowered his voice and looked around. "That's the last we heard. Chances are, he's dead now and that ship's on the bottom of the sea, but he was on *our* side, fighting bad Japs. And most of the Japs that made it here have wound up with the Grik—and the Grik are *much* worse than Japs!

"The Grik keep people . . . Lemurians, anybody they catch, I guess, in the holds of their ships as rations. I've seen that, the aftermath, so I can kind of imagine what it *looked* like in the hold of *Mizuki Maru*. That said, I can only guess what it *was* like to be a prisoner of the Japs. I'm sure it was hell, sir, and the Japs who put you there *belong* in hell. With all due respect, though, Commander, you can't have any idea what it was like for us when we first wound up here, all alone and practically sinking." He gestured around. "It seems like we've done pretty well for ourselves, and I guess we have, but at first it was only us and we had less idea where we were or what had happened to us than you do." He shrugged. "That hasn't changed, really, besides some wild-assed guesses, but where we are isn't the all-consuming question it once was, and at least we've lived long enough for some of us to kick it around a little.

"Now, if you think you're going to just show up out of the blue and *pull rank*, there's something you better know." He held his thumb and forefinger about a quarter inch apart. "When we got here, we were *that* close to coming completely unwrapped, and only two things kept that from happening: the Skipper and the 'Cats. Captain Reddy never gave us a chance to wring our hands and worry and never *allowed* us to fall apart. He just kept doing his duty and expecting us to do ours . . . and we did. Not because of any oath or for a country we'll probably never see again, but for each other." He looked hard at Herring. "And for the skipper." He lowered his voice. "It never even occurred to anyone until later that maybe we weren't in *the* Navy anymore, but by then, it didn't matter. The skipper was still the skipper, and *Walker was* the Navy." He sighed and scratched his nose. "So the Navy's a lot bigger now, and there aren't many of us guys from *Walker* and *Mahan* and S-19 left, but, by God we did the right thing, the only thing, and Captain Reddy deserves most of the credit.

"As for the 'Cats, we never would've made it without

them, and, of course, all the ones here at least would be dead by now if we hadn't become friends. We've been through a hell of a lot together, side by side, so you'll have to excuse me if I'm sort of fond of the little guys. These 'Cats . . ." He paused and shook his head. "We just *like* each other. It's hard to explain. They had their ways and we had ours, but compared to the fix we were all in together, the differences that cause separate drinking fountains back home just never mattered, see? We—us and them—never *let* it matter much, and when trouble came up over various things, it got squared away fast." He chuckled. "Eventually, the little differences started going away. You've probably noticed how many of our ways most of them have taken on, particularly Navy and Marine 'Cats, and most of us probably seem a little weird to you too. I think, in all the ways that matter, we were a lot alike to start with."

He stopped again, and his smile turned downward. "One thing we have in common is that we've got ourselves one hell of a war. I've seen things . . . done things. . . ." He gestured helplessly at the others. "All of us have. . . . I'm sorry, sir, you just had to be here. This war is downright modern now compared to what it was. We've got guns and steamships and airplanes, for crying out loud, but it started with spears! I've heard it got pretty old-fashioned against the Japs in the Philippines, so maybe you can imagine a little of what I'm talking about, but this is a real war, a big war, and it's mean as hell. It's also for the whole enchilada: we win or die. It's that simple."

"What *Commander* Letts is getting at, Commander Herring," Ben Mallory interjected, "is that despite the fact that Captain Reddy's done his best to uphold the traditions and organization of the Navy here, for a lot of reasons, you really don't want to make a fuss about your seniority. That can only cause distractions that might cost lives. Right now, you're not senior to anybody. Captain Reddy might see it different because that's the kind of guy he is, but you won't find another soul who thinks this is still *your* Navy. The U.S. Navy on this world belongs to Captain Reddy."

"I see," Herring replied thoughtfully. "Do you agree with . . . Colonel Mallory's assessment, Mr. Letts?"

"I do, and as he said, I think you'll find the sentiment universal."

"What will become of us, then? What if we decide this isn't our war?" Herring actually chuckled. "If this isn't *my* Navy, then its suspension of discharges for the duration can hardly apply." The growing tension ebbed a notch.

"That's true. We'd love to have you—we *need* you—as long as you've got your heads straight about the setup around here. But your old oath doesn't bind you, not to us. Captain Reddy made that clear when he asked the guys—all the humans in military service—to voluntarily reaffirm their oaths." Letts eyed Herring closely, then glanced at the others. "Nobody backed out. This is a good cause, Commander. And what else would we do?"

"Forgive me for asking, but what exactly *is* your cause ... besides survival?"

Alan suddenly realized that wasn't a bad question.

"Well ... it started out as just survival, but it's way beyond that now. Believe it or not, this isn't a bad setup. Lots of growing pains, but we're trying to build a kind of, well, republic, I guess, along the lines of the constitution we all swore to defend. I know it seems weird, and it *is* weird to the 'Cats. Some of their 'states' are those aircraft carrier–size ships." He shrugged. "I guess if something as small as Rhode Island could be a state back home ... Anyway, it's kind of screwy, but in the end I guess we're fighting for the same things we always have. Freedom, security, the *principles* we stand for ... and each other."

Herring was silent a long moment. He too was looking at the graves now and the plaques. His companions were watching him, but by their expressions, Letts thought Gunny Horn and the Australian sailor had heard enough.

"You make a compelling argument, *Commander*," Herring said at last. "And yes, you've clearly earned your rank. To inspire such loyalty and confidence, your Captain Reddy surely has as well." He paused again. "I need to think, to get up to speed, but I'm a quick learner. If I decide to join you, to 'ship over,' as it were, perhaps you might have need of an officer with intelligence training?"

"I'll say!" Letts and Brister chorused.

Herring looked at his fellows. "I presume we could find civilian employment, but what are the terms of enlistment?"

"It's voluntary, but it's for the duration," Letts replied. "The 'Cats don't have many rules, but they're serious about the ones they have. All military personnel are governed by Rocks and Shoals. We're still sorting out the pay scales—they didn't even use money here before—but I think you'll find the wages sufficient. In your cases, you'd go in with your current ranks or ratings, and we'd put you where we need you most."

"Sounds fair," Herring said softly, looking at his comrades. "Well, men, I hate to break up the gang, but it's up to you. It *is* nice to be able to choose our fates for a change."

"I have only one question," Conrad Diebel said, pointing at another pair of P-40s sporting over the bay. "Can I fly one of those?"

"You'll have to *earn* one of those," Ben answered immediately, "but you'll fly."

"Then I'm in."

"How's the chow?" Gunny Horn asked abruptly.

"Weird," Alan confessed, "but good, I guess—and regular."

"Hmm. Well, hand over the enlistment papers, Commander Letts. We'll ship over," Horn said, speaking for himself and Lance Corporal Miles, while looking at Commander Herring as if for permission. Miles didn't speak, but he frowned.

Herring nodded. "Thanks for . . . everything, Gunny."

"No thanks necessary, sir." He looked at Letts. "You've got a lot of these 'Cats running around calling themselves Marines. Maybe I could help with their training?"

"Maybe so, Gunny," Letts said thoughtfully. "But I think you'll find they know their business pretty well. I may have another, more independent assignment for you."

"I'll join," said Leading Seaman Henry Stokes; then he hesitated. "But only if Commander Herring does. Even then, I'd like to stick with him. He might need a hand."

"Glad to have you, Stokes," Herring said, glancing at Alan. "*If* I join. Like I said, I've got some thinking to do. . . . And I believe I will go down and observe those Grik captives you mentioned. Have I your permission to talk to others? In the various industries and military commands as well?"

"Knock yourself out," Letts replied. "But don't take too long making up your mind." He shrugged. "There's a war on. When you decide, we need to talk to Chairman Adar. You'll like him. If he's not in too big a huff over the way you ran us around, I'm sure he'll be delighted that we may soon have our own Office of Naval Intelligence. Less work for all of us, and maybe as a new eye, you'll spot an opportunity we've been too close to the problem to see." He looked at Stokes. "And you'll need a staff."

CHAPTER 3

First Fleet
***TF* Arracca**
SE Coast of Grik India
February 24, 1944

Commodore James Ellis, *Walker*'s former exec, had a virtual fleet under his command. His task force was built around the reconfigured and recently arrived carrier *Arracca*, her battle group of four new steam frigates, or "DDs," and a train of oilers and supply ships. The latter were mostly converted Grik Indiamen taken at Singapore, and more of them arrived every day. In addition, he had another thirteen DDs, including some of the older ones, such as his own *Dowden*, and almost forty other ships clustered out of range of anything ashore but in full view on the horizon. Those ships were mostly oilers and supply ships, and there were a few of the new destroyer and seaplane tenders. It was hoped that the Grik would think all were troopships.

Dowden, as flagship, had temporarily joined *Arracca*'s screen. The thirteen other DDs of Des-Div 4 steamed inshore, just south of the low tide crossing between Ceylon and India, adding their fire to a furious bombardment. Nearly a hundred field pieces already floated on barges parallel to the crossing, pounding Grik positions within the bordering forest on the India side. There was very little answering artillery. It was a stirring sight, as Jim watched through binoculars on *Dowden*'s quarterdeck. The ships streamed smoke from their guns and stacks and moved slowly with all sails furled and broad American battle flags flowing taut to leeward. To Jim, the sound came as a continuous, rumbling thunder, and dense woods beyond the beach churned with smoke, geysers of earth, blizzards of splinters, and tottering trees. *The screams are probably pretty loud too,* he thought with grim satisfaction, *but they just can't compete with the rest of the noise and the distance.* Something caught his eye and he raised the binoculars higher. A squadron of "Nancys" from *Arracca* swirled above the enemy, occasionally adding their own bombs to the abattoir below. Other planes flew higher, spotting and scouting and ready to raise the alarm if any Grik zeppelins appeared.

The thought of the shocking and totally unexpected appearance of enemy dirigibles over First Fleet, Aryaal, and even Baalkpan itself still burned Jim's soul. In his mind's eye, he again saw the mighty Lemurian Home–turned aircraft carrier *Humfra-Dar* erupting like a fiery volcano as bombs fell on her crowded flight deck. There'd been very few survivors of the holocaust that engulfed the great ship. Some had been aloft flying missions and were recovered aboard Keje's *Salissa*, or "*Big Sal*," (CV-1), but perhaps the only thing that preserved the few awkward swimmers, flailing in the terrifying sea long enough to be rescued, was the stunning underwater acoustics of the terrible explosions.

The zeppelins had swarmed them in their scores, loosing sophisticated bombs in a density a flight of B-17s might have envied that not only destroyed *Humfra-Dar*, but also heavily damaged several of her screening DDs. The only consolation was that many of the Grik "air lizards" must have been extreme amateurs at the time, and a large number of their airships made no compensation for the sudden loss of their bomb load and practically rocketed into the sky and were destroyed by structural failure or the catastrophic expansion of their gasbags. The resulting spectacle created a viscerally satisfying, almost grim amusement, but little comfort for their loss. Most of the surviving zeppelins escaped over India to God knew where, although Captain Jis-Tikkar "Tikker," Commander of Flight Operations (COFO) for the First Naval Air Wing, managed to claw high enough to get a good look at the things and even bring one down.

Only a few airships attacked Aryaal, and they were repulsed after inflicting only minor damage. The larger raid on Baalkpan was decimated by Ben Mallory's P-40s. No zeppelin that survived either raid was likely to have had the fuel to return, so their losses had probably been total, but First Fleet had seen groups of the things again, several times, so they must have established bases for fueling and maintenance somewhere in India. Jim frowned. *Every time we think we've got the damn Grik figured out, they pull something new out of their hat. That crazy Jap Kurokawa is probably behind a lot of it, but not all. Apparently not all the Grik, their Hij, at least, are fools. We KNOW they're building a new fleet. I hope to God it doesn't come as big a surprise as their zeppelins did!*

"What's the dope?" he asked aside as he became aware of Niaal-Ras-Kavaat, his dark-furred exec, standing beside him.

"The scouts report that the enemy continues to gather, preparing for our assault." Niaal blinked pleasure and grinned, showing his wicked young canines. "And we continue to kill them!"

"Good. Hopefully we can keep it up for a while, before they get wise."

"Not much chance of that," Niaal said in a contemptuous tone.

"Of them catching on? I don't know," Jim countered softly. "Pete—I mean, General Alden—thinks the Grik have a new cheese who knows what he's about. Flynn's Rangers—shoot, the whole Third Division of Queen Maraan's Second Corps—ran into something that nearly ate it alive, and it sure gave everybody the creeps."

"What did General Lord Rolak's pet Grik, Hij-Geerki say about it? And weren't a few prisoners taken at Colombo?"

"Geeky didn't know what happened. Said he never heard of such a thing. Of course, he was just a clerk . . . sorta . . . at Rangoon. He was from Ceylon, originally, but hadn't ever been anywhere else. Besides, we caught him before all this new stuff kicked in." He paused. "He does seem loyal to Lord Rolak now, though, and everybody's pretty sure he's adopted the glorious old goat as his new pack leader, or whatever. He questioned the prisoners, but all he got was a little more about that new Grik General Halik"—Jim's face turned grim—"with a Jap tagging along, who seemed to throw just as much weight."

"Kuro-kawaa himself, perhaps?"

"No such luck. Kurokawa's apparently General of the Sea, or something, for the whole Grik Empire now. This new Jap is a soldier. My guess is he's one of those special Navy Jap Marines, or something, who was part of a contingent on *Amagi*, kind of like Alden was a shipboard Marine himself."

"That could be . . . bad."

"Right. All the more reason to stay on our toes." He nodded at the seething shoreline. Case shot continued to burst among the trees a mile or more inland, and he imagined what it must be like to be caught beneath that clawing, shrieking hell. "At least we're killing 'em now, and I bet we have their undivided attention!"

"Indeed."

"We'll keep this up all night. At dusk, *Arracca* will 'secure from air ops in all respects' and move in to replace the DDs with her big guns." Lemurian/American carriers were also heavily armed with large guns, but after *Humfra-Dar*, they'd determined they shouldn't function as battleships and aircraft carriers at the same time. The combination of bombs and highly flammable aviation gasoline was bad enough, but add gunpowder and open magazines to the mix, and they'd just been asking for trouble. With the freak hits on *Humfra-Dar* at exactly the wrong time, probably nothing would have made any difference, but they'd made as many adaptations as they could to prevent accidents from achieving the samc rcsults. Everyone knew the new safety procedures were stopgaps, but for now, it was the best they could do. "We'll get ammunition lighters to replenish the DDs; then we'll spread things out a little."

"Does that mean we will get in on the fun ourselves, at long last?" Niaal asked.

"Sure. Everyone will. We want it to look like we're building for the jump-off here, so the Grik'll keep swarming in. It's the most logical place, after all. When the sun comes up, *Arracca* will 'secure from surface action' and launch everything she's got, loaded to the gills with incendiaries—those gasoline and sticky-sap bombs." His eyes narrowed. "Then we'll burn this whole corner of India to the ground! Even if they're starting to get reports from other places, they'll have to worry those are the diversions. One way or another, they should stay tied up in knots for at least a couple of days!"

400 miles NNE
Near Maa-draas
Grik Indiaa

General Pete Alden, former Marine sergeant in USS *Houston*'s Marine contingent, splashed across the last few feet between the barge and the moonlit beach. He did it quickly, with a chill down his spine. The thick forest beyond the beach might harbor unknown threats aplenty, along with an only guessed-at number of their enemies, but he had confidence he could deal with that. Any opponent he could shoot remained just that: an opponent that he had a growing confidence he could best. The waters around Indiaa were some of the most dangerous they'd encountered yet, however, and maybe a little like Tony Scott, Captain Reddy's long-lost coxswain, any physical contact with them gave him an almost supernatural case of the creeps. Maybe there weren't as many flasher fish—tuna-size piranha, for all intents and purposes—as they endured within the Malay Barrier, but there were *sharks* out there that could sink a ship!

His staff and their guards hopped across the gap with similar uneasiness and joined him amid the tumult of an army trying to sort itself out in the darkness of an unfriendly shore. In front of them was the malignant black blob of the forest. Behind, the wave tops glittered like they were strewn with floating foil. The deceptive peacefulness of the night was marred by the now-familiar chaos of amphibious operations. There was shouting, cursing, and the wailing of the vaguely moose-shape paalkas being hitched to clattering limber traces, and the deep creaking of wooden wheels as guns, wagons, forges, and all manner of vehicles were drawn through the sand. Drummers beat regimental tattoos, drawing wayward troops into growing formations—which were often thrown into confusion by other columns of troops or teams of paalkas grunting the heavy guns through their ranks. More shouting ensued. Occasional musket shots thumped in the forest as pickets or skirmishers from advancing regiments fired at lurking Grik, other frightening creatures, or perhaps nothing at all. Drowning out much of this was the constant surf sound of thousands of hushed voices and the sea.

"Thank God we took 'em by surprise," Pete said, referring to the congestion. Really, though, he had to admit to himself that this *seemed* much better than when they went ashore on Ceylon, and it was infinitely better than the assault at Rangoon. Still . . . "I keep telling Alan we've got to have better landing craft," he complained, "that don't take so long to clear out of. We ever hit a heavily defended beach, we're going to get our heads handed to us—or eaten."

Keje-Fris-Ar, High Chief of *Salissa* Home, Reserve "Ahd-mi-raal" in the American Navy, and Commander in Chief of operations in the West (CINCWEST), nodded. "I am sure Mr. Letts is working on it, along with countless other things. He may already have solved the problem, but much depends on supply priorities, and I maintain that new weapons and ammunition, not to mention troops and provisions, take precedence." He grinned, and if his red-brown fur was indistinguishable from the night, his stocky form and bright teeth were plain. "And we do not need better landing craft as long as you continue to outwit our enemy into believing our blows fall elsewhere!"

Pete grunted. "You shouldn't be here at all. It wasn't exactly a cakewalk for the first wave. There was maybe a battalion of Grik with those weird matchlock muskets hanging around here—I don't like the way we keep seeing more of those, by the way—and I doubt Billy Flynn and his Rangers got 'em all. There might be a sniper aimin' at you right now!"

"Or you, General Aalden," Keje said blithely.

Pete grunted again and continued churning forward in the loose sand toward a hastily erected CP tent. The frequent rains meant that their precious comm gear must always be protected, and there was usually someone near such devices who had some idea where people might be. "Either way," Pete resumed, "the word's going to get out, and we can expect company shortly. You belong on *Big Sal*."

"And I shall return soon—I promise." Keje paused and his voice changed. "I can only send my people into battle so often without at least standing on the same ground they strive for, from time to time."

Pete had no response to that. He understood it perfectly. "Well, where the hell is everybody?" he demanded loudly of those under the tent.

"Just what I would like to know," reinforced General Safir-Maraan, Queen Protector of the island of B'mbaado and commander of II Corps, as she appeared out of the gloom. Only her polished, silver-washed breastplate and helmet were visible at first in the dim gri-kakka oil lamps of the CP, but her exotically beautiful, sable-furred face and otherwise black raiment grew more resolved as she drew near. She saluted Alden, and he returned it as the comm 'Cats jumped to attention. "Where are my Sularans—and their aartillery?"

"It . . . is confused," admitted a 'Cat lieutenant whose Home regiment could only be discerned by the crest on his rhino pig–leather armor. As the war in the West became less . . . linear, the Sa'aaran practice of tie-dyeing a kind of camouflage pattern in Army kilts and smocks and the painting of armor had grown almost universal. It made eminent sense, and not only did it simplify production and supply; it made troops harder to see from the air, which was a growing concern. As new supplies came forward, the regional uniforms were steadily being replaced. Even the Marines painted their field armor now, though they insisted on keeping their blue kilts. Blue blended well enough in the dense forest, Pete rationalized, as did the black of Queen Maraan's regiments, who similarly clung to their traditions—although they also darkened their armor now.

"*How* confused?" Pete demanded.

"Well . . . General Rolak has apparently personally supported Colonel Flynn's push inland, with elements of General Taa-leen's First Division and most of the First Battalion, Second Marines, and perhaps some of Colonel Enaak's Maa-ni-la Cavalry . . ."

"Goddammit!" Pete seethed almost resignedly, and the lieutenant flinched, but the Army and Marine commander's wrath was not aimed at him. "Which elements? Flynn was supposed to lead his Rangers and the Second to find that road or path junction—whatever it is—and seize it, then send runners back to show the others the way! You mean Taa-leen and Rolak just . . . went along? Besides, General Rolak's a *corps commander*, not a brigadier! What the hell does he think he's doing?"

"He is an old warrior 'marching to the sound of the guns,' as I think you would say, Gener-aal," Safir soothed in a softer tone. "He must see some advantage."

"I *know* what he's trying to do," Pete admitted. "He's trying to do *Flynn*'s job! Well, Flynn knows what to do. Once we control that junction, that goofy Grik berg where Madras should be will be cut off. We *need* Madras and its port to keep the beans and bullets on the road! I'm not really worried Rolak'll get in the way, but he does have a real job of his very own, and he's liable to get his overeager ass killed!" He looked almost pleadingly at Safir. Possibly she alone knew how much Pete counted on the old Aryaalan. "I just wish he wouldn't go romping off like this," he added.

For the first time, really, with Hij-Geerki's aid, some odd but decent captured maps, and aerial reconnaissance, the Allies had a good idea of the geography of their objectives and could finally make strategic plans. They'd spent the last month sucking the vast majority of Grik combatants into South India, and now they meant to cut them off and destroy them before possibly countless reinforcements could be summoned. Their main goal in this, besides killing Grik, was to destroy what Pete suspected was this dangerous new team of Grik leaders. After that, they would establish a temporary defensive perimeter around what they saw as the resource-rich—including iron ore, some coal, and perhaps just as important, a kind of rubber-producing forest—industrial heartland of Grik India. That should oblige what they hoped was some ordinary Grik commander to come at them in the same old way, and they'd bleed him white before resuming offensive operations.

Pete admired Rolak's guts and initiative; he just wished the wily old warrior would finally come to grips with how important he was and quit taking such spontaneous personal risks. The fact that Pete sometimes did the same thing himself didn't even enter his thoughts.

"Okay," he said with a sigh, squinting in the darkness toward where he heard the snuffling and heavy breathing of muzzled me-naaks, or "meanies," the long-legged, crocodilian, Maa-ni-la Cavalry mounts. "We'll send runners ahead to drag our . . . fiery old gentleman back here, where he can resume his proper duties and get this mess squared away." He looked at Safir. "How's Second Corps shaping up?"

Safir Maraan flicked her long black tail. "Third Division landed north of Maa-draas, as planned, and moves against the city. I came ashore on the south bank with the Third B'mbaado and Sixth Maa-ni-la Caav. I have, as yet, no idea where Colonel Grisa's Ninth Aryaal or the First and Third Sular have found themselves, and they, of course, bear the bulk of my aar-tillery." Somehow, Sularans were natural artillerymen who had an almost instinctive grasp of ballistics. Maybe that was a result of their millennia-long reliance on slings and thrown missiles instead of arrows? There was no telling. Regardless, their regiments were always gun-heavy. Safir suddenly went silent, and they listened for a moment as a furious cannonade abruptly erupted several miles to the north, the booming echoing back at them from the ships offshore.

"Ah," she said with a predatory grin. "There had been no report, and it never occurred to me that the Sularans might make landfall exactly where they were supposed to! Perhaps, with practice, things grow less confused at last?"

Pete rubbed his neck with relief. Safir was right. After some recent . . . catastrophes, he always assumed their landings would be botched. But after Alan Letts's visit, things had improved dramatically, and maybe practice did make perfect. Well, "perfect" was relative, of course. . . .

"Okay." He gestured around. "But we've still got to get *this* mess squared away, and Rolak should have been here to do it." Another wave of barges loaded with Surgeon Commander Kathy McCoy's medical division and hospital corps was hitting the beach, threatening to stack things up even more. Pete growled in frustration and held his watch to one of the lamps. "Third Division is attacking from the north right now. That'll draw the enemy. In less than an hour, we need to be hitting Madras hard from the south, so let's get these other guns on the move while we still can. General Maraan, Madras is your nut, so see if you can push things along up the beach. That attack has to go in before the Grik have a chance to get their shit in the sock."

"And you, General Aalden?" Safir asked.

"I'll stay here until we round up General Rolak; then I'll join you. If we can take the city and the crossroads before the end of the day, they'll never push us out." Pete looked at Keje. "Sir, I know your bombardment element is already in place, but we have to have that combat air patrol up with the sun, in case our lizardy friends start poking around with zeps to see what the hell we're up to. I'd also love to know if there's anything unexpected heading our way on the ground."

"Of course, General Aalden," Keje rumbled. "I shall take your hint and return to *Salissa*." He nodded at Safir. "May the Maker of all things be with you all."

CHAPTER 4

Ghaarrichk'k Madurai
Provisional capital of Grik India after the loss of Ceylon

N'galsh, Vice Regent of India and Ceylon, was almost keening with woe in the Speaking Chamber of the ancient temple. He was one of the few beings who knew that the odd stone structure festooned with the curious weathered remnants of unknown creatures carved on nearly every exposed surface actually predated the Grik conquest, which had occurred perhaps five hundred years before, but he cared nothing about that now. General Halik had been intrigued by the structure when he first arrived, and General Niwa assumed a troubled expression. But Halik's interest had quickly turned to the subject at hand, and now he glared at N'galsh with a loathing he could no longer conceal. He'd had just about enough of the officious, elitist, fear-crazed creature, and wondered that N'galsh had not already turned prey despite his Hij status. It had been a rough day for them all. Why could N'galsh not contain himself?

"They are coming, probably with the dawn!" N'galsh cried. "The world burns. It heaves! They *will* cross the Ceylon Tongue, and if you do not send more warriors, they will soon have all India as well! You must bring your warriors forward!"

"Silence!" General Halik finally snarled. "You lost any entitlement to make demands of me that your exalted station may once have afforded you, N'galsh, when you abandoned Colombo while the Battle of the Highlands was at its peak! It is *you* who cost us Ceylon, and you attend me now only at my sufferance!"

N'galsh's mouth snapped shut with a stunned, toothy *clack*, but he was clearly preparing to open it again when General Orochi Niwa of the Jaaph Hunters, Halik's implicit co-commander, stepped beside him.

"Consider before you speak, Lord Vice Regent N'galsh," he warned. "This war was never meant to be decided in India. The enemy was supposed to extend his lines to the breaking point before we struck in earnest. Now, largely because of you, India increasingly becomes the focus of both sides—and our lines of supply are even more tenuous than those of our foes. Regardless of whether General Halik is right or not, the Celestial Mother herself appointed him to command here, and in martial matters even you must no longer interfere." He shrugged slightly. "The only matters remaining in India now are military and within the province of the Great Hunt. Right now, he may feed you to his lowliest Uul, if he likes."

N'galsh shrank back from the strange creature who so rarely spoke to or around him.

Niwa turned to Halik. "Anything more you send into that . . . grinder of meat will be wasted, General. Too many are already being wasted there, and our reserves are not what they were. I know you sent word that we could hold this land if General Esshk would send us the . . . more mature of his 'Chosen Warrior' hatchlings, and I even agree, but we must meet the enemy on ground of our choosing to gain the time for them to arrive."

Despite himself, N'galsh hissed. Until recently, the chosen hatchlings Niwa referred to were selected by the Chooser, or members of his order, to be eaten at birth. The world as he knew it had gone insane.

"*If* he sends them," Halik growled, glancing darkly at N'galsh.

"If, indeed. Nonetheless, this can be *our* kind of fight."

Halik nodded, still staring at N'galsh with contempt. "Yes, it can, and you are right. We will send no more warriors into the fight for the Tongue. The enemy will cross and he will be blooded by the Uul that survive there—those not already made prey." He took a long breath. "Perhaps it might be different with the chosen warriors, as it is said. Perhaps they *can* defend. But they are not here now, and we will make this fight for India in the old way, even if just for one final time. But this time, we will strike when *we* choose."

A mud-spattered First of One Hundred suddenly dashed into the chamber and sprawled on the stone floor amid a clatter of equipment. In Halik's army, such creatures were not necessarily elevated to the exalted rank of Hij, but they were no longer just Uul either. Halik had been such a creature himself and understood the potential of older, experienced Uul. In a sense, they *were* Hij—in all but education—and they could think.

"Speak!" Halik commanded. Still groveling, the creature hissed without looking upon him.

"The prey comes!" it said.

"So soon," Niwa mused. "I had expected a dawn attack, although that is not long now."

"As had I," Halik admitted. He considered how to get the most information out of the underofficer. "Do they come in force? Are there many of them on the Tongue?"

"Not the Tongue, Lord General!" the creature whined. "I runned here, long way. Others runned long way first! I told to repeat, 'The prey is ashore in strength at Madras!' "

Niwa straightened, and Halik stood from his lounging hassock. "Madras!" they chorused, and looked at each other, both their faces hardening in their own way.

"They have done it to us again!" Halik breathed bitterly.

"Yes," Niwa said, thoughtful, even with a touch of admiration, "but where they have landed changes nothing. True, we must deploy to react, even launch spoiling attacks to keep them off balance, but the bulk of our army must remain concentrated! We can still choose our ground!"

"Yes," Halik replied, looking at the great map on the broad table. "But first we must see where they turn, how they face." He stared hard at Madras on the map. "Not this time, my clever foe!" he softly swore. "We are learning, you see. This time, you have leaped upon the back of the radaachk'kar, and it will snatch you off. This time I will have you!"

Madras Crossroads

The sun was above the horizon now, and Colonel Billy Flynn's Rangers remained crouched behind what cover they could find. The ground in front of their position heaved with mewling, wounded Grik, and feathery reptilian corpses lay sprawled before and among the bloody, exhausted troops. The Rangers and 1st of the 2nd Marines had reached their objective after floundering in the dense, almost junglelike forest for unanticipated hours before they finally cut the road that led them here. Only the most meager protective breastworks had been thrown up before the first sizable Grik force arrived and charged headlong in their singular, terrifying way to slaughter them. As usual, there'd been little organization to the attack, just a pell-mell, roaring sprint up the south fork of the road. But the blow fell with such sudden ferocity, Flynn nearly lost his tenuous grip on the strategic choke point. That initial attack was finally crushed only by concentrated volleys of loose-fitting "buck and ball" from the muzzle-loading Baalkpan Arsenal rifled muskets in the steady hands of Flynn's veteran regiment, and the rapid fire of the Marines' "Allin-Silva" conversions. In many places along the hasty line, the issue was settled with bayonets.

Sporadic flights of crossbow bolts still *thrumped* out of the woods on the south side of the cut, and General Lord Rolak's guards ringed and defended him with their bronze-faced shields as he paced along, congratulating the defenders. Things were firming up now, with the arrival of General Taa-leen's 1st "Galla" Division—mostly regiments from Baalkpan and B'mbaado—and the weight of General Rin-Taaka-Ar's 2nd Division was starting to be felt on the left flank. There were still plenty of Grik in those woods, however, and Rolak wished the comm 'Cats of the signal corps would hurry and catch them so he could get reports directly from the aircraft beginning to crisscross the sky above.

"General Lord Rolak!" cried a 'Cat in a Maa-ni-la accent. Rolak turned to see a meanie blowing through snot-slinging nostrils and clenched teeth. Several crossbow bolts festooned the ugly beast and blood leaked down its flanks, but the wounds were shallow and didn't seem to have worsened the creature's normally foul disposition. A Maa-ni-lo, still in Saan-Kakja's black-and-yellow livery, sat atop the surly mount.

"Get down from there, you fool!" Rolak cried. The rider ignored the order, but saluted.

"General Rolak, my orders are to locate you and ask if you do not agree that a corps commander's proper place in battle is a suitably removed position from which he can coordinate the movements of *all* the troops under his command, and not only the handful around him."

A tired cheer arose from the nearby troops, but Rolak slumped a bit. "Please tell my dear Queen Protector that I am withdrawing, duly chastened, to such a suitable place as we speak," he said a little ruefully. The cav 'Cat saluted again and lashed his animal with a heavy quirt. With another shower of snot, the meanie bolted back the way it had come, chased by another flurry of bolts—which provoked more musket fire.

"Colonel Flynn!" Rolak called, as the former infantryman/submariner-turned-infantryman-again rejoined him in a crouching rush. "I must retire. Thank you for your forbearance. General Taa-leen should join you shortly. Please express my compliments to the commanders of the Fifth and Seventh Baalkpan, and tell them I said they should advance behind a wall of fire and clear those archers from the woods! Your Rangers and Marines have done enough for now, and deserve a rest." He paused. "But I suppose even division commanders should not expose themselves as I have." He sighed heavily, and from another the gesture might have seemed overly theatrical, but with Rolak . . . that's just how he was. He looked back at Flynn. "Sometimes the old way of things, for my people, at least, overcomes my senses."

Flynn, with his white-streaked red hair poking from under his helmet, laughed. "Aye, sir, I know how you feel.

That's how I wound up back in the infantry!" Flynn had been a foot soldier in the Great War before joining the Navy and the submarine service. "I'll pass the word," he added. "Then, once those archers are cleared, we'll get back to work on the breastworks. They'll probably have at us again before long."

"No doubt." Rolak glanced around, taking in the bodies and the height of the sun once more. Then he gazed northeast, where a mighty column of smoke towered high enough that he could see it above the trees. Madras was burning. "The enemy certainly knows we are here now, Colonel. They will be back, and this position must hold."

Marine Captain Bekiaa-Sab-At, Flynn's exec, scrambled behind the protective shields, her hot musket in her hand. "The enemy fire is slacking," she said, even as the replying musketry around them continued to taper off. A Grik horn boomed in the distance. It might have been calling for a while.

"That is a redeployment call," Rolak said, "if Hij-Geerki described it properly." He'd left his pet Grik aboard ship—for now. He actually trusted the pathetic creature, but no sense in tempting him, he figured. "They may have learned to use it for the same effect as a retreat call, to preserve their warriors from Braad-furd's Grik Rout. I wonder . . ." He looked at Flynn. "Don't rely on it, though. It is just a thought." He blinked apologetically. "Now *I* must retreat, I fear." He gestured back at the sun. "Your deeds have been noted this day, my friends! Farewell!" He turned and strode away, back up the road they'd so recently found, against the tide of marching troops coming to their relief.

"He is a good one," Bekiaa said. "He reminds me a little of Captain Garrett. I think troops would follow anywhere he chose to lead them."

"Sure," Flynn agreed. "*We* did. And he is a little like that Garrett kid—just older, with a tail, gray fur, pointy ears. . . ."

Bekiaa chuckled. She was the only Marine still with the regiment; the others had been reassigned. She'd commanded USS *Tolson*'s Marine contingent, and she and some sailors and Marines from *Donaghey*, *Tolson,* and *Revenge* had volunteered for Flynn's outfit after *Revenge* was sunk by a fish, and Russ Chapelle's *Tolson* and Garrett's *Donaghey* went aground. Greg Garrett had inspired her by leading them through the terrible shore action that followed. *Tolson* had been destroyed, but *Donaghey* was ultimately salvaged. Bekiaa still meant to go back to sea when Chapelle got a new ship or *Donaghey*'s refit was complete. As much as she liked and admired Russ Chapelle, however, for some reason, she really wanted to join *Donaghey*—and Captain Garrett. Maybe it was because *Donaghey* was the last of the first new-construction frigates and still relied entirely on sails, or maybe it was because she'd spent most of that nightmare fight at Greg Garrett's side. In the meantime, she and Flynn's "amalgamated" Rangers had fought across Ceylon, and now they were here. *Donaghey*'s exec, and "Salig Maa-stir," Lieutenant Commander Saraan-Gaani—whom Bekiaa had a mountainous crush on—had also been with the regiment for a time, but had been sent as an envoy to his native Great South Island in hopes of bringing that land into the war.

"You know what I mean," Bekiaa said at last.

"Sure I do. Some folks have it, like Rolak, Garrett, the Skipper. I think General Alden and Queen Maraan have it . . . and so do you."

"Me?!"

"Yep."

There was an awkward almost silence punctuated by a few occasional shots as Rangers slew the least-wounded Grik they saw. No ammunition would be wasted on the rest. The Grik were gone for now, Flynn judged. The 5th and 7th could take a break. He'd get some pickets out, though. "All right," Flynn said brusquely, loudly. "They ain't payin' us by the hour. Company commanders to me! Even-numbered companies will take the first shift on the breastworks detail. Let's move the whole thing forward a little, and get a better alignment with the Tenth Baalkpan on our right!"

A PB-1B "Nancy" roared by overhead, its OC (observer/copilot) dropping a weighted note with a colorful streamer attached. A squad from the 1st Marines went for it and brought it to Flynn, who was acting division CO. "Okay," Flynn drawled after he unwrapped the dispatch and read it. "This says there's a bigger Grik force charging up the road through what's left of the one we pushed around. Ought to be here inside an hour."

"That is as we expected," Bekiaa said.

Flynn's face scrunched into a skeptical expression. He waved the note. "Sure, but the flyboys say there's nothing behind *that* force at all. Not on the south road, anyway. Weird."

"Then we should be grateful. Perhaps we did achieve surprise. It might take them days to react in force."

"Maybe . . ." Flynn shook his head. "Never mind. Maybe I'm still spooked by how they hid tens of thousands of their warriors in those mountains east of Colombo—and I figure it would be a lot easier to stash them in a jungle!" He snorted. "Well, big-picture thinking's not my job, thank God. There's still a lot of Griks coming our way and we'll be plenty busy before long. Better get at it on the breast-works—and tell the fellas to expect a *million* of those Grik buggers by morning, from any damn direction! I don't care what the flyboys say."

CHAPTER 5

Respite Island
February 29, 1944

The response to USS *Walker*'s return to Respite Island was notably different from when she first appeared there. The beautiful anchorage at the bright-beached foot of the fortified peak overlooking the crystalline water was packed with ships of all description, and where there'd been uncertainty and hesitant wonder the first time the destroyer appeared, now there was genuine delight at the sight of her. The guns in the high, white-walled fortress boomed in salute, the reports dull in the stiff breeze, but they were repeated by many of the anchored ships, and steam whistles whooped exuberantly. *Walker* fired a precise, four-gun salute salvo, symbolically emptying her guns, and sounded her shrill whistle and mournful horn in reply. The harbor pilot who'd boarded the ship beyond the dangerous reef had been brought out by the same pretty little single-masted topsail cutter that met them before, but this time its crew was grinning and talkative as it paced *Walker* through the channel. The pilot himself made no attempt to take the wheel or assert any control whatsoever over the unfamiliar vessel, but diligently and professionally directed them through to the anchorage. He was used to steamers, but had no notion of *Walker*'s handling characteristics.

The Honorable New Britain Company had been extremely unpopular on Respite, and the Governor, a man named Radcliff, had strongly hinted that if the Empire continued down the self-destructive path the Company had been leading it, his island might have no choice but to break away. The success of *Walker*'s mission to the heart of the Empire had clearly come as a great relief to the people here—yet now the Empire was at war with the Holy Dominion and had joined the Alliance against the Grik as well. Matt hadn't been sure how they'd be received by the independent-minded Respitans, knowing their isolated island would become an important strategic nexus of contact between the two powers. They'd been willing to help before, with limited basing and fueling facilities and a powerful wireless station, but it had been understood that the Allies would leave them alone once the situation in the Empire was sorted out. Now that was out of the question, and despite cordial correspondence via that wireless facility, Matt expected some resentment. He couldn't be more pleased by this new attitude on display.

"Thank you, Lieutenant Busbee," he said when the pilot pronounced them free to maneuver in the anchorage. He scanned the shoreline with his binoculars, taking note of the new fueling pier and much-enlarged government dock. "You have the conn, Mr. Kutas," he said to the badly scarred first lieutenant and former chief quartermaster. "Lay us alongside the dock first, if you please. After we've paid our respects, we'll make Spanky happy and shift her over to the fueling pier."

"Aye, aye, Captain. I have the conn," Norman Kutas replied formally, and Matt stepped out onto the port bridgewing. Moments later, Sandra and the Bosun joined him there.

"Bashear's assembling a side party to pipe you and the ambassador ashore, Skipper," Gray announced, anticipating the order, and Matt smiled his appreciation. "Thanks, Boats." He knew Gray, Silva, and Stites would accompany Sandra and him ashore, no matter what he said or how safe it was, so there was no point telling them not to. Down on the well deck he could see the ambassador's party, including his aide and Midshipman Brassey, already waiting, peering excitedly over the solid railing there. He was surprised to see Diania, Sandra's own dark-skinned, raven-haired steward waiting to go ashore as well. Diania had been Sandra's first human female recruit into the American Navy. She'd found the striking but somewhat . . . odd woman in Maa-nila, but Diania was from Respite and Matt hadn't expected her to want to go ashore. She'd never been forced into any . . . disreputable pursuits—she'd been a "carpentress"—but he'd still supposed she'd resist revisiting her former life of forced labor. On the contrary, she seemed even more anxious to go ashore than the others. Sandra followed Matt's gaze.

"She still has family here—or friends she considers family." She looked squarely at Matt with a slight grin. "She also has a kind of . . . evangelical air about her today," she warned. "I wouldn't be surprised if the Navy had a number of new recruits shortly!"

Matt exhaled an exasperated breath, but then noticed the way Gray was staring at the dusky beauty and his eyes went wide. The Bosun glanced at him, probably expecting a response to what Sandra said, and saw his expression. He actually blushed!

"Uh . . . that's all we need!" Gray grumbled defensively. "More damn women aboard—no offense, Lieutenant Tucker!" Hurriedly, he excused himself and practically bolted from the pilothouse.

"Good Lord!" Matt said, astonished. "You'd almost think he was sweet on her, and he's what—three times her age?"

"He *is* sweet on her," Sandra confirmed, looking sternly at him. "I know that look pretty well. What's more, I think Diania's sweet on *him*. She goes on a little too much about that 'grate, beastly ogre, Mr. Gray,'" she added, slipping into a passable re-creation of the girl's convoluted brogue. "And so what if he's a little older than she is—"

"A little!" Matt spluttered.

"They've both had it rough. Diania's been a virtual slave most of her life, with no real prospect of a decent life—not to mention a decent *man*. And Fitzhugh Gray lost his only son aboard *Oklahoma*. The only other things he's cared about in years are this ship and you! Give him a break. I hope they *do* get together."

Matt shook his head, eyes narrowing. "You haven't been pushing that along just a little, have you?"

"What if I have?"

Matt's full entourage, or, more properly perhaps, Ambassador Forester's escort, included Sandra, Diania, and Lieutenant Bachman. Gray, Silva, and Stites represented the Captain's Guard. Chack led an honor guard of six 'Cat Marines—all they had left aboard—in his immaculately turned-out Marine major persona. When aboard *Walker*, his Home, Chack reverted to what he considered his permanent role as a "mere" bosun's mate who happened to be in charge of all the Marines, in spite of his growing reputation and increasingly greater status ashore.

Governor Radcliff greeted them himself, accompanied by a large, enthusiastic gathering and an . . . unusual little band that played an oddly familiar fanfare as *Walker*'s party marched down the gangway and assembled respectfully as the music played. While he waited, Matt evaluated the Imperial Governor of Respite. He was dressed as finely as before, though Matt now knew his clothes were slightly out of date by the fashion standards of New London. He remained portly, but radiated the bloom of a less-taxed constitution and didn't seem nearly as harried and concerned as he had during their first meeting. Matt briefly wondered if he'd come down the mountain from the governor's mansion on the grounds of the high fortifications, riding his unassuming burro once again. When the music finally stopped, Radcliff strode, with an expression of happy anticipation, to face Matt.

"My dear Captain Reddy," he boomed warmly, sketching a return to the salute Matt and the others offered. "Ambassador Forester!" he added, returning Forester's bow. "You come extremely highly recommended, sir!" He straightened and addressed them all. "I can't wait to hear your news. I am still amazed by the wonder of wireless, but nothing can substitute for words spoken by one friend to another!" He beamed. "I am so happy to see you all! Please, I would receive you more properly at my home, where we can discuss in greater comfort the heady advances you have wrought. I have taken the liberty of providing sufficient transportation."

"Of course, Your Excellency. We're at your service," Matt said, then paused. "Sir, you know my other companions, but if I may present our Minister of Medicine, Lieutenant Sandra Tucker? I believe you may remember that I've mentioned her before."

To Sandra's amazement, Radcliff snatched her hand and knelt over it, brushing it with his lips.

"I am deeply honored to meet you at last, my lady!" he told her earnestly, then his smile returned. "The last time I saw this man of yours, he was prepared to raze the entire Empire to the ground if a hair on your head—or that of our own Princess Rebecca—had been harmed. I naturally assumed that you must be the beauty of the world to inspire such devotion, but now my eyes chastise my imagination for the woeful disservice it did you!"

Beneath her tan, Sandra's face went dark red.

"You are . . . flattering and very charming, Your Excellency," she somehow managed, then gave Matt a knowing glance he'd seen before that always seemed equally proud . . . and afraid for him. "And it seems you got to know Captain Reddy very well indeed."

"Quite," Radcliff replied softly, gently squeezing her hand before releasing it. He turned back to Matt, his enthusiasm reborn. "There is so much I want to tell you, I feel that I may burst!"

•

They sat in the shade of the vast, wraparound porch encompassing the lower floor of the governor's residence. Moisture condensed on glasses of cool beer arrayed on a wide wicker table, surrounded by the visitors and the half-dozen advisors and members of the governor's staff. As when he'd first visited there, Matt was struck by the glorious view beyond the sloping parade ground of the fort. To the northeast, the sky was clear and bright. Due east, a few lazy clouds lingered. South of there, a dense, dark squall lashed the sea, and wispy white tendrils of the thing extended out to either side. The road that brought them to the summit wound around the back of the mountain, giving them a slowly rising view of the lush, scenic valley where the bulk of Respite City lay. Cultivated fields surrounded the population center, and beyond them loomed the dense, dark jungle. The contrasts were so sharp, so extreme, it was as though he'd glimpsed several entirely separate worlds since leaving his ship. The impression was similar wherever he went, he supposed, but only here was it quite so profound.

Matt turned his attention to his more immediate surroundings. He was pleased to see Radcliff's wife, Emelia, again, particularly when she took her place with the rest of them, right beside her husband. The daughters he'd met on the last occasion weren't present and he wondered about that, but he knew Chack must be relieved. Imperial ladies couldn't seem to resist petting his soft, brindled fur, and it mortified him. Chack wasn't the only Lemurian there, however. They'd been joined by two others, both seemingly in a state of reverential awe toward the men and the 'Cat just returned from the east. Lieutenant Haan-Sor-Plaar commanded another new Fil-pin-built steam frigate, USS *Finir-Pel*, and Lieutenant Radaa-Nin was in charge of a pair of fast fleet oilers and three munitions and supply ships—all new sailing steamers, and all bound for New Scotland. Matt would get with them later and brief them on what to expect at their destination. In any event, he knew Radcliff had certainly become acquainted with many more Lemurians since they'd first met, and maybe he'd banned his daughters because he'd finally noticed the . . . discomfort their attentions caused his furry guests.

Interestingly, this time Matt didn't sense the slightest resentment toward Emelia's presence from the governor's other advisors, and she smiled warmly at him when he caught her eye. That was new as well. Matt knew that, despite Imperial custom, Emelia had long been the governor's most influential advisor, and she'd been as worried about the Alliance as she was about the deterioration of the Empire. He was glad to see that her concerns in that regard seemed to have been put to rest. He looked to Emelia's right, where Sandra had taken a seat, and was surprised to see the older woman pat her hand occasionally as if to reassure her. He'd never known Sandra to *need* reassurance, particularly from strangers, but he'd never seen her around such an almost motherly, astute observer as Emelia before. . . . He shook his head.

"Captain Reddy," Governor Radcliff began, "first let me extend my most sincere condolences for the sad losses your people and your remarkable ship suffered during the recent, glorious campaigns, not to mention the terrible losses sustained on the Grik front. . . . I saw the casualty lists, of course, when they were passed along to you, and I understand some of them constituted direct, personal losses to you and your ship. Friends and former shipmates." He sighed. "We have never seen such a war and can hardly imagine what it must be like. . . . I am not glad our Empire is beginning to find out, but I recognize and even embrace the necessity." He met Matt's gaze. "You will return home with a strong alliance with my country, for what you are doing for us, and we will help you in every way we can as well." He straightened in his seat. "We have raised a full regiment here on Respite, for service in the west."

"That's very generous, Your Excellency," Matt said softly. It was. Respite was the oldest Imperial territory, established even before the Empire existed, but the population there and on all the islands under its jurisdiction probably amounted to less than two hundred thousand.

"It only makes sense," Radcliff said. "Wherever our people fight, it will be far from home, and with the Doms pushed back to their continental holdings, the Grik are actually closer." He took a sip of beer, then forced a smile back on his face. "But enough of that! Congratulations are in order for many things! You have doubtless observed that the Grand Alliance is extremely popular here?"

Matt nodded. They'd ascended the mountain aboard a kind of carriage reminiscent of a San Francisco streetcar drawn by burros, and the road had been lined with enthusiastic well-wishers, quite a few of whom were women. "Indeed, Your Excellency. I'm glad to see it."

"Take my word, Captain, the greeting is quite sincere. You accomplished everything we could have wished and more. You personally may not have saved the Princess Rebecca—and your lovely bride-to-be—but your people did. And then *you* avenged their abduction and mistreatment!" He leaned forward with a genuine grin. "The official version of that is colorful enough, I assure you, but I beg a firsthand account!"

"Perhaps this is not the setting or the time to press him on such a personal matter, Mr. Radcliff," the governor's wife gently admonished him in a mellow tone. Radcliff spared her an exasperated but indulgent glare.

"Later, then, if you please, Captain. Over dinner? Still, not only did you destroy the beastly Company's domination of our lives and hasten the end of the inhumane institution of indenture, but you also did no less than save the Empire itself from conquest or at least dissolution. You have my most profound thanks."

"We didn't do it alone," Matt said quietly.

"No, but you struck the spark and fanned the flames of liberty to life! I wish to God I had been with you! As you know, I had begun to despair, but to be there and see my emperor restored and country saved . . ."

"Please do save your speech for the ball, Mr. Radcliff," Emelia chastised. "I fear you are embarrassing the good captain!"

"Embarrassing!" Radcliff huffed. "Heroes are always embarrassed. They are supposed to be."

"Ball?" Sandra suddenly interjected with an expression close to fear on her face.

"Oh yes!" Emelia gushed, grasping both Sandra's hands in hers. "As soon as I learned of yours and Captain Reddy's desire to wed here—on our island!—I began planning the most glorious celebration! The romance of your . . . situation has resonated quite deeply with our people, and you stand as a figurehead for what all women in the Empire can achieve! The event will celebrate your wedding to the captain, of course, but it will also honor the Allied victories in the east, the resurrection of the Empire, and even what contributions our small land has made to facilitate those accomplishments. And, incidentally, as I said, I mean to stress your own achievements to inspire our people! It will be an event to rival an Imperial coronation, with repercussions that will be felt for decades, at least!"

"Oh, my God," Sandra whispered, and Matt barely suppressed a laugh.

"I guess it isn't *your* 'operation' after all, Lieutenant Tucker," he said with a straight face but a twinkle in his eye.

The discussion resumed, returning to more serious matters, and shortly, Matt dismissed the honor guard to return to the ship and whatever duties they had there. He knew Spanky meant to commence repairs as soon as possible now that the ship was at rest, and Marines were part of the deck division when aboard as far as Chack—and certainly the Bosun—were concerned. The Bosun himself, as well as Silva and Stites, remained. They may have been a little bored, but habit kept them alert and listening to the conversation. Matt didn't mind. Chairman Adar would likely pump Silva for his impressions of the governor once he returned to Baalkpan, and that was okay with him. Adar needed as many impressions of their new allies as he could get, and he'd be able to read between the lines of Silva's likely flippant description.

"And I am glad to see that we will have an official envoy to the western allies at last, Ambassador Forester," Radcliff continued dryly. "It is long overdue."

"Indeed," Forester agreed with a chuckle. Two envoys, one from Respite and another selected by the Imperial Court of Proprietors, had already gone to Maa-ni-la. Each had adamantly opposed the presence and credentials of the other, and Saan-Kakja sent them both away in disgust. That was before the Imperial situation had stabilized, but all it accomplished was to annoy the High Chief of all the Fil-pin Lands even further, and make her more reluctant than ever to send troops and ships to defend the Empire. "I understand I may have my work cut out for me, in regard to the . . . charming young Saan-Kakja, at least."

"With all due respect, sir," Matt warned, "whatever you do, don't let her age fool you into thinking you can push her around."

Forester held his hands up and laughed. "Oh no! As a friend of the Governor-Emperor, I have known Princess

Rebecca all her life. I'm told she and Saan-Kakja are fast friends and very much alike. I have seen firsthand that fewer years do not necessarily equate to lesser wisdom—or determination. Quite the opposite, on occasion. And I wouldn't dream of trying to push *Her Highness* around! I want nothing less than Saan-Kakja's—and Adar's—complete satisfaction with our membership in the Alliance."

"Good. In that case, I'd also caution you against pressing for a larger commitment in the east, from either of them. At least for now. You may not see this yet, but I believe the Grik are the most pressing enemy, and the western allies have been more generous already than anybody there—including me—is really comfortable with."

Forester's face turned grim. "It is difficult to understand how the situation on the Grik front could be more pressing than the menace posed by the Holy Dominion, but I am prepared to concede it. You have fought both enemies on both fronts, and I trust your judgment. But do you really believe these Grik—mere savage . . . reptilians—may actually surpass our own technology?"

"Maybe not surpass, Your Excellency, but they can match it—particularly with the help of the Japanese Captain Kurokawa. I honestly don't know what motivates him—other than insanity, I guess. But he's already brought the Grik too close for comfort, and with their numbers—and frankly, ferocity—all they need to be is close."

"But the Dominion has vast reserves as well," Radcliff observed, "and other than your *Walker* and your flying machines, there is little material difference between us."

"True, but we've hammered a big chunk of their fleet, and for now, our tactics are better. The Enchanted Isles are at risk because the Dom fleet is still respectable, particularly if it concentrates, and those islands are strategically placed to support future operations against them. That's why I agree that Harvey Jenks needs to relieve them as soon as he can, because we're going to need them. But otherwise, the Empire and its continental colonies are secured by a vast ocean, and I'm told, impassable territory between the colonies and Dominion territory. Our navies control that ocean.

"On the other hand, the Grik industrial base may actually be broader than the Dominion's. We know they're building a new fleet, and when they're ready, we expect them to hit us with something huge and likely unexpected. Kurokawa—and some of the Grik Hij—aren't fools. They've already hit us with flying machines of their own—much larger and more complicated than ours, and they had a lot of them." He shrugged. "Ours were faster and better armed. That was the difference." He looked at Sandra, then at Chack and the other Lemurians. "Trust me. The Grik have to come first."

"Well, then. I will not argue it with you or anyone else at present," Forester conceded. "Your people . . . your friends . . . *have* been generous. I do pray your evaluation is correct, however."

"So do I."

A servant attired in the white coat and knee breeches of the Respite militia appeared. "Dinner, if ye please," he announced.

Matt was too accustomed to the spartan shipboard fare to fully appreciate the sumptuous feast prepared for them. The food was just too rich. The governor and his wife ate theirs with obvious relish, but Sandra, seated beside him now, only picked at her plate. She seemed to blush every time he caught her eye, still embarrassed by the sheer scope of the spectacle Lady Emelia was planning. She'd said she expected a big wedding on Respite, but the description Emelia continued whispering to her during the meeting outside was beyond anything she'd ever imagined.

The visiting Lemurian officers were enjoying their meal, and Chack was curiously sampling a little of everything. Matt was amazed when Silva caught a server's sleeve and ostentatiously asked if another of the chicken-size, broiled "lizardy-lookin' guys," might be brought out. When the server went to fetch it, Stites leaned in to Silva and muttered: "Good thing Larry ain't here. He'd have to go hungry or turn cannibal."

"Wouldn't be the first time. I seen him eat lotsa critters more like his relations than these little boogers," Dennis answered in what his damaged hearing probably thought was a whisper, then looked up, surprised by the sudden silence around the table. "Course, maybe he woulda ate the fish," he offered.

Chack couldn't help it and burst out in a hacking laugh, blinking apology at the same time. The other 'Cats joined him, and soon everyone was laughing, even Sandra, who'd needed something to break her tension. Matt explained about Lawrence, and the comment better understood, the laughter redoubled. When it finally died down, it was replaced by a more lively conversation.

Silva can break anything, Matt thought with amusement, *even ice.*

"Oh, my dear captain," Radcliff said at last. "I wish you had brought the creature along! I simply can't wait to meet him."

There was a knock on the great door that led to the dining chamber, and another servant went to investigate the cause.

"We don't consider Lawrence a 'creature' anymore, Your Excellency," Matt explained mildly. "He's a Tagranesi . . . well, Sa'aaran, now, and if his Grik cousins are capable of achieving his level of intelligence, we've got a lot to worry about."

The servant hurried over to stand beside the governor, a frown on his face, and waited for Radcliff's attention.

"Yes, yes. What is it, Gomez?"

The dark-skinned servant, probably a descendant of the Spanish/Indian mix in the Dominion, handed over a bifolded page sealed with wax. "Which it's a dispatch from the Allied wireless station, Guv'ner," he said with a typical Imperial accent. "An' it's marked 'urgent,' as ye can see. Yer orders are never ta delay d'livery o' such."

"Indeed, indeed," Radcliff replied, taking the folded square. After a brief hesitation, he offered it to Matt. "It's most likely meant for you, after all."

"Go ahead, Your Excellency," Matt said, but his chest tightened. It was his sad experience that urgent communications rarely carried good news.

Radcliff nodded and broke the seal, then unfolded the sheet and held it at arm's length to better see the words. The diners around the table were silent now, watching with curiosity. Matt's stomach churned with dread when he saw the governor's growing frown. Without a word, Radcliff passed the message across and Matt looked at it. Sandra caught her breath when she saw the expression forming on his face as he read, and she put her hands on his shoulder. Finally, he looked up and his gaze was bleak.

"Well, it's started in the west. Alden has invaded India and has a solid beachhead at Madras. First and Second Corps are pushing inland, and Third Corps has crossed from Ceylon in the south. So far, the Grik are on the run." He paused and there was a spatter of applause, but Matt's tone didn't reflect the good news. He continued.

"A little closer at hand, it would seem Commander Sato Okada's *Mizuki Maru*, the armed . . . freighter that Saan-Kakja sent after the Jap tin can *Hidoiame*, met the enemy . . . and was apparently lost with all hands."

Sandra gasped and Gray cursed aloud.

"Where . . . when?" Chack asked.

"The Sea of Japan." He waved the sheet. "The position's here. 'When' was almost a month ago!"

"But . . . why wait until now to tell us?" Sandra demanded.

"Because we were too far away to do anything about it, and Saan-Kakja's fully aware of our damage and our weapons limitations," Matt answered bitterly. "She probably didn't want us to push things and hoped she could handle it on her own. Three ships sent to the last known position to search for survivors didn't return, and the only one with a transmitter reported being under attack before contact was lost. Several squadrons of 'Nancys' were sent to locate the enemy. One squadron actually found her and bombed her, but no damage was seen—and four of the six planes were shot down!"

"Oh, my God!" Sandra whispered, her hand over her mouth.

"Nancys," or PB-1Bs were single-engine floatplanes that looked like miniature versions of a PBY Catalina, and they were the current backbone of the Allied air arm. More advanced aircraft were in the works, but "Nancys" had proven to be reliable and versatile little planes. Each had a crew of two.

"The only good thing, I guess," Matt continued, "is that nobody reported seeing the destroyer's tanker consort, and she can't go far without her. She probably ran around for a while trying to throw us off the trail to where the tanker is—but now she's going to have to find someplace else to hole up, and she's got to get her tanker and maybe break down and pack up whatever shore installations they've spent irreplaceable resources on first!"

"That could take some time," Gray said, scratching the stubble on his chin. They finally had razors again, and Matt wasn't the only clean-shaven human in the Alliance anymore.

"Yes," Chack said, "and we know where they must be!"

"*If* Okada was right and they really did set up around where Sapporo ought to be . . . Damn, I need a chart!" Matt said. The Imperials knew almost nothing of that region. "Governor Radcliff, could I trouble you to send a runner to my ship? Or maybe to Lieutenant Haan's *Finir-Pel*? His charts may be more up to date than *Walker*'s. If we can compare where *Hidoiame* was last seen to where we suspect her base might be, maybe we can catch her before she scoots!"

"What are you talking about?" Sandra suddenly demanded, looking at Matt with stormy eyes. "*You're* not going after her!" The Imperials around the table were visibly shocked by her outburst, but Matt just looked at her. "It's not that you shouldn't go or I don't want you to," Sandra continued. "That's true enough. But I *forbid* it because you *can't*!"

"You *forbid*?" Matt demanded, eyes wide.

Sandra stood and crossed her arms beneath her breasts. "Yes! As Medical Officer of USS *Walker* and Minister of Medicine for the Allied Powers, I declare you, your ship, and her crew unfit to pursue *Hidoiame*! None of you are sufficiently recovered from your wounds, physical and psychological, and you have neither the strength nor material means to accomplish the mission!"

"Shit!" murmured Silva, too loud again, in a tone that showed admiration for her angle, if not her message. "Look at her go!" The Bosun, face purple, made a savage "cut it" gesture at him.

"I and I alone am the judge of whether or not my ship is fit for action!" Matt said coldly.

"And I say that if you intend to pursue *Hidoiame* at this time without the rest your crew needs and the refit your ship requires, then your judgment must be impaired by exhaustion, Captain Reddy! You can't be everywhere at once. You and your crew, your ship, have been too close to the fire for too long, and sooner or later it's going to burn you up! You know that yourself, but if you can't see that going after *Hidoiame* will turn 'sooner' into *'now,'* then you can't be thinking clearly! She's a new ship—faster, heavier, and better armed! How close would you have to get to even damage her with the primitive shells you've been forced to use? All that time while you're trying to close, *Walker* will be taking fire. And it won't be cannonballs—it'll be high-explosive shells, accurately delivered, to kill your crew and your ship!"

Sandra's argument was beginning to take its toll. She was right, and Matt knew it. *Walker* had a full load of ammunition for her main battery, all but the Japanese 4.7-inch dual-purpose that had replaced her own damaged number four gun on the aft deckhouse. They had almost shot it "dry," and other ships and installations armed with the rest of *Amagi*'s salvaged secondaries had priority for resupply. The black-powder four-inch-fifty shells *Walker* had taken east and that supply ships had begun stockpiling for her at almost any friendly port she might touch, had worked better than they had any right to expect, but they just didn't have the range to go up against *Hidoiame*. But the rogue Japanese destroyer they'd left Okada to deal with had proven she was just too dangerous to run loose anymore. If they didn't catch her now, how would they find her later? What if, God forbid, she managed to make it all the way to join Kurokawa and the Grik?

"Aah, Cap-i-taan Reddy?" said Raada-Nin reluctantly. "My manifests include supplies dispatched for the . . . main-tin-aance of your ship. Among those supplies is a quantity of ammunition for your main baat-tery. *New* ammunition." He blinked apology at Sandra, but he couldn't keep it secret.

"New?"

"Ay, Cap-i-taan. From Mr. Saan-dison in Ord-naance."

He fished in his belt pouch and extended a letter. "This is from him to you. I would have left it for you had we already off-loaded and sailed for New Bri-taan Isles, but may-be you look at it now?"

Wordlessly, Matt took the letter and read.

To: Captain Reddy, CINCAF,
HCAC, and CO USS Walker
(DD-163)

From: Lt. Cmdr. B.
Sandison, Acting Minister
of Ordnance

Dear Skipper,

I don't know if this will find you, but if it does, I hope it finds you well and already on your way home. You'll be glad to hear that we've finally solved the guncotton issue and I'm really kind of embarrassed how easy it was once we quit trying to make it so hard. Evidently, cellulose is cellulose, to a larger degree than I had imagined. Anyway, we now have some four-inch-fifty shells I think you're going to like. I won't go into all the tech stuff here—some is stenciled on the crates and there's more for Campeti in an insert pamphlet—but basically, pressures look good (17.4 tons). I'm sure glad we didn't fork over the copper rods for making the pressure disks! Who knows what kind of "copper" they are, and how to duplicate it! We tested the shells in Old Number Four, as we call her (she's shipshape again, by the way), and S-19's deck gun. I'm happy to report that the trajectories matched book specs. There's still something screwy with the burn rate or the alloy we're using for the brass shells is a little off, because sometimes (around 10 percent) they split, but no chamber damage has been observed.

The projectiles aren't armor piercing—what's out there to pierce?—and we stuck with the old, specified 1.1-pound black-powder bursting charge, but the projectiles are the proper 33-pound iron with brass bearing bands. They shoot straighter, hit harder, and pack nearly the same wallop our old HE did. I think you'll like them.

I've sent close to a full load out with Lieutenant Raada-Nin. He has orders to leave half at Respite and take the other half to Scapa Flow if you don't meet. More are already at Manila, along with all the specs to start production on them, as well as the Jap secondaries scattered around.

Other projects are proceeding in every department, and I hope to have some very pleasant surprises for you soon.

Respectfully,
B. Sandison
Lt. Cmdr.
USNR

Still without speaking, he handed the letter to Sandra, who scanned it incredulously. "So?" she demanded harshly, tossing the sheet toward the Bosun. "What difference does that make? Maybe you've got better ammunition now. What chance will that give you?"

"An *even* chance," Matt replied, "and that's better than usual."

"Even," Sandra snorted. "Right. That's like saying an old man is 'even' with a teenager because he can spit just as far."

"Lady Sandra!" Emelia gasped. She was not above such disputes with her husband, but never like this, in front of others, and she was keenly aware of the presence of all the Imperial men—something Sandra seemed to have forgotten.

Sandra suddenly looked around at the uncomfortable or disapproving stares, and realized with sick certainty that her outburst had doomed her cause. If only she'd waited, tried to reason with Matt in private, she may have stood a chance. But now she'd backed him into a corner, in front of men—their allies—who would think him weak if he conceded to her . . . and they *could not* think the Commander in Chief of All Allied Forces was weak. The Lemurians would understand how crazy it was for Matt to risk himself and his ship like this unless the situation was utterly desperate. The whole Alliance could crumble if something happened to him; he was still the primary unifying force. But as much as she knew the Imperials respected and honored Matt as a warrior and even as the savior of their country, they had a strong emperor again, and a country with a long tradition of unity. They just wouldn't get it yet, wouldn't *think* that way. . . . It was then that she caught the very distressed expression on Ambassador Forester's face. *Or would they?* she thought.

"The young lady may have a point, you know," Forester said in a soothing tone. "Granted, her outburst was . . . unseemly, but the traditions of the Americans are different from ours and it is understandable if she is upset. We were discussing her wedding just a short time ago, after all."

Sandra's ears burned at the thought they would believe that was her primary motivation, but she kept her mouth shut.

"I know little of *Walker*. Her design is foreign to me. But even I can see that she has suffered serious damage that cannot all be repaired here. Is it wise to risk her and her brave, valuably experienced crew to destroy a single ship?"

"No," Matt himself agreed honestly, "but wise or not, I don't see a choice."

"Keep sendin' planes after her. Bomb her to scrap, I say," said the Bosun.

"And lose how many? Six already tried, and four were lost without even scratching her paint. That's eight precious flyers we can't afford to lose." Matt shook his head. "*Walker*'s more important to me than to anybody, but in many respects, this war has passed her by almost as thoroughly as our war against the Japs did. She's not going to decide this one either, Boats. Not by herself. Lieutenant Tucker's right about *that*. Sure, she might as well be a battleship in a surface action against *what we've seen*, but air power will most likely be the tipping point. In the meantime, though, it's not even close to 'even' for whatever *Hidoiame* runs into. Apparently, not only did she destroy *Mizuki Maru*, but two feluccas and a frigate. That's close to seven hundred people she's killed, beyond her previous . . . atrocities."

"One of our big carriers with *Amagi*'s secondaries could take her," the Bosun speculated.

"If it could draw her in," said Chack, "but it would never

catch her. An entire wing of 'Naan-cees' could overwhelm her defenses and probably sink her. . . ."

"But the losses would be terrible," Matt repeated, "and the question's moot anyway. Saan-Kakja's building two more flat-tops for deployment to the east, but though they'll be heavily armed with conventional weapons—muzzle-loading cannon, and big ones too—they're still limited to a couple of thousand yards, tops. Besides, neither of them will be ready for sea sooner than three months from now. That's too long."

"So you're going to do it," Sandra stated. It wasn't a question.

"No choice. I wish we'd been close enough to do it when we first heard about her, but all our major ports and strategic outposts are well enough armed to protect themselves, and besides, we had other priorities." He shrugged. "And I thought Okada would handle her." He was silent for a moment, and everyone saw the thoughts colliding behind his eyes.

"Hell!" he said suddenly. "I hate it how things sneak up on me! I just realized that she represents another, more pressing threat I hadn't even thought of before. She had an oiler in tow when she came through her squall—or whatever it was—so we've been thinking she'd just hole up. But what if the oiler wasn't full? What if she's starting to run low on fuel, or what'll she do when she does? The longer she's on the loose, the sooner that'll happen. If she's based where we think she is, she can't even drill for oil like we did because there isn't any there. She can't take it from any of our facilities or set up shop nearby without us knowing it . . . and she can't even know everywhere we are!"

Matt's face turned even grimmer as he looked around the table. He saw Chack blinking furiously in thought.

"That means this bad Jaap will have only one other way to sustain himself, at least in the short term," Chack murmured, his tail swishing behind him.

"Right," said the Bosun thoughtfully. "She'll have to go after our ships like a g—dad-blasted pirate! Take oil from the steamers, probably the food and supplies from other ships in the pipeline, headed either way. She might already be doing it!"

"That Jap tin can's a major threat to our shipping lanes, all around the Fil-pin lands, at least," Matt confirmed. "With her range advantage and speed, she might as well be the *Graf Spee*!"

"And us without the old *Exeter* to chase her down," Gray agreed, oblivious that most of those present had no idea what he was talking about. He remembered when he and his captain had watched the Japanese sink the famous British cruiser, almost effortlessly.

"Yeah . . ." Matt's sigh was almost a groan. "This *Hidoiame* can cripple our overall war effort, on both fronts, whether she's become Kurokawa's stooge or not." He paused. "Lieutenant Raada-Nin, would you mind taking Chief Gunner's Mate Stites out to look at these new shells?"

"Of course not, Cap-i-taan Reddy."

"Good. Silva, go with 'em. Pick up Campeti on the way. We'll have to test them, obviously, and recalibrate the gun director, but I want to know what all of you think immediately. Ask Spanky and Tabby to join us up here as well." He looked around the table, his gaze fastening on Governor Radcliff. "I don't mean to impose, sir. If you'd rather I go back to my ship . . ."

"Absolutely not! No imposition at all. Battles are complex things, I'm told, and though I've no notion how to fight one, perhaps I can learn a bit about preparing for one, at least."

"Thank you, sir," Matt said sincerely. "And if you or your officers have any questions—or suggestions—I'd love to hear them." He looked at Sandra then and saw her desolate expression. He'd called her bluff and she'd backed down, as he knew she would. He actually agreed with many of her arguments . . . and maybe his judgment *was* affected? He *was* tired; everyone was, and they'd desperately needed this . . . respite. He could also tell that she knew he was right as well, however. Particularly as the new threat sank in. She never would have retreated otherwise. Not for the first time, the two absolute necessities they advocated were irreconcilable. But this time, for the first time, he was afraid it might tear them apart. He longed to hold her, reassure her, and wished they could take some time alone. Maybe later, if she'd allow it. For now, he had to plan. So did Sandra, it seemed, because Emelia Radcliff suddenly rose and tugged her by the hand.

"You men may draft your war," she said a little harshly. "Lady Sandra and I will try to salvage her wedding—if it is still to occur at all." She stared hard at Matt, and though he could tell she was angry, he was surprised to get the impression she wasn't only mad at him. Sandra wouldn't—couldn't, he thought—meet his gaze. "I presume you won't be steaming away again at first light, Captain Reddy?"

"No, ma'am," Matt replied quietly. "We couldn't if I wanted to. We'll have to remain here several days, at least."

"Gomez!" Governor Radcliff suddenly called. "You may clear away the debris of our meal now. And do bring brandy, if you please!"

CHAPTER 6

Respite Island
March 2, 1944

Shockingly well-crafted, almost *furniture-grade* wooden crates of dazzlingly polished (four each) four-inch-fifty shells came aboard in the early-morning light and were shifted to the magazines fore and aft. Campeti crouched beside one such crate, the lead-painted lid prized off, shuffling thoughtfully through a sheaf of pages. Stites was poking around in the cluster of carefully swaddled, white-painted Baalkpan bamboo tubes protecting the ammunition, and Silva sat on the deck with one of the heavy, gleaming, fixed cartridges on his lap, fingering the waxed-paper seal at the nose of the projectile where the similarly carefully shipped fuses would be inserted. They were surrounded by nearly the entire ordnance division, as well as many onlookers.

"Looks like a sculpterin!" Silva said, beaming. "And we don't even have to put 'em together."

"Prob'ly don't trust us to," commented Stites.

"Yeah, this reads like a novel," Campeti agreed, waving the spec sheets. "It looks like ol' Bernie's done us proud, though. Get a load o' this! He's detailed everything they put into these beauties. There's bagged—he calls it 'Explosive B,' for 'Baalkpan,' or maybe 'Bernie'!—charges in the shells on top of a priming charge." He chuckled belatedly. "Bernie bullets! Anyway, he swears they'll fly like they're supposed to. Now I can scrape my paint markers off the gun-director dials!"

"Quit screwin' around with that ammunition out here," Gray roared, suddenly surging through the gaggle with Bashear in tow. He stopped and saluted when he noticed Campeti for the first time. "Sorry, *Mr*. Campeti. We didn't know it was *you* playin' with dangerous explosives on *our* deck."

"Don't apologize, SB!" Campeti said sheepishly. It hadn't been that long since he'd been a chief, and the Super Bosun's word was still law as far as he was concerned. "It's my fault. I just couldn't wait to see what was under the Christmas tree." He turned to the others. "You heard the man. Silva, put that thing back in the tube and secure the crate. You other guys, get the rest of this stuff stowed away. Stites, get a count on what we have to offload to make room for all this. I know it's weird having *too much* ammunition for a change, but we just have to cope."

The ordnance strikers snatched crates and took off, blinking rapidly, and the onlookers scattered before Gray or Bashear could think of more duties—like chipping paint—to keep them properly occupied. A strange sound froze them in their tracks, however, and most stared up at the sky, shading their eyes. With excited shouts and chittering, they began pointing into the air, and many crowded toward the starboard safety chains to gawk. Wordlessly, Gray and Bashear joined Campeti as he followed suit. Soon, most of *Walker*'s crew was lining her starboard rail, watching with the awkward amazement of children allowed through the tent flap of the traveling freak show for the very first time, while two lumbering behemoths passed overhead and began a banking descent toward the bay.

The aircraft were obviously the promised "Manila Clippers," and they were . . . quite a sight. They were the first real departure from the initial aircraft designs the Alliance had put in production. Nancys had a single, central-mounted "pusher" engine, while the bigger "Buzzards" had been built along the same lines, with an extra pair of outboard engines. But the "Clippers," or PB-5s, had four larger, more powerful versions of the Wright Gipsy–type power plant that had become so ubiquitous, mounted atop a much bigger, broader wing attached to the top of a deeper, longer fuselage with an enclosed cockpit. Instead of wingtip floats, there were bulbous, aerodynamic protrusions on each side of the fuselage to provide stability in the water.

Even Captain Reddy was not immune to the excitement, and he stepped out on the starboard bridgewing with his binoculars. Looking through them, he caught his first glimpse of the latest thing in long-range aircraft on this world.

"Holy smoke," he muttered appreciatively, adjusting the focus. He suspected that the contraptions were actually a little bigger than their old, lost PBY, while still lighter and possibly even stronger, with their diagonally braced and laminated bamboo-and-fabric construction. They sure looked more robust than a Nancy, although the high, exposed, forward-facing engine mounts appeared a little delicate.

"Big suckers," Spanky said beside him. "Ugly, though."

"How can you say such a thing?" Matt demanded with a grin, watching the morning sun wash across the blue-and-white-painted planes as they lined up for their approach, maintaining their somewhat gangly-looking formation. "Ben say's they'll carry ten passengers—or almost a ton of bombs! Maybe they're not B-17s, but that makes them beautiful to me!"

"Why send two of 'em? We're not even sending ten people."

"Insurance. One is carrying extra fuel and parts. It'll also be there in case the one carrying passengers has to set down. They're pretty important passengers, you know, and this is their longest flight to date."

"Surc. Say, that reminds me. You still sending Silva home? What with us maybe—hopefully—catching that Jap tin can. He's mighty useful in a scrape."

"I know, but he goes. Adar really wants his 'expedition,' and it's a good idea. It's also liable to be dangerous as hell, and Silva likes Cook. He'll take good care of the kid. I know we don't have a lot of guys left who've seen action against a modern opponent, but Campeti's got Stites, and with Silva helping train them, the gunnery division's in good shape." He grinned. "Besides, if we let him tag along, we'll never get rid of him, and the expedition'll start without him. Remember the last time he was supposed to get on a plane in Maa-ni-la? He gave them the slip. Most of the yard workers familiar with *Walker* are in Baalkpan, but I'll put her in the Maa-ni-la dry dock if I can, and we might be there for a while." He chuckled. "You have to give the devil his due; Silva knows how to stomp all over the line without—exactly—crossing it. Better to get rid of him now, while I can *watch* him get on the damn plane."

The planes thumped down on the still water almost in unison and began motoring closer to the dock.

"Larry likes Cook too," Spanky said, referring to the Grik-like Sa'aaran. "I bet he'd blow if he thought Silva was going to try to skip the flight. Next to Princess Becky, I think Silva's his best friend, but he's got his own people to worry about now. I know he's hoping to recruit more . . . lizard folks to join Chinakru's new colony on Samaar."

"Probably," Matt agreed, as the big planes wallowed toward the pier—and the hundreds of spectators gathered there.

"Speaking of passengers," Spanky said, then hesitated. He saw Matt looking at him expectantly and forged ahead. "Uh . . . what are you going to do with Lieutenant Tucker?" He suddenly felt his face heat. "I mean, uh, after tonight, damn it!" Spanky took a breath. "Are you going to send her home too?"

Matt glumly returned his exec's gaze. "No, Mr. McFarlane," he said in a formal tone. "Despite the imminent change in her . . . marital status, the Nurse Lieutenant will accompany us in search of *Hidoiame*. She's been *Walker*'s medical officer, and there are no competent replacements currently on hand." He took a deep breath and looked back into the pilothouse before speaking in a lower tone. "I had to make a deal, damn it. Since the wedding will be a hurry-up affair, and the honeymoon will consist of two days in a beachside hut—while you, Commander McFarlane, do all the work necessary to get this ship underway—I had to bend the regulation about married personnel aboard the same ship. Technically, she's already been transferred back to her duties in Baalkpan, but considering the very real possibility we may sustain casualties, she's 'volunteered' her medical services for however long it takes for her to report."

"The plane would be 'first available transport,' Skipper."

"No, Mr. McFarlane. We will maintain the fiction that the planes had already departed before the decision to proceed with the . . . nuptials was finalized, and since we are no longer technically part of the same ship's company . . ."

"I got it, Skipper," Spanky said with a spreading grin. "I can't say 'Remind me never to play poker with that woman,' because I don't much like the game. But I guess I'd be careful wagering against her in a chess match, after this."

With plenty of fresh water now aboard, Matt indulged in a long, hot shower. He had a lot on his mind. There was so much he *should* be doing right now—preparations and decisions to make—but for now, the work really involved only his ship, and he had to admit that Spanky and his other officers were fully capable of filling his shoes in that respect for the next few days. Isolated as he was, there was little he could contribute to the grand strategy of the overall war effort as it unfolded on the far-flung fronts. He'd agreed to the proposals of his commanders on the scene and trusted their judgment, based on their much better appreciation of their circumstances. He couldn't—wouldn't—second-guess their decisions while he was thousands of miles away. They'd planned the overall strategy together, and it was up to them to carry it out.

He still felt uncomfortably as if he were playing premeditated hooky, and it gnawed at him. There was also a sense of unreality that tended to mask his excitement and dull his anticipation regarding the evening's . . . event, and he was almost grateful, because the dreamlike nature of it all helped keep his lurking anxiety at bay.

Despite his . . . unusual feelings, he was in a good mood—almost giddy—and seemed possessed of an abundance of almost jittery energy. He turned off the water, wrenched the tattered green curtain aside, and grabbed a towel. Mostly dry, he pulled on his skivvies and started aft, whistling "Deep in the Heart of Texas" while still vigorously toweling his freshly trimmed hair. He almost didn't see Diania standing at rigid attention and holding a salute as he padded through the wardroom.

"Jesus, girl!" he shouted defensively, quickly wrapping the towel around his middle. "What are you doing here?"

The forward crew's head had—of necessity, in Matt's view—been reserved for all "female" personnel. It made things inconvenient for everyone, and there was a lot of griping, but the human destroyermen still aboard simply weren't ready, in any sense, for coed crappers. Exceptions were made when the crew was at battle stations, but even then, some care was exercised—a knock on a bulkhead, a shout of warning. While *Walker* was at anchor, a meagerly screened "fantail crapper" was rigged over the starboard propeller guard, and anybody could use that. It took a little of the pressure off.

"The Lady . . . Lieutenant Sandra sent me ta' fetch somethin' fer her . . . an' I coudnae find Mr. Marcos!" Diania stuttered fearfully. She deeply admired Captain Reddy, but she was scared of him too. In her mind, he had more power than the Governor-Emperor—and she knew he was against women in the Navy.

"Well, get whatever it is and scram!" Matt said less harshly. "And in the future, don't go running around officers' country without an escort!" he added a little apologetically, suddenly struck by his hypocrisy. They probably had to deal with this all the time in the crew's berthing spaces, and despite her status as engineering officer, Lieutenant Tabby had remained in the aft crew's berth. But Sandra lived in "officers' country." Of course, she'd been there long enough to know the rules, to make her presence known, and, besides, well, she was a "doctor."

That didn't mean the arrangement was fair, and things were bound to get more complicated soon, particularly as more women inevitably joined them. He realized that without thinking about it, and *because* he hadn't thought about it, he'd left a glaring, possibly hurtful hole in his otherwise blanket insistence that Lemurian females—and he guessed women too, now—had to receive, to *count on*, equal treatment in all respects. It seemed just like the Lemurians, Matt's men were always having to make adjustments. He sighed.

"Forget it, Diania," he said. "And, by the way, we don't salute indoors." He tightened his towel and marched down the passageway to his stateroom, realizing he needed to pass the word for Tabby to shift her gear forward—and the chiefs' quarters were going to get more crowded too. The men might bitch, but with the bigger jobs came the few perks that helped reinforce a chief's or officer's authority. He determined then that aboard *Walker*, and in *his* Navy, discrimination of any sort would never be tolerated—*Except when it comes to the heads,* he amended.

By the time he pushed his own curtain aside and hung up the towel over his little sink, he was whistling again.

Resplendent in their immaculate Whites—and God knew how Juan and his small division of stewards and laundry 'Cats had accomplished *that*—Matt and his party stepped ashore and boarded the trolley waiting to take them to the Cathedral of St. Brenden in the heart of Respite City. It was the first covered trolley Matt had seen and it was generously carved and gilded. The driver told them that it once belonged to the Company director, but Matt was grateful for the protection it afforded them, because the humidity in the valley where the bulk of the city lay was oppressive and afternoon storms were common. Other trolleys would bring a large percentage of the rest of the crew to join them, leaving a small but alert watch aboard the ship. Maybe Matt had grown paranoid, but it seemed to him that far too many bad things seemed to happen whenever their guard was down, and even Governor Radcliff agreed. The Respite militia was in a high state of readiness, and a couple of picket ships had been sent beyond the reef to reinforce and broaden the range of the guard ships stationed there.

The smallish trolley was filled almost to capacity because Spanky, Gray, Chack, Kutas, Campeti, Juan, and even Silva all attended Matt on this fateful journey. Midshipman Brassey would join them at the cathedral as an Imperial representative in the party. Little conversation passed among the group, and what did was somewhat awkward. Of those in the trolley, only Gray and Campeti had ever been married before, and the adventure ended in disaster for them both. In neither case had the proceedings been accompanied by such fanfare, and they began to get a real dose of that as they wound through the outlying streets and approached the center of the city. The roadside grew increasingly choked with happily waving well-wishers.

"I . . . wasn't expecting this!" Matt muttered, looking at the throng. He wasn't whistling anymore and even looked a little pale. "I guess I wasn't this nervous before we fought *Amagi*!" he suddenly blurted, shocked by the admission his mounting tension released.

"That's okay, Skipper. You're *s'posed* to be scared to death before jumpin' into somethin' like this," Gray assured him. "Hell, that's one o' the reasons I only ever did it once!"

"Skipper's not scared of anything," Spanky denied. "It's Juan's coffee that has my guts in an uproar. That's probably what's bothering him too. Sorry, Juan, but by God, it's time somebody spilled the beans you been murderin'."

"I don't think Juan's coffee is to blame," Matt objected bleakly.

"Course not!" the Filipino declared, glaring at Spanky. "Snipes poison themselves on burned bilgewater," he added, referring to Spanky's previous, longtime status as engineering officer. "I've seen it take years to get that sooty swill out of their system! Here, Cap-i-taan Reddy!" he offered, trying to pass him a sick-berth urinal. "In case you feel . . . ill. I sterilized it myself!"

"Put that goddamn thing away, you idiot!" the Bosun growled incredulously, then snatched the cylinder himself and tossed it under the bench they sat on. "What the hell's the matter with you?"

"But his uniform!" Juan objected.

"The Skipper's uniform won't get a spot on it, 'cause he ain't gonna puke. Sure, he's a little edgy. Who wouldn't be with all this fuss? I guess if he was the sort to spew, he woulda done it the first time he ever stuck a Grik with his fancy sword!"

The thought of that very sword at his side right now caused a queasy stir in Matt's stomach.

"Just shut up, everybody," he murmured. "About . . . being sick, anyway." He looked at Juan and offered a weak smile. "Thanks for the thought, but I'll manage."

Dennis Silva muttered something and chuckled.

"Think I'd prefer a quick pass by the JP myself," Lieutenant Kutas said. His scarred face looked pinched as he stared at the crowd.

"It does seem quite a . . . fuss," Chack observed. "We do such things much differently, as you know. Why could you not have just a simple ceremony like you performed for Mr. Letts and Nurse Theimer, Cap-i-taan?"

"Because we were all fixin' to die then, Chackie," Silva said. "This is politics!"

As was often the case, Silva was more astute than he generally pretended, because politics were definitely involved. Governor Radcliff wanted to capitalize on the popularity of the destroyermen to reinforce Respite's dedication to the Alliance—and the Empire they'd helped to save. Emelia, as she'd stated, wanted to showcase Sandra and the respect her own people gave her to emphasize the advantages inherent in dismantling the system of female indenture and the advancement of associated social reforms. The . . . spectacle was also clearly intended to display strong friendship not only to *Walker*'s crew, but also to the large number of allied personnel now stationed on the island and the crews of other ships in port. Of course, Matt and Sandra's decision to wed on Respite demonstrated their esteem for the people there and the Empire in general.

The donkeys pulling the trolley were finally reined to a halt in front of the Cathedral of St. Brenden, and the passengers gawked up at the impressive edifice as they stepped out of the vehicle. It wasn't as big, and certainly not as Gothic as its old world counterparts the humans had seen, or seen pictures of, but the white-plastered stone fairly gleamed and massive columns supported the front of a truly impressive bell tower that soared perhaps a hundred feet high. Broad steps led to a massive conical wooden door that

Radcliff had told them was hewn from the very timbers of the "passage" Indiaman *Hermione* herself.

Militiamen and two of *Walker*'s Marines flanked the huge door, and the thunder of the cheering crowd echoed back at them from the cathedral face like a breaking surf.

Matt straightened his tunic and adjusted his sword belt. "C'mon," he said, with what seemed a brittle confidence. "I guess we better go inside."

The doors swung wide as they ascended the steps and the scent of burning candles met them as they left the bright sunlight and entered the relative gloom inside. At first, in equal contrast to the tumult outside, there was hardly a sound within as their eyes adjusted, but then the applause began as they were ushered forward toward the lighted altar at the far end of the long, arched chamber. Matt heard a muffled "Belay that shit!" from the Bosun behind him and he wondered briefly what Silva had done, before he focused his attention on the gathering that awaited them.

Several men, ranging from relatively young to ancient, stood on an elevated platform and were dressed in flowing white robes with little ornamentation. They flanked a man in a silky blue robe with gold accents whom Matt had briefly met during his first visit to Respite, and he was further discomfited to realize that the ceremony would apparently be performed by Bishop Akin Todd himself! His stomach clenched again when he remembered that previous meeting had not been completely cordial; the bishop had harbored deep suspicions of the Alliance in general, and its social meddling in particular. Now, however, the tall, white-haired man with the conical "pope hat," as Gray had called it, practically beamed at him as he motioned Matt and his party to find seats in the right-front pew.

Glancing down the length of the long, wooden bench as his men preceded him with awkward, sideways steps, Matt was surprised to see Ambassador Forester and Midshipman Brassey standing at the far end, waiting. Brassey he'd expected, but he wondered why Forester had chosen to sit on the groom's side. He glanced to the left, and was equally surprised to see Governor Radcliff, Emelia, their daughters, and several others he didn't know sitting for the bride. As had been arranged, Dennis Silva, of all people, joined them there with a beatific smile, and Matt suppressed a groan. Sandra had insisted, and he supposed he understood, but he sensed a disaster in the making. With a final glance behind him, taking in the various attendees with his eyes better accustomed to the gloom, he noted the garish colors of Imperial finery interspersed with numerous Navy uniforms, and he jerked a nod in their direction and sat. Periodically over the next quarter hour, the great door admitted light, warm, humid air and more members of *Walker*'s crew. Each time, the local attendees clapped their hands for men and Lemurians, and Matt was again pleased by their reception.

The applause abruptly stopped when the Bishop finally extended his arms to his sides. A choir stood behind him, from seats arranged beneath a massive cross that Matt only then fully appreciated. The thing appeared to be made of thousands of shards of multihued volcanic obsidian, from clear to blue to almost black, and it sparkled in the candlelight like hot blue, flickering flames. The bishop lowered his arms, and the choir commenced an unfamiliar hymn. Matt didn't understand the words, but the voices were clear and strong and the melody was moving. The admirable acoustics of the cathedral added an impressive power to the music, and Matt felt his tension ease to some degree. The song was kind of long, but when it finally ended, Bishop Todd raised his hands again in the sudden silence and boomed:

"Let us pray!"

The prayer was pretty straightforward and not unlike many Matt heard in church as a kid, and he duly bowed his head for its duration. When it ended, he was surprised to hear the bishop call Governor Radcliff to speak. The melodious words that followed were essentially a highly complimentary account of the past campaign that highlighted Matt's, *Walker*'s, and even Sandra's contributions to its success. Matt knew Radcliff had prepared a major speech to kick off the "reception," and didn't know how he'd keep from repeating a lot of what he'd just said, or even much further embellish it. The address closed with flowery compliments of "Supreme Commander" Captain Reddy's military prowess and unerring leadership—while Matt's face burned—and Radcliff added his personal assurance of "Minister Lady" Tucker's purity, chastity, courage, and medical genius.

After a respectful silence while the governor made his way to his seat, the choir erupted into another unintelligible but hauntingly familiar chorus, while priestly ushers advanced toward the forward pews. Matt recognized his signal to stand, and suddenly rubbery legs reluctantly obeyed him. Spanky, Gray, Chack, Kutas, Campeti, Juan, and Brassey all shepherded him before the altar. Dennis Silva, shoulders square and mouth grim, erectly escorted Emelia Radcliff toward the front of the cathedral, where they stepped inside an alcove Matt hadn't seen when he entered. They emerged a moment later, each on the arm of . . . a short, white, shapeless cloud, and Matt almost barked a nervous laugh at what Sandra must think of her Imperial wedding dress.

The gown was fancy enough, Matt supposed, with plenty of frills, lace, and sparkly stuff, but it was also cut in the Imperial style that deliberately de-emphasized and obscured the female form to protect the modesty of ladies of quality and status. Matt had always been struck by that, since indentured or lower-caste women in the Empire wore little more than civilian Lemurians—which was next to nothing. In the Imperial case, he supposed that was the easiest way to differentiate the classes, but there was little wonder why there were so many "fatherless" children running around Imperial port cities, particularly when lower-caste women had so little expectation of legal recourse or protection.

Matt knew Sandra wasn't vain, but doubted she'd ever expected to wear such an amorphous thing to the altar—or that she'd preserve it unaltered for the future use of any daughter they might have! For the first time since the . . . ordeal began, a broad grin spread across his face—and grew even broader when Sandra drew close enough for him to see her savage blush. His anxiety all but fled, and he felt a sudden swirling rush of anticipation. In spite of the ridiculous dress and her brightly flushing cheeks, at that moment, Sandra was the most beautiful thing he'd ever seen, and her features softened and her lips ticked upward into a tentative smile when she saw his expression.

Diania and Tabby brought up the rear of the bridal procession, and Diania was dressed in a similar, simpler version of Sandra's dress. Tabby, however, wore what had evolved as the Lemurian version of dress whites: a well-tailored, high-collar tunic that did *not* de-emphasize *her* shape in any way and a long white kilt. Belted around her waist was a standard pattern 1917 cutlass, but it was sheathed in a tooled and brass-accented leather scabbard. Diania might have preferred similar garb, but Emelia had virtually insisted that the formerly indentured woman appear as a "lady."

The singing ended just as the procession arrived at the altar, and in the ensuing silence, the bishop thundered: "Who comes here before God and this congregation to be joined in holy matrimony?"

They'd been warned that it was customary for the groom to recite his name, titles, and lineage at this time, though it was not, of course, usually expected of the bride.

"Matthew Patrick Reddy," Matt answered in a voice that surprised him with its firmness. "Captain of the United States Ship *Walker*, High Chief of the American Clan, and Commander in Chief, by acclamation, of all Allied Military Forces united beneath the Banner of the Trees." He paused, remembering to add the lineage part, and continued proudly: "I'm the son of former Chief Quartermaster's Mate Donald Vernon Reddy, recipient of the highest military honor for bravery that my birth nation can bestow. He's now a cattleman—a large landholder—in the great state of Texas, U.S. of A.!"

He heard murmuring to his right in response to his revelation. It sounded like Kutas asking Gray what Matt's dad had done. He suppressed a head shake. *How on earth do they think I got in the Academy*?

"Sandra Cayce Tucker," Sandra interjected before the bishop could proceed. She spoke a little softly at first, but with growing strength. "Nurse Lieutenant and Minister of Medicine for Adar, High Chief and Sky Priest of Baalkpan and Chairman of the Grand Alliance. I'm the daughter of Malcom C. Tucker, ah, Norfolk industrialist, in the great state of Virginia, United States of America."

The congregation murmured, but Bishop Todd cleared his throat.

"And who giveth this woman to be wed?" he demanded.

Silva straightened. "Me!" he boomed. "Chief Gunner's Mate Dennis Silva of the United States Ship *Walker*, DD rate, number one-sixty-three! Famous slayer o' Japs, Griks, Doms, super lizards, mountain fish, an' various other dangerous critters, includin' a Dom Blood Cardinal I spattered at most of a quarter mile! Protector o' women an' small princesses, an' rescuer o' same! I'm the son o' Stanley an' Willa Silva, who was actually married when I was born but passed on soon after, God rest 'em, an' I hail from Alabama—also in the U.S. of A!"

The bishop was taken aback and Gray muttered something, but Matt supposed it could have been far worse.

"And do you swear before God that this woman is here seeking the solemnization of matrimony of her own free will, and has no just impediment, nor moral or legal obligation that might entangle, complicate, or prohibit the honorable estate she seeks?"

"Ah . . . yes, sir. I swear," Silva replied with less exuberance. "If all that means what I think it does."

Matt saw Sandra roll her eyes.

The bishop paused, again perhaps taken aback by the unorthodox reply. "Then I entreat this congregation to bear witness that this man and this woman have entered this house and the sight of God to be joined together in holy matrimony, an institution created by God in the time of man's innocency, which signifies the mystical union betwixt Christ and his Church, and which He adorned and beautified with His presence. With that understanding, it must be admonished that this estate be not enterprised lightly or wantonly solely to satisfy men's carnal lusts and appetites like brute beasts, with no understanding, but reverently, advisedly, soberly, and in the fear of God, duly considering the causes for which matrimony was ordained.

"First of these is the lawful procreation of unobligated children, to be reared in the fear of the Lord and to praise His holy name.

"Secondly, as a remedy against sin and fornication and other base temptations of the flesh, so that those who enter into this, the greatest of obligations, might keep themselves undefiled members of Christ's body, and righteous members of His Church.

"Thirdly, for the mutual society, help, and comfort that the one ought to have of the other, both in prosperity and adversity.

"Only through due obedience to God's matrimonial decrees may those who are scattered, and children begotten in the lonely places of this savage world, remain servants of the Lord, and not degrade themselves until they become unknown to Him."

Matt was struck—vaguely—by the many similarities as well as differences to other wedding ceremonies he'd witnessed. He supposed—vaguely again—that the differences were mostly rooted in the odd society the Empire had created as far as women were concerned, but at that moment it really didn't matter to him—except insofar as how damn long the thing was taking! They both answered in the affirmative at the end of the long, familiar, if somewhat archaic vows, and Matt duly, somewhat ironically, noted the extra-heavy emphasis on service and obedience that Sandra agreed to. He honestly wasn't entirely sure what "plight thee my troth" meant, but a plight was like a predicament . . . wasn't it?

Spanky stood next to Matt as his best man, and at the appropriate moment, he fished in his pocket for the ring: a simple golden band traditional for all Imperial weddings. It was growing increasingly hot in the still, unventilated cathedral, and the ring suddenly squirted from Spanky's fingers just as he triumphantly produced it.

"Goddammit!" he muttered, instantly flushing red as the ring hit Sandra's dress. Instead of being captured in the shapeless folds, it fell and struck the floor with a tiny *chink* and rolled away down the aisle. Silva stomped on it before it could escape completely, and Spanky quickly retrieved it and stuck it in Matt's hand. Matt then laid the ring on the large, leather-bound Bible on the altar, as he'd been instructed, and the bishop held it up before passing it back to him. That's when Matt turned to put it on Sandra's finger. Her eyes were . . . chuckling, either at Spanky's embarrassment or Matt's grim, nervous expression, and Matt felt his own grin return as he repeated what the bishop told him to say.

"With this ring, I thee wed. With my body, I thee worship." There was nothing about "worldly goods" in Imperial ceremonies, but Matt didn't have anything to offer but his ship. "So help me God," he almost whispered. They both knelt then, and Bishop Todd held his hands out over their heads.

"O eternal God, creator and preserver of all mankind, giver of spiritual grace and author of everlasting life: send thy blessings through Christ our Lord upon this man and this woman, whom we bless in thy name. May they ever remain in perfect love and peace together. Amen."

There was more, but regardless of how interesting or even beautiful it might have been, from that point on, Matt and Sandra might as well have knelt there all alone, as far as they were concerned. Only later, after all was done and the choir had been singing again for some time, did it suddenly occur to Matt that the song was "Eternal Father, Strong to Save." He didn't know how old the "official" Navy hymn was, but doubted it was old enough that the Imperials would know it. He was touched by the gesture, both on the part of their hosts and whoever had thought to give them the words and music. He hoped he could somehow reflect the words into a prayer of his own as he looked into Sandra's eyes—not only for himself and this woman he loved, but for *Walker* and her crew and all those she'd lost.

"O, Trinity of love and power, our brethren shield in danger's hour.

From rock and tempest, fire and foe, protect them wheresoe'er they go.

Oh hear us when we cry to thee, for those in peril on the sea."

CHAPTER 7

Zanzibar
Sovereign Nest of the Jaaph Hunters

General of the Sea Hisashi Kurokawa, former captain of the lost Japanese Imperial Navy battle cruiser *Amagi*, almost chortled with glee as his new personal yacht, the double-ended paddle steamer *Tatsuta*, backed her paddles and crept up to the dock. He knew General Esshk was wildly jealous of the vessel. *But, then, General Esshk is in a poor position to complain just now. Isn't he?* Kurokawa thought with smug amusement. Esshk had hitched his fortunes to a waning star, and after the catastrophic losses in airships during the recent raid on the enemy fleet and bases, all in a desperate gamble to save Regent Tsalka's precious Ceylon, Esshk's "star," had been slowly, painfully snuffed.

A quick, high-pitched giggle did escape then. An irony was that Ceylon had already fallen by the time Tsalka's mission took place, but Tsalka had promised his life in exchange for the stupid, wasteful attempt to salvage his regency, and Kurokawa had "sadly insisted" that he must pay his own set price for failure. He'd argued vigorously against the gesture, as he'd described it. The airships should have been held back until they could accompany his new Grand Fleet into battle, thereby ensuring complete and total victory. Tsalka's selfish insistence was what cost so many machines, trained crews, and time to replace them. For that, if for no other reason, he had to be held to his pledge! Now Tsalka was dead—having wagered against the Traitor's Death!—and with him had vanished yet another obstacle to Kurokawa's ultimate scheme.

Another giggle escaped compressed lips when the image of a naked Tsalka, teeth smashed, claws ripped out, convulsing against his bonds—and shrieking in wild, animalistic terror and agony while dozens of famished hatchlings fed on his living body—floated behind Kurokawa's eyes once more. He'd maintained a somber demeanor at the time, which cast a pall on his enjoyment of the proceedings. It wouldn't do for his allies at the court of the Celestial Mother to recognize his deep pleasure. Even the Chooser would have been horrified. Instead, he'd been forced to assume a mask of regret that accompanied his sad insistence that Tsalka's debt be paid.

First General Esshk had actually been shocked by Kurokawa's attitude, as if he'd expected something resembling *loyalty* from him! How ridiculous! All along, Kurokawa had been nothing but a tool for Tsalka and Esshk, and they'd shown no loyalty to *him*! Did they think they were *friends*? They'd become his tools now, and the expenditure of Tsalka was a first, necessary step toward achieving *his* goals, for a change.

Perhaps the greatest irony of all was that though Ceylon was lost, the air raid had actually accomplished far more than Kurokawa ever dreamed. An enemy aircraft carrier was destroyed—and not every airship was lost after all. Some had survived, and a pair of bases had been established in India that more and more airships could make use of as they were completed. They now also had reasonably quick communications with the garrison there, under Halik and Niwa's command. At least once a week, airships came and went bearing messages, fuel, weapons, and priceless reconnaissance intelligence. For the first time, Kurokawa knew what his fleet would face.

The American-Lemurian Alliance had been busy indeed! The quality of the enemy aircraft—and their carriers!—had come as a particular surprise, and he'd instructed that certain modifications be made to his capital ships accordingly. He'd long been a member of the conservative, battleship school, and though he'd come to respect the role of aircraft at sea, he still believed he could sweep the waves of the comparatively puny Allied fleet once he came to grips with it. Regardless of their ingenuity, the frail Allied aircraft couldn't possibly threaten *Hisashi Kurokawa*'s battleships! Besides, he had geniuses of his own, now.

He was in a very good mood, and he smiled with real benevolence while Japanese crewmen tossed lines to Japanese sailors and steam rushed skyward from the tall, thin funnel behind the pilothouse. Kurokawa had a dozen Grik guards that attended him at all times, even to this place, but by the grateful order of the Celestial Mother herself, the entire island of Zanzibar had been set aside as a Japanese preserve—a temporary homeland for the 350-odd remaining survivors of *Amagi*. Kurokawa considered the acquisition of his own "Regency" a major coup for a variety of reasons, and a sure sign that his grand scheme to insinuate himself irreplaceably within the upper echelons of Grik society was bearing fruit.

Incidentally, Kurokawa began to realize that by securing that boon, he'd also secured a new, burgeoning, and strikingly real loyalty from his own countrymen at last. It was fortuitous, because as his schemes moved forward, he needed that loyalty more desperately than ever. It rankled that he'd been forced to essentially *bribe* his men for what should have been his natural due, but amazingly, this small thing he'd done—for them, they thought—had worked wonders. He'd never been more respected, actually appreciated, before. It *was* maddening, but he would accept their loyalty on whatever terms now, as long as it was real. Living with and dealing with the Grik for so long had forced a measure of . . . pragmatism upon him, a realization that every so often, he must make unpleasant compromises, at least for the short term. In spite of himself, his survival had depended on his ability to become a long-term thinker, to plan far ahead, and it had not been easy.

Less than a third of his men were ever on Zanzibar at

any given time. Most were employed in the Grik war industry, designing and overseeing the construction of the tools of battle. Those not critical to their posts were allowed "liberty" on a rotating basis and shipped from the hellish Grik factories and industries where they worked to this comparatively idyllic place. Though close to the equator, almost constant breezes kept the temperature refreshing, compared to the mainland jungles, and the air was fresh and clear of the stench of death and filth. It was a place where they could get away from their vile Grik "allies" for a time, enjoy the scenery that was little spoiled by the few previous Grik inhabitants—large prey could not sustain themselves there, even if imported—and try to remember what it meant to be Japanese. They worked here as well, even harder than they did for the Grik, but here they enjoyed the illusion that they were working for themselves.

Kurokawa enjoyed "vacationing" away from the Grik as well, but the most important thing, from his perspective, was that he finally had a base secure from Grik interference, where he and his countrymen could gather and discuss their own plans and work on Kurokawa's own projects. He had secretly collected certain—he believed—trustworthy notables who had distinguished themselves through their technical efforts on his behalf. Men who finally seemed to understand that what reflected well on Kurokawa benefited them. Other pragmatists, at least, if not patriots. Men unswervingly hitched to *his* rising star. They would be his captains in the heady times to come. They were fully versed in those aspects of his scheme that had brought them this far, but no one knew its ultimate, audacious scope. Today, he would share with them, and as many of his department heads, trusted technicians, and upper-level advisors to the Grik who could reasonably get away, a further portion of his strategy. It was a thing that had been growing and maturing in his mind like a perfect flower for over a year, but it would never do to reveal it all. Not yet.

For now, he would tell them only what they needed to know to get him to the next level. Once there, it would be time to reveal at last that his ultimate goal was not merely to continue to rise as a respected figure at the Celestial

Mother's court, but to *rule* the entire Grik Empire—on behalf of Emperor Hirohito, of course. He and his loyal captains would rule the world! The other remnants of his own people—once treacherous, but benevolently forgiven—would bask in the radiance of his glory! They would reap the benefits of his achievement—and owe it all to him!

He smiled again. Today there was much to do and plan, and he had left his provisioning fleet across the channel at the premier Grik naval base to preside over a meeting he'd set several weeks before, time enough for all the men he needed to find reasons to attend. He could hardly wait. Soon would begin the final campaign to destroy the hated Americans, their Lemurian lackeys, and the Grik he hated most of all.

A young signals lieutenant met him on the dock with an honor guard. Kurokawa's Grik protectors were gently but forcefully led aside and fed. They were used to that here, and made no complaints. The lieutenant led him past a large steam-generator building that provided power for their own, apparently modest repair facilities. Other generators and engines, beyond the view of unexpected guests, powered more ambitious enterprises. From a distance, their smoke resembled only a humid haze. They passed a cluster of long, thatched-roof barracks, supported on high pilings in the Lemurian way, and continued on to a slightly smaller but more traditionally constructed building. The honor guard was more than ceremonial, and was armed with some of the few Arisaka Type 38 6.5 mm rifles they'd managed to carry away when *Amagi* went down. In addition to countless colorful flying reptiles that fed on an even more numberless variety of insects resembling butterflies, there were some fairly small but surprisingly dangerous creatures on Zanzibar.

The building had gun port–like shutters, all raised to allow the breeze to circulate inside, and he heard murmuring within as he approached. All went silent when he stepped on the porch, and an enlisted servant quickly opened the door, then knelt and briskly wiped the dust from his finely crafted boots. Kurokawa ignored the man but waited until he was finished, then strode through the door. The dozen occupants rocketed to instant, rigid attention, staring straight ahead at other men arranged around the conference table. His eyes swept around the long room, inventorying the faces he saw, tight-lipped, intense, some wearing beads of sweat. He continued on to the far side of the room, walking slowly, enjoying the respect. Finally, he halted and turned beside a chair.

"Be seated," he barked. Only once he began his descent did the others comply. "Everyone seems to be here," he said, again counting the faces around the table. "This trip may have been . . . inconvenient for some of you—it certainly was for me—but some of what we must discuss is rather sensitive. We cannot risk writing any of it down, even in Japanese. We had traitors once, and the Grik may have subverted others." He let that sink in, then proceeded. "I would like to begin by taking direct reports of your activities. Spare me nothing. I know much of what many of you do is for the Grik, but that may not always be the case. I must know exactly what is available for the coming campaign so I will know what I may use and what I may choose to . . . reserve." A few eyes flicked at him before resuming their forward stares.

"General of the Sky Muriname?"

Hideki Muriname was a small man, a pilot of the old Type 95 floatplane they'd used to bomb Baalkpan. The aircraft—*Amagi*'s last—had been damaged in the raid, and though it was maintained and preserved—on Zanzibar now—he had always claimed it could not be made airworthy for any serious operations. When Esshk had asked about it, Kurokawa reported that its structural integrity had been compromised, and without aluminum to repair it and spare parts for the engine, it remained only a model for their own designs. Esshk finally accepted that, and for a long time only Muriname and Kurokawa knew their report was a lie. They *did* use it as a model; its structural-assembly techniques helped them design the framework for the great dirigibles that currently constituted the backbone of Grik aviation. Its gauges and instruments provided patterns for more. But here on Zanzibar, they also copied its wing shapes, and even its engine.

"Ca . . . General of the Sea, aside from our . . . projects

here, we continue to build airships and train crews. As you know, I kept only a few machines back from the raid, for training purposes, but since all were not lost after all, I have the benefit of observations made by some veterans of that attack. There are a number of . . . difficulties and unforeseen characteristics apparently unique to airship operations. I had no previous experience with the machines myself, so did not know to prepare my aircrews for them."

"*Your* aircrews?"

Muriname gulped. "So I have come to . . . encourage them to consider themselves, sir. I apologize. . . ."

"No, no, General. Do not apologize for *that.* I sometimes promote a similar perception of . . . mutual reliance myself. Most interesting. Tell me, do these flying Grik return any of the . . . dedication you show them? I have made a study of the phenomenon, you see."

"I . . . I believe they do, to a degree."

"*Most* interesting," Kurokawa murmured. "That may be of use someday." He shook his head slightly and his eyes narrowed. "But perhaps you go too far."

"Sir?"

"The emblem, the insignia you paint on your machines, is a perversion of our own sacred flag. What is the meaning of that?"

Muriname had wondered how long it would take for Kurokawa to bring that up. The insignia in question was a representation of the Rising Sun flag, cradled by stylized images of the sickle-shaped Grik sword. The swords—and fewer rays—were the only deviation. "Sir, with my utmost respect to you and our glorious flag, the aircrews are all Grik, and the minor adjustment to the flag . . . pleased them beyond my expectations. Sir," he added earnestly, "I can see no disadvantage. Symbols are important things, and the more closely they associate themselves with ours, the more closely they will be bound to us. . . ."

Kurokawa stared away. It was genius, of course, and he'd never even considered it. He must immediately supply his fleet with similar flags. He doubted Esshk or even the Celestial Mother would care. All the inclusive Grik banners of the Celestial House that represented all the Grik were simply red. Sometimes the shapes varied, but it was the color that mattered. Even if anyone noticed, or possibly objected, he would merely excuse it as a design meant to signify that they were all in this together. It *was* red, after all. In the meantime, the Imperial flag—his flag—would increasingly be associated with unity and authority. He suppressed a smile and looked impatiently back at Muriname.

"You may continue the practice, but you will seek my permission for such things in the future. So. What 'unforeseen characteristics' did you neglect?"

"Of course, sir. Ah, most egregiously, though I cautioned them to compensate for the release of their bombs, even I did not expect just how radically and catastrophically the airships would lunge skyward when the full weight was dropped. Some particularly bright, quick-thinking crews managed to stabilize their craft through procedures that have become part of the training curriculum, but quite a few were lost due to that . . . miscalculation on my part."

Kurokawa stared at the almost-cringing man who'd demonstrated such brilliant initiative, then not only admitted a failure, but took responsibility for it! His initiative required greater control, and he would have to be punished for his mistake, of course, but not too severely—this time. Kurokawa needed men who could think and learn from their mistakes. He'd talked the Grik out of destroying all their own warriors who turned prey, after all. Even if only a few recovered, it was wasteful of those few. He would have to guard against men like Muriname thinking *too* much, however. He sensed danger down that path.

"This is a serious matter, and I will deal with you later. But the problem is solved?"

"It is."

"And production?"

"Still improving. The techniques have reached a perfection of simplicity similar to what you have seen in the conventional shipyards, and since the labor is not as intense, the attrition of trained workers is lower."

"Excellent. How soon will you replace what we lost?"

"In merely a month and a half, we have already replaced over a third. As efficiency continues to improve, I expect to be back where we started, with one hundred airships and even better-trained crews, within another month."

"Hmm. And how will they protect themselves from enemy aircraft?"

"For now, imperfectly. As you directed, all efforts toward modern small arms go toward equipping our own people here." He quickly glanced at another man named Riku, with a brooding mouth and wispy mustache, who was head of Ordnance for the Grik, but covertly served in that same capacity for Kurokawa. "But I understand the production of the matchlocks is quite simple and proceeding at a rapid pace. We will arm the airships with them, as well as with light swivel cannon that can fire blasts of lead balls. It is . . . dangerous, of course—with only hydrogen for a lifting gas—but the best we can do at present."

"Very well. They will have some protection, then. I do not wish to give those creatures any technology beyond what we already have. You must make do." He paused. "And what of the 'new' bombs?"

Muriname grimaced in spite of himself. "I presume Commander Riku has prepared a presentation on the more . . . specialized weapons we are making here, but as far as the new bombs we have made available to the Grik, training in their use is the most difficult challenge. The design and construction is fairly simple; resources are abundant. They are also light enough that they do not tax the payload of the airships. They *are* tragically wasteful," he interjected with an almost bitter tone that Kurokawa let pass. "But they work well enough. I . . . have tested one myself."

Kurokawa raised his eyebrows. "Indeed? Very well. You will stand ready to deploy your forces with whatever ordnance we have made available to the Grik at the appropriate time."

"Yes, General of the Sea."

Kurokawa looked at another man, bigger than Muriname. "Speaking of technology we will *not* share with the Grik, have there been any . . . further developments in your department, Signal Lieutenant Fukui?"

"No, ah, General of the Sea. Not since those few"—he looked around—"odd transmissions."

One of the things they'd never revealed to the Grik was the existence of radio or any kind of remote communication. The Grik used horns operated by a bellows, and sometimes a crude form of semaphore. Kurokawa was content to let them remain ignorant. Fukui's department had the still-operable radio from the grounded plane, and they'd produced other crude sets like they knew the Americans had done, but they could no longer eavesdrop on enemy communications because they knew they'd been burned once and always used codegroups now. Those in Fukui's department led profoundly boring lives, sequestered from any possible contact with the Grik, and constantly listening for stray, unguarded transmissions from the Allies—or anyone else who might be out there. They never transmitted anything themselves.

Then, a couple of weeks before, they'd picked up—on the radio—a very weak voice transmission! Shortly after, there was another transmission from what sounded like a different source. The problem was, neither message sounded like English, but they didn't think it was Japanese either. They just couldn't tell. They considered the possibility it might have been Lemurians speaking, but whatever language the voices used, they sounded like human tones. It was a mystery.

"Hmm," Kurokawa said thoughtfully, drumming the table with his fingers. "Keep listening," he commanded.

Almost as an afterthought, he cocked his head and regarded Fukui. "I wonder if it might have been Miyata. Perhaps he reached the southern hunters at last, and they had some means of communication?"

Young Lieutenant Toryu Miyata had been on an expedition south to the cape of Africa, to contact some obscure, probably human "hunters" the Grik knew resided there. The Grik considered the region too cold and uninviting to conquer, especially while locked in an unprecedented battle for survival. General Esshk had sent Miyata and two other men, along with a Grik escort to make the Offer to the southerners to join the Great Hunt. This had never been done before, making the Offer without first testing the foe, but these were extraordinary times. The choice Miyata was to convey was basically "Join or die," and Esshk told Miyata to stress that regardless how busy the Grik might be elsewhere, they could easily spare the meager force it would require to crush the people in the south.

Kurokawa had not been pleased by Esshk's summary order, not that he cared anything for Miyata and the others, but at the time, he was in no position to refuse. *Yet another slight that Esshk will one day regret!* he promised himself.

"I . . . cannot say, General of the Sea," Fukui answered his question.

Kurokawa shook his head and waved his hand dismissively. "It is of no consequence at present, but do get word to me, however you must, if you hear the voices again and are able to make sense of them."

"Of course, General of the Sea."

The conference continued into the early afternoon, while Kurokawa listened to reports, made comments, and occasionally harangued the speakers, but with only a shadow of his old venom. As much as it sickened him, he knew he needed to coddle these men for now, and in dealing so long with the Grik, he'd learned to hide his true thoughts well. At last, he stood abruptly, quickly followed by the other men.

"Soon," he said, "within days, the Great Fleet we have built for the Grik vermin will move at last, and I—*we!*—will crush the enemy that invests India! It is the same enemy, my people, who brought us to this world and marooned us here! Again we will face the Americans, our *natural* enemy, and the Grik will face theirs: the Americans' ape-man lackeys! In that, if nothing else, we share a common cause! It is still the Americans—and now their puppets too—who stand between us and our destiny. And only by destroying them utterly shall we achieve it!"

CHAPTER 8

Respite Island
March 3, 1944

Sandra woke slowly, savoring the soft, clean sheets that felt so smooth against her skin, and the large, firm mattress she sprawled upon. She'd always been a sprawler, and the tiny, claustrophobic berths she'd slept in for most of the past two years had been excruciating, despite her small size. Golden sunshine streamed through the open, curtained windows and a steady, cool breeze circulated in the bedroom of the surprisingly luxurious little bungalow. For just a moment, she was disoriented. Her eyes opened wider when she saw the dark hair and firmly muscled back of the man still sleeping beside her, and it all came flooding back: the hurried, awkward, glorious wedding; the boisterous reception that followed; the carriage ride to the secluded beachfront bungalow; and the night of gentle, soaring, laughing, whirlwind . . . electric passion that followed. She smiled, utterly content. They'd waited a long time, and sometimes she'd despaired that last night would never come, but it had been worth the wait, and more.

Matt lay on his side, taking only a small portion of the bed. *He's far more accustomed to tiny beds than I am,* she reflected. *He's . . . economical in many ways; in tastes and often in words, but he's extravagant in all the things that matter,* she realized. He'd proven many times that his love for her knew no bounds, and he was maybe a little too generous of himself for his own good as far as his ship, crew, and cause were concerned. She gloried in the former, and had learned to accept the latter. That was part of the deal she'd made to have him, and she was wise enough to know he couldn't—wouldn't—ever change in that respect. As much as it worried her, she also loved him for it. It was why he was *who* he was.

She focused on the numerous white or purple puckered scars on his back. She remembered when he got most of them. The big, ugly one across his left shoulder blade had come from a Grik spear at Aryaal and had nearly killed him. Clusters of smaller scars had not been serious, mostly caused by tiny fragments of steel or glass she'd plucked from just under the skin. There was a long, jagged, older scar across his lower back, and she traced it softly with her finger, wondering what had caused it. She'd seen it before, of course, but it predated their acquaintance, and she'd forgotten about it. Suddenly, how he got it—like so many other things about him she didn't know—became vitally important to her, and she cuddled up to him, molding her body to his.

"That can get you in a lot of trouble," he warned in a pleasant, muzzy tone. She chuckled huskily.

"*That* kind of trouble I can handle, sailor," she said.

"Well, never say I didn't warn you," he said, mock serious, rolling over to embrace her.

"Wait!" She giggled. "We barely know each other!"

He blinked. "What do you mean?"

"I'm serious! I want to know everything . . . like, where'd you get that scar on your lower back?"

"I was bitten by a whale!" he said, clasping her close and kissing her.

"Tell me!" she insisted, and he paused.

"Right now?" He looked at her. "You're serious!"

"Sure, I am! We're *married* now. I want to know."

He started to speak, then paused. After all this time, they really didn't know a lot about each other. They knew all the things that *mattered*, of course, but almost nothing about each other's lives before they met. He shrugged. "I fell off a horse on a barbed-wire fence when I was fourteen."

"That's it?"

"Scout's honor."

"Were you a Boy Scout?"

"No."

Sandra laughed. "You're terrible!"

"Absolutely." Matt brushed back her hair and smiled. "I'll tell you something else, now that we're married. You've got to quit looking at me—that way you do—when you think I'm about to pull some nutty stunt that'll get me hurt. You know which look I mean! I've always been a sucker for big-eyed, pretty girls, and when they stick out their lip and squirt tears at me . . ." His smile faded slightly. "It makes it a lot harder to do what I have to do."

"I do not 'squirt' tears at you!" she denied. "My arguments against your sometimes very foolish behavior are based on reason and practical concerns!"

"And when I don't see 'reason,' you resort to anger. When that doesn't work, you hammer me with the Look."

Sandra frowned, creating a face much like the one he'd described but without the tears. "Reason should be enough," she said at last, as if surprised it wasn't. "Reason *and* anger work with everyone else, but not you! You're too damn stubborn!" She sighed. "So maybe the tears come with frustration because I *love* you, you big dope! I don't make them come—you do!"

"So . . . no deal?" he asked with such a pitiful tone and solemn expression that she burst into a fit of giggling. She struck him with her pillow—which disrupted the bedding in a pleasantly revealing way—and Matt embraced her again.

"Look," he said, softly laughing, his hand gliding across her skin. "I'm sorry I brought it up. You're right, though. We have a lot to talk about. I'll tell you every little thing you want to know about me: every scar, every hobby, even my favorite ice cream. We've both got in-laws . . . somewhere . . . we don't know anything about! I want to hear all about that privileged childhood you said you had, about every scraped knee, and even your favorite color . . . but later. We don't have an awful lot of time together—like this," he reminded gently. "I respectfully suggest we make the most of it."

They did.

The Bosun slogged through the sand, breathing hard, and stepped up on the porch of the servants' bungalow where Diania was staying and where Juan joined her during the day to prepare meals and such for the newlyweds, or in case Matt and Sandra wanted them for any reason. Both stewards had, for all intents and purposes, insisted. Even so, there was considerable distance between the two structures, and Gray wasn't too happy about that. He didn't like it whenever the Skipper—or Sandra—didn't have anybody around to protect them. Captain Reddy had specifically prohibited a guard detail this time, however, and Gray could even understand. The location of the honeymoon was supposed to be a secret, and he doubted any Company sore losers would find them in the short time they had. He supposed somebody might have followed *him* out from the ship . . . but he doubted it. Why would they? Who here would know that he was an overprotective mother hen?

Besides, he reassured himself as he glanced surreptitiously at the other bungalow, *even with just one leg, Juan's got plenty of guts, and he can shoot.* He hesitated before going inside, stomping the sand off his shoes. *Okay, that's all true. So why am I here?* Was it just because he was overprotective, or did he have another reason to leave the ship when he had so much work to do?

Suddenly, the lightly built door swung open in his face and Diania confronted him, surprised. She'd ditched the goofy dress, he saw, and was back in dungarees and T-shirt. He gulped at the . . . glaring effect of the transformation.

"Why, g'marnin', Mr. Gray!" the girl said a little nervously. "I hared a tarrible stampin', an' thought the island was a-tremble."

"It was just me, uh . . . Miss Diania," Gray stammered.

Diania was stunned. The Bosun had never actually addressed her before, other than to give her summary commands. She'd heard him refer to her as "that damn woman" a time or two, which set her apart from the other female humans aboard only in that he called them "that *other* damn woman" or "those other damn women." At best, he might refer to them occupationally, like the "water-tender broad," or something like that. Diania had to admit it hurt her feelings, because she rather admired the Super Bosun, and everyone else treated her much better than she'd ever been treated before. The thing was, she knew he didn't resent her for being a woman suddenly elevated from her obligated status, like an Imperial man might. He just resented her for being a woman on his ship. She hadn't understood at all until Lady Sandra explained the metaphor of old dogs and new tricks, and described the way things used to be in the Bosun's "old" Navy.

"What did ye call me?" she asked, almost breathlessly.

"Well . . . Miss Diania, I guess," Gray growled in a more normal tone. "We ain't on the ship, and neither of us is on the watch bill, so we ain't really on duty. 'Sides, this is kinda like me showin' up at your off-base housin'. I got manners." He looked around. "Where's that little Flip on a stick?"

Diania collected herself. "Ah, ye mean Mr. Marcos? He took coffee yonder ta the Captain an' Lady Sandra." With a small smile, she pointed at the strange tracks in the sand. "He was very insistent that the Captain'd never forgive 'im if he neglected that duty."

Gray grimaced. "Jeez. That's a helluva way to bring the newlyweds back down to earth!"

Diania chuckled warily. She didn't drink coffee and had taken Juan's statement as fact. She took a breath. "So, ah, what brings ye here?"

Gray waved his hand. "Oh, I was ashore, roundin' up a few lost sheep after the shindig last night, and then I had to make personal sure that maniac Silva got on the damn plane—and stayed on it this time! Skipper's orders." He shook his head. "Wasn't really such a chore once I found the big lug, and then he went peaceably enough . . . not that he was in any shape to make a fuss!"

"Where was he?" Diania asked, boldly she thought. She was amazed that she was actually carrying on a conversation with the terrible Bosun.

"Hidin'. At least he thought he was. He must've picked

his spot while he was . . . less devious than usual. And besides, Chack ratted him out." Gray didn't mention that he'd finally found Dennis Silva curled up and passed out inside an overturned barrel in the . . . sailor's recreational district, and that he and Chack had rolled the barrel almost three hundred yards down to the dock. His sea bag was already awaiting him there, but they had to hose the insensible giant down before the "Clipper" pilot would let him aboard the plane. Gray shrugged. "Anyway, so then I thought I'd wander out here and check on things."

Diania steeled herself. "Then ye must stay fer yer breakfast," she said as firmly as she could. "I'm about makin' it, anyway . . . as soon as Mr. Marcos returns ta oversee me skills. One more mouth'll make no difference, an' . . . I've so many questions about the Navy life!"

Gray looked at the exotic, dark-skinned girl—*She* is *just a girl, damn it!*—and scratched the white stubble on his chin.

"Well, I s'pose the fellas on the ship can make do without me for a little longer. Thanks."

CHAPTER 9

Imperial Port City of Saint Francis
North American Colonies

Imperial Commodore and newly appointed CINCEAST (Commander in Chief—East) of the Grand Alliance Harvey Jenks stood on *Achilles'* quarterdeck, gazing about at the small fleet preparing to get underway. The North American sun that bathed him with its rays was unusually warm for the latitude at this time of year, making for a beautiful day that displayed his ships, the city, and the strange land beyond to best effect. If not for his lingering frustration over the endless series of delays that postponed this movement for so long, he would probably be utterly charmed. Instead, there had been weeks of ship repairs, organizing, arming, and properly training the . . . hotheaded colonial levy, and streamlining the local bureaucracy (in the aftermath of more high-level treason!) so his force could be properly supplied and victualed. . . . The list had been endless. As it was, his chest still roiled with an impatient anxiety that threatened to plague him all the way to the Enchanted Isles. The fact that most of the delays hadn't really been anyone's fault did little to mitigate his concern that they might already be too late to relieve the beleaguered garrison at that strategic place.

Many of the delays may have been unavoidable, but there

was plenty of blame for the haste they retarded. The Dominion had indeed attacked the Enchanted Isles, just as Admiral McClain predicted, though not in sufficient force to justify his diversion of the greater part of his fleet in that direction, leaving Jenks, Captain Reddy and his USS *Walker*, and only a handful of ships to face the bulk of the Dom fleet and invasion force all alone. The result was a vicious battle, and the narrowest of victories.

McClain then compounded his error by sending most of his ships *home*, instead of securing the isles he believed must have already fallen when he heard of the battle south of Saint Francis—then coming *here* himself! Jenks already knew this war had spiraled beyond their experience and even comprehension—the reports of the fighting for New Ireland proved that—and he'd seen the unprecedented nature of the war in the west, against the Grik, firsthand. He bitterly understood that compared with the experience the Americans and Lemurians had amassed, his people were literally amateurs. But there could be no excuse for the lethargy, vacillation, and incompetence High Admiral McClain had demonstrated. Jenks had relieved him on sight and sent him home as well. In retrospect, he supposed he could have been hanged for that, but the Governor-Emperor endorsed his decision, and approved his elevation to CINCEAST.

Jenks caught himself absently twisting his braided "Imperial" mustache again, and snatched his hand away and grasped it with the other behind his back. *Won't do for the lads to see me so restless,* he chided himself once more. His force was bound to rendezvous with a much larger one designated TF *Maaka-Kakja*, built around the massive new aircraft carrier it was named for. Once together, the combined force, with all its ships, aircraft, and troops would again constitute Second Fleet, and he, like his counterpart Keje-Fris-Ar in the west, would assume overall command. It was a daunting prospect. He was sure the fleet would be sufficient to relieve the isles—if they still held!—and then they could take the war to the Doms at last. He yearned for that more than he had anything in his life. He'd seen the terrible Grik and understood why Captain Reddy had to return to that front, aside from the repairs *Walker* needed.

But the Doms had shown themselves to be just as terrible as the Grik, and perhaps even more inhuman—*because* they were human!

He wasn't sure what they'd do if they found the Enchanted Isles had fallen. The almost-certain annihilation of the garrison was bad enough, but they desperately needed those islands as a staging area at the end of unprecedented, almost unimaginably long lines of supply. Only once they were secure could they control the sea and air around them, and perhaps other islands, and amass the vast armies and war material required to end the Dom menace forever. *We will take them back! That is what we will do!* He promised himself. Brevet General Tamatsu Shinya would command his ground forces, assisted by Jenks's old Marine lieutenant—now colonel—Blair, and some well-seasoned Lemurian officers. All had extensive combat experience, and Captain Reddy trusted Shinya completely. They *would* take the islands back; they had no choice. But it would be costly and another delay that could have been avoided!

Standing there, he tried to will the ponderous preparations of his fleet to greater speed so they could get to sea at last. Only nineteen ships of the now thirty-odd in port were raising steam, beginning to move. Some had to remain behind to protect Saint Francis, after all. He wasn't surprised to see that USS *Mertz* and USS *Tindal*, the Fil-pin-built frigates—or DDs, as they called themselves—had already weighed their anchors and were jockeying near his own *Achilles*. The two "American" ships had been badly mauled in the battle but quickly restored to order. He grimaced, remembering they'd replenished their savaged crews with *female* volunteers!

"Up and down!" came the cry from forward, relayed back to the raised, bridge-shaped "quarterdeck" control station between the large amidships paddle boxes.

"Very well," Jenks replied. Despite his new position as CINCEAST, he still personally commanded his ship. At least for now. Lieutenant Grimsley would take over once they joined the rest of the fleet. "Helm, Quartermaster, maintain position with the engines until the anchor is secure!"

"Aye, sir!" the two men chorused, the quartermaster's

hands grasping a pair of handles attached to either side of a device almost exactly like the Americans' engine-room telegraph. *It is odd,* mused Jenks, *how form follows function across so vast a gulf!*

The other ships of the small fleet eventually signaled their readiness and with *Achilles* in the lead they slowly steamed past the fortress island, through the mouth of the bay and into the wide sea beyond.

***TF* Maaka-Kakja**
East Pacific 130 Longitude
N Equatorial Current

Second Lieutenant Orrin Reddy, Acting Lieutenant Commander and COFO for the 3rd Naval Air Wing aboard USS *Maaka-Kakja* (CV-4), waggled the wings of his PB-1B Nancy flying boat to get the attention of the 'Cat flying the ship off his starboard wing. *Damn kid never can seem to pay attention to what he's doing when he's in the air,* he grumbled to himself, even as he recognized his hypocrisy. He'd had the same trouble when he first learned to fly, to soar so high above the world and all the cares and even thoughts that seemed so firmly rooted there.

Regardless, he'd also learned the hard way that losing focus for even a moment in the air was the quickest, maybe most surprising, way to die that he'd ever seen. Two of his '41-C classmates at San Diego were killed in a situation just like this: two ships, all alone, flying straight and level. One drifted into the other, a wing tangled with a prop, and it was all over but the fall. Neither pilot even got out of his tumbling craft. Of course, the Japanese and their agile fighters visited all sorts of deliberate, sudden death on his 3rd Pursuit Squadron mates in the Philippines. It added a whole new dimension when somebody was actively trying to kill you. Then he'd heard how his pal and fellow survivor Jack Mackey bought it after his first action in the west—against zeppelins! He still couldn't get over that—when he stuck a wheel in a bomb crater on the airstrip and TL'd one of the few precious P-40s that somehow made it here. That just wasn't fair at all.

Orrin knew he hadn't yet discovered nearly as many ways to die on this world as his illustrious cousin and "Supreme Commander" Captain Reddy. The closest things he'd seen to Grik were Lawrence and the Sa'aarans in the Fil-pin Lands, and those few wild "flying Grik" that gave them so much trouble on New Ireland. But he was *Maakaa-Kakja*'s COFO now, like it or not, and he didn't intend to lose any of his pilots to woolgathering.

"Zap him, Seepy!" he shouted into the speaking tube beside his shoulder. "Seepy" was Orrin's copilot/spotter/wireless-operator backseater, or OC, in the little plane. The brown-and-gray-furred 'Cat's real name was Kuaar-Ran-Taak, and unlike so many others, his squadron handle hadn't come from what his name sounded like to a human American. Orrin was the only one of those in the whole 3rd Naval Air Wing, anyway. Seep was an intoxicant made of the ubiquitous polta fruit that also produced, when properly prepared, the miraculously curative polta paste, so Orrin could only guess what inspired Seepy's name, but the guy was the best backseater in the wing, and a good pilot in his own right.

"I zap him already!" Seepy answered indignantly through the same tube. His voice came dull and tinny over the sound of the air gushing past the two open cockpits and the drone of the engine above and between them. He'd sent the long, harsh keystroke from his wireless transmitter that basically meant "heads-up!" It was not something pilots wanted to receive on scout-training flights—particularly since everyone in the wing could hear it, or would hear *about* it, and the zap was followed by the miscreant's tail number.

Orrin watched with satisfaction as the other plane contritely returned to its proper station, and he realized with a start that he *was* satisfied not only with his wayward pilot, but with his whole new setup. He'd honestly been dubious at first. He'd been through hell in the fighting in the Philippines, but that hadn't compared to the ordeal he and only a few surviving others endured at the hands of their Japanese captors before and during their transport on *Mizuki Maru*. Arriving on this world and surviving the massacre that followed left him starved and mostly dead, but he had survived and he was actually starting to like it here.

It took him a while to get used to things, of course. The presence of dames—of any race—in his cousin's Navy, as well as commanding some of its ships, required some adjustment, but Admiral Lelaa-Tal-Cleraan, commander of *Maaka-Kakja* and her task force, was an absolutely swell gal—with more guts than *he* had, he was sure. Nancys weren't P-40s, or anything close, but they were decent little kites and they were probably even more reliable. He wasn't quite sure how he felt about this whole new war he was in the middle of; he had no experience on the western front, but the 'Cats were good guys, and if they hated the Grik as much as they did, he was willing to take their word how bad they were. He knew firsthand how lousy the Doms were, so he guessed the reasons he fought really hadn't changed that much for him.

He *did* like being COFO, he realized. He liked his pilots and he liked 'Cats in general. He'd always liked cousin Matt, even when he treated him like a kid—when he was a kid. He even liked most of the officers he'd met attached to the task force—except Colonel Shinya. He *respected* Shinya and believed he knew his stuff, and he knew Matt trusted the guy, but he was a *Jap*, damn it! He just couldn't get over that yet. All in all, though, he guessed he could have wound up in a lot worse situation. He stretched.

"Hey, Commaander," came the muffled voice from behind, "look tree o'clock down, mebbe six miles. There some mountain fishes down there."

Orrin looked. *Sure enough. Damn, those things are big!* At five thousand feet and several miles, they looked like whales a few hundred yards off, cruising slowly, their massive flukes never breaking the surface. The bow wave they pushed in front of what he'd been told were kind of their foreheads looked like breakers on a distant beach.

"We go mess with them?"

Orrin chuckled to himself, but spoke sternly. "No, not this time." On occasion, they used the mighty beasts like practice targets, but Admiral Lelaa had forbidden actually dropping anything directly on them. They'd already discovered they could kind of herd the massive creatures by dropping bombs around them, and they'd done it a couple of times to clear the dangerous things out of the task force's path, but so far, for some reason, mountain fish in this region seemed totally disinterested in ships—or anything much *but* bombs—that might divert them from whatever destination they had in mind. Generally, they took a "leave them alone as long as they leave us alone" approach out here.

"But we got two practice bombs," Seepy reminded. They also carried a crate of live, hand-droppable mortar bombs aboard. That was SOP now, but Seepy didn't mention those.

"I know, and we'll use them when we get back on one of the towed targets. Even when we miss, the guys watching will get more out of it than if we use 'em out here where no one can see." Orrin shook his head. "We're not going to pester the big fellas today!" He paused, glancing at the little mirror that showed him the fuel gauge bobbing in the tank, then looked at the bulky, windup clock embedded in the instrument panel. Watches were scarce these days—he sure didn't have one—but it was essential for flight leaders, at least, to keep track of the time.

"About thirteen thirty. Time to head back," he shouted. He'd been keeping an eye out for their replacements for a while. Sometimes the guys liked to "bounce" each other, like real pursuit pilots, and trying to get the "old man" added extra spice to the game. He didn't discourage it, as long as things didn't get out of hand. Nobody wanted to end up in the drink! But he also knew the Grik had aircraft now, and it was probably only a matter of time before the Doms did too. They already had their pet flying lizards. They'd been promised new planes with better performance, as soon as Colonel Mallory got the new radials on line. For some reason, nobody seemed to doubt he would. Then they needed rubber for tires, which was supposed to be coming out of Ceylon and India soon. It was widely rumored the new ships would not be floatplanes, though, and Orrin had mixed feelings about that. He loved the idea of the performance upgrade, but also liked something that would float if he was ever forced down on the scary sea.

USS* Maaka-Kakja *(CV-4)

Admiral Lelaa-Tal-Cleraan paced the bridge of her mighty ship with undiminished pleasure, despite the presence of her scruffy, greasy chief engineer, who dogged her every step. She knew what mice were; there were similar, if not identical, creatures on her world, and she had to admit that Gilbert Yeager, one of the original fireroom "Mice" aboard USS *Walker*, certainly reminded her of one, even if he was taller than she was. As much as he physically resembled a mouse, she'd heard that he'd once been just as quiet. No longer. Now he never hesitated to bring his daily reports straight to her, and if those reports sounded more like the nasal, squeaky whining of an angry mouse, she had only herself to blame. She'd encouraged it.

"... an' after I tole 'em to fix it, they just oogled at me an' asked me *how*!" Gilbert ranted. "How many times I gotta show 'em how to do the same god d... gut-dumpin'... thang, again an' again, afore they get wise?"

Until you learn to explain what you are doing and why, Lelaa thought.

"How we ever come this far without stallin' out, sinkin', 'er just rollin' belly-up, is a myst'ry to me," he droned on, "since mosta my division cain't find their swishy tails with both hands, let alone figger out which end of a wrench ta' grab!" He shook his head, then stared at the deck. "I'll admit it. I'm tired, Skipper."

"This entire crew is inexperienced, Chief Gilbert," Lelaa replied pleasantly. "It is fortunate we have a core group such as yourself to help the others along."

"Well, ain't that my point? They ain't *gettin'* much along, even with all my helpin'!"

Lelaa didn't know Isak and Tabby, the other "Mice," but she knew that while Gilbert might be a font of engineering wisdom, the tap was perpetually closed to a trickle. Despite his newfound ability to communicate, he still couldn't pass ideas and technical information very well. His division seemed eager enough to learn, as far as she could tell, but Gilbert was, frankly, a crummy teacher. Considering the situation threatened to suppress her fine mood. It was a serious issue. So far, most of *Maaka-Kakja*'s machinery had functioned flawlessly. It was overengineered to a point of almost gross inefficiency, after all. But what if? They were steaming toward certain eventual combat, and they had little real notion of the Dom defenses or domestic capability. All they'd seen so far was what the Doms could do at the end of a very long rope—like they would soon be.

"Relaax, Mr. Yay-gar. Actually, you *must* relaax. You—how do you say?—own a plank of this ship, as do most aboard her, so I understand your concern. I will give this matter the thought it requires, I assure you. In the meantime, you do have some good people. Not all are as green as you say. Make use of them."

Gilbert shrugged. "Well, maybe they ain't *all* useless, but them who ain't are as wore down as me. Some folks just don't get it that this gal has the biggest . . . dern . . . power plant we've ever thowed together, an' there ain't nothin' light down there. Stuff one fella could do on my ol' *Walker* takes a dozen fellas aboard here . . ." He stopped and blinked. "Which that don't compare, 'cause she has turbines an' we got these jug jumpers. . . ."

"I believe I know what you mean," Lelaa said.

"Well, maybe you do, but it boils down to as wore out as I am . . . I'm just as tired o' worryin'. I don't want none o' my fellas gettin' hurt. See? It's like a Chinese fire drill down there half the time."

Lelaa didn't know what that was, but his other words reinforced her belief that his primary concern was for his division and the ship. That spoke well for the very strange man.

She cast her eyes over the surrounding seascape and the, to her, unprecedented numbers and power of her element of Second Fleet. Besides *Maaka-Kakja*, there were steam-powered and fast-sailing oilers, tenders, colliers, and transports. All of the newer Company steamers had been seized or requisitioned as troopers, and if they were the slowest ships in the task force and set its pace, they could at least be counted on to manage the same creeping station every day. Another task force, built around the even slower, heavy, Imperial ships of the line, or liners, would be along later. Around and among all those ships present were dozens of Lemurian-American and Imperial DDs, and nearly everything out there was driven by steam. There were the usual mechanical casualties, but there were a lot of competent engineers in the fleet. Maybe she could borrow a few to give Gilbert a hand—if only to interpret his grunts and disapproving stares for his snipes. One thing was sure: Gilbert couldn't keep *Maaka-Kakja* running essentially by himself forever. He *was* wearing out. Lelaa suddenly wondered how he would take it if she brought in some professional help. Mice could be sensitive creatures.

"Then maybe you need a *larger* division as badly as experience."

"If they could stay outta each other's way . . . that might help. Manilly Bupers seems ta' think this tub didn't need any bigger black gang than a harbor tug." Lelaa saw he was studying the vast fleet surrounding them now. He stuck his hands in his pockets, then jerked them out. "Could maybe . . . a bigger, *more experienced* division happen?" he asked hesitantly, and Lelaa blinked amusement.

"I am sure we can work something out."

After Gilbert left the bridge, Tex Sheider approached her, grinning. He'd been S-19's radioman, but, like all of them, his capacities had expanded amazingly. Not only was he one of Lelaa's best friends, but he was also her exec.

"Getting that squirrel to *ask* for the dose you wanted to make him take is one of the slickest things I ever saw!" he laughed.

"He may be a 'squirrel,' but he is a good man. It was only a matter of discovering what he really needed, so I could help *him* know."

"Figuring out anything bobbing around in that weird little head is bound to be a miracle. Spanky said it can't be done."

A pair of four-cylinder Wright Gipsy engines roared on the flight deck below as the great ship eased slightly more into the wind, and one after the other, a pair of Nancys were hurled into the sky ahead, assisted by the hydraulic catapults. (Those were other devices Gilbert Yeager passionately despised.)

A signals 'Cat entered the bridge from the separate comm shack dedicated to air ops. "Commaander Reddy's flight has rejoined the other flights of the Eleventh Bomb Squadron and has the task force in sight. He asks permission to proceed with the scheduled training exercises."

"Of course," Lelaa said. "Signal *Icarus* to stream the target."

"Ay, ay, Cap-i-taan!"

They watched through Impie-made telescopes as the twelve planes crept toward the task force in a long, echelon formation. Two planes suddenly banked away from the others and dove on the target barge *Icarus* had unreeled about two hundred yards in her wake. Tall white splashes straddled the barge on the first pass, and again on the second. Only one splash marked the passage of the third pair, so one of them must have hit the barge itself. The exercise continued, with similar, satisfactory results. Only one plane missed dramatically, nearly hitting *Icarus* on its second pass, but its pilot was likely one of Orrin's replacements. The wing had lost a lot of pilots and machines in the New Ireland fighting, but as a whole, it had gained a lot of experience as well. Replenishment ships out of Maa-ni-la had brought the wing back up to strength in both flyers and aircraft, and not only were there now *extra* pilots; there were also thirty spare Nancys aboard, still in crates. Perhaps sixty more were scattered through the fleet, and the tenders each had an assembled plane mounted on a new directional catapult amidships. *Walker*'s precedent of carrying a plane aboard for long-range reconnaissance had been as successful here as the same practice had been for larger ships on the world she'd come from.

In total, Orrin would eventually command more than 120 aircraft when they reached the Enchanted Isles—*if* the islands were still in friendly hands, and *if* there was a protected waterway to operate them from when they got there. Hopefully, they would have answers to those questions within the next week, even before they rendezvoused with Jenks's elements. There was no transmitter in the Enchanted Isles, and somebody had to either get there or at least get eyeballs on the place before they'd know the situation. Fleeing ships had confirmed the attack, but since then there'd been no news.

Orrin even had a couple of pursuit planes. The P-40s that arrived in Baalkpan in *Santa Catalina*'s hold had been designed for six .50-caliber machine guns each. Colonel Mallory had decided not to mount them all on the planes, with a couple of exceptions. The P-40s could carry four times the bomb load of a Nancy, fly four or five times as fast, and with an auxiliary fuel tank and minus the weight of four of their guns, they even had slightly greater range. With the spare guns aboard the ship, the Alliance now had almost 150 extra of the powerful weapons. Several had been hurried out to Scapa Flow before the fleet put to sea, with instructions on how to mount one gun each in the noses of Nancys in such a way that they wouldn't shake the little planes apart. The same had been done for First Fleet with more urgency and in greater numbers, considering the airship threat and what had happened to *Humfra-Dar*. It wasn't much, but at least Second Fleet had some air to air protection now.

"Orrin's shaping up just fine," Tex observed.

"He is. I had some doubt at first. He is . . . very different from his cousin, Captain Reddy."

"Yeah, and he'd already been through a lot when we got him. He didn't have a lot of time with Captain Reddy when they were both in the New Britain Isles either, but he definitely respects the 'old man,' and he's plenty committed to fighting the Doms, at least."

"Indeed, and perhaps more important than his commitment to the cause, Commander Reddy has become even more committed to his aircrews. That is good."

Tex shrugged. "Sure. Gilbert's right, though. The ship *is* green, but at least Orrin's given her some damn sharp teeth."

"Yes," Lelaa replied. She turned to the officer of the deck. "I believe Commander Reddy has almost completed his exercise. Stand by to begin recovery operations. The fleet will assume its appropriate stations and observe all signals."

"Ay, Cap-i-taan!"

CHAPTER 10

La Plaza Sagrada del Templo de los Papas
The Holy Dominion

Signals Ensign Kari-Faask, attached to USS *Walker*'s Special Air Division, sat huddled in a corner of her iron cage, glaring hatred at the stares from the surging mob of dark-skinned humans beyond the bars. She'd been there long enough that few usually seemed to notice her, and fewer poked or threw things at her anymore. She'd become a fixture; yet another curiosity within the vast plaza surrounding the massive, severe, pyramidal temple to whatever wicked gods were worshiped in this evil land. She knew little about those gods; she hadn't heard a word she understood in weeks. She'd once been under the impression that the people of the Holy Dominion revered essentially the same God, or Maker, as her human friends, but now she knew that couldn't be. The Doms used a barbaric caricature of the cross worn by Sister Audry and a number of the human destroyermen, but that was apparently the only similarity after all.

The attributes and virtues of her friends' God were almost the same as the Maker of All Things, whom she'd been raised to revere, and many had begun to suspect that He was, in fact, truly the same supreme being, despite some liturgical differences. From what she'd seen, just from her cage, whatever creature or creatures demanded the faith of the Doms could not possibly be more different.

He/it/they possessed so many different, conflicting attributes that it was impossible to reconcile them all. Apparently He was all-powerful, yet required the assistance of a huge panoply of frightening creatures to impose his will—the plaza was festooned with carvings and sculptures of all manner of beasts—who seemed to require similar devotion. He was supposedly merciful, yet besides her own suffering, she'd witnessed monstrous barbarity on the high steps of the temple, acts committed in cold blood that rivaled the horror of battle. And the people here seemed convinced that those acts were not only endorsed but required by their God. It was abominable. Twice now, once a month she supposed, she'd seen hundreds of naked humans herded, shrieking, up the steps of the temple, where they were slaughtered in the most hideous fashion. She couldn't see everything from where she was kept, but she saw the heads come tumbling, bouncing down the steps, followed by rivers of blood—all amid the desolate cries of the victims and the approving roar of the crowd. Not even the Grik could be so loathsome, and she wondered how anyone could worship such a terrible, bloodthirsty God.

One day, they would probably take her to the top of those steps, she suspected, and when they did she would not wail—she would fight them. Her nail-claws had been torn from her fingers and her sharp canines had been broken off, but now that they'd begun feeding her and keeping her cage cleaned out, she exercised as much as she could within her small enclosure to maintain her strength. She'd wondered once what she was doing in the new war against these people, but they were her enemies now, as surely as the Grik. When they came for her, she would surprise them with her strength and kill as many as she could.

Some ceremony was underway—they happened all the time—and though she didn't think a slaughter would ensue, there was a . . . different kind of excitement in the air. Hordes of people swelled the plaza; more than usual for other festivals she'd seen. Gradually, she noticed that fewer crosses were in evidence, compared to the number of other icons;

strange little figurines dangling from thongs around necks that looked oddly like the small cat creatures that ran loose in the New Britain Isles. She knew those animals came from the old world of the destroyermen and had inspired the friendly diminutive of her own people, even if they weren't really that similar and seemed little smarter than bugs. They were rather attractive little things, she thought, and they came in all sorts of colors, so the comparison wasn't without some merit. But the cat icons worn by the Doms were all black, or yellow with dark spots. Strange. Even stranger, she realized: she was drawing more attention than usual that day, and some of the spectators seemed to be comparing their icons to her own nearly black, tan-blotched pelt.

A commotion began directly in front of her cage and people started practically climbing over each other to make way for . . . something. Brightly uniformed guards with red neck cloths forced their way to the bars with muskets, plug bayonets inserted in their muzzles, forming a gap in the throng. Kari tensed. Maybe the time had come? She discovered with a thrill that she wasn't even afraid. Her father had been a great warrior in Aryaal and had died a hero's death. She'd never considered herself brave, but she suddenly realized that maybe his blood ran thicker in her veins than she'd ever suspected.

Two figures moved toward her between the barrier of troops. As they drew near, she recognized one as that Blood Cardinal, Don Hernan, who'd caused so much turmoil on New Scotland and then somehow escaped. He wore his usual bloodred cloak and strange, ornately decorated white hat. Despite the rest of the mob, he still wore the garish gold cross he'd always worn as well. She'd seen him twice since she was captured. He'd never spoken to her, even though she knew he spoke English and she'd yelled enough of it at him that he had to know she spoke it too. She'd expected to be tortured for information, but though she *was* tortured, no one ever asked her anything! It was as if they heard her . . . but didn't! In their view, she was an animal. She couldn't possibly speak, so they couldn't hear her when she did. She wondered what he was doing here. Then she recognized the second figure.

"Fred!" she blurted, unable to restrain the shout. Some of the soldiers twitched, surprised, then studiously ignored her. Lieutenant (jg) Fred Reynolds was her pilot and her very best friend. She hadn't seen him since they were forced down in the Caal-i-forniaa surf and taken prisoner by the retreating Doms. She'd figured he was dead.

"Fred!" she cried again, scrambling across the floor of her cage to crouch nearer as he approached. Then she saw the dull look on his face; the sunken eyes; the scabbed, shaved scalp. His cheekbones stood out in bruised relief and he looked half-starved. He was dressed in a long white robe that covered his feet. He halted beyond the bars—and he was standing, without restraint, beside Don Hernan. She was stunned. Could her friend be dead, after all?

"Here is the creature we found you with, my son," Don Hernan said in his deceptively gentle voice, his black mustache quirking upward at one end of his mouth. "I preserved it, as I promised."

"Of course, Your Holiness. I never doubted," Fred whispered. His voice sounded . . . strange, rough, unused.

"Look upon it," the Blood Cardinal commanded softly. Fred obeyed, and his eyes passed across Kari, but his expression never changed. "You realize now that it is a mere *thing*, an animal unworthy of thought or concern? One cannot befriend an animal. They have no place in the kingdoms of God, but to serve Him as the beasts they are, as they are made to do?" He gestured around. "This festival commemorates the service of one such beast, and some heretics"—he glowered around—"still cling to the belief there is thought behind that service." He shrugged. "But there is not. No thought crosses their minds beyond their own comfort and what they will eat. They have no room in their minds and hearts for God. They serve God and us as draft animals, guards, and even such as the small dragons that brought your flying machine down because we feed them and make them comfortable!"

"Of course, Your Holiness," Fred agreed in a firmer tone.

"Excellent. Then you cannot object if I do away with this . . . thing?" The question seemed almost a test.

"I have no moral or spiritual objection, Your Holiness,"

Fred replied slowly, and Kari's heart skipped a beat. She was stunned not only by Fred's words, but by the utter lack of inflection. *Oh Maker! What did they do to him?*

"Not anymore," the former aviator continued. "But from a practical standpoint . . ." he looked at the crowd beyond the barrier. "Since . . . it was placed on display and some have grown accustomed to it, there may be unrest if it's destroyed. Besides, the Empire is allied to creatures like it. Having it captive here, for God's soldiers to see in its vulnerability, may reduce the shock or even fear of meeting them in battle."

Don Hernan's eyebrow rose. "Most interesting. I had not even considered that." He appraised Fred for a long moment. "I believe you are sincere." His tone sounded surprised. "The Cleanser said you had embraced the faith with unusual earnestness, but I was skeptical at first. Since then, you have unstintingly assisted with our project to build our own flying machines, and held nothing back that I could see. It is rare enough for the heretic to gain true salvation, but to then go forward and strive so hard to perform God's work . . . I am proud of you, my son!"

"Thank you, Your Holiness. I am yours and His to command."

"And yet you still think!" Don Hernan enthused. "Very well. We will preserve this specimen until the enemies of God are destroyed; then we shall wipe it away along with all vestiges of this infantile predisposition of some of our flock to cling to ancient habits and associations!" He sighed and glanced at the sky. "With the death of this creature, even this silly festival will pass away at last! Come, my son. Let us go to the temple. It is almost time to pray—and I think you may be ready to be presented to His Supreme Holiness at last!"

Don Hernan and what had been Fred Reynolds quickly retreated, and the armed cordon closed and vanished behind them. Kari was still too stunned to speak, and even though she wanted to scream and bash through the iron bars with her bare hands, all she could do was crouch there, numb. She was stung and hurt, but mostly she felt a welling rage. Not at Fred or what she knew would be her ultimate fate, but toward the monsters that had already destroyed her friend.

"Oh, Fred!" she keened to herself.

"So you *do* speak," came an English voice with no accent she could place, and she almost jumped out of her skin. The crowd had reverted to what it had been before, but one man, more bedraggled and disheveled than most, peered in at her like the urchins of the city often did. He had dark hair and dark skin like the multitude around him, but it *was* he who'd spoken, and he held her gaze—which was more than most would do.

"Of course I speak, you dope!" she flared, and caught herself when he shushed her and looked around.

"You . . . your species . . . truly is allied with the Empire?" the man asked urgently.

"It . . . I am."

"The war goes badly?"

"Not when I left it," she quipped. "The attack against the Imperial Isles failed, and we were going to the aid of the colonies."

"Not what they tell the masses," the man said ironically.

"Who are you?"

"No time. I cannot linger here. Just know that you have friends, and we will do what we may for you."

With that, the tide of humanity swept the strange man away.

CHAPTER 11

Baalkpan, Borno
March 9, 1944

Chief Gunner's Mate Dennis Silva, brightly attired in his very best shore-going rig and a fresh black eye patch, marched up the pier from the exhausted "Clipper" with a powerful, rolling gait that left his companions hard-pressed to keep up. His sea bag was balanced on one shoulder, and his Thompson hung from the other by its sling. The web belt around his waist was festooned with a bizarre variety of weapons. In addition to his beloved 1911 Colt and a pair of magazine pouches were a 1903 Springfield bayonet and a hard-used pattern of 1917 Navy cutlass. Perhaps most incongruous, a long-barreled, ornately carved flintlock pistol dangled from the belt by a long bar hook. The flight from Respite had taken almost a week, with numerous refueling, maintenance, and rest stops for the planes and pilots, and the trip had been hard on all of them but, apparently, him. He reached the dock and paused, gazing about, as if expecting a band. Many workers were present, but no fanfare awaited him and his companions.

"I swear," he grumbled to Midshipman Stuart Brassey, who'd arrived panting beside him. Larry had matched his pace, but Lieutenant Laumer hadn't tried to keep up. Now he joined them with a chuckle on the dock.

"What were you expecting, Silva? Ticker tape and dancing girls?"

"Maybe not for me, but ol' Larry here deserves some notice, and so do you . . . sir." He shrugged. "Anything I done to deserve praise was just me bein' me. Mighta got me hung, in different circumstances."

Laumer nodded thoughtfully. He admired Silva but wasn't sure he liked him. He considered Silva a loose cannon and didn't understand why his behavior was tolerated. He'd finally come to understand that Silva's . . . talents were an asset to the war effort, however, and Captain Reddy apparently knew best how to handle the dangerous man. With that realization came another: Silva wasn't his responsibility, nor was he really subject to Irvin Laumer's command or discipline. Once that was clear, he no longer felt like he was neglecting his duty by not *trying* to enforce discipline on a man he was actually, well, maybe a little afraid of. He remained convinced that Silva set a bad example—but, somehow, with very few exceptions, nobody ever *followed* his example . . . or at least they never lived to do it twice. Ultimately, the big man probably wasn't as corrosive to discipline as Irvin originally thought, and he was good at what he did. He could accept that.

"Might still get you hung, if what I hear is true. Did you really go AWOL?"

"Not exactly," Dennis answered absently, gazing about. "I hate what they've done with the place."

"It looks like what Manila has become," Laumer agreed. "It's necessary, though, if we're going to win."

"Used to be so pretty," Silva sniffed. "Now it's all noise an' smoke an' marchin' troops. Stinks too. Looks better than it did after the big battle, I guess, but now it's like . . . Mare Island, the Palms, and Shanghai all wadded up." He slowly grinned. "Which could maybe be a *good* thing!"

"Well," Laumer said, "you're not my problem, beyond making sure you report to Mr. Sandison. I'm supposed to report to Mr. Brister at the War Room in the great hall . . . I guess."

"May I accompany you, sir?" Stuart asked. "I suppose I must report to Mr. Cook, but I've no idea where he may be."

"What a'out Lawrence?" the Sa'aaran asked.

"Guess it never occurred to anybody to peel you offa me, Larry."

Silva's statement was punctuated by a high-pitched shriek of delight, and he turned his head just in time to tense before a short but muscle-heavy missile impacted his chest and wrapped its arms around him.

"Sil-vaa!" squealed Risa-Sab-At, hugging him almost painfully, but not—thankfully—licking his face this time. "You got here early," she scolded fondly. "We had to scamper to meet you!"

"We had a tailwind," Silva defended, pecking Risa's furry head between her ears. He looked at Laumer. "So there woulda' been a parade after all if that air 'Cat hadn't been heapin' on the coal so!"

Risa laughed. "No paa-rade, you dope, but plenty of happy people!" She released him and slid to the ground, grinning hugely up at him and blinking with glee. "I'm so glad you are home—and safe! You always scare poor Risa with your stunts!"

"Well, as you know yerself, the hee-roin' bid'ness don't always respect a fella's priorities." He gestured at the city beyond the growing, laughing crowd, and his gaze caught Laumer's . . . priceless expression, likely the result of the exuberant greeting.

"I heard you'd be here," Dennis resumed, "buildin' yer own regiment! We prob'ly shouldn't carry on so in front of the children. Besides, you're a officer now! I oughta *salute* ya!"

"You never were in *my* chain of command!" Risa retorted archly. "Speakin' of commands, though, how's that silly brother of mine?"

Silva recognized other faces approaching and inwardly cringed just a bit. Sister Audry was all smiles, for some reason. Ronson Rodriguez was smiling too, but his eyes looked serious. Young Ensign Cook seemed embarrassed, but he quickly advanced and shook Brassey's hand. Commander Bernard Sandison actually looked grim.

"Chackie?" Silva asked, distracted, then looked back at her. "He's swell. He came as far as Manila with us." He hooked his thumb back at the "Clipper." "The flyboys needed a nap, so I went with him to meet Major Jindal and his Impie boys. They got there just before we did." He cocked his head. "We also met Chackie's new commando outfit. Some strange ducks there. Some o' them China Marines and Army guys from the old world weren't too impressed with our Chackie at first, like they didn't care to be commanded by a 'Cat." He shrugged. "We commenced to impress 'em."

"I can imagine how you did that," Ronson said, as he and the others joined the group. Silva and his fellow passengers saluted.

"Hey, Ronson," Silva greeted. Rodriguez might be an officer now, and Silva would salute him, but he remembered when the dark, skin-headed Hispanic with the Pancho Villa mustache had been a second-class electrician's mate. "*Mr.* Cook," he added, and Abel blushed.

"We didn't hurt nobody," he continued to Risa, "but now they know this war ain't a cakewalk—and that maybe we know more about fightin' it than they do." His gaze swung to Bernard Sandison. The former torpedo officer was standing there with something long and skinny and wrapped in canvas held at his side. It was nearly as long as he was tall. Unlike Ronson, whom Silva still considered an equal, Bernie had always been an officer. "Mr. Sandison," he added, hesitantly. "You gonna hang me?"

"He is *not*!" Sister Audry declared, and to Silva's amazement, embraced him. He stiffened with surprise and the Dutch nun stepped back, smiling.

"The prodigal has returned, but has not squandered our trust! You are our Samson, Mr. Silva, and I am very proud of you!" With a glance at Risa, her smile cracked slightly. "Perhaps there are Delilahs in your life . . . but none seek to betray you."

"Why . . . thank you kindly, Sister." Silva's eye narrowed. "Samson? Long hair? Got his eyes poked out?" He rubbed his freshly burred scalp, then fingered his patch. "Not me, Sister, and I aim to keep the peeper I got left! Say, what's got into you?"

Audry just shook her head, still smiling, but backed away.

"C'mon, you," Bernie said gruffly. "Mr. Letts says you're

to report to Mr. Cook here, and you're not going to be around long, but I've got you as long as you are. I've got things to show you that I want your twisted opinion on, and I haven't got all day." He frowned. "I've got less than a week before Torpedo Day."

"What the hell's Torpedo Day?" Dennis asked.

"It's the big day Bernie told everybody we'd be ready to test the new torpedoes!" Ronson muttered accusingly. "Adar's turned it into a giant, freak-show spectacle, when we're all supposed to trot out the new gadgets we've been working on. I ain't ready either!"

"You don't say? Torpedoes, huh?" Silva grinned. "Sure, let's go. That is, if Mr. Cook considers me 'reported' an' releases me!"

Abel blushed even deeper. "Ah . . . yes, of course, Mr. . . I mean, Chief Silva. We won't be departing for a few weeks yet. Plenty of time to discuss our expedition."

"Thank you, sir," Silva said in a respectful tone that wasn't—quite—destroyed by his expression. He paused for a moment then, and gestured at the long object in Bernie's hands. "Whatcha got in your poke? Some kinda tor-poon?"

Bernie sighed. "No! Well, kind of. Alan and Mr. Riggs wanted to make you an officer, and we all know how that went over. Then they figured they ought to give you a medal or something, God knows why. I told 'em you'd just use it for a fishing weight." He shrugged and started unwrapping the object. "So . . . knowing how bent you'd be over losing your old 'Doom Whomper,' I had the fellas—and dames, if you believe it!—over in Experimental Ordnance, slap this together for you." Bernie waited while Silva wordlessly lowered his sea bag and handed the Thompson off to Larry, then fully revealed what looked like a gargantuan version of the new standard issue Allin-Silva breech-loading musket and handed it to the big man.

For a long moment, Silva was speechless. He just stood there, staring at the massive weapon in his hands.

"It's basically a breech-loading version of what you had," Bernie said a little awkwardly. "We had the barrels off of four more busted twenty-fives, so we built them all up like this, using as many of the same parts we use on the . . .

normal Baalkpan Arsenal rifles as we could. Same locks, triggerguards, and springs, so most of the things that might break are interchangeable. Of course, we had to make way bigger breechblocks and barrel bands. It uses pretty much the same hundred-caliber bullet you came up with too, but in a metallic cartridge." He hesitated. "I don't know who's going to get the other three, because they kick like . . . well, I don't know what they kick like, because I'll never shoot one of the damn things. But some 'Cats have big enough shoulders to pad the poor bones underneath, and we got them all proofed, tested, and rough sighted in." He stopped and waited. Still, Silva didn't speak.

"Well? What do you think, damn it?"

"She's a dandy, Bernie," Silva whispered. "I guess I don't know what else to say. Nobody ever gave me nothin' before but orders an' whuppin's."

For a moment, Bernie was just as speechless; then Sister Audry spoke.

"That's not true, Mr. Silva. You also have our trust, appreciation, and friendship—all freely given." For the first time since Dennis saw her, she frowned. "Some have even tried to give you their love." She shrugged. "Much as I approve of your new weapon, that is an even more precious gift."

Silva winced and took a deep breath. "Yeah. Maybe so." He looked at Risa and offered a half smile. "Where's Pam, doll?"

Risa shook her head. "She's out at Kaufman Field—with the airplanes. She always goes out there when they fly a lot . . . and sometimes she sees Colonel Maallory."

Silva nodded briskly. "Good choice. He ain't so bad for a Army man." He looked at Bernie. "C'mon, Mr. Sandison! I can't wait to see all the new toys! I'll . . . pay my respects to Pam later. Larry, take my chopper and my sea bag wherever it is they're stowin' us bachelor types, willya?"

"Goddammit, Pepper, they cain't *do* this to me!" Isak Rueben whined in his reedy voice. He was one of the original Mice, along with Gilbert Yeager, who was now CV-4 *Maaka-Kakja*'s chief engineer in Second Fleet. Both had once been simple—and very squirrelly—firemen aboard USS *Walker*. They'd adopted Tabby, and made her one of their own, but she was the engineering *officer* of their old ship now, and Isak, at least, resented that a little. He'd been stuck in Baalkpan toiling on "that goddamn floatin' hog trough" that had once been a beached, abandoned freighter, but everyone else was now proud to refer to as the "protected cruiser" *Santa Catalina*.

Isak's intense, narrow face looked beseechingly at the salt-and-pepper-furred Lemurian behind the bar of the Busted Screw. "They cain't just slurp me off right when I'm startin' to get my bizness ready ta percolate!" Isak moaned. He and Gilbert had spent a year and a half trying to turn the chewable but utterly unsmokable tobacco of this world into something that could be smoked—without making the smoker puke. Isak thought he finally had it and planned to establish "Isak's Sweet Smokin' Tobacco," and start raking in some of the gold everybody was being paid with now—until he got his new orders.

"Now I'm s'posed to fly—*fly* in one o' them clatterin' death traps—to join *Walker* once she puts in at Manila, so I can help with her refit!"

"I'd think you would like to be back with your Home," Pepper observed, wiping down the bar. It was between the morning and midday rush.

"Well . . . sure I would, but all my makin's—ever'thing I need to build my smokes—is *here*! An' besides, Tabby'll be my boss! *That* ain't right. I taught her ever'thing she knows!"

"And *she* knows that, Isaak," Pepper said patiently.

"Well . . . maybe we'll still get along, even if she's a officer. But what about my bizness? With that damn Laney still here, snoopin' around, he's bound to swipe my rice bowl!"

"You leave it with me," Pepper offered offhandedly. "I can handle Laney. Beside, scuttlebutt says Laney's gonna be an officer soon too; take engineerin' on *Saanta Cata-linaa*."

"Yah," Isak smoldered. "Ain't that a gas? Makes me even gladder I'm gettin' off her." He winced and shrugged. "Just as well, I guess. He does know her guts inside an' out, an' they've tried to make his sorry ass work at just about ever'thin' else. Can't kill 'im . . ."

He suddenly peered suspiciously at the 'Cat. "Yah! An' Earl Lanier left you his bar to watch for *his* useless, fat ass, an' you took it plumb over!"

Pepper blinked and shrugged. "He still my partner, if he ever comes back alive."

Isak's eyes went wide. "So you wanna be *partners*, huh? Damn it, Pepper, I'm already partners with so many of yer cousins, I can't keep track of 'em all!"

"I keep track of 'em," Pepper said, "an' I keep bizness goin' while you're gone too. You still get your half when you come back. Gilbert gets his half, cousins get one half for all, an' I take only half for me."

Isak scrunched up his face in a frown. "I dunno . . ."

"What else you gonna do? Let Laney take it? I don't know when *Saanta Cata-linaa* sails. . . . He might be here a long time after you fly off!"

"No, dammit! I don't even want nobody *sellin'* smokes to *him*!" He paused, then stuck out his hand. "That's an awful lotta 'halfs' but I guess we got a deal!"

Suddenly, he jerked his hand back with a sharp "Ook!" and vanished below the level of the bar.

"What?" Pepper demanded.

"I just seen *Dennis Silva* yonder! With Mr. Sandison!"

Pepper turned. Even amid the crowd, Silva stood out. "Yeah! There he is! I heard he was coming to Baalkpan!" He leaned over the counter and peered down at Isak. "Hey! How come you hidin' from him? Is he going to kill you for something?"

"Not that I know of . . . but *he* might have a reason!"

Pepper tossed his rag down on Isak's head. "Why are you scared of Silva? He's a right guy. You ain't scared of Laney, and he's a jerk."

"Yeah, but no snipe ever wants Silva to *see* him!" He looked up at Pepper. "You oughta get down too!"

Pepper snatched his rag back and blinked consternation. It was going to be another strange day at the Screw.

CHAPTER 12

New London, New Britain
Empire of the New Britain Isles
March 12, 1944

Courtney Bradford flapped his strange, wide-brimmed sombrero to cool himself while sweat beaded on his ruddy, balding pate. He was wearing a finely woven maroon wool frock coat cut in the local style, appropriate for the formal event he was already late for, and, except for the hat, he looked fairly respectable in the outfit, which included tan breeches and a black cravat cinched tightly around his neck. The wool was cooking him though, and he suspected that before the day was done, he would probably die. Fortunately, hats like the one he flailed at himself were the style on Respite, and there was enough demand for them in the Imperial capital of New London on New Britain, or the "Big Island," that they were relatively easy to find here. He'd been relieved to discover it after losing his previous one of similar shape at sea.

He leaned forward and peered out the coach window at the throng of humanity, and despite his discomfort, was utterly charmed. There weren't nearly as many indentured women on New Britain Isle, at least here in the capital city, and for a time he could push that unpleasant aspect of this society to the back of his mind. Here, for the first time in his travels on this world, was a familiar civilization. The streets were paved with smooth, rounded stones, and the architecture was even reminiscent of the timeless parts of the old London he'd visited many times. There were no automobiles of course, but there weren't any brontasarries or paalkas either. Real horses pulled carriages and wagons and quaint streetcars with dozens of occupants. Iron tires grating on stone and clopping hooves replaced the sounds of motors and tooting horns, but he was old enough to remember when that had been the case back home as well. He understood there was an impressive library and even several museums, and he couldn't wait to visit them. One museum contained relics of the Founders, including preserved portions of their ships. Another was devoted to specimens of creatures acquired from other lands the Empire had visited or claimed during a brief exploratory period some decades past. Like Scapa Flow, but on a much grander scale, New London resembled an oasis of familiarity on an otherwise wildly exotic world. Only the superabundance of parrots and small, flying reptiles as ubiquitous as pigeons seriously undermined that illusion of normalcy. He grunted and leaned back in his comfortably cushioned seat to examine his companions.

Sergeant Koratin's white leather armor practically gleamed, and his red-striped blue kilt was immaculate. He had graying, dun-colored fur, and the manelike beard around his face was almost white. He was an "odd duck," as Courtney's American friends would say. He'd been a noble, a lord of Aryaal, on faraway Jaava where Surabaya should have been. There, he'd been a political creature: venal and corrupt, swept along by the winds of expediency, foul or fair. His devotion to the moral and physical well-being of younglings had always been his passion, however, no matter how poor an example he set. The war, the loss of his family—including his own precious younglings—and the consequences of real corruption backed by limitless power, had caused an epiphany.

Sister Audry's teachings—and Courtney's explanations of them—had made him a Christian, if not yet a Catholic, and though he was not wild about the political structure emerging within the Alliance, he was devoted to destroying its enemies. Now he was an enlisted Marine, not even an officer, who'd distinguished himself repeatedly in battle. He stayed as far from politics as he could, but he was still a keen observer of them. Bradford thought his insights might prove useful and had tapped him as his aide while Koratin fully recovered from wounds he'd received at the Battle of the Imperial Dueling Grounds.

Beside Koratin was Lieutenant Ezekial Krish of the Imperial Navy. He was dark-skinned with black hair, and wore his very first attempt at an Imperial mustache on his upper lip. Courtney wondered what kind of name Krish was, but decided it didn't matter. The Imperials were descendants of polyglot crews of a pair of lost East Indiamen, and their population had grown with the help of "acquisitions" from the east. Likely, Krish didn't even know the original foundation of his name. Courtney swept the thought away. The young officer seemed a conscientious lad and took his duties as liaison to the Allied ambassador seriously. Today, his help was particularly critical, because he would have to guide Courtney through the protocol of his appearance at the Imperial Court of Directors. Currently, the young man was staring significantly at a large watch in his left hand. A silver chain disappeared between the buttons of his white coat.

"We'll arrive in plenty of time, Lieutenant," Bradford assured the man, trying to conceal his own resurgent unease. "As you said yourself, my own part in the proceedings is quite limited. I doubt I'll even be required to speak." Despite his calm words, he suddenly tugged almost desperately at the cravat, as if on the verge of a claustrophobic fit. Adjusting the ridiculous thing was the primary reason for his tardiness.

"Perhaps, Your Excellency," Krish replied with brittle calm, reaching across and stilling Courtney's hands, "but their majesties specifically charged *me* with your punctuality." It was no secret that Courtney Bradford needed keepers. "Much of the Governor-Emperor's address concerns the Alliance, and he wanted you there as its representative."

"Of course. But if I'm not mistaken, he meant to begin with a description of the state of the Empire, the war, and the implementation of the various reforms." His tone grew almost plaintive. "The heat of the glares I expect to be directed my way will probably *melt* me, and the shorter the time I'm exposed to them, the more likely I am to survive."

Krish said nothing because Courtney was probably right. This would be Governor-Emperor Gerald McDonald's first address to a full assembly of the Imperial Court of Directors since the abortive Dom invasion and the Dom-assisted rebellion on New Ireland were crushed. During that time of emergency, the very foundations of the Empire had been shaken and Gerald McDonald had exercised unprecedented executive powers without consulting the courts of Directors or Proprietors. Of course, so many members of the Court of Proprietors—including Prime Proprietor Sir Harrison Reed—had either been high officials in the subversive Honorable New Britain Company or directly in league with the enemy, that the Proprietors had virtually ceased to exist. Krish was personally surprised and a little disappointed that the Governor-Emperor hadn't simply abolished the Proprietors *and* Directors. After the fighting and all the arrests, the shrill finger-pointing began and nearly every member who'd been taken into custody spilled compromising information against many who weren't, in an effort to mitigate their own transgressions. Long after the true traitors had been hung, the papers were full of lurid details of graft, kickbacks, vote buying, and election fraud. The illegal "stacking" of indentures, a process that kept its victims in perpetual servitude, had been far more common than anyone dreamed as well. Now even the most stalwart defenders of female indenture had been forced to moderate their stance. The resultant feeding frenzy and open display of just how corrupt the government had been stunned the Empire.

Special elections had been held to fill the many sudden vacancies in the Court of Directors, and most of the winners reflected the new attitudes toward their human and Lemurian allies, a willingness to consider a change in the status of women within the Empire, and a grim determination to not only destroy the Holy Dominion forever, but to repay the debt owed to the western allies by helping them against the Grik. Regardless, many hard-liners had retained their seats. Not all had been corrupt. Krish believed the Governor-Emperor would have a majority for his new, radical proposals, but it would be slim and perhaps even tenuous.

"Did Gerald speak much to you about the contents of his address?" Courtney asked, making conversation to distract himself from his misery.

Krish cringed slightly over the man's casual use of his monarch's first name, but nodded. "The Governor-Emperor truly means to abolish indentured servitude entirely. He will reaffirm the alliance between"—he glanced at Koratin—"your people and mine, and make a formal declaration of war against the Holy Dominion and the Grik Empire. He will underscore the social reforms by letting his wife, the Lady Ruth McDonald, address the assembly as well."

"Amazing! Has that ever been done? I mean, has a woman . . . ?"

"Never, Your Excellency. Even when his grandmother, the Lady Verna, was Governor-Empress before her son was born, her factor appeared in her stead."

"Poor woman," Courtney sighed. "Gerald spoke of her. She remained sequestered for years." He looked at Krish. "Understand, this . . . system of yours remains quite foreign to me. My people have a history of powerful, headstrong queens, and my *new* people, the Lemurians, have many strong female leaders as well. Safir Maraan, Saan-Kakja . . . Did you know that Saan-Kakja is roughly the same age as your dear Princess Rebecca, yet rules perhaps more land than your Empire, even including your tentative holdings in the Americas?"

"Yes, Your Excellency . . ."

"Of course you did. A dear, sweet creature, yet bold and quite willful! She will doubtless be mollified to some degree by this new policy." He leaned forward, flapping his hat again. "She remains distrustful of your Empire, you see," he whispered conspiratorially.

Koratin flicked his ears in amusement, but said nothing.

Courtney leaned back and wrenched at his cravat again. "Gerald and I discussed his address at great length, of course," he went on. "I consider him a fine fellow and a friend, but I was frankly afraid to rely on such an abrupt change. But the current emergency makes this the perfect time to push for it, I suppose."

"It is unfortunate that so many had to die in the course of this 'emergency,'" Koratin suddenly interjected in a cynical tone, "but in crisis, there is always opportunity."

"What a dreadful thought," Bradford said, regarding his aide.

"But true."

"Of course it's true, and in this instance, the overall Alliance shall be the beneficiary—but you just prodded to mind the realization that the crisis is ongoing! We know there are still subversive elements at large, and some must be highly placed! How else would the enemy have gained such intelligence of our plans for the New Ireland campaign?"

For several moments Bradford sat, fulminating, the city outside his carriage window and his irritating cravat both forgotten. "We mustn't be lulled into complacency," he finally stated. "All may seem well for the time, but we must remain on our guard for treachery. If I am called to speak to the assembly, I believe I shall forcefully remind everyone of that!"

Koratin's eyes narrowed. "Indeed, Your Excellency. Never forget, there are always people like me—like I was—waiting to pounce."

They rode in silence after that, Courtney and Krish digesting the implications of what Koratin said. The traffic on the narrow avenue grew more congested as they neared the Ruling District, and the carriage slowed to a crawl.

"There's nothing for it now," Krish muttered impatiently. "Even if we left the carriage and sprinted the rest of the way, the conclave will already be well underway before we could possibly arrive."

"I hope you don't really mean to attempt it," Courtney warned. "If we try to get there on foot, the two of you might make it, but my finely dressed corpse won't be of any use to their majesties whatsoever. Don't worry, Lieutenant Krish. You did your best. I'm quite comfortable accepting all the blame. I'm used to it, you know." He smiled. "I do try to conform to the imperatives of others, but I fear I'm ill equipped for it. My former employers used to get very annoyed—as did Captain Reddy, before he learned to make allowances.

"Regardless how hard I try, my attention is easily diverted," he admitted, looking at Krish appraisingly, as if gauging his discretion. "I began writing a book once, a modest little thing describing the flora and fauna I'd encountered throughout the Malay Barrier. Even then I expected it to take years to complete since I had barely scratched the surface. Well, despite my . . . relocation, I've decided to carry on, but just imagine how I've been forced to broaden the scope of my studies! My earlier research has little bearing now beyond vague references for the purpose of comparative anatomy, but I've also rather ambitiously decided to broaden the scope of my work to include contextual observations! It shall now be a history as well! The Journals of Giles, Stewart, Park and Livingstone, Lewis and Clark, and even Sir Stanley—without the controversy, I should hope!—shall be my inspiration."

Krish's eyes had glazed over and Koratin wasn't even pretending to listen, staring out his own window at the passing city. "We here?" he asked suddenly, and Krish stirred, looking for himself. The congested avenue had broadened significantly, and the previously uninterrupted cluster of shops, stores, and other buildings abruptly ended. A large number of coaches and smaller, stylish buggies were gathered on the broad lawn in front of an impressive, columned edifice. Horses stood, cropping long, luscious grasses with coachmen attending them or still sitting patiently atop their vehicles. "Yes, almost, thank God." He raised his voice so the driver could hear. "Take us directly to the main entrance and let us out there. You'll have to find a place to wait as best you can."

A whip cracked and the coach lurched forward, curving around a long oval drive toward the front of the Imperial Court of Directors. A moment later, the coach ground to a stop amid the rough, grating moan of wooden brakes on iron tires. Through the window Bradford could see a pair of Imperial Marine guards approaching.

"Can't we just sneak in the back way?" Courtney asked,

mopping his forehead with a handkerchief and running a final finger between the cravat and his neck.

"No, Your Excellency," Krish replied, his voice harried, "but I will enter first. Aides come and go all the time. I'll call you forward when it looks like your entrance will cause the least distraction." Krish reached for the latch on the coach door.

With a brain-jolting crack of indescribable thunder and pressure, a roiling wall of opaque white smoke and dust swept over the Marines and flung the coach on its side like a child's tiny toy. Bradford was slammed by one side of the coach, then hurled downward against the other. Dust and smoke invaded the interior through shattered windows, and it quickly grew too dark to see. Deafened by what could only have been a stupendous blast, the occupants of the overturned vehicle still felt the thing being slammed and battered by large, heavy objects. One particularly large fragment of one of the columns smashed down on the front of the coach, crushing open a new path for even more debris to enter. Smaller pieces pattered against the wooden shell for some time, but then there was only stillness and dark.

Courtney was stunned. He couldn't breathe and felt something yanking at his neck. He tried to protest, but all he could do was cough, and his left side didn't seem to be working. Suddenly, he felt something pressed against his face, and he lashed out with his right arm. His hand struck the pebbly rhino pig leather of the armor Koratin wore, and for an instant, he thought the strange Marine was trying to smother him. Then, through his panic, he realized he could breathe! Gratefully, he reached up and replaced the 'Cat's hand with his own, holding what he now realized was the damned cravat over his mouth and nose. His eyes were full of grit and he kept them closed, but he sensed Koratin move away, probably trying to locate Krish in the gloom.

His hearing began to return. It was a dull thing at first, heralded by what sounded like a squealing belt inside his head, but he thought he could hear muffled voices as well. The squealing grew louder, but now it was *out*side, and he grimly recognized the sounds of agony. The loudest came from horses, he knew, but he'd also grown far too accustomed to the gut-wrenching wails of hopeless, terrified, dying men. He dared a peek through his gravelly, tear-soaked lids and saw the darkness had begun to fade. His left side was still numb, but he discovered he could move all his arms and legs and decided he must get up. He had no idea what had occurred; he was still too rattled to much consider it yet, but he had to get out of the shattered coach.

"Sergeant Koratin!" he croaked. The dust gagged him and he moved the cravat just in time to retch. He sucked in more dust and a coughing spasm threatened to overwhelm him. Finally, forcing deep breaths through the tightly woven cravat, he brought himself under control. "Koratin!" he called again more strongly, though his throat and lungs seemed on fire.

"Here," came a clipped, strained voice, and a shadow reentered the coach through the shattered forward end. Courtney blinked repeatedly, letting the tears wash the worst of the grit from his eyes.

"Where's Krish?"

"I don't know. Maybe smushed." Koratin rummaged through shattered timbers until he found his musket. The stock was broken right through the lock and the rear portion was missing. Swiftly, he slid the bands off the barrel and unscrewed the tang screw, letting the lock and triggerguard fall. Then he drew his bayonet and affixed it to the muzzle of the barrel, making a formidable, makeshift spear.

"What are you doing?" Courtney demanded. "Stop that foolishness at once! I need to get out of here and see what has happened!"

"I don't know what I am doing," Koratin growled in reply, helping Bradford to his feet. "When I do, I will know if I am foolish or not! Somebody has just killed many of the people here on our side. If we were not late, we would now be dead as well."

Courtney suddenly realized the damned cravat had saved him twice! He let Koratin lead him through the shattered coachwork and into the open, chalky air. A dense fog of limestone, pumice, and powdered stucco still hung heavy, but there was also the unmistakable, acrid hint of gunsmoke. He looked in the direction of the building they'd been about to enter but couldn't see anything. The haze was still too thick. Horses continued shrieking nearby, but their own team lay still, half-buried in debris. Of their driver there was no sign.

"My God," Courtney murmured. "It had to be a bomb!"

"A very big bomb," Koratin agreed.

There was shouting and dark shapes started running past them, toward the court building. There were just a few at first, but then the trickle became a torrent. Koratin tensed, but no one paid them any heed. All were running toward what was slowly resolving itself into a tremendous heap of rubble.

"My God," Courtney repeated. "The Governor-Emperor—both their majesties were inside!"

"What remained of the entire Imperial government was inside!" Koratin snapped.

"Your Excellency!" came a cry, and they turned toward the voice. A man emerged from the thinning haze on the other side of the overturned coach. He was covered in dust and looked like a ghost except for the reddened eyes and the tears streaking the dust on his face.

"Why, there you are, Lieutenant Krish!" Courtney exclaimed. "I wondered what became of you!"

"I don't really know, sir, but thank God you're all right." Krish turned his own gaze toward the court building. They could all now see that it had been completely destroyed. Only the far northeast corner still stood, and men were crawling all over the debris, shouting and calling for survivors. With an anguished sound, Krish started to run and join the rescuers.

"Wait!" Koratin demanded.

"But . . . the Governor-Emperor!"

At that moment there was another explosion far away, a dull boom they would have taken for thunder if the sky hadn't been perfectly clear above the billowing dust. Even so, it sounded like it came from high in the air, and the report rolled down the flanks of the mountains that stood northeast of the city.

"That was the wireless station!" Krish exclaimed. "They've . . . whoever has done this has destroyed it as well!"

"To isolate us!" Koratin guessed immediately. "To prevent word or warning of this reaching . . . who?"

Courtney's eyes grew wide and flashed at the men passing by. Most were civilians from the nearby shops, but he suddenly bolted toward one, a Naval officer, and caught him by the arm. "Wait, sir!" he cried. "Have you a ship? Equipped with wireless?"

The man tried to shake him loose. "Release me! I must . . ."

"What you *must* do is help us send word of this, and pass a warning to New Scotland!"

The man paused and glared. "And just who are you to command me?" he demanded.

Krish rushed forward. "Captain, this is His Excellency Sir Courtney Bradford, the ambassador for the western allies to the Imperial throne, and a particular friend of His Majesty!"

The man stopped straining to escape, and Courtney let go. "So?" he said. "That gives him no authority over me, but I will hear the reason for his request."

"Um . . . Captain, is it?"

The man nodded.

"You may not have noticed, but we heard another explosion that likely took down the wireless aerial above the capital. With the preponderance of naval and newly arrived air power in the vicinity, I highly doubt this attack is a precursor to another Dom invasion, so destroying the wireless station must have been done to prevent us from sending a timely warning!"

"To whom?"

Courtney was growing agitated. "I pray His Majesty has survived, but clearly he must have been the target of this attack! Assuming that, who is the *next*-most-likely target?"

The officer's face was not yet white with dust, but it suddenly drained of color. "Good Lord! The princess Rebecca!"

"Precisely! She remained on New Scotland while her parents came here to make this address today. She must be warned!"

With a final glance at the ruins of the Imperial Court of Directors and the small army now combing the rubble, the man grasped Courtney's arm in turn. "Very well. My ship has no wireless set, but the instruments at the harbor master's office have been completed, and I'm told they can signal Scapa Flow directly! The harbor master there can dispatch a warning *and* marshals to Government House within minutes! Come, I will take you there—and across to Scapa Flow myself, if I must!"

CHAPTER 13

New Scotland Island
Empire of the New Britain Isles

A shimmering, brightly feathered shape made a trilling, *flupp*ing sound as it exploded from the dense highland scrub and took to the air. Princess Rebecca Anne McDonald, barely thirteen years old and heir to the Empire of the New Britain Isles, immediately snatched the fine double-barrel fowling piece to her right shoulder, planted her left foot, put the bead on the nose of the rising creature, and fired. The target staggered in midair but didn't fall. Without thinking, her finger found the rear trigger and she fired again. It was just windy enough to carry the smoke from her shots away and she saw the creature, now perfectly lifeless, drop like a stone.

"Well struck, Yer Highness!" boomed Sean "O'Casey" Bates, the Imperial Factor and Chief of Staff to Gerald McDonald. The big, one-armed man was behind and slightly to the right of her.

"Indeed!" complimented Lieutenant Ruik-Sor-Raa, the almost-blond-furred Lemurian commander of USS *Simms*, a Fil-pin-built steam frigate undergoing major repairs at Scapa Flow. The ship had followed *Walker* in after the naval battle off Saint Francis. She'd been the only American frigate able to make the long trip, and her consorts had been forced to seek repairs at the hard-pressed facilities at the continental colony where San Francisco would have been. "It rose so fast, I never had a chance!" Ruik continued. He carried a Fil-pin Armory version of a nineteenth-century smoothbore Springfield, and it was a heavy weapon for wing shooting. Its percussion-ignition system was more advanced than its Imperial counterpart, but even it was already obsolete compared to the newer weapons being made by the Alliance. *Rifled breechloaders* were in the pipeline now, but the Dom Front was at the end of a very long supply line, and the more pressing Grik Front had priority when it came to modern weapons.

Four men—Bigelow the gamekeeper, and some beaters he'd hired to flush game—politely applauded the shot, and the princess smiled at them. "Thank you, Mr. Bates. Lieutenant." She looked at Sean. "I believe my shooting has benefitted much from your advice."

"That may be, but poor Ruik's at a disadvantage. No Marine musket's the equal o' a fine fowler—fer fowlin'! Leslie's makes arms ta fit a body, not pile bodies on the ground." He nodded at Ruik's gleaming weapon. "An' that one, with a fine, wicked bayonet, an' a lively sort behind it, is a wee bit better fer that!"

Sean Bates appreciated good weapons for whatever they were designed to do. He couldn't carry a common musket or fowler of any sort, but he did have an extremely long-barreled pistol—long enough, almost, for a cane—with a light, tapered barrel. Currently, the barrel rested on his right shoulder, but he was perfectly capable of hitting a bird or hare when the unusual weapon was loaded with small shot—or anything else within a reasonable range with a load of buck and ball. The only truly dangerous large animals on the island were other descendants of the passage that brought humans there—feral hogs—and the strange pistol worked well on all but the largest of those.

A peculiar creature, little bigger than the fallen prey and with many similar features, suddenly dashed ahead, leaping into the air and coasting over the shin-high scrub. It violently pounced on the dead lizard fowl.

"Now, Petey," Rebecca scolded kindly after it, "be a dear and do take it to the gamekeeper."

"Eat?" the creature pleaded, clutching the prize that so resembled him. He couldn't fly, but the feathery membrane that joined his arms and legs allowed him to glide amazingly. He was obviously related to the lizard fowl in many not-so-subtle ways, but there were profound differences as well. For example, the game was omnivorous and Petey was most emphatically a carnivore.

"You will eat quite enough later," Rebecca said sternly. "Perhaps if you are a good boy, Mr. Bigelow will give you the head to chew upon." Reluctantly, and with a great show of sullen obedience, Petey did indeed drag the lizard fowl to the gamekeeper and solemnly left it in his charge with a warning hiss. Bigelow took the animal, careful of his fingers, and put it in the bag with several others. He was the only other armed man in the group, but his devotion to the princess kept him from murdering the obnoxious reptilian rodent she so doted on.

"Ye don't think that ridiculous creature understands ye, Yer Highness!" Sean said. It wasn't a question as much as an incredulous statement. Ruik chittered respectful amusement.

"Some," Rebecca replied, a little huffy, beginning to reload her weapon. Mr. Bigelow's offer to load for her had already been politely but firmly refused. Rebecca Anne McDonald had recently become *very* proficient with firelocks, and intended to stay in practice. "He obviously knows his name," she continued, "and he did obey me. I'm sure he knows what 'no' means, and he is intelligent enough to sometimes *pretend* he doesn't. . . . Apparently, he knows 'take' and 'later' and possibly other words." She chuckled. "He knows Mr. Bigelow has our other birds, particularly the parrots—he does like parrots!—and there is no doubt whatsoever he understands the meaning of 'eat.'"

"Aye ta that," Sean agreed. "The beastie's a famous eater, an' no mistake." He glanced ahead, surveying the gradual slope of the mountain that reared high above the naval port city of Scapa Flow. The princess was in his personal care while her parents were in New London, and there were still shadowy elements, either Dom agents or Company loyalists forced into hiding, who posed a very real threat to the child's safety. Bored out of her mind in Government House, with nothing to do but read or visit some of her friends in the Allied delegation, she'd talked him into this outing. She had no friends near her own age now that Abel Cook and Stuart Brassey had steamed back west with *Walker*. Even Dennis Silva, whom she considered a demented older brother, and her beloved Lawrence had left her. She could no longer relate to the few children she'd considered friends before her departure and long exile. Her girlfriends had become young ladies, preparing for the hopefully long, possibly happy, but certainly dull (in comparison) domestic lives that were expected of them. Perhaps it was unseemly, but she couldn't help but pine a little "for the boys," in general, and maybe Abel Cook in particular. She'd seen and endured too much to be content with what was expected of *her* in Imperial society. Hopefully, those expectations were about to undergo some radical revisions, but even if she hadn't been heir to the Imperial throne, and therefore subject to fewer restraints than other girls, she'd tasted too much of life to just stop and settle down and wait for it to *happen* to her anymore.

Sean had finally relented to her pleas to get out for a while, hoping this little excursion might give her a brief taste of adventure and self-sufficiency for however short a time. Maybe it would help. But Sean Bates had been her protector for a long time, through a variety of terrifying adventures, and wasn't about to let anything happen to her now that she was home again at last.

"I think ye've shot us quite a supper, yer highness," he said. "Best we get on back to Guv'ment House an' turn them birds over ta missis Carr afore they spoil. It's cool up here, but they'll ripen quick enough once we return to the carriage yonder." He gestured down slope a mile or so, but then paused suddenly, squinting.

"There are armed horsemen at the carriage," Rebecca stated, shading her eyes. "Half a dozen? More?"

"I think eight," Ruik said seriously, his long tail swishing behind his blue Navy kilt. "I can't see their dress, but they . . . are not Marines."

"They ain't in Guard or marshal livery neither, Your Highness," said the sharp-eyed gamekeeper with a hint of concern.

The Guard was a small, elite security force dedicated to the protection of the Imperial family. The marshals were the much more numerous Imperial Police. Otherwise, the Empire had always relied on its powerful navy and a small but competent corps of Marines. There was no army. Instead of building an army from scratch, however, the corps of Marines was swelling dramatically, borrowing heavily on the instruction, organization, and experience of their Lemurian-American allies. Until the recent battles on New Scotland and New Ireland, those Marines had never coordinated any large-scale operations however, and there'd been some severe growing pains. In any event, Imperial Marines, Guards, or marshals were the only ones with a legitimate reason to assemble such an armed party, particularly here in an Imperial preserve. That left only brigands, and everyone seemed to realize that fact at once. The reaction was . . . unexpected.

One of the beaters, a bearded man in a long, threadbare coat, suddenly dove at Mr. Bigelow, driving the gamekeeper to the ground with a startled cry. Another lunged at Sean, grabbing his pistol by its long barrel with a guttural shout. The third beater stood, just as stunned as everyone, his eyes wide in confused panic.

Sean allowed his assailant to yank the barrel from his shoulder and grasp it with both hands, pulling and wrenching savagely. He had only the grip to hold on to, but in this circumstance, for the instant it took, that was enough. He heaved backward suddenly, straightening the other man's arms, and squeezed the trigger. The pan flashed and a heavy load of small shot blasted out, and its tight pattern at that range struck the man full in the face with the diameter, if not the weight, of a four-pound shot. It didn't decapitate him, but his head erupted bloody gore and brains back at Sean like an exploding melon and his corpse dropped to the ground without a twitch.

"Goddamn!" Petey squealed, and launched himself toward Rebecca.

Ruik recovered his wits while the first attacker fought with Bigelow to gain control of his fowler that had fallen about two yards away from them. He raced over and aimed his musket, but loaded with bird shot, he feared he couldn't hit one without the other. Bigelow was crawling on the ground, toward his weapon, while simultaneously trying to hold on to the traitor and keep him from it. But the bigger, bearded man was raining blows upon him, trying to loosen his grip and drag himself over the gamekeeper. Immediately, Ruik reversed his musket. He was a Naval officer, not a Marine, but everyone had to train with the new weapons to some degree. With a trilling cry, backed by his literally inhuman strength, he delivered a creditable butt stroke to the head of Bigelow's adversary, who went limp and rolled senselessly onto his back.

"Thankee, sir," Bigelow managed through broken lips, and Ruik helped him to his feet.

"Swell," Ruik said, pushing him aside to see Princess Rebecca grimly aiming her double at the still-motionless third beater. The man—more of a boy, really—was obviously terrified.

"And what about you, sir?" Sean snarled, stepping toward him. The long pistol was thrust in this belt, leaving his tunic smeared with bloody chunks, and his sword was in his hand.

"I . . . I . . . didn't—couldn't!"

"Quit jabberin', boy, an' speak up!"

"I don't know those men!" the boy finally managed. "Before God! I never seen 'em before today!" He looked beseechingly at Bigelow. "You used me before, sur! For His Majesty! I'm as loyal as can be!"

Bigelow nodded slowly, a strange expression on his face. "Aye, we've used him before," he confirmed, "an' he seemed a good lad." He glanced at the faceless corpse. "Them others, they was . . . recommended." He turned to look back at the man he'd fought, and his eyes went wide. The bearded beater, his hair matted with blood from Ruik's blow, was sitting up now. In his hand was a pistol of a cheap, common sort that the Company had long traded in the colonies. The things were hopelessly inaccurate beyond a dozen paces, but they were reliable, and it was pointed at the princess just a few steps away.

"No!" Bigelow roared, and lunged forward just as the pan flashed and fire and smoke bloomed from the muzzle. At that same instant, Ruik, who'd been distracted by the interrogation, brought his musket all the way back up and fired. The long coat covering the assassin's torso shivered like a sail that just took a broadside and the man fell back, screaming. Ruik didn't have a bayonet, but he pounced on the man, prepared to smash his skull this time, but his eyes, like everyone's, went to the princess.

She seemed bewildered, her hand pressing a bloody spray on her bright green hunting frock, just above the belt around her waist. Petey was staring at her, eyes bulging.

"Lass!" Bates yelled. He'd been halfway to the killer, his sword raised. Now he dropped the weapon and rushed to the girl, stripped off her belt, and eased her to the ground.

"It really doesn't hurt much," Princess Rebecca softly murmured.

"I must see yer wound, lass," Sean told her apologetically but forcefully. Tears already streaked his face.

"Of course."

Sean ripped the coat open, but paused in surprise. There was no blood on her blouse.

The Imperial gamekeeper suddenly coughed, swayed, and collapsed.

"Mr. Bigelow!" cried the boy, kneeling beside him. "It's him that's shot!"

Suddenly Sean knew what must have happened. The pistol ball had torn through Bigelow and sprayed the princess with a stream of his blood. The ball may have even been turned downward by a rib and struck her itself, thankfully spent. He quickly opened the blouse over her midriff to assure himself and saw there was indeed a ripening oval bruise, but that was all.

"Thank God!" he breathed.

"I'm not shot?" the princess asked.

"No, but Mr. Bigelow is. He saved your life!"

"Go to him, I beg you!"

"Aye." Sean stood and looked down at the gamekeeper, but the poor man was clearly gone. "Did he speak?" he asked the boy.

"Aye," replied the boy through tears of his own. "I understood but a single word—but it made no sense!"

"What was it?"

"McClain."

"Sur," Ruik interrupted over the screams of the wounded man he still guarded. "Those other men, on horses—they shot the coach driver. They come this way now!"

"Bind that man," Sean directed Ruik, "an' gag 'im. We need 'im ta live, fer a time at least, but I've had enough o' his screamin'! Have ye other than small shot fer that musket?"

"Some," Ruik said.

"Load it, then." He paused a moment, deciding whether they could really trust the youngster. He snorted. "Boy? Can ye use Mr. Bigelow's fowler? He keeps ball in 'is pouch."

"I know how to load, but I've rarely shot."

"But ye can?"

"Aye."

Princess Rebecca had restored her clothing and was already pulling the wads atop the bird shot in her double with a corkscrew-shape device on the end of her ramrod. She poured the shot on the ground, then dropped a single large ball down each barrel. They *thunked* against the powder wads. "They're loose," she said in a strange tone. "I have never loaded a weapon for the express purpose of shooting a man before."

Sean looked at the girl. Despite her words, she still sounded so . . . calm that it worried him. He fished in his pouch and handed her a portion of a paperlike insect's nest. "Those're not men," he snarled. "Ram more waddin' ta hold the balls in place, lass," he added. "Ye have a few fixed charges with which to reload. Do ye not?"

The princess nodded. The riders were coming hard now and were barely half a mile away. Sean clasped the long pistol to his side with the stump of his left arm and proceeded to load it. The process may have looked odd, but he managed it quickly enough.

"How . . . what you want to do? How we do this?" Ruik asked. With the excitement, his normally excellent English had slipped a bit.

"Well, clearly we must kill 'em or drive 'em off. Don't fire till I give the word, but then choose yer target wi' care. We'll not fire a volley! Princess, yours an' mine'll be the least-accurate shots, an' we must save 'em till they're nearly on us."

"I don't think I can hit a man on a running horse!" the boy cried.

"Are ye daft? Ye an' Lieutenant Ruik'll shoot at the horses! Surely ye can hit a target such as that! Wi' luck, ye'll dump the riders, an' p'raps goad the others into firin'!"

Even Ruik knew it would be next to impossible for the riders to hit a mark at a gallop—more difficult than deliberately striking a distant ship with a single, aimed shot from the pitching deck of his own *Simms*. *Walker* could do it, but she had advantages no other ship—or man—could match. "I hate to shoot horse," he said sadly. "They not want to hurt us."

"Aye," Sean agreed, "but ye've no choice." He'd seen how delighted Lemurians were to "discover" horses. Most, except possibly some he'd heard of on the Great Southern Isle, had never imagined forming communicative, even emotional bonds with any animal. But so far, every Lemurian he'd seen meet horses automatically liked them and considered them almost people. "Make ready!" he warned.

With a terrified squawk, Petey bolted upslope, running and soaring as fast as he could. "Useless bugger," Sean said with a grunt. "But maybe smarter than I thought."

Ruik took a knee to aim his piece, and the boy followed his example.

The six horsemen galloped in against the four of them, short capes flowing behind them. Most apparently carried pistols or some kind of shortened musket, but two had long, heavy swords in their hands. Sean warned tersely that those might be the most dangerous. The range closed rapidly and the tension mounted.

"They coming right at us," Ruik advised the young man

beside him, his pronounced accent the only sign of his nervousness. "That make it easy. Just aim high." The gamekeeper's fowler had no rear sight to adjust for elevation, and he'd heard that one of the problems the Imperials had with training novices for their expanding forces was that they tended to jerk their shots low.

"H-how high?" the fellow stuttered.

"That depends," Ruik confessed. "Faactor Bates know better the range to . . . trip a horse. I tell you when he say!"

Just waiting for the charge was one of the most terrifying things Princess Rebecca had ever faced. She knew they had to stand their ground, but the fearsome horses and the killers atop them came on with an energetic, remorseless purpose. She knew Sean Bates loved her as his own and would give his life to save her. She also knew he was a skilled and confident fighter, despite his handicap—but, oh, what she would give to have Dennis Silva with them at that moment! The range narrowed inexorably, the horses gasping as they barreled up the slope, hooves thundering, spraying damp clods of earth high in the air.

"At yer convenience, Lieutenant Ruik!" Sean cried at about a hundred paces. For an instant, nothing happened, and in that time, their enemy advanced another twenty or thirty yards. Then Ruik fired, and Rebecca thought she actually saw the vapor trail of his ball cross the humid gap. A deep *thwack!* followed the sound of the report, and one of the horses staggered and slowed.

"At its nose!" Ruik shouted, and the boy fired next. His ball had an even more dramatic, if accidental, cffect. It struck another onrushing horse square in the knee, and it shrieked hideously and tumbled, likely crushing its rider, who was thrown clear, but couldn't move before the horse rolled over him. The other four assasins sank their spurs and charged in, almost on top of them, pistols aimed and swords raised to strike. Rebecca and Sean took careful aim. Pistols barked, but the balls *vrooped* harmlessly past, and Rebecca fired at a man. She missed! Maybe the pistol shots had rattled her—but she was already rattled! Despite what Sean had said, her target *was* a man! Determination swept her fear aside and she squeezed the rear trigger, blowing the same man backward out of his saddle. A terrible scream drew her gaze to the left. Ruik had avoided a sword stroke with an ease that had to have disconcerted his attacker, and with a powerful leap, he snatched the man from his horse. The loyal beater wasn't as skillful or agile, and another sword had slammed diagonally across his chest as its wielder galloped past.

Without thinking, Princess Rebecca dropped her fine fowler and pulled her short hunting sword from the leather sheath at her side. She charged the mounted murderer as he yanked his reins back and turned for another pass. She knew she didn't have a chance, but in that instant, her fury overrode all other concerns. A heavy boom roared behind her and the target of her rage pitched and dropped his weapon with a yelp. The horse bolted, but after only a few strides the rider toppled from his lurching mount and lay still in the scrub. Princess Rebecca whirled and saw Sean toss his long pistol aside.

That quickly, somehow, only one mounted assassin remained. His horse stood still, perhaps forty paces away, and the rider was jamming his empty pistol into his belt.

"You are the very spawn of Satan!" he screamed at her. "Cast forth from the underworld, from the chambers of fire and darkness to do his bidding! On behalf of His Supreme Holiness, Emperor of the World by the Grace of God, I shall strike you down yet!" He wrenched his own sword from its scabbard then and came for her, urging his horse to a gallop. Princess Rebecca merely stood there, unable to run, her short sword raised to deflect the blow she knew she couldn't stop. She felt small and all alone in the face of utter evil—until Sean Bates stepped in front of her, raising his own sword.

At that moment, another shot sounded—deeper, louder—and the assassin fell, wailing, to the ground. The horse passed by harmlessly, and the princess and Bates rushed to the fallen man. An instant later, they were joined by Lieutenant Ruik. He was covered in blood and his musket stock was dark and slick. A wisp of smoke still curled from the muzzle of the weapon. Together they regarded the would-be killer. He'd spoken without the accent of the Holy

Dominion, but clearly he was a devout follower of its twisted faith. The man had a gaping, bloody hole in his lower-left chest and he spat blood at them.

"You will all die." He coughed. "This entire land, and yes, even that of your unholy, demon friends will be washed clean with your own blood!"

"Yer makin' quite the putrid puddle on this land now," Sean said coldly. "Nothin'll ever grow on this spot again!"

"I am dying," the man conceded, "but soon I will be in paradise. You will burn in the lowest chamber of hell!"

"I just may," Sean conceded, "But I'll tear yer black heart out wi' me teeth when I find you there!" He paused, vaguely disappointed, suspecting the assassin hadn't heard him. He was dead. Briefly, he hugged Princess Rebecca close, then turned to Ruik. "A fine, timely shot!" he complimented. "But how did ye get ta be such a mess?"

"I needed to reload," Ruik replied, flicking his ears toward the man he'd dragged down. "He not let me."

Sean stared at the bloody heap Ruik indicated. "What did ye do? Tear 'im limb from limb?" Ruik didn't answer, but Sean knew many Lemurians had amazing upper-body strength, particularly sea folk—from which the Navy drew nearly all its officers. "Aye. Well, *he's* dead, then. Did we take any alive?"

"Just the one we start with," Ruik said, "if he's not dead too now. The one whose horse I shot, he run for coach." He pointed. "He take fresh horse, I bet. We never catch him."

Princess Rebecca shaded her eyes. "We won't, but perhaps they might!" Some distance beyond the coach, charging up from the city, was a squadron of Horse Marines, the Imperial standard flying at the head of the column.

"Aye, here's the Marines—just in time!" Bates muttered sarcastically. He looked at the Lemurian. "The boy?"

"Dead," Ruik replied, blinking regret.

"He was loyal," said the princess, "and we never even knew his name."

"We'll find it out," Sean promised her.

"I just . . . something just occurred to me," Ruik said, his English beginning to return to normal. "Those Marines that are coming so fast. Why are they coming at all? Nobody can see us from the city."

"Maybe the shots were heard?" the princess speculated doubtfully.

"Nay," Sean said, his brows knitting. "We've been shootin' all mornin'. That's what we came here to do. The lieutenant's right; somethin's afoot. P'raps they already *know* what this was all about."

CHAPTER 14

Grik India
March 12, 1944
First Fleet "Northern" Allied Expeditionary Force

"Would you look at that!" Colonel Billy Flynn blurted when Captain Bekiaa-Sab-At led him to the vast open clearing and he viewed the . . . extraordinary sight before him. He wasn't the only one staring. Many of his Rangers had already fanned out to secure the discovery, and most of them were gawking as well. The First Amalgamated and elements of the 6th Maa-ni-la Cavalry were responsible for screening the northern flank of II Corps' leapfrog advance along the western road toward the looming, sawtooth escarpment ahead. The objective was another major crossroads beyond the mountain gateway on the more open land beyond that had been identified by reconnaissance flights as a potential marshaling area for significant Grik forces. The enemy might infiltrate through the forest, but they could only move artillery and massed troops by road.

Unfortunately, the time it took to secure the frontiers around Madras, and the recon required to confirm or amend Allied strategy previously based only on captured Grik maps and Hij-Geerki's notions, had delayed any "lightning" thrusts to seize that next strategic crossroads. The Grik command had likely used that time to catch its breath. In several respects, maybe that was a good thing. The "Northern" AEF had needed a breath itself after the sporadic but fierce fighting that punctuated the consolidation, resupply, and reorganization required after the improved but still chaotic aftermath of the invasion. Also, the enemy had reacted to the capture of Madras as hoped, and sent most of its known armies northeast. This allowed III Corps and the newly constituted V Corps (together constituting the "Southern" AEF) to cross the narrow land bridge from Ceylon with little resistance, and secure that vital approach. The Cavalry-heavy V Corps was now racing north across a relatively open coastal plain to link up with Rolak's I Corps as it began its push south. Hopefully, the V would take the Grik assembling to oppose Rolak in the rear.

The Allied High Command, from CINCWEST on down, was pleased with the campaign so far. Not only had they avoided a bloody smash-up at the crossing; they believed they'd dispersed the enemy into smaller, more manageable packets. They'd done the same with their own forces of course, but the Allies' superior training, discipline, weapons, and growing cohesion *should* justify that risk. The Allies had uncontested control of the air after destroying a few snooping Grik zeppelins, and the rest, wherever they were, seemed reluctant to come up. Ultimately, they also had the only real deepwater port on the east coast firmly in their hands, and they were just now coming to grips with what an important industrial center Madras had been for the enemy. The sheer tonnage of enemy shipping and stockpiles of coal, timbers, and plate steel they'd captured was mind-boggling. The plate steel was an ominous discovery, but correspondence from Courtney Bradford had predicted that much of the enemy's entire coal reserves would be in northeast India, and losing Madras had to hurt them.

Consequently, however, along with the element of surprise, II Corps' ability to move quickly had also been lost. It couldn't simply march down the rough road in column, so scout regiments were tasked with the difficult chore of moving forward through the dense forest on either side of the broad dirt "highway" one at a time, until they found defensible positions or land features where they forted up in the old Roman style. Only then did their opposite number do the same. Once the flanks were secure, General-Queen Protector Safir Maraan brought her corps up the road. It was a drawn-out process that slowed the rapid advances they'd made following the invasion, but only the Grik knew all the forest pathways that might allow them to strike a longer column in the flank. This way, they hoped, the corps as a whole would maintain greater cohesion and more rapid internal lines of support, and could rush troops to any major point of contact with the enemy.

"I already *have* looked at it, sir," Bekiaa responded dryly, blinking mild frustration. "That is why I thought you would wish to."

"Jeez," Flynn murmured, ignoring her tone. "I bet no damn Grik ever built *that*."

They'd seen some very weird things since the landing at Madras almost three weeks before; things unlike any they'd encountered yet. Again, the Grik noncombatants—if there really was such a thing—had fled or been slaughtered, but there were giant, furry, buzzard things, kind of like flying skuggiks, that had "cleaned up" the countless Grik dead. They were almost as big as the dragons Second Fleet had encountered, but they had beaks instead of toothy jaws and avoided anything alive. There were deadly snake . . . things . . . in abundance, much to their unpleasant surprise, most of which lived in the trees instead of on the ground. They had short, grasping claws along their bodies that allowed them to cling tightly to trees and limbs instead of drooping about. Lemurians as a race weren't accustomed to snakes and only a few had ever seen one. Courtney Bradford actually suspected that the rare snakes described to him were probably transportees themselves, since there were so many things that would happily root them up and eat them. Rhino pigs would keep them off Borno, for example. Regardless, Lemurians instinctively hated anything that looked like a snake, and God knew how much ammunition they'd wasted before fire discipline had been restored.

Other new discoveries included bizarre gliding and tree-leaping rodents that infested the forests as thickly as insects, and there were tiny hummingbird-like creatures that behaved like mosquitoes. Added to the real mosquitoes, the needle-nosed little devils contributed significantly to the misery of the Allied troops.

They saw very few large animals besides Grik—and the adolescent Griklets that had apparently been released to harass them once again. As on Ceylon, it grew evident that without the Grik, there was a big hole in the local food chain. Almost nothing substantial or easy to catch had been seen, leaving everyone to wonder again what the Grik ate besides one another—and their enemies, of course. Hij-Geerki had been a "frontier clerk," basically, and though he'd been to Ceylon and had given them some useful information, he'd never been in a position to explain how large populations of his species fed themselves in older, more established parts of its empire. It was well-known that frontier and expeditionary Grik relied on "prey" and even each other for sustenance, but he had no idea what else they ate in the sacred ancestral lands. Prey—of any sort—had to be scarce and, obviously, no species could rely entirely on itself for sustenance, particularly when it needed more numbers, not less.

Another new mystery had taunted them in Madras. Mixed with the usually simple adobe Grik architecture they'd grown accustomed to, were ancient, far more sophisticated ruins that didn't make any sense at all. So far, they'd discovered only tantalizing fragments, incorporated directly into Grik construction, but now Flynn gazed at a granite cliff face adorned with strikingly ornate ruins carved from the living rock. His first impression was of a temple of some sort, and arched entryways surrounded by crumbling columns extended deep into the cliff. His second impression was that it was very, *very* old. Only when his focus expanded and he began to digest the entire scene did he begin to form a possible answer to one fundamental question about the Grik, at least the "locals."

The ruins they'd found had been incorporated into another structure as usual, but in this case it formed one wall of an immense, recently cut, tree-staked pen that nearly filled the clearing. Inside the pen, shuffling and lowing, their ribs becoming visible along their sides, were hundreds of large, greenish gray beasts with long tails and oddly duck-shaped heads. They were actually bigger than the Asian elephant-size brontasarries in Baalkpan, and maybe two-thirds the size of a super lizard. Their hind legs were much larger than their forelegs, and they stumped around, cowlike, mostly on all fours, vainly rooting at the dirt for something to eat.

Me-naak mounted cav 'Cats eased forward, their slathering mounts snorting and sniffing, but the penned animals showed no fear. Some merely raised their large heads and gazed disinterestedly at the new arrivals. Flynn was glad to have cavalry, even if meanies gave him the creeps. They were a pain in the ass to feed; worse than medieval heavy horse, he suspected, because there certainly wasn't any forage for the dedicated carnivores and they always seemed tempted to forage on his troops. Oddly, they obeyed their riders about as well as any horse Flynn had seen, and even appeared to bond with them to a degree. Sometimes, in a capricious fit, they might try to eat one, but that was rare.

The point that struck him then was that whatever they were, meanies were obviously predators—yet the penned ... whatever the hell they were weren't afraid of them. That meant there *likely* weren't any large predators around, other than Grik of course, and hadn't been for a very long time. Also, since the pen had to have been made by Grik, the creatures inside apparently didn't consider *them* predators either, in the traditional sense.

"My God," Flynn exclaimed. "Dino-cows. They're *cattle* for slaughter, I'll bet. Orderly!" he shouted back down the trail Bekiaa brought him. A young 'Cat scampered up, slate and chalk in hand. They had paper now and ink, but it was simpler and more economical for orderlies to carry the older tools. First, not all of them could read or write English. And second, their dispatches would be transcribed before transmission or distribution.

"I tripped on a root," the near youngling apologized, blinking too fast for Flynn to decipher the meaning. "I thought it was snake!"

"Caap'n Bekiaa!" cried a Ranger sergeant who trotted up and slammed to attention, tail straight.

"What have you found?"

"There is rolls of leaf fodder, stored in those . . . cave holes, an' a . . . gizmo for diverting spring water to the pen, but no sign of Griks here for days."

"Get this out," Flynn snapped, suddenly terse, and the orderly 'Cat poised his chalk. "Have discovered more goofy ruins of non-Grik origin. More important, we've found a big . . . herd of large animals, apparently corralled as live rations for the enemy. Most of the structure enclosing the animals is of recent construction, and I must therefore assume a large enemy force is nearby." He rubbed his eyes. "Maybe they were expecting us to stick to the road and we took 'em by surprise. The caretakers here probably weren't fighting Grik, anyway." He looked at his orderly. "Forget that part, write this: "Recommend Air Corps keep a lookout for similar sites. Placement may give clues about enemy plans." He looked at Bekiaa. "They can't count on us or each other for rations until after the fight, and they'll damn sure need something to tide them over if they want to gather up anything big enough to face us." He paused a moment, then nodded at the orderly.

"Run on. Get that to the Division runners as quick as you can, then get back here."

"Yes, sur!"

"You think they eat these things all the time?" Bekiaa asked, gesturing at the pen. "Scuttlebutt says the flyboys been seein' dino herds on the high plains we're headin' for, specially round water, but nothing in the woods or coastal plains."

"Maybe the Grik live mostly down here, but herd these things down from up there. Who knows? Maybe they raise 'em and just let 'em graze up high." Flynn waved at the trees. "Flyboys can't see crap down in these woods from above. There could be a million Grik within five miles of the damn road at any point."

"But . . . no dino-cows were in Maa-draas."

"Maybe not, but I bet if somebody looked again, they'd find pens where they'd been." He shook his head. "Or maybe they just carted in the meat. Killing something that big in the middle of a city might drive all the Grik there wild!"

"Then what about the bones? We should have found bones."

"I may not be Courtney Bradford, but I know a thing or two. There's lots of industrial uses for ground or powdered bone—and, hell, maybe they eat that too. The point is, if I'm right, the Air Corps should be able to tell us soon." He looked at the pen again, then back at the sergeant. "Form a detail to feed and water those damn things, then tell Captain Saachic some of his cav 'Cats are going to have to learn to be cowboys. I want them all herded to the rear. Whether we can eat 'em or not, I'm not leaving them here for the Grik."

The next morning, the Rangers returned to the road near a narrow lake just west of 3rd Division and the rest of Safir's II Corps. They were moving to shoot the gap through a rocky, wooded pass bordered by a swift, steeply falling river and high, jagged crags. They were joined by the 1st Battalion of the 2nd Marines, as Flynn had requested, and were screened by Captain Saachic's company of the 6th Maa-ni-la Cavalry. An hour after daybreak, they proceeded to do what they'd been doing all along: leaping forward to establish a defensive position to support the 1st Sular (this time), and another company of the 6th. The difference was that Flynn's leap would also be a reconnaissance in force at the end of a longer limb, and the 1st Sular and 6th Maa-ni-la would follow almost immediately. In the confines of the gap, the only avenue for support was from the rear, so Safir would bring the rest of the Corps through as quickly as she could. No one had forgotten the near-catastrophic ambush this new Grik commander had laid for them on Ceylon, so Safir didn't mean to leave any real spaces between the various regiments for the enemy to exploit.

The river formed an impassable barrier on the south side of the gap, snug against the sheer cliff it had carved through the ages. The gap on the north side of the river was strewn with great, undermined boulders but was reasonably wide, enough that the troops could negotiate most of it in a series of block formations instead of long columns. Against the Grik, massed firepower was still the only defense. Any open-order advance was suicide. The rise in elevation was significant, but fairly consistent. There was good visibility to the front and behind, at least where the road was straight, and though it couldn't guarantee there were no Grik on the high, forested ridges, the Air Corps assured them they would face no artillery.

As usual, it was a hot, grueling day, and the rough, rocky, uphill passage made transporting their wagons and artillery difficult. Paalkas had hooves, but they weren't hardened against this type of terrain, and many were lamed. Those too far gone to heal quickly were butchered for the cavalry. Others moaned and squealed in pain loud enough to be heard over the tumbling water, but labored on as if they somehow knew what awaited them if they gave up. Even the cavalry's me-naaks weren't immune to injury. None were lamed, but they did grow testy.

Pairs of Nancys occasionally rumbled by overhead, sometimes low enough to drop weighted messages with streamers attached. These would be carried back to Division HQ, but the pilots rightly thought Flynn needed the results of their forward observations first. Some of the messages disturbed him. Apparently, once they'd been told what to look for, the Air Corps had increasingly begun to notice odd clearings in the forest. Where before pilots might have been content to report that no Grik were seen, now they reported the clearings as possible corrals, whether dino-cows were present or not. Flynn was compiling his own mental map of the sightings and the picture practically confirmed, if he was right, that there were a *lot* of Grik in the area.

Nothing of the enemy had been seen on the more-open plain beyond the pass, but the patrol patterns the Nancys flew didn't allow them to scout more than about twenty or thirty miles ahead. Twice Flynn sent requests for special flights to scout beyond that, hopefully as far as the Corps' next objective. More planes eventually flew by, and he hoped they'd gotten the word.

Hours passed in the thick, humid heat within what was quickly becoming known as Rocky Gap, before advance scouts reported they were nearing the western end of the pass.

"Captain Saachic!" Flynn shouted. "Take your company forward, if you please, and scout the flanks as they broaden out. Then find us and the Sularans a couple of good places to park. You know what to look for. Remember, it may take a couple days for the entire corps to move up, so high ground would be nice. Feel free to detail a couple of platoons to begin laying out the position."

"Yes, Colonel," Saachic replied, whirling his mount. His orderly, mounted beside him, blew a series of shrill calls with his whistle.

The gap gradually widened, and the daylong tension caused by the confining passage began to ebb. A breeze stirred the regimental flags for the first time that day, and even if it was hot, it was welcome. Flynn didn't know what he'd expected to find beyond the pass—maybe some kind of prairie, the way it had been described. It *was* a grassland, but the trees hadn't surrendered to it entirely. They stood singly or in clumps amid and atop gently rolling hills. They didn't look much different from the trees in the forest below, but the tall, straight trunks were bare much higher up and were topped with bright green leaves several shades lighter than the dark, thick grass. A line of denser trees followed the river that receded in the distance. In Flynn's mind, it was beautiful country.

"I've never seen anything like it," Bekiaa admitted beside him. "Maybe north Saylon is kind of the same, but the trees are different. Only at sea have I ever felt the world was so . . . big."

"Yeah," Flynn agreed. "There's an awful lot of sky up there, and these craggy, hilly, mountainy things we passed through turn into real mountains to the south. See?" He pointed.

One of Saachic's troopers galloped up and halted, his me-naak blowing. "Caap'n pick two hills," he said, pointing north, then south. Flynn looked. Both were about the same size, but were a little farther apart than he would have preferred. As the rest of the corps moved up it would fill the space in between and have two solid anchors, however. When they advanced again, the leapfrogging would no longer be necessary. They should be able to rely on conventional scouting in the relatively open land ahead.

"Okay. We'll take the northern position, as usual. Ride back until you meet the next company of the Sixth and lead it up. You can show 'em where to go. The First Sular won't be far behind us." He paused, looking out at the lovely landscape. *Pretty land. Two perfect hills just a* little *too far apart. . . .* He shook his head. *Getting paranoid.* He knew he'd faced this new Grik general before, and the bastard was sneaky. He hated his guts but had to admire him too, compared to other Grik generals they'd faced. He rubbed his bristly chin, introspective. He wasn't *really* a colonel, after all. His only infantry experience prior to this was as a corporal a quarter century ago. *Maybe I should've stayed with Mr. Laumer and that goddamn sub*, he thought.

He shook his head again. *No, that Grik honcho may be sneaky, but taking advantage of this would take subtlety—and a lot better understanding of strategy and tactics than any Grik has ever shown.* Flynn often based his decisions on what human—or 'Cat—opponents were likely to do and then threw in a double handful of "wild-ass Grik" to compensate for the unpredictable nature of the enemy, but he supposed he usually gave the Grik, and even their new leader, too much credit. Better safe than sorry. Right now he suspected he was giving the enemy way too much credit. He looked at the cav 'Cat. "Well, get on with it."

"Yes, sur!" cried the 'Cat, and jangled away, back in the direction they'd come. Like all the cav, he held his shortened, carbine-length Baalkpan Arsenal musketoon tight against the sling that kept him from dropping it—but also let it beat the crap out of him if he didn't hold it that way when his mount was moving quickly. Flynn thought the cav was probably the only Allied force in the west to retain the old smoothbores. His Marines had the Allin-Silva .50-80 breechloaders and soon the whole army should, but the cav liked the ability to fire heavy loads of buckshot at close range.

The Rangers reached the summit of the low, broad hill and began digging in and throwing up breastworks around the perimeter. Axes *thocked* against the trees that stood fairly dense atop the hill, and the trunks and brush joined the defensive structure. Two batteries of artillery—a full dozen of the much-improved twelve-pounders—and carts of supplies loaded with food, ammunition, water butts, even the field transmitter/receiver joined them. The comm 'Cats in charge of the wireless set began to assemble the apparatus and prepared to string an aerial in the remaining trees. The 1st Battalion of the 2nd Marines maintained a rear guard back to the pass with their quick-firing breechloaders and another battery of guns, until the leading elements of the 1st Sular pushed out of the gap and headed toward their own position about seven hundred tails away. The Marines remained in place until the first Sularan companies began to establish themselves. Then they limbered their guns and pulled back toward the northern hill. By then, as the sun crept closer to the western horizon, two more companies of the 6th Cavalry had deployed in the mouth of the gap, screening the advance of the rest of the corps.

"That went very well," a satisfied Bekiaa said to Flynn. "Though it has been a long day," she amended. Everyone was tired, but Flynn had been limping slightly for most of the long march. In his forties, he'd spent most of his life in submarines. Those had been dangerous years, but they'd left him ill prepared for a return to infantry life and he ached from his back to his toes all the time, it seemed. Even his shoulder ached from carrying his '03 Springfield. Sometimes in the past he rode a paalka to give his ankles a rest, but that day he'd refused.

"Mmm," Flynn replied, listening. "Say, I think our long-range recon is coming back."

The breeze was laying with the late afternoon, and soon the distinctive sound of Nancy engines was plain. "There they are!" someone cried as the planes grew against the evening sun. One plane banked toward the north hill, the other to the south, and streamers fluttered down. A rider fetched the closest one and brought it to Flynn. He unwrapped the note from the small rock it was tied around and spread the sheet to read it:

MANNY MANNY GRiK AT CRosRoADs AROWND RiVER BRiJ ABouT 80–90 MiLEs WEsT YoR PosisHiN. MosT CoMiNG FRoM WEsT oF THER, BuT soM NoRTH. SAW LoTs oF DiNo CoWs.

"Damn it, I knew it!" Flynn said, waving the sheet at the planes as they disappeared east over the crags. "I wish somebody would teach those airedales how to make a report, though. 'Many' is awful vague, and what were they doing? Were they crossing the river or just plopped there? And where were the dino-cows? Orderly!" he shouted.

"Here, sur," came a voice directly behind him.

"Tell those comm 'Cats to get a move on. I need comm!"

In the distance, beyond South Hill, a rumbling, roaring horn suddenly sounded, and all conversation stopped. A second horn joined the first, then another. In seconds, the air was filled with the bone-chilling and utterly unmistakable bellows-powered calls that signaled a general Grik charge! The slopes beyond South Hill, so still and peaceful just moments before, erupted with movement as seemingly dozens of shapes burst from beneath every tree and joined the growing, howling swarm flowing down toward the narrow plain below the Sularan position.

"My God," Flynn exclaimed. "That lizardy son of a skuggik really did it this time! He Custered us! Drummers, sound 'Stand To'!"

"What does that mean, Colonel?" Bekiaa shouted over the thundering drums that suddenly competed with the horns. "What's 'Custered'? You said something like that in the highland pass on Ceylon, before the battle there."

"General Halik, or whatever the hell his name is, figured out where we were going, how we were moving, then let us stick our necks through that damn, rocky noose! There *were* Grik all over those damn heights on our flanks all day, just waiting for this! He tried the same stunt in the highlands, but this time it worked—and *I* let it!"

"But their guns! The planes saw no artillery, and no way they could get any up there!"

"Don't you get it? They don't *need* artillery, not yet. They aren't going after the whole corps right now, just us! They can keep General Maraan bottled up in the Rocky Gap while they eat us alive. Between us, the Marines, the Sularans, and the Cav, that's around thirty-five hundred troops, and a fair-size chunk of Second Corps!"

A gun flashed on South Hill, downward and away, the

vent jet stabbing at the sky. Then another fired. Both reports were drowned by the growing, snarling, hissing shriek of thousands of Grik charging down out of the hills, where they must have remained hidden to crossing aircraft.

"What have we got coming at us here?" Flynn demanded when a 'Cat lieutenant raced up from the west side of the hill.

"Nothing yet. They seem all go at First Sular, yonder. They lots still not to top of hill. No dig in."

The sun had touched the horizon at last, and the long shadows would soon be replaced by a very long night. Musket flashes and more cannon firelit the distant hill.

"They mean to take us one at a time," Flynn decided. "My guess is they've probably got a lot more out there than are even coming off the hills. Probably have some guns stashed too. If they wipe us out, or even if they don't, they can keep Second Corps stopped up in that gap until that 'many' force gets here from the east. After that, it's all attack, attack. Their kind of fight."

"But even they get us, Second Corps get away!" the lieutenant said, blinking furiously.

"Boy, have you even been *with* us the last couple of days? Remember the dino-cows? They didn't cook this up on the fly. I guarantee they're hittin' Second Corps from behind and in the flanks right damn *now*! They'll cork General Maraan in that lousy gap from both sides!"

"But . . . well, what *we* do?" the young officer almost wailed.

"You're relieved, Lieutenant," Flynn said, almost gently. "At least until you pull yourself together." He looked at those who'd gathered around him. "*All* of us better do that right quick, or we've had it. Saachic!"

"Sur?"

"Take all the cav and scoop up both companies of the Sixth in the gap. Whoever's behind 'em will have to take the load when it lands. After that, haul ass to South Hill. If it looks like they can hold off the first shove, help them do it, then tell them to run, not walk, the hell over *here*."

"Yes, sur . . . but what if they not holding?"

Flynn took a breath. "Then spike what guns you can and

get everybody out who can climb in the saddle with you. We'll cover your run back here."

"Meanies don't like extra riders," Saachic warned. "And even if we all get some, we can't get all."

"I know."

The battle for South Hill intensified as darkness fell, flaring and slashing with fire. Every instinct Flynn had told him to march to the aid of the Sularans, but he knew that was probably exactly what the Grik wanted him to do. With the darkness, he had no way of knowing how the enemy deployment was developing. The cavalry was keeping a clear line of communication between the hills—the Grik seemed to respect their me-naaks—but he already had reports of Grik circling around South Hill to threaten that line. One way or the other, the Sularans had to pull back here soon.

In the meantime, his Rangers were digging like fiends and heaping the damp earth in front of their lines. Stakes were being cut, sharpened, and driven into the ground, and details were busy spooling out the new barbed wire they'd just recently received from Baalkpan. It was crummy, lightweight stuff compared to what Flynn had seen in France as a youngster, but this would be the first time the Grik ever ran into such an entanglement, and it was going to cost them. Other details were starting work on several bunkers to give them some overhead protection, and revetments were taking shape around the guns. The Marines maintained their position on the south side of the hill, throwing breastworks in front of their own forward battery, which was prepared to fire down the flanks of the gap held by the cavalry when the Sularans finally came out. When they were withdrawn into the fortifications, their guns would serve as a mobile reserve for any hot spots that might develop.

Flynn looked around. He'd done his best to prepare, he thought. There was little more he *could* do but make North Hill so costly to take that the Grik would choke on it.

"Col-nol Flynn! Col-nol Flynn!" he heard called in the deepening gloom.

"Here!"

One of the comm 'Cats hopped closer. "Col-nol, we got

contact with Maa-draas HQ! Gener-aal Taa-leen wants to know what the hell is going on! We can't get Division or Corps. Them damn hills round the pass block us, I bet."

"I'm on my way." He paused for an instant, listening. High above, he heard the sound of motors, lots of them, and they weren't Nancys. The night suddenly brightened with the lights of what looked like falling meteors that illuminated the bellies of Grik zeppelins in the sky. The things didn't light up until they'd fallen some distance from the ships, and he guessed that made sense. They were using some kind of delayed-ignition system to protect their hydrogen-filled airships. The first meteor struck out on the plain and burst amid a roiling ball of spreading flames. It was followed by many more. None landed on North Hill. They probably couldn't see it in the dark. Some probably burned Grik when they fell, but several splashed fire on South Hill, and Flynn swore.

"C'mon," he said to the 'Cat. "Now they're throwing Grik fire at us! If the Air Corps can't keep those bastards off us, they'll burn us out for sure!"

"What the hell's going on out there?" General Pete Alden demanded, storming into the briefing room adjacent to the comm shack in Madras.

General Taa-leen commanded 1st Division, and while it occupied the city, he was essentially Pete's Chief of Staff. "A counterattack, General. A big one. Beyond that?" Taa-leen spread his arms.

"Where?" Pete asked, shoving through milling, confused staff officers to stand before the most current map they had, tacked to the wall. He did a double take when he saw Hij-Geerki lying on a pair of the common Lemurian cushions in a corner, as inconspicuous as he could make himself. He'd thought Rolak had taken his pet Grik south. He shook the distraction away.

"Everywhere. Or so it seemed at first," Taa-leen answered.

"Show me what we know; then we can wonder what it seems like."

"Of course. In the south, Third Corps has not been directly attacked, but a strong force has assembled opposite it. Fifth Corps is heavily engaged and has been forced to pause its advance and assume a defensive posture. Its supply lines south have been cut. General Rolak has encountered increasing spoiling attacks, he calls them, but continues to push First Corps south even now. He thinks the large enemy force that he hoped to fix in place for Fifth Corps to hit from behind has turned to crush Fifth Corps, or at least drive it south and prevent it from linking up with him."

"Nobody could ever call Rolak timid," Pete said respectfully.

"No, sur." Taa-leen blinked. "And perhaps he is right to push. Where he had been the anvil, he might now become the hammer, and the result could be the same."

"Is that what you think?" Pete asked, eyebrow raised.

"It is. The Air Corps saw no indication that fresh enemy troops had moved against Third Corps. Co-maander Leedom believes it faces the same battered troops that the fleet gave such a pasting."

Lieutenant Commander Mark Leedom had been assistant Commander of Flight Operations on *Salissa*, and was acting COFO of the 5th and 8th Bomb Squadrons and the 6th Pursuit—all from the lost *Humfra-Dar*. He also had two new squadrons that had literally been assembled in Madras, right off the transports.

"If true," Taa-leen continued, "it cannot be a steady force and is likely there only to fix Third Corps in place."

"Okay," Pete agreed. "We'll give General Rolak his head. If anybody can keep it together in a night march, it's him. We'll know more about the big picture in the morning. In the meantime, if he runs into anything he even thinks he can't handle, I want him to pull back."

"Yes, sur."

"So, what's the worst of it? There's got to be more, or you wouldn't have sent such an urgent message. There's nothing going on here, so that leaves Second Corps."

"Yes, Gener-aal," Taa-leen admitted, "I don't *think* the Orphan Queen is in a jaam; I *know* she is. All physical lines of communication have been cut between here and the place they were calling Rocky Gap. Wireless transmissions report that her situation is dire indeed."

"What happened?"

Taa-leen explained what they knew so far; that II Corps was basically trapped in the gap and the 1st Amalgamated, the 1st Sular, the 1st of the 2nd Marines, and several companies of cavalry were independently trapped beyond it. At first they'd been on separate hills, but now they'd consolidated. Losses, particularly to the 1st Sular, had been high. To make matters worse, a very large enemy force was assembling, and likely advancing from the west. "We are in wireless contact with Colonel Flynn and General Maraan," Taa-leen continued, "but they cannot communicate with each other. Of the two, the smaller force is in the greatest jeopardy. I have just received confirmation that zeppelins are bombing it with Grik fire! I suspect the rest of Second Corps will soon receive the same treatment."

"Get Leedom in here," Alden barked at an aide, who dashed out of the briefing room.

"You will send planes up there? In the dark?" Taa-leen asked, blinking concern. "The air crews are all tired. Most have flown numerous sor-tees, and we lost two more aircraft today for no apparent reason. Commander Leedom blames hasty maintenance caused by the pace of operations."

"Night flying here is different than it was for those guys in Second Fleet," Pete conceded. "India's a hell of a lot bigger than New Ireland! But Leedom'll take care of those damn zeps, if he has to do it himself," he ground out. "I'll tell him to ask for volunteers." He looked at Taa-leen. "He'll get 'em too. You know why? Because nobody in Ben Mallory's Air Corps could sleep a wink tonight knowing the damn Grik are burning our people!"

He turned back to the map. "So," he muttered. "That's the deal. I think you're right about the south. It's clever and might even work, but I think this General Halik has deliberately tossed his best dice at Second Corps, hoping to wipe it out. The question is, what the hell are we going to do about it?" He turned and looked at Hij-Geerki, who was watching attentively. "What do you think?" he blurted with a sour expression.

"I no t'ink," the creature answered tentatively in its strange but improving English. "I . . . 'e-long to Lord Rolak. I t'ink what he t'ink. I *can't* . . . self t'ink like Gen'ral." Geerki hesitated. "Ony . . . 'aybe dis Gen'ral Halik not t'ink like *Grik* Gen'ral."

North Hill was ablaze and the trees that stood atop it flared like great vertical matches in the dark. A lucky hit by the first flight of zeppelins had landed on its flank and ignited one of the Marine artillery caissons and the resultant flashing detonation had drawn the attention of the other airships. Most had already dropped their firebombs and the plain between the two hills was dotted with dying fires. The tall, damp grass just wouldn't burn, at least without a wind to fan the flames, but the few airships that still carried loads quickly dumped them on the illuminated hill. Finally out of ordnance, the zeppelins departed, but they left plenty of misery in their wake.

"Get the wounded in the ditches!" Flynn roared over the hideous, wrenching screams. Bad as the cries of the wounded were, the agonized, squealing wails of scorched paalkas were probably worse. "Throw dirt on those fires . . . and put those poor damn animals out of their misery!"

"What about the trees?" someone cried.

Flynn wiped the soot from red, streaming eyes and looked up at the crackling trunks and naked limbs above. The flames were already diminishing. The tree bursts had been the worst, spattering the Grik fire over a broader area than the ground impacts. "Nothing for 'em. They'll have to burn out." He stared a moment longer. "I don't think they'll burn once the fuel is gone. Pretty wet wood." For the first time, he was grateful for the almost daily rains and high humidity. "Jesus," he mumbled, taking in the rapid activity and smoldering bodies around him. He didn't know how he'd escaped with little more than a few light burns; most of the Grik bombs had fallen right around him. He coughed on air that was thick with smoke and the stench of burning fur.

Bekiaa appeared out of the swirling gloom and stopped beside him, gasping, her hands on her knees. Flynn offered his canteen.

"You better save that, sir," Bekiaa grated. "We lost all the Sularan water butts, and I don't know if ours made it through this or not yet." She waved around.

"Take a drink," he ordered grimly. "We have only about half the Sularans to worry about."

"We were lucky to get that many out," Bekiaa reminded him, and relenting, took the canteen. "The Grik nearly got them all, and the caav, once they figured out they were retreating." She took a small sip and handed the canteen back, blinking admiration. "The caavalry earned their pay today! I confess I never imagined such a . . . quickly moving fight on land! And the Marines who covered them at the end!" she added proudly. "Those new breechloaders are a wonder! The Grik pursuers melted before them like wax!"

"Yeah, the cav did swell," Flynn agreed. "Everybody did. And those Allin-Silvas are great—but they use a lot of ammunition, fast." He looked around. "Just swell," he muttered. "So, now everybody's here with us, in one place, being burned alive." He paused, steeling himself. "What's left?" he asked at last.

"It was bad," Bekiaa admitted, "but the work you had us do paid off. We lost over a hundred dead in the bombing, and many more wounded." She sighed, her tail swishing in the glow. "A lot of those will not live. I estimate twenty-eight hundred effectives remain." She stood up straight at last. "We brought out some of the Sulaaran's caissons, with many people clinging to them—but then lost several of our own to the fires. I am not sure exactly what our ammunition situation is, but we can still fight."

Flynn pointed at the sky. "We can't fight *that*! Where the HELL is the Air Corps?"

Bekiaa shook her head. "I do not know. The communications equipment survived, but the aerial is down—for now. Saachic has taken out a patrol, but the Grik stay back."

"Makes sense," said Flynn. "No point in them getting burned by their own zeps when they come back."

"You think they will?"

"Why not?" Flynn said bitterly. "The fires are dying down, but we can't put 'em all out. We make a fine target from the air." He grunted.

"What?" Bekiaa asked.

"Oh, just a weird thought. There might be fifty thousand Grik out there—plenty to go over us like a steamroller—but *they're* waiting for *their* high-tech weapons to finish *us* off!"

An hour passed, then two. Axes dropped most of the rest of the smoldering trees and they were shifted into a checkerboard of revetments, fighting positions, and overhead protection. The aerial was restrung, but now there was a problem with the batteries. Apparently, one of the trees they felled landed heavily against its cart and cracked their mobile power supply. A Ronson wind generator was rigged, but there was no wind. The handles for the hand generator couldn't be found, and the comm 'Cats were trying to make some with the help of a battery forge. It was all infuriatingly frustrating and exhausting work—on top of a long, difficult march the day before and the events of the late afternoon.

Heavy, echoing thunderclaps of massed artillery fire and ripping sheets of musketry drifted toward them from the Rocky Gap, and flashes like lightning beyond the horizon lit the sky above it.

"Second Corps is in it now," Flynn said to Bekiaa, still by his side. None of the 1st Sular's senior officers had survived, and she remained his exec. An exhausted Captain Saachic returned and blearily reported that there very well *might* be fifty thousand Grik surrounding North Hill, but for now they were holding back, waiting, as Flynn had predicted. Flynn ordered him, and everyone who could, to get some sleep. The long night wore on and the flames faded almost entirely, giving them hope that the enemy airships might not return. Of course, they could just be waiting for daylight now. The fighting in the gap ebbed and flowed, but never ceased, and all that William Flynn, Bekiaa-Sab-At, and much of what remained of the 5th Division could do was stand, sleeplessly, and wait.

Eventually, just as the sky was beginning to turn gray in the east, the dreaded sound of the odd little Grik zeppelin engines reemerged. Inexorably, the airships drew closer, nearly invisible in the dark sky above.

"Sound 'Stand To,'" Flynn sighed, and shortly after, the drums began to rumble.

Staring up, Bekiaa thought she could just make out the enemy craft, the sun beginning to reach the higher objects. She was startled when a stream of reddish, flaring dots suddenly arced through the air and impacted against one of the dingy cylinders. Almost immediately, it erupted into bright, hungry flames and began to fall out of the creeping formation!

"Col-nol!" she cried, grasping Flynn's arm.

As was customary at that latitude, aided by the elevation, dawn came swiftly—particularly to the "furball" that suddenly erupted in the sky. A squadron of white-bellied Nancys swarmed the remaining eight zeppelins, hosing them with tracers from the single .50-caliber machine gun mounted in their noses. The weapons were further gifts from the salvaged *Santa Catalina*; either spares or guns that had been removed from the P-40s. It had been deemed unnecessary for all the Warhawks to carry their full complement of six, particularly those deliberately lightened to increase their range or carry bombs. Now the slowly resolving sea of Grik around the hill emitted a rushing wail as the Nancys slashed their own machines apart.

Blazing, crumbling airships stumbled from the sky, some intact, but most in disintegrating, fire-breathing sections. Some even fell on the gathered Grik below. Firebombs vomited flaming fluid from the impacting machines, or drizzled fiery tendrils down on clots of Grik between the hills. Shrieks echoed and seethed. A flight of Nancys rumbled low over the horde and *Allied* bombs tumbled among it, detonating and spewing fire, weapons, and parts of Grik in long, roiling ovals.

"All batteries, commence firing with spherical case!" Flynn roared. "Fire at will!" The Grik were too far for canister to be effective. "Mortar crews, stand by! Action south!" Mortar 'Cats scrambled from their various positions around the perimeter, lugging their tubes and crates of ammunition.

Chest-thumping concussions ringed the hill and white smoke billowed outward as exploding case shot soared among the Grik, popping with gray-white puffs above or within their ranks, and scything them down with hot, jagged shards of iron. More bombs fell from another flight of the strange little seaplanes before it clawed its way back into the sky. A huge mushroom of smoke chased them this time, and one of the planes staggered. Its port wing fluttered away and it spiraled down amid a smear of fire.

"Damn!" Flynn growled. "Must've been those antiair mortar things of theirs again!" The cumbersome Grik weapons had made their first appearance on Ceylon.

Another Nancy was in trouble high above. A long stream of gray smoke chased it as it peeled away from a final, plummeting zeppelin. The plane steadied for a moment, but the smoke grew thicker and darker and it dove for the earth.

"Caap-i-taan Saachic!" Bekiaa shouted over the pounding guns. "That plane looks like it will try to set down there, near where the Marines had their works last night! You must rescue the crew if they survive the crash!" Nancys had no wheels—but wheels would be useless in the tall grass, at any rate. Maybe a hull designed for landing on water would fare better?

Saachic, already mounted, whirled. "First Squad!" he cried to the ready unit that had been around him throughout the night. "Follow me!"

With a clatter of equipment, swords, and carbines, 1st Squad's me-naaks vaulted the breastworks and raced toward where the wounded plane was leveling off above the long grass that glowed golden green under the bright sunrise. The Nancy was burning now, its engine gasping and popping in agony. It nearly stalled, but the pilot dropped the nose and it swooped low, into the very top of the grass, and practically fluttered to the ground. Even with such an amazingly light impact, the high wing immediately sagged to either side of the engine and the fuel tank in front of it ruptured with a searing *whoosh*!

A man leaped out of the forward cockpit, coveralls smoking, and did a somersault in the damp grass. Immediately, he jumped to his feet and tried to get around the collapsed port wing to the aft cockpit, where his observer/copilot sat. It was no use. The plane was fully involved by then. Ammunition for the .50 cal started cooking off and finally forced the man back.

"Look!" someone shouted. "The Grik!" A mob of the enemy several thousand strong was sweeping forward despite the fires and the other pursuit ships that had followed their comrade down. The planes began making strafing runs to keep the Grik back, but it wasn't working.

"Damn it, they're going for him!" Flynn growled, eyes darting from the Grik to Saachic's cavalry, now streaming toward the man. It was going to be close. He had a sinking feeling; not only because of the danger to the flyer, but about the Grik they faced. Once, the trauma of the last quarter hour would have rattled them badly. They'd stood against unusually determined Grik in another pass, on Ceylon, but even they had finally broken off. The Grik trying to take the flyer showed no hesitation at all, and Flynn suddenly noticed that the vast majority of the rest of the army surrounding them had remained steady as well.

"I think we may really be in for it," he whispered.

"Mortars!" Bekiaa roared. "Commence firing in support of Captain Saachic and the flyer!"

Saachic's cavalry won the race, and Saachic himself scooped the pilot onto the me-naak's back. A flurry of crossbow bolts and even some musket shots chased the squad as it bolted for the safety of the breastworks. Flynn wondered if the shots came from the new Grik matchlocks or weapons captured on South Hill. There was a flurry of *toomp* sounds as mortar bombs arced into the sky and began snapping among those closest Grik, sending geysers of earth, screaming Grik, and shredded grass into the air. The enemy fusillade was interrupted and none of the galloping cav 'Cats were hit. A couple of me-naaks may have been, but they all flowed back up over the barbed wired entanglements, and the hasty berm.

"They're not stopping!" Bekiaa shouted suddenly, still staring at the Grik. The whole mob that had gone for the flyer—and some other groups as well—kept right on coming, straight for the south slope of the hill. A couple of planes dropped two more bombs into the mass, and the gun-armed Nancys made another firing pass but then they flew off, into the rising sun, maybe low on fuel but certainly out of ordnance.

"Battery!" Bekiaa yelled. "Load canister! Mortars, increase elevation. First Marines and Company-A Rangers, make ready!"

Saachic's meanie picked its way through the fallen trees to rejoin Flynn and Bekiaa, and a bloodied, scorched man slid down from the animal and stood before them. He saluted absently.

"Goddamn!" he gasped, taking an offered canteen. "Thanks!"

"Leedom?" Flynn asked, remembering the man's name.

"Yes, sir," the man replied, taking a gulp and wiping his mouth. "Lieutenant Commander Mark Leedom, acting COFO for Army and Naval air out of Madras! You're Colonel Flynn?"

"I am."

"Battery!" Bekiaa roared again. "Marines and Rangers! At my command . . . Fire!"

The yellowish white smoke that always seemed to accompany their canister gushed downhill in an opaque, rolling wall, and the deafening thunder of the guns overwhelmed the volley of muskets.

"Independent, fire at will!" Bekiaa ordered, her voice cracking, and with a glance at Flynn, she dashed toward the guns for a better view. With the stirring breeze, the smoke would clear there soonest.

"What happened, Commander?" Flynn asked.

"I got shot down!" Leedom replied defiantly. "They had some kind of gun mounted in the gondola; like a little cannon loaded with shot. It hammered us just like a damn duck!" He looked at the plane, burning amid the surging Grik. "Tacos—my OC—got hit . . ." He looked down. "He was a good 'Cat. God, I hope he was already dead before . . ." He looked back at Flynn. "Colonel, you're in the shit." Artillery and the firing of the fast-loading Allin-Silvas almost drowned his words, but Flynn heard.

"Don't I know it," he agreed grimly, watching the slope below the guns, willing the Grik to break. But they just kept coming, running or crawling over their own dead in places.

"Shit! Just a minute!" He spun toward a 'Cat beside him wearing the painted bars of a captain on his leather armor. "Get your company up there right damn now! They ain't stopping!" The 'Cat bolted, and the crackle of rifles increased amid the hissing roar of the Grik. Two guns bucked at once, spewing canister and scything down dozens, maybe a hundred of the enemy, they were so tightly packed. Mortar 'Cats, no longer able to bring their primary weapons to bear, were throwing grenades like baseballs, as fast as they could pull the pins. The wailing shrieks were terrible, and with the combination of concentrated fire, canister, and now the storm of grenade fragments, the swarm finally seemed to balk.

"Reserves already, Colonel?" Leedom muttered. "God, I hope not!"

"Flying reserves," Flynn admitted, troubled. "We have more—but we're surrounded, as you can see, and I can't strip much around the perimeter." He pointed at the south slope. "So far, this is the only attack, but if they see a hole somewhere else, they might go for it." He hesitated. "Why? What did you see?"

Leedom stripped the goggles off his head and threw them on the ground. "Colonel, you have *no idea* how surrounded you are." He snorted. "*We* are."

The reserve company formed, standing, behind the junction of the Marines and Rangers, where the two battalions had become intermingled, firing as quickly as they could. That's where the most densely packed Grik thrust seemed to be headed, as if deliberately *aimed* there, like a wedge.

"What the hell?" Flynn murmured.

Four guns snarled with distinct, separate thunderclaps of fire, and the reserve company poured in a volley of buck and ball at less than thirty yards. Finally, *finally*, the Grik charge staggered, shrouded in smoke, lead, and a blizzard of downy fur and reddish vapor. Only then did something like Grik Rout grip what remained of the bloody stump of the enemy thrust. Maddened by wounds, pain, and panic, some Grik turned on each other, fighting to get back, aside, away from the hail of bullets and buzzing canister. These, as always, were hacked down by their comrades, but not before the charge stacked up behind them and the withering fire spread the effect. Hundreds fell in the next few moments while those behind pressed against others that retained no notion other than an instinctual imperative to escape.

All the veteran troops had seen Grik Rout before, and they cheered when they saw the symptoms now—but the cheer slowly died and the stunned Marines and Rangers resumed firing with a will when it didn't really *happen*. The charge came apart, and many did flee mindlessly, but the great bulk of the surviving attackers *backed* away, still shooting crossbows or firing the weird matchlocks, if they had them. Only the Rangers had ever seen the enemy retire before, and they'd been beyond musket shot then. The rifled muskets still picked at them and so did the big guns, but it hadn't really been a retreat under fire. Not like this.

Flynn gave the order to cease firing after the Grik moved beyond a hundred yards. Leedom's words still echoed in his mind, even without a proper explanation, and he instinctively knew that explanation would mean they had to conserve ammunition. The smoke slowly drifted away and dissipated in time for them all to see the attacking force rejoin the multitudes that ringed them—and be welcomed back into those ranks.

"A hell of a thing," Flynn muttered. His gaze turned to the field below the breastworks and the dark mounds bearing down on the tall grass. He couldn't see them all, of course, but there were surely thousands; maybe half the force that broke ranks to go after the fallen plane to start with. He could see inside the breastworks as well, now that the smoke was gone, and stretcher bearers climbed out of the ditch with their grisly, moaning burdens. These were carried to the centrally located medical section that had set to work under lean-tos erected around a tree-trunk stockade. After they deposited their burdens with the surgeons, the stretcher bearers returned to the ditch for more.

Bekiaa rejoined them. The white fur around her mouth was smudged black with powder from tearing open musket cartridges with her teeth, and her painted armor was dingy and streaked with blood. She'd slung her rifled musket, but seemed to sag under its weight.

"That was . . . closer than I expected," she said softly, barely audible over a loud, eerie chant the Grik had begun. None of them had ever heard anything like it, but its newness didn't compare to the other changes they'd seen in the short fight.

"Yeah," Flynn agreed. He turned to Leedom. "What were you saying? What did you mean?"

Bekiaa looked at the flyer and blinked tired curiosity.

"I'm afraid we're cooked," Leedom said, almost matter-of-factly. "Have you got comm?"

"I hope so. The guys were trying to patch up the generator," Flynn admitted.

"Listen, sir, I gotta report what shot me down so other guys don't get it!"

"You need to tell me what you saw!" Flynn demanded.

"Okay. General Alden needs to hear it too. If comm's up, I'll tell you while we send it. Fair?" He suddenly looked around with an almost-desperate expression for the first time, and patted the holster under his arm. "Say, uh, I sure could use a weapon besides my pistol!" He looked dubiously at Bekiaa's rifle musket. "You got any oh-threes around here?"

CHAPTER 15

March 14, 1944
USS* Salissa *(CV-1)

Lieutenant Sandy Newman banged on the bulkhead beside the door, or "hatch," to Admiral Keje-Fris-Ar's quarters, despite the Marine sentry standing there, who blinked astonishment at the breach of protocol. Keje opened the heavy door and stepped into the passageway.

"I was just on my way," he said. "Cap-i-taan Atlaan-Fas called me over the bridge voice tube. Come, you can fill me in as we walk!"

"Yes, sir," Sandy said, hurrying to keep up with the bear-shaped 'Cat. "One of Tikker's scout planes spotted a fleet, sir, a *hell* of a fleet, about four hundred miles west-northwest, the other side of the south India coast. Two advanced pickets have confirmed; the DDs *Naga* and *Bowles*. They're shadowing now, and also confirm the contact is definitely headed in this direction."

They reached the companionway to the bridge, and took the steps two at a time.

"Ahd-mi-raal on the bridge!" someone cried, and Keje waved irritably. It was well-known he didn't like to disturb the watch, and the warning was probably the result of a case of nerves.

"Ahd-mi-raal," Captain Atlaan-Fas greeted him.

"Cap-i-taan. Show me." They moved to the large chart table. Unlike on many other "Amer-i-caan" ships, *Salissa*'s charts often retained the ancient texts of the prophet Siska-Ta written on the margins. Few passages were pertinent to this part of the world, however, so the margins on this chart were almost blank. Almost. There were a few passages, and they gave Keje comfort now as Sandy pointed to a place on the "scroll."

"What do we know?"

"Little. There are many Grik ships of the type we've seen before, perhaps only a hundred, but all with cannon. There are also perhaps a dozen massive steamers, almost as big as *Salissa* herself, that look most odd, according to reports."

"Speed?"

"Only five or six knots, Ahd-mi-raal, but there are zeppelins above them, perhaps being towed! The pickets report a string of three or four trailing above each steamer! This in addition to the zeppelins we know have been sneaking past our air patrols at night and landing on fields across the western coast. The Third Bomb Squadron located one of their fields this morning and destroyed as many as ten airships on the ground, but there must be more." He blinked exasperation. "The Ancient Enemy learns to conceal himself from us."

"They are learning far too many things of late!" Keje confirmed darkly, absently dragging a nail-claw around the bulging southern coast of India. "Order *Naga*, *Bowles*, and the other pickets to break contact and withdraw at their best possible speed to here, just off the cape. It concerns me that they are out there on their own, and if they can see the Grik, the Grik can see them. We will observe the enemy movements with aircraft. This battlegroup and *Arracca*'s will join them at Point"—he squinted—"Point Comorin. Pass the word for COFO Jis-Tikkar. He must prepare a strike against the enemy fleet with every aircraft we have!"

Sandy shifted uneasily. "Uh, Admiral, as you know, General Alden's in kind of a fix. He's finally got a handle on what they ran into, and it's bad. He's ordered Fifth Corps to withdraw back south and dig in with Third Corps. He also ordered Rolak back to Madras, after all." He shook his head. "Those poor guys pushed south all night without a break, and now they've got to turn back the way they came, and maybe fight their way through! Second Corps is way out on a limb, and one of its divisions—Colonel Flynn's command—is dangling by the very last leaf. In the meantime, Madras itself is dangerously exposed. They're all counting on us for air support!"

Keje was silent, and stared at the chart. Then he looked at the map that showed the updated disposition of the expeditionary elements. "What remains of Lieutenant Leedom's squadrons?"

"They're down about twenty percent, mostly mechanical casualties, but they've lost some planes and crews too. Leedom himself is with Flynn now, said he was 'shot down,' and the Grik zeps have some kind of defensive weapons now."

"Make sure Cap-i-taan Tikkar is aware," Keje warned.

"He is, sir."

Keje sighed. "Very well. Ask Cap-i-taan Tassana-Ay-Arracca if she might spare General Alden one of her squadrons. We are all suddenly so very stretched and pulled in every direction. I cannot risk this fleet in close combat with the enemy until I know more about its capabilities, particularly of these new steamers of theirs!" He paused. "Advise General Alden that we will soon have a battle of our own. He may land every Marine from every support ship in Madraas to bolster his defenses there, and I will send him every plane I have when and if I can."

Madras HQ

General Pete Alden was staring at his own map, the fingers of his left hand massaging his forehead. "So. No dice, huh?" he asked General Taa-leen.

"No, sur . . . I mean, yes, we will have another squadron from *Arracca*, and it will provide support for General Rolak on its way here, but we cannot expect more from the Ahd-mi-raal at this time."

"Yeah. And I can't really blame him. We're in the shit, but we know we're in the shit now. He's about to jump off the pier in the dark." He snorted. "Glad he's bein' more careful than I was."

"You couldn't have known, General," Taa-leen consoled.

"I should have! Damn it, we caught a glimpse of it on Ceylon!" He looked at the ancient Grik, Hij-Geerki, still curled on his cushion. As far as Pete knew, the lizard hadn't left the room. *Damn,* he thought. *Doesn't he ever eat? Or take a dump?* "Hell!" he continued, "Geeky there *told* us! Those nine civvy Grik we captured at Colombo told him about this new General Halik and his Jap sidekick, but I never dreamed they could pull something like this together. They saw what we were doing, what we *wanted* to do, then figured out a way to clobber us when we did it!"

"I ser' you, lord!" Hij-Geerki croaked piously.

"Yes," Taa-leen agreed, ignoring Hij-Geerki. "This Haalik, or his Jaap, can design battles. We know that now. We will design better ones! I am concerned only about that in the short term. What worries me most are the reports of how the individual Grik are fighting! Few are suffering from Braad-furd's Grik Rout, and now there is this other report!"

Pete nodded, and felt a chill despite the hot afternoon. They knew a large force had been massing at what had been II Corps's objective, but Leedom had been the first to report a very frightening thing. Subsequent flights sent to firebomb the Grik surrounding Flynn had carried on and confirmed what Leedom saw. The "many" Grik west of Rocky Gap *were* advancing. In the Grik scheme of things, the fresh force wasn't particularly large, perhaps numbering less than fifty thousand. That was more troops than Alden had in all of India, but no more than a properly handled corps had defeated in the past. But this new force was no mob rampaging along like a plague of locusts; it was a real army, uniformly dressed and equipped with matchlock muskets and long spears, and it was *marching* toward the Rocky Gap—and Flynn—in a long, fat column, complete with a supply and artillery train.

Pete looked back at the map. Fifth Corps was having little trouble moving back south—so far—but Rolak was hitting some serious opposition. It was still mostly savage spoiling attacks, but each time he had to deploy part of his corps, and his troops were utterly exhausted. Once they made it back to Madras, they wouldn't be of any use to Safir Maraan and II Corps. Pete thought Safir *might* hack her way back to Madras, but that still left Flynn. He rubbed his eyes.

"You know, General Taa-leen," he said, "we've got a lot of wild-ass Grik causing us fits down here in the low country, but we're kind of used to that. I'm like you. I don't like what Second Corps is up against one damn bit. I think, all of a sudden, that stupid, shitty Rocky Gap is something we need to hang on to—if for little more reason than the Grik want it so bad. Besides, it's the only place a real army can get through to Madras from the west. I hate to rush him, but I think we have to tell Rolak to punch back through to here quick as he can. His guys can rest up then. As soon as he *gets* here, we take your division, the Marines off the ships—hell, the sailors from the transports, if Keje'll let us—and *we* punch through to Second Corps and *keep* that crummy gap!"

"Yes, sur, General. But what about Flynn?"

Pete shook his head. "I . . . don't know. It all depends on his position and whether he has the supplies—and troops to hold it."

March 15, 1944
Below North Hill

"They *cannot* resist much longer!" Halik ranted aloud to himself as a third, properly coordinated (this time) attack ground up the corpse-choked slopes of that wickedly tenacious hill on the long grass prairie. The horns brayed insistently, and his army roared with something he remembered as akin to glee as the bloody banners swept forward and up. A thunderous staccato booming erupted in all directions and smoke churned down the slopes, engulfing the front ranks of the charge. Halik knew those first ranks had been flayed, but there were more behind them, many more. The stutter of enemy muskets—*Better than mine,* he seethed—became a continuous crackle, like dry sinik wood in a roaring flame. Still, this portion of his army, a quarter the size of that attacking the mouth of the mountain gap, still outnumbered the enemy at least eight to one, and he'd sent nearly all of it this time. The enemy had to be running out of ammunition—and warriors—by now.

This was the first time General Halik had led an entire battle alone. He and General Niwa had realized that staying together had been the greatest mistake they'd made on Ceylon. Neither had been in a position to avert several disasters that occurred too far away for them to influence, and they'd determined never to allow such a concentration of command again. Niwa was in the south, coordinating the various actions there, and Halik wasn't nervous, exactly, but he did feel a measure of unease. He believed he'd planned this battle well, and the enemy had done exactly as he hoped—at first. The resilience of the defenders on that cursed northern hill and the speed with which the force in the pass had reacted to his attack there had surprised him, but he didn't think he *needed* Niwa here. His battle was taking longer than expected, but he believed it was still in his grasp—yet he *missed* the Jaaph officer. Niwa's cool counsel was always welcome at times like this, when Halik's blood began to boil.

A shadow flitted across him, and he looked up. *Not again!* Several of the blue-and-white enemy aircraft swooped low, directly over his converging horde, and released more of their hideous firebombs. The things exploded, flinging streams of fire among his precious, disciplined Uul more vigorously than his own similar weapons could ever manage. He raged. He didn't have any of the large fire throwers here, nor did he have enough artillery. What guns he had were deployed against the force in the gap. Worse, he had no more airships to use here either—all that remained in India had been taken from his command for "something else," even General Niwa had no details about. He assumed General Esshk and General of the Sea Kurokawa were coming at last, but he had no confirmation. His rage dampened just a bit. It barely mattered. The enemy machines would make short work of his airships again, even if he still had them at his disposal.

This fight would have to be decided the old-fashioned way, but he still needed to win it quickly. The first "new" Uul had been landed a few weeks before in the Cambay Gulf, just as he'd asked. He'd actually been surprised by that, but he was grateful. Now they were hurrying here, even as the battle raged. They were not "attack" troops. Not yet. They had been designed from birth to *defend*. They were very young, barely mature, but he'd been assured they could do what they were made to do: stand and fight to the bitter end—just as his enemies now did atop that thrice-cursed hill!

This attack had to succeed, but at what cost? What price *could* he pay for that wretched hill? He still needed these attack warriors in the gap, and they were withering before his eyes! Had he become distracted from his own plan? He might yet win the hill and lose his primary objective. Only once the enemy in the gap had been pushed back could *he* fortify a defensive, impervious position with invincible troops! The enemy would never break out onto the prairie where its better, more coordinated mobility could be fully employed. Again he wished he had fast animals his own troops could ride! The enemy cavalry, as Niwa called it, had been nearly as dreadful a surprise as its aircraft! He wondered if there was not something, somewhere, in all the realms of the Grik, that could be tamed for such a purpose.

More bombs fell, and now the summit of the hill was all but invisible through the roiling black smoke of burning fuel and bodies, and the white smoke of guns. He tensed, watching closely.

Flynn's defenses had been forced back into secondary positions all around the perimeter by the amazingly well-executed attack. A couple of Sularan guns had been overrun in their forward positions, but not before they'd been disabled. Most of the paalkas were dead, either riddled by Grik bolts or burned to death two nights before. Unlike meanies, the stupid damn things wouldn't lie down under cover. Billy Flynn had heard from the Maa-ni-los that they *couldn't* lie down or they'd suffocate. He figured they would know, but the result was that his draft animals had been effectively exterminated. The rest of the guns had been heaved, by hand, into a contracting circle around the central hospital stockade, where new positions had already been dug. At the moment, it didn't look like it would matter. Ammunition was dwindling fast, particularly for the new breechloaders and mortars, and they were almost out of canister. All they had was what they'd brought with them, and there was little possibility of resupply. General Maraan probably had the power to reach them, but she couldn't *deploy* it in the narrow gap and pop the cork the Grik had shoved in. Worse, from what Flynn heard through Madras HQ, if she did break through to them before General Alden could support her, Flynn would probably have to find room on North Hill for all of II Corps! What a crazy mess.

"Hammer 'em," Flynn yelled as he moved, crouching, behind the secondary breastworks. The Grik crowded so densely in front of it that it was impossible for a shot to miss. Crossbow bolts thrummed past or stuck in the shields that a pair of Marines insisted on defending him with as he moved. "Chew 'em up! Shred 'em!" he chanted. "Stomp 'em like the goddamn lizardy roaches they are!" He wasn't even sure his troops could hear him, but they poured in the fire or stabbed with their bayonets at anything that got close enough. *This would be a swell time for grenades,* he thought, but they'd already run out of those. It was terrible and horrifying—and magnificent all at once.

One of his Marine guards dropped suddenly, his head misshapen by a Grik musket ball that punched right through the shield and hit him above the ear, sending his helmet flying. A Sularan quickly slung his musket and snatched up the shield. *Dammit, I wish they'd just use their weapons!* Flynn seethed to himself, angry that yet another of his guards was dead—but this was the crisis, the tipping point, and he thought he had no choice but to expose himself so. If there was any consolation, he didn't think he was being specifically targeted. The smoke was so dense and visibility so poor, few of the enemy could even see him. Besides, the Grik leaders in this attack, if there were any, seemed to be leading from the pack, and the common Grik warrior probably didn't know to single him out.

"Captain Bekiaa!" he shouted, finally slipping down into the trench beside the female 'Cat, where he sensed the greatest enemy pressure. *Trust her to find the hottest spot first!* His guards followed and he yelled for them to get back in the fight, which they gladly did.

"So, *you're* our reserve now. Huh, Colonel?" Lieutenant Leedom asked ironically. He'd found a bloody Lemurian helmet and had tied the straps beneath his chin. He also had Flynn's own '03 Springfield, since he wasn't as familiar with a musket. Flynn had kept the weapon but hadn't used it himself since they invaded Ceylon. Apparently, the '03 was in good hands. The long bayonet was reddish black, and Leedom was pushing bright brass shells through a stripper clip into the magazine.

"I'm all that's left," Flynn confirmed, raising his musket and firing. He nodded at the guards as he started to reload. "Me and those fellas."

"We're almost out of ammunition!" Bekiaa yelled.

"There's more on the way," Flynn assured her, "but it's about the last of it." He nodded at the surging enemy. "Won't need it in a second. Bayonets!" he roared as the Grik hurtled forward.

Few in what remained of Flynn's division had shields anymore. Only the Marines still habitually carried them, and that was mainly because the Marines at the Dueling Ground had done so, and it had been reported that they could turn musket balls—for a while—if held at an angle. Flynn realized now that letting his Rangers discard their shields had been a mistake. The weird Grik matchlocks fired bigger balls than the Dom muskets did, and if they didn't always punch through a shield, they made very short work of it. But shields still came in very handy against crossbow bolts, and at that moment, as in the jungles around Raangoon, a wall of shields would have been very welcome. The Grik must have recognized that too, because the biggest Grik charge didn't come against the Marines; it came right at Flynn, Bekiaa, and Leedom, and the now utterly mixed "company" of Rangers and Sularans.

One very important thing Flynn suddenly—vividly—remembered from his time in France was that once the enemy reached your trench, you didn't stay in it and let him land on top of you unless you wanted to die.

"Up!" he roared. "Up and at 'em! Charge bayonets!" Shrilly, the order swept down the defending line like a crackling electric current. Even as the Grik charge waded through the entanglements and reached the breastworks beyond, the Rangers and Sularans flowed up out of their trench and met them in a slashing, shooting, stabbing melee. As had long been observed, the Grik were better armed, physically, for such a fight, but the training and discipline—not to mention the bristling bayonets and thundering muskets that fired in their faces—left the Grik stunned for an instant. An instant was all it took.

Saachic's cavalry, dismounted and without orders, joined the countercharge with a stutter of carbine fire and their long, deadly blades. A clawing, shrieking, hacking brawl ensued like hadn't been seen since the fighting for the south wall during the battle of Baalkpan. Grik claws slashed and tore past their own small shields, which were suddenly in the way. 'Cats screamed and rolled back into the trench, bleeding or dead, but the long bayonets on the Allied muskets were sharper, better, and more horrible than any spear. Also, if a 'Cat had a chance, he or she could still load and shoot—and the steel butt plate on the other end of the musket was a far better weapon than the butt of a spear.

These Grik were better trained than any they'd faced before, and they fought with greater skill. But if they'd largely learned not to wildly break, to "turn prey" in what Bradford had once coined "Grik Rout," that ability was achieved only through greater awareness—an awareness that permitted a variety of somewhat normal, genuine fear. They didn't break in the face of the sudden, ferocious countercharge, but they did recoil from it just enough to allow it to gain some momentum.

Other Grik regiments pressing forward on the flanks also paused, bewildered and frightened as their comrades gave ground. That allowed other Ranger companies, Marines, and Sularans, to push back as well, and soon the Grik were falling back, still fighting savagely, all around the hill. The last few dozen grenades exploded among them, and cannon sent hoarded canister sleeting through the disconcerted ranks.

"At 'em!" Flynn kept screaming, over and over, stabbing with his long bayonet as he'd been taught so long ago. Bekiaa appeared beside him. She'd lost her musket, but she plied her cutlass with practiced, savage ease, hewing heads and grasping, slashing arms. The Baalkpan Armory copies of the 1917 Navy cutlass were outstanding weapons. Just like those that inspired them, they were the culmination of thousands of years of human experience. Fairly short, they were handy in close quarters, but their sharp, heavy-spined blades were ideal for slashing and chopping flesh and bone. Grik swords were great for hacking or slashing too, Flynn had seen, but generally lighter and even shorter, and shaped more like a sickle or claw, so they tended to turn in the attacker's hand if they struck another sword, shield, or even musket barrel. Bekiaa and many other veterans were well aware of this and exploited it mercilessly.

Flynn took a clawed slash across his chest, unable to block it in time, then had the wooden forearm gnawed off his rifle while he tried to wrench it from clinging jaws. He finally yanked it free in a shower of splinters and shattered teeth and drove his bayonet through the eye of the Grik that tried to eat his gun. He thought he heard a squeal. Another lunged for him, batting at his rifle with its small shield, but Leedom drove it back against those behind it with a roar and sixteen inches of Springfield Armory steel.

Bekiaa was down! A Grik stood over her, sword raised for the killing blow. Flynn flung his rifle at the beast and chased after it, drawing his own cutlass. He hadn't practiced with it much, but great skill would've been wasted just then. The Grik deflected the thrown musket, but screeched when the cutlass tore into its chest. A blow on his helmet hammered Flynn to the ground as well, but somebody must have killed or distracted his assailant, because there was no second strike. For a moment, he was knocked back and forth on his hands and knees by the legs and feet of friend and foe alike, and couldn't get up. Grik hind claws slashed his thigh, and he gasped. Finally, a harried 'Cat hauled him up and pushed him out of the way. He saw Leedom then, Springfield on his shoulder, dragging Bekiaa back out of the fight while firing his pistol in the crush.

Flynn could sense the enemy was still afraid—he saw it in their wide eyes—but they just wouldn't break. There were too many, and he was so tired! His wonderful Rangers—and all the others, of course—had done all they could. The Grik were firming up now, and his countercharge had stalled. There was nothing for it. He started to yell an order for his troops to fall back to their trenches when he suddenly heard the dull, thrumming roar of Grik horns in the distance. Obediently, but almost reluctantly, it seemed, as if the warriors themselves had known how close they were to finishing it, the Grik started backing away.

"Don't chase 'em, for God's sake," Flynn croaked. "They wanna retreat, let 'em!"

He didn't give the order to cease firing, however, and able to reload at last, the horribly diminished troops around him sent a patter of musketry after the Grik until they were beyond crossbow range. Few fired after that. They couldn't have had much left to fire with.

"All right," he said at last, his knees turning rubbery. "Form details to get our wounded out of this mess." He waved at the carpet of corpses strewn around. "And pick up any weapons and ammunition you can find." He stopped a furiously blinking Sularan lieutenant who was pulling cartridge boxes off the dead. "You take charge here, son. Get somebody else to do that." He lowered his voice. "The guys and gals love to see their officers fight, but they'd rather we tell them to do stuff like this, while we pretend to think about what's *next*."

The lieutenant looked at him, his tail still swishing erratically from side to side, but the blinking stopped. "Yes, Col-nol," he whispered.

"Lord General Halik!" the warrior cried as he flung himself into the grass at Halik's feet. "I beg to report!"

"Rise, General Ugla," Halik said almost mildly.

Ugla instantly rose to his feet, perhaps surprised he still lived. "Yes, Lord General!"

Halik looked at him, eyes steady. Ugla had reason for concern. Halik had not always been kind to those who brought ill tidings. But that was before. General Niwa had taught him a great deal. "Your assessment, General. Withhold nothing you perceive as truth."

"Yes, Lord General." Ugla still paused.

"Only your silence will anger me at this point," Halik warned.

Ugla removed his helmet and shook out his crest. Halik noted that it was stiff with . . . anger?

"Lord General, we had them in our grasp. The prey was at bay and could not escape. It had gone to earth! It fought hard, still, and many Uul were slain. Many more would still have been lost . . . but we *had* them! Only you . . . Forgive me! Only the horns called us back before we gained all the prey atop that hill to feed upon!"

Halik said nothing for a moment, but only gazed into the west. Then he looked back at Ugla and pointed his sword at the smoldering hill.

"You are right, General. You *would* have had them. I know that as well, and I am . . . unhappy that I was forced to stop you." He took a deep, rasping breath. "Not long ago, I wouldn't have, no matter the cost, but the price of that stinking hill has grown too great to bear at present." His own crest flared. "I like to believe I have grown wiser in the ways of war and I need your seasoned warriors, those that remain, for a far more important task we must set them to immediately." He pointed back to the west. "We are out of time to pursue this sport. As you can see, the hatchling host draws near," he said, using the somewhat derisive term he'd heard his generals use to describe the barely mature army of culls—some said—that had been bred to defend. "There are their banners now."

It was true. Cresting a nearby rise, hundreds of bloodred pennants streamed in the afternoon sun, each signifying a hundred Uul warriors.

"We cannot linger here," Halik stated. "As you say, the enemy on the hill is crushed, cut off from resupply or reinforcement. They can no longer threaten us. Leave a few thousands of your warriors to ensure they do not escape, but we must rejoin the bulk of our army and push the greater force of the enemy back, deeper into the gap. There we will hold him while the hatchlings deploy." He paused.

"You have shown great promise, General Ugla, and I *need* you and your warriors there." Hesitantly, he patted Ugla's shoulder as Niwa had often done to him. It wasn't his people's way to touch each other at all, other than while killing or mating, but Niwa's touch had become oddly . . . comforting. Ugla recoiled, as Halik expected, but then let him pat him again. "Once that is done," he continued, "we can finish our business here."

He stared hard, thoughtfully, at the smoking hill, imagining the scene on it. "We know you had them, General," he repeated, "but perhaps more important, and far more interesting, is the fact that the prey—the *very worthy* prey—you faced must know it as well. I wonder what they will think of that."

Colonel Flynn stared at the withdrawing Grik a moment longer. They'd mauled them badly and they didn't seem as numberless as they had, but he knew his guys were done. They'd never hold off another assault half as big as this one. They just didn't have the numbers, ammunition, or strength left to do it. *They should have had us,* he thought. *Hell, even the common Grik warriors probably knew it. I wonder why they pulled back*. Suddenly, over the throbbing of his wounds, he felt a chill, and there wasn't enough of a breeze to blame it on his sweat-soaked shirt. "*How* in the hell did they pull them back?" he muttered. He'd been amazed to see the growing discipline the Grik displayed ever since Ceylon, but pulling the Grik off the shattered remnant of his division must have been like pulling a pack of dogs off a tree full of raccoons. Wearily, he shook his head and turned back to the trench to check on Bekiaa—and what was left of his troops. He was perplexed and uneasy, but he wouldn't complain.

"Col-nol!" cried a filthy, blood-spattered Marine corporal.

"Yeah?"

"My cap-i-taan send me. Make sure you see!"

"See what?"

The corporal blinked agitation. "Pease come, sur! You see better on right."

Almost reluctantly, Flynn followed the corporal around

and over the tangled heaps of dead. The hill was a little higher on the west side, the slope a little steeper, and that was probably another reason the Grik had concentrated where they had. That didn't mean the Rangers and the company of Marines emplaced there had gotten off without a scratch, but the enemy dead did extend considerably farther away from the breastworks, slain by the more accurate .50-80s. As Flynn drew near, he saw that his troops were moving forward to reoccupy their forward defenses. Then he saw something else.

"Oh, good God," he muttered. A few miles to the west-southwest, an *army* marched in long, dense, serpentine columns with the precision of a machine. The corporal's captain joined them and handed Flynn his telescope without a word. Flynn raised it with shaky hands and managed to adjust the focus. "Jesus, Mary, and Joseph," he whispered without even realizing he'd spoken. Leedom had *told* him, but he just hadn't grasped it, hadn't understood. Marching under the midday sun with a grandeur and geometric inflexibility Napoleon would have envied, an honest-to-God *army* of Grik churned rapidly, relentlessly, through the tall, green grass, as yet unspoiled by the battle that had raged around the hill.

"Are . . . are they coming for us?" The captain asked hesitantly but almost formally.

Flynn slammed the telescope shut.

"No," he said. "They're angling for the Rocky Gap. And look"—he pointed—"the Grik reserves that didn't come at us are already moving that way." He shook his head and snorted an ugly laugh. "Now I know why we're still alive. That General Halik's got bigger fish to fry, that's all. There's not enough of us left up here to worry about, and he knows it. Shit!"

William Flynn was as Irish as any American could possibly be, and despite his pain, even fueled by it, his temper soared. "We gotta report the absolute hell out of this. Pray God we've still got comm. Whether we do or not, we're *going* to get word out somehow—and make General Halik wish he'd wiped us out when he had the chance!"

CHAPTER 16

Baalkpan
March 15, 1944

ennis Silva walked with Bernie Sandison and Ronson Rodriguez at the head of a virtual army of young torpedo techs and strikers, ordnance 'Cats, EMs, and other "sparky" types. Lawrence trotted exuberantly alongside Silva, his crested head swiveling rapidly back and forth, taking in all the changes to the city. Within the column were carts piled with weapons, tools, and crated ammunition, and it snaked its way through the crowded, festive pathways toward the area between the vastly enlarged new fitting-out piers and the massive shipyard.

Dennis was still stunned to see how packed, bow to stern, the piers were, with completing ships of all descriptions. There was *Santa Catalina*, smoke coiling above her funnel, looking almost predatory with all the armor and weapons they'd lavished on her. Silva hadn't seen the ship before—and had fluttery feelings when "her" P-40s thundered overhead—but he'd been told she looked like the old Asiatic Fleet destroyer tender *Blackhawk*.

Maybe once, he decided with a critical eye. *The lines are still similar. Most of the cargo booms are gone, though, and she looks kinda . . . tough now.*

His gaze wandered as he walked. He was particularly amazed by the monstrous, almost Home-size floating dry docks fitting out at a completely new facility in the far distance across the bay. These weren't the same as the ones he'd seen under construction when he left. Those were finished now, and already in use either here or elsewhere. The new class was a powered, self-propelled variety that could steam wherever they were needed, and even fight!

The original permanent dry dock had even more smoking engines around it, and the place was wreathed in a perpetual cloud of steam. A brand-new carrier was taking shape inside the now *concrete*-reinforced, 'Cat-made canyon, and mighty wooden cranes were poised over mountains of bright timbers like impossible insects. He'd known concrete was in the works. Many of the ingredients were abundant in the highly volcanic region, and they'd been cooking limestone for acetylene. He'd heard that was related somehow. But to see it already in use . . . His eyes strayed to a pair of the old floating dry docks, side by side, and sure enough there were S-19 and the salvaged remains of *Walker*'s sister, *Mahan*! The wrecked destroyer and practically wrecked sub were both in the process of becoming something maybe a little different from what they'd been, though major alterations on S-19 had only just begun with Irvin Laumer's arrival a few days before. Not much to see there yet but a nearly stripped pressure hull. But *Mahan*! He couldn't believe it. He wondered how they'd managed to fish her up. Almost half the damn thing had been blown off, but she was beginning to look kind of like her old self again! Maybe shorter . . .

"Silva!" Bernie snapped—maybe the third time.

"Whut?"

"That nasty, creepy thing you use for a brain must be off on the moon! Listen up, and quit woolgathering! You and Risa will be the first ones at bat with all the new small arms, after Adar says his piece. I'd *order* you not to screw it up—with half the city watching—but then you'd probably start the show by seeing if you can whiz farther than you can shoot!"

Silva shrugged. "Maybe I *can* . . ."

"*Please* don't screw it up!" Bernie groaned. "I'm *asking* you, damn it! I'm nervous enough as it is without worrying about you! And whatever you do, don't carry on with Risa out in front of everybody! Besides . . . everything else, she's a Marine and an officer now!"

Silva grinned and patted the sling that supported his new "Doom Stomper."

"No sweat, Mr. Sandison! I'm your man! I'm still feelin' mighty friendly and a-bleeged! Besides, shootin' stuff is what I do! Me and Cap'n Risa'll shoot off the good stuff, an' show 'em why the junk won't work." Clearly, Silva had already formed strong opinions about some of the experimental weapons. "Relax," he continued. "Torpedoes and . . . other things . . . are what you do. It ain't like you got to *sell* the stuff!"

Bernie stopped, wordless for a moment, and the whole column ground to a halt behind him. "That's *exactly* what we're here to do today!" he finally insisted. "We have to decide what weapons and systems to devote our resources to, then *sell* them to the guys and gals who'll make them—as well as those who'll have to bet their lives on them! We all bitched about the useless crap the Navy gave us to fight the Japs: the crummy torpedoes, the dud shells. Stuff that cost lives! Now *we're* the ones responsible! All this time, we've been making do, but the time's come to put some real weapons in the hands of our people, and I'll be damned if one sailor, soldier, flyer, or Marine gets killed because something doesn't go off when they're counting on it!"

Silva arched an eyebrow. "Zat what yer workin' on, off in the jungle east o' town? *Real* weapons?"

Bernie stiffened. "I don't know what you're talking about."

"Bull flops. I seen some o' the brightest ordnance 'Cats we got headin' down a trail at first light yesterday, an' they didn't never come back. They all get ate, an' you forget to mention it? What're you doin' off in there you can't tell *me* about?"

Bernie looked at him. "I wouldn't tell *you* I had a hangnail!" he said, then paused. "Look," he almost whispered, "you try to fool everybody, but you're not stupid. Of *course* we've got secret stuff going on—you sniffed it out easy enough. Must be the way your mind works. Anyway, some things—big things—have to stay secret now. The war's changing. We've got Impies and all these women running around. Who's to say not one of 'em is a Dom spy? It would still be tough for the Grik to spy on us, but we have to stay tight-lipped about things here that somebody who gets deployed might blab to a Jap interrogator—or a Grik who understands English!"

Silva nodded. "No sweat, Mr. Sandison," he murmured back. "I won't blow. You workin' on anything that might interest me?"

Bernie hesitated, then shook his head. "No."

"Then I don't care what it is." Something caught his eye and he grinned.

Ensign Abel Cook and Midshipman Stuart Brassey appeared and hurried to join them as several paalka-drawn carts, heavily laden with fresh meat, took the opportunity to cross ahead of the stalled column.

"Good morning, Commander Sandison. Commander Rodriguez," Cook said in his vestigial, high-class British accent, and saluted. "Hiya, Dennis."

"Mornin', *Mr.* Cook," Silva replied, stressing Abel's new status. "Mr. Brassey!" Cook's freckle-tanned face reddened, and Brassey smiled uncertainly.

"'Ister Cook!" Lawrence tried to repeat, and saluted as well.

"Lawrence," Abel managed, then turned back to Bernie. "Ah, may we assist in some way, sir? We have no other duties, at least until we report back to Mr. Letts in the morning."

"Sure, kid . . . I mean, Mr. Cook," Bernie said, catching on to Silva's unexpected reminder that despite a degree of informality among them all that harked back even to their Asiatic Fleet days, distinctions between officers and enlisted men must always be maintained.

"Thank you, sir," Abel and Stuart chorused, stepping into the column that was now waiting for the meat carts to pass.

Dennis suddenly did a double take and then trotted over

to an old Lemurian, swatting a paalka clear of the pathway with a long, dried bamboo shoot. "I'll catch up, Mr. Sandison!" he called behind him. "I gotta talk to this guy a second."

"No screwin' around!"

"No, sir."

"Hey, Moe. What's up?" Silva asked the ancient 'Cat. Moe looked good for his age—whatever that was—and was still just as tough and sinewy as Dennis remembered. Now, in addition to the ragged kilt he usually wore to town, he also wore dingy rhino-pig armor with sergeant's stripes.

Moe looked up at him. "Si-vaa," he said. "Where you been? Lotsa huntin' to do."

"Oh, I been here and there." Silva answered. He waved at *Santa Catalina*. "Heard you went on a little jaunt yourself."

"Damn weird place," Moe nodded. "Weird critters too. Glad I back here."

Silva gestured at the heaps of meat on the carts. "I see you ain't run outta pigs. They gettin' harder to find?"

"No. We kill all we want. They make more." He shook his head.

"Look. They're sendin' me and Larry and the kids over there—you remember them—up the river, north, into Injun Jungle Lizard territory. We're s'posed to say howdy to 'em. You wanna go?"

"No," Moe answered truthfully, but then twitched his ears at his stripes. "But I Army scout now. They *make* me go, an' I been helpin' plan the trip." He shrugged like he'd learned to do and gazed northward. "We go up there, we gonna die, I betcha." He grinned. "But I old. Gonna die soon, anyway!" He laughed at Silva and swatted the paalka again. "See you around, Si-vaa!"

A grandstand had been erected near the water overlooking the old seaplane ramp, and it was packed to overflowing. Nearby buildings were covered with 'Cats and women as far away as the Screw in one direction and the main dry dock in the other. Sailors and yard workers lined the rails of the completing ships, and others skylarked in the masts and rigging. Below the grandstand, beside the ramp, with deep water in front of it, was *Walker*'s refurbished number-one torpedo mount. Some distance to the rear of the triple-tube mount, resting securely fastened on cradle trucks exactly like the one Silva remembered from *Walker*, were three long, shiny cylinders with rounded noses in front, and four fins and two propellers at the back. Compressors and large accumulators for charging the air flasks were close at hand. Whatever the things were actually capable of, they sure *looked* like torpedoes to Dennis.

"Nice fishies, Mr. Sandison. Do they work?"

"God, I hope so," Bernie whispered, then raised his voice. "The torpedo division will assume their posts!"

Dennis was surprised to see Ronson join a crew beside one of the weapons.

"We're trying three kinds," Bernie explained. "Two are reverse-engineered Mk-14s like that wadded-up fish we carried around so long. The only difference is one's hot and the other's cold. You're probably thinking the ship's sailed on that one, but we're not talking the same ranges here—yet. If the cold fish can do the job for now, it'll save a lot of effort."

Dennis wasn't sure exactly which ship Bernie meant. He didn't much care about torpedoes and didn't trust them. He firmly believed you should never send a fish where you could send a bullet, and though nobody knew what kind of ships the Grik were working on, he hadn't seen anything on this world since *Amagi* that needed a torpedo. His attention was already focused on something else.

"The other one uses the same gyro, Obry gear, everything," Bernie continued, unaware he'd lost his audience. "But Ronson talked me into letting him try an electric motor and batteries in place of the air flask." He shook his head. "I think it'll work eventually, but I'm afraid our batteries just aren't there yet."

"The only thing I care about is if the damn things'll go off," Silva said absently but darkly.

"Yeah, they'll go off," Bernie assured him. "They're contact exploders all the way, no horsing around."

"Good," Silva said, still distracted.

About forty yards from the torpedo mount, on the old ramp itself, was *Walker*'s glisteningly restored number four,

four-inch-fifty gun. Mounted beside it, bolted to a similar concrete pedestal, was an almost exact replica of it, except the mount was taller and more reminiscent of the Japanese 4.7s they'd salvaged. Bernie had told Silva to expect it, but he hadn't had time to come down and see the thing. He'd been too busy familiarizing himself with the small arms. Now he knew he truly was looking at a dual-purpose four-inch-fifty!

"I'll be derned," he said. "Ain't that a pretty thing? What did you make her out of?"

"All our modern weapons are made of Jap steel, from *Amagi*." Bernie shrugged. "Not sure how good it is, but it's better than what we can make so far. Somebody calculated that we salvaged enough steel off her to make every single rifle and pistol used by everybody on both sides in the Great War. I find that hard to believe, but there's a lot—and we can use local iron in projectiles and nonordnance applications. We are making some steel of our own now, like I said, and we're doing it by the book—but there's no way to know if it's really worth a damn, since Laney's the closest thing we've got to a metallurgist. He worked in a steel mill for a while before he joined the Navy."

"Got fired, I bet," Silva quipped.

Bernie shrugged. "Probably. I wish Elden hadn't got himself killed. He really knew stuff." He brightened. "Spanky does too, but until he gets back, Laney's the expert. We've had to do a lot of guessing and experimenting with heat treating and stuff."

"I know heat treating—on small parts an' springs an' such," Silva said, and Bernie glowered.

"All the more reason why . . ." He stopped and sighed. Silva had long ago taught what he knew about making springs and case hardening. That knowledge was widespread now. Silva knew nothing about making steel for heavy ordnance. "Well, for now, the new breechloading guns like that one will still use the black-powder shells we've been making, to keep pressures down. They're basically wrought iron—or wrought Jap steel."

"It *is* a four-inch-fifty? Why didn't you standardize on the four-point-seven? We've actually got more of those scattered around, and I guess you could eventually convert the four-inch-fifties."

"We thought of that," Bernie admitted. "We've got salvaged Jap gun directors and everything, but production on 'our' shells was already so far along and performance being so close, we figured it would be easier to line the four-point-sevens when the time came. You got us on this lining kick with your Allin-Silvas, and it made sense."

"Sure," Silva nodded. "And you can *reline* 'em when the bores are shot out."

"You got it."

The rumble of the crowd softened when Adar, High Chief and Sky Priest of Baalkpan and Chairman of the Grand Alliance, stood from his seat at the center of the bleachers. Near silence was achieved when he raised his arms. As always, he still wore his old "sky-priest suit" as the humans called it. It was deep purple with a scattering of embroidered silver stars across the shoulders and hood, which today was thrown back, revealing his gray fur that glistened like silver in the morning sun. Beside him, Alan Letts stood as well, his whites almost painful to look at. Other high-ranking members of the Alliance flanked them, and also stood as a group.

"Who's the skinny guy there by Mr. Letts?" Silva asked. "In the officer suit."

"New guy," Bernie replied. "Name's Herring. *Commander* Herring, he made a point of rubbing in at first. He came in from Manila with a couple China Marines, an Aussie, and some Dutchman Colonel Mallory grabbed up. They were off *Mizuki Maru*, poor devils. That one was ONI, and Letts tapped him for the same job around here, once he decided he was on the level."

"Our very own snoop brain, huh?"

"Looks like."

"A fella like that might come in handy," Silva probed.

"He might," Bernie answered, noncommittally. "I've only talked to him a few times. Kind of an odd, Ivy League sort. The first time I saw him, he was poking around the powder-blending tower, asking a bunch of screwy questions, and he hadn't even joined up yet!"

"What about the Grumpys? They goin' to Alden?"

"The Marines?" Bernie asked, rightly suspecting another one of Silva's odd, often unexplainable nicknames. "I snatched one of them, a corporal, for Ordnance. He's kind of a snot—like a Marine version of Laney—but he earns his keep. I think Letts is sending the other one, a gunny named Horn, with you." Bernie looked around. "He might be around here somewhere, or maybe he's at the drill field."

"Gunny Horn," Silva said, brows knitting. "*Arnie* Horn? Big guy, black hair?"

"I don't remember his first name, but that sounds like him. I swear, Silva! Did you know *everybody* on the China Station?"

"Most everybody that'd been there a while," Dennis replied, reflecting.

"Well . . . if he's who you think he is, is he a problem?"

"No. Shouldn't be. Arnie's a right guy. I just figgered he croaked—and I owe him one."

"One what?"

"Oh, nothin', sir."

Adar began to speak and his voice carried in that strange, Lemurian way. "We are gathered here, at the first Torpedo Day celebration, to behold the latest wonders wrought by our fine technicians to smite the evil foes of peace and freedom! Even as those foes grow in numbers, so does our capacity to slay them!" A thunderous cheer ensued that was quieted only when Adar raised his arms again. "Today we will view the performance of new weapons that the forces of the evil Dominion or even the Ancient Grik Enemy cannot possibly be prepared to face, and some of them are already in the hands of our precious troops, or en route to them. Their force will be felt!"

Another great cheer built and slowly died away.

"Yet we will also see the future! Experimental weapons that are not yet ready for battle, but soon will be! Bear in mind that as the day progresses, you may see some few contrivances that do not perform as hoped. Do not be disheartened by such setbacks or scorn those who suffer them, but honor the effort and remember: the greatest triumphs are built on the adversities encountered and defeated beforehand!"

There was some laughter mixed with the cheering this time, and Bernie's face turned red. "All right, Silva. You're almost up. Get ready. I've got to oversee the final preparation on my 'fishies.'"

"You bet, Mr. Sandison."

At that moment, two loudspeakers Dennis hadn't noticed before suddenly squealed raucously, like maddened rhino pigs, until the piano prelude to "Beat Me Daddy, Eight to the Bar" defeated the feedback and delighted the assembly, many of whom tried to sing along with the harmonizing Andrews Sisters. The recording was rough; it was a big favorite at the Screw and had nearly been played to death. New phonographs had been built, copies of Marvaney's original, but the ability to broadcast was new. He looked at Ronson.

"Yeah," the former electrician's mate said. "And we've got real radios now too, even if they're big as a steamer trunk. And our tubes are the size of cantaloupes! We're shrinking everything as fast as we can, and pretty soon we'll have VHF radio-telephone—TBS sets—for every ship in the Navy! A dozen sets should be arriving at First Fleet any day. Mr. Riggs based them on our old HT-Four on *Walker*. The good thing is, we can actually *use* them since they're short-range, line of sight only. Not likely to be picked up by anything the enemy might have." He looked around conspiratorially. "We're working on Huff-Duff too, so our planes'll be able to find their carriers or airstrips if they get lost, and also detect enemy transmissions!"

Silva blinked. "That's swell, Ronson. Sounds like you sparky guys have been busy as a buncha little bees!" He grinned and shuffle-danced away, in time with the music, toward the carts. There he met Risa, already sorting through the weapons.

"Hi, doll," he said. "Wanna dance?" Risa spared him a grin as she selected one of the new Baalkpan Arsenal Allin-Silva "conversion" muskets and a cartridge box. This specimen, like all the new rifles they were issuing, had been built as a breechloader. Conversion kits consisting of new barrels with breechblocks already attached and altered hammers were being sent out as quickly as possible for installation in the field. The old barrels were to be returned for conversion by lining the barrels and installing the breechblock.

Silva chose one of the muzzle-loading rifled muskets and a cartridge box, just like those still in the hands of all the home troops, and many of those deployed elsewhere. With the vast scope of the war, it would take time to equip everyone with the new rifles, and most of the troops with Second Fleet in the east still had smoothbores. At a glance, all the weapons looked identical, but Risa's had a trapdoor at the breech into which fixed, metallic cartridges could be inserted.

"Wanna race?" she challenged.

"What do I get if I win?"

Risa's grin faded, and she blinked regret. "You can't win, Dennis. Everything is different now."

"Yeah."

The music ended, and a Lemurian with a speaking trumpet that magnified his already powerful voice explained to the spectators that they would now compare the accuracy and rate of fire of the old rifles against the new. Floating targets had been placed in the bay at one hundred, two hundred, and three hundred tails, and other targets dotted the seascape at intervals that reached beyond easy view. Silva and Risa were both well-known warriors of extraordinary skill, he continued, but skill alone, and certainly size (Silva made two of Risa) would make little difference when all Allied troops were armed with the wondrous new weapons.

Everyone knew the Allin-Silvas weren't Springfields or even Krags, but they also knew they were a big step in the right direction. Enough of the troops in the crowd remembered when the Grik were defeated with virtually no firearms other than crude cannon. And the new rifles might not be repeaters, but the big fifty-caliber bullet on eighty grains of powder had been proven even deadlier against large beasts than the .30-06 Springfields and .30-40 Krags. The lower-velocity and much heavier bullets of the .50-80 afforded them better penetration against the dangerous animals in the vicinity—and they inflicted gruesome, charge-stopping wounds on Grik. That was more important than flat trajectories to people accustomed to fighting berserk enemies at close range.

At the sound of a whistle, the competitors commenced firing. Silva was good with the muzzle loader, no question about it. Each shot he fired rang off the iron gong and caused the float to bob. But it was very quickly apparent that he was outclassed. Risa also hit every target, the butt slamming against her muscular shoulder with each booming crack, but she'd already moved to the second target by the time Silva loaded his second shot! She finished with all her targets before he fired his last shot at the first. Without a word, she handed him her rifle. He flipped the rear sight up and shot at a target bobbing in the bay about five hundred tails away. He operated the weapon almost mechanically, recocking the hammer, flipping the breechblock open and ejecting the empty, smoking cartridge. Inserting a new one, he closed the breech, raised the rifle, and fired again. Even offhand, he hit the distant, swaying gong four out of five times.

The crowd cheered and stomped enthusiastically at the demonstration. The superiority of the new weapon was clear, and by exchanging rifles, Silva and Risa showed just how little adjustment the troops would have to make. Ostentatiously, and to instill the conscientious need to do so, the pair then gathered their empty brass off the ground and the speaker explained that it could be washed and loaded again.

They next selected two more weapons off the cart. The first was Silva's heavy Thompson. He inserted a twenty-round magazine, racked the bolt back, and fired at the first of several barrels floating about forty tails offshore. A cloud of white smoke erupted around him, since these were some of the shells loaded with black powder. He stitched the barrel, but many of his later shots went wild as the smoke obscured his aim.

"Suckers kick a little," he muttered ruefully as he squirted gri-kakka oil in the action around the bolt and inserted a magazine loaded with their dwindling Rock Island ball. "Raises the muzzle more than I'm used to." He stitched the barrel again with the old world military ammo. This time, he kept all the rounds on target and left the barrel sinking amid a swarm of splinters. After the appreciative applause, the talker announced that he would now use ammunition made entirely—brass, bullet, powder and all—at the Baalkpan Arsenal!

Silva inserted the third magazine, the bolt already back, and aimed at another barrel. This string of twenty shots left the smoking-hot barrel at the same apparent velocity and even better accuracy. There was a little more smoke, but it was dark and probably came from the burning lube on the lead bullets. The bullets themselves may not have penetrated both sides of the barrel, but they shattered it even more thoroughly when they deformed on impact. Silva lowered the scalding weapon with a grin amid happy cheers.

"Yes, friends!" the talker said. "We have now matched the amazing, less-smoking ammunition the first Americans brought us here! But as wonderful as that is, there are few of the Thompson guns. How will that help the Alliance as a whole?" Risa stepped forward with an odd cylindrical device with a pistol grip, a thin wooden butt stock, and a skinny barrel with a tall front sight. She inserted a standard Thompson magazine into a rectangular well forward of the trigger-guard, and pulled back a large knob located on the side of the tubular receiver.

"Cap-i-taan Risa-Sab-At will now demonstrate the Baalkpan Arsenal Blitzer Bug!"

The "Blitzer Bug" was the simplest thing in the world; basically, a pipe with a barrel on one end that fired from a spring-loaded open bolt. Originally called the Bug Sprayer during development, because it kind of looked like one, Commander Brister had suggested that it would be most useful in a Kraut-like blitz assault, and the name just naturally evolved. It was fully automatic only, so far, and fired very fast as long as the trigger was depressed. To make it shoot only once or twice required serious practice. That was of little concern today, when the idea was to impress.

Risa clutched the weapon tight against her shoulder, holding the pistol grip and the magazine, and leaned forward as she aimed down the sights and squeezed the trigger. There was a long, raucous *buuuurp*! And the third barrel was blown apart. Risa grinned hugely and held the weapon up while the crowd erupted once more.

"How was it?" Silva asked, muttering in her ear.

"You were right. It's a handful," she replied, still grinning. "It took all my strength to keep it on target. I think it will be very wasteful of ammunition."

"Yeah, but maybe in the right hands, like these commandos Chackie's workin' up in Manila, they might shine."

"Could be."

The demonstrations continued, with Silva and Risa, then Abel, Stuart, and even Lawrence putting various pistols through their paces. Most of these were junk in Silva's view, or required too much potential machine time and handwork to make. A nice revolver based on the Single-Action Army Colt Russ Chapelle had discovered aboard *Santa Catalina*, and intended to give to the Skipper, was very accurate, but got out of time after two cylinders were fired. Silva thought it had potential, but the guts needed work. A copy of a Mauser "Broomhandle" in .45 ACP fired once, then locked up. Probably the best was a copy of Silva's beloved 1911 Colt. It was a pretty thing, he had to admit. The slide was color case hardened, and the frame was a kind of purplish blue. A few machining shortcuts had been taken, but it felt right in his hand. Firing quickly but carefully, he managed to empty three magazines on target before it started getting tight and failed to function. Abel and Lawrence both fired others like it until they too started having problems. Dennis figured the pistols might be *too* well made, in a sense, and needed more "slop."

During these exhibitions, Bernie, Ronson, and their strikers continued fooling around with the torpedoes. The small-arms demonstration at an end, Ben Mallory and a couple of his pilots wowed the crowd with modest stunts in the ever popular P-40s overhead, while Silva took charge of the four-inch-fifties. As acting gunnery officer, he merely designated the targets and gave the command, "Commence firing in local control!" After that, he appraised the quality of the gun's crews drill as much as the performance of the weapons. On the whole, he was pleased. The crews were young recruits who'd never seen combat, but they were well trained and confident.

Walker's old number four gun performed well with the

new shells, just as Bernie said it would. It had been tested quite a bit already, and the people of Baalkpan were used to its rushing crack and the associated pressure. Dennis frowned when he saw a couple of the shell casings had indeed cracked, but was satisfied, particularly by the much-improved explosive force of the new "common" shells and the glorious shocks of distant spume they threw up in the bay. The new gun did fine as well—at first—with the black-powder shells provided. Accuracy was good, and several of the farthest targets were destroyed before the left recoil cylinder split on a seam and the right fill plug blew out, both spewing oil all over the gun and its crew. The spectators laughed and cheered, but even then, Silva—who'd avoided a dowsing—wasn't disappointed. The gun worked and so did the mount. None of the elevating and training gear had failed. The new telescope sights made with Imperial lenses seemed as good as the old ones. A recoil cylinder was just a pipe. They could make better pipes. He gave the command to cease firing and secure, and over the rumble of the people nearby, he heard a new, different sound.

"What the hell's that?" he demanded as a tiny aircraft blew past overhead. It sounded like a giant mosquito, but even as little as he knew about airplanes, he noticed several things at once. The craft was an open-cockpit, single-seat monoplane with a smallish radial engine, and it had fixed landing gear—with wheels!

"People of Baalkpan and the Grand Alliance, the Air Corps presents the P-1 Mosquito Hawk!"

Dennis guffawed; he couldn't help it. "Skeeter Hawk my ass! That's a homemade, pint-sized 'Fleashooter!'"

"You're right," confirmed a female voice behind him in a flat, distant, tone. "That's Colonel Mallory's latest; a pursuit ship for the carriers. He says it's a scaled-down cross between a P-36 Hawk and a P-26 Peashooter."

"Pam!" Dennis said, turning to face the short, dark-haired woman.

"What? No 'sugar pie'? No 'honey dew'?" she asked sarcastically in her strong Brooklyn accent.

"No," Silva answered simply.

"I oughta hate your guts."

"Yep. Why don't you?"

Pam took a deep breath and let it out. Around them, all eyes were on the little plane as it swooped low over the shore and snap-rolled to the right, over the water. "'Cause I can't, that's all. You're a jerk, a turd, the worst asshole in the world, for not comin' back to me when you were supposed to—not even comin' to *see* me when you finally got here, but . . . did you know Sister Audry thinks you're some kinda Holy Warrior called to 'smite' our enemies?"

Dennis blinked. "Hell, no! Huh. Maybe that explains why she was so nice to me the other day. All my hee-roin' musta impressed her after all, back when we was marooned. She really thinks that?"

"Yeah . . . an' *I* don't know what to think anymore."

"*You* don't believe that stuff!"

Pam shook her head. "I told you I don't know what to believe," she snapped. "But maybe you did help out more where you were than you would have back here. At first I figured you just like the damn war too much to leave it, but she talked a little sense, and I guess it's not my place to judge whether you were 'called' by God or some goofy sense of duty."

"Hey, don't knock the war, doll," he said, trying to keep his tone light. "It's the only one we got."

"Damn you! Can't you ever be serious? About anything?"

Dennis looked around and saw that Risa, Abel, Stuart, and Lawrence had moved a short distance away, clearly leaving them to hash this out in relative peace while the crowd enjoyed the antics of the new plane.

"Bein' serious can get a fella in a lotta trouble," he admitted softly.

The small plane performed a barrel roll that caused the spectators to cry out, and Dennis pointed at it. "Colonel Mallory in that thing?"

"Probably. He's like you in that way. Always jumpin' in the fire when he doesn't have to."

"Somebody has to."

"But why does it always have to be guys I care about?" Pam flared, loud enough for Risa to hear, and she came to embrace her friend.

"Because you, like I, are drawn to the sort who care enough about you—and the cause we fight for—to do their duty as they see it, no matter what," Risa murmured.

Tears came then. "Are you tryin' to tell me this big dope stayed away because he *cares* for me?"

Risa looked at Dennis and blinked discomfort. "Of course he did, my sister. He cannot protect you here . . . and ultimately, neither can Col-nol Maal-ory."

"But I don't *want* protection!" Pam whispered into Risa's fur, then paused. "You know, that's what Sister Audry said too."

The new plane dove toward the bay, and with a grumbling stutter, bullet geysers erupted around yet another target barrel, and amid more thunderous acclaim, the odd little pursuit ship pulled up and raced back toward Kaufman Field. When Silva looked back to where Pam and Risa had been, they were gone.

"Dames are nuts," he muttered, "all of 'em." He moved toward the torpedo mount. "Hey, Mr. Sandison! What's with the Fleashooter? I thought we needed rubber before we got anything with wheels."

Bernie was adjusting the depth controls on the torpedoes with a ratchet, setting them to run at five feet. "We're starting to get a little rubber from Ceylon. We'll get more in India. Colonel Mallory began testing the 'Skeeters with leather tires, but when we were coming up with the recoil cylinders for the guns, he came by and had us make Oleo struts to take the shock on his gear."

"What did he use for guns?"

"Basically, Blitzer Bugs mounted in the wheel pants, with long magazines following the struts up and through the wings. All they need is light springs for the followers, since they're pushing the cartridges down. They work pretty good."

"Forty-five-ACP *airplane* guns?" Silva asked doubtfully.

Bernie sighed in exasperation. "Sure. What are they gonna shoot at? Creeping zeps and packs of Grik." He waved at the sky. "There aren't any Zeros up there, and the Flea—I mean, the Mosquito Hawk—can even outrun that damn Jap spotting plane if it ever shows up again. Besides, the principle of the Blitzer Bugs should work with bigger stuff, like thirty-ought six, when we get around to it." He rolled his eyes. "You'd've *known* all this if you'd been here, instead of running loose in the east! Now leave me alone. I've got 'fishy' stuff to do!" he added angrily. Silva stepped back and watched while the strikers started slathering lard all over the first torpedo, already poised at the rear of the left tube.

"I've been watching them," Abel offered at his side. "The first one is the 'cold' torpedo, and it utilizes only compressed air that operates a three-cylinder engine to turn the counter-rotating propellers. That is all very straightforward, but the complexity of the guidance system is most fascinating and impressive!"

"They ain't got a warhead on the end of that thing, do they?" Silva asked.

"No. It is a practice head, they called it."

"Good. Let's ease back a little, just the same. C'mon, Larry. It's been my experience that torpedoes are more dangerous to them around 'em than they are to who you're shootin' at!"

"I want to watch what they do," Lawrence objected.

"You can watch with us from back a ways. Like Mr. Sandison said, let's leave him be."

Small motor launches loaded with several observers each eased into the watery range at predetermined distances, while the crowd talker described the first weapon as a Mk-I cold-air torpedo and proudly described the complexity of the device. Bernie finally stepped back and ordered that it be pushed the rest of the way into the barrel of the tube. The gyro had been set for a simple, straight run. When the weapon was fully inserted to the spring-loaded stop, a striker removed the propeller lock and closed the circle door just like he'd done it a hundred times. Finally, he inserted a big brass cartridge into the firing chamber at the top rear of the tube, gently closed the little door, and stepped back to Bernie, presenting him with a lanyard attached to the hammer.

The torpedo had no warhead, but the air flasks were the first of their kind made on this world and were stoked beyond a thousand PSI. They'd tested them, of course, but Bernie didn't want anyone on the mount when the charge went off and all that air tried to dump into the complicated little engine under somewhat stressful acceleration. He didn't *think* anything bad would happen, but there were an awful lot of pieces to fly in all directions if it did.

"Ready!" he cried, stretching the lanyard and looking nervously at the suddenly silent grandstand. By prior arrangement, Adar stood and made a grand, throwing-away gesture.

The impulse charge detonated with a hollow, muffled *boomp!* and the slimy torpedo squirted from the tube with a high-pitched skirl of air, followed by a billowing cloud of white smoke. It *splapped* noisily into the water and vanished from sight, but a surge of bubbles rose to the surface in a gratifyingly straight line.

Bernie, Dennis, and nearly everyone near the mount raced to the water's edge to watch the bubbling wake. Deadly flasher fish and other finned . . . things . . . leaped into the air or churned away from the weapon's path. Swirling lizard birds took notice of the disturbance in the water and angled down, swooping and pacing the trail of rising air. The torpedo *was* going straight—but it was clearly also going disappointingly slow. It seemed to take forever to reach the first boat stationed two hundred tails offshore, and when they raised a little flag signifying its passage, Bernie looked at his watch.

"Eight, maybe ten lousy knots!" he ground out, barely heard over the happy cheering and shouts from the spectators.

"Least it's runnin' true," Dennis consoled, "and those 'Cats on the boats'll be able to tell us if its runnin' at about the right depth."

Bernie brightened. "Yeah. And I knew it would be slow compared to the hot air torp." He grinned tentatively. "I think it works!"

The second boat raised a flag at four hundred tails, and Bernie confirmed his initial speed estimate, but he was in a better mood by then. Finally, the eight-hundred-tail boat waved its flag but heaved out a net with a marker that indicated the torpedo had come to a floating, exhausted stop. The net would snare the wallowing weapon and mark its position. They wouldn't have used it if the propellers were still turning.

"Kind of pitiful," Bernie muttered aloud, "but it proves all the really complicated stuff works."

The second torpedo was prepared, with Ronson shadowing the strikers like an expectant mother. Externally, the "Mk-2" looked exactly the same, but the starting lever would complete a circuit instead of opening a valve. It was loaded and made ready just like its predecessor, but this time Ronson took the lanyard. At the same signal from Adar, the electric torpedo leaped into the bay, but there were no bubbles this time. The crowd cheered, then waited expectantly. Ronson snatched his binoculars to his eyes, staring at the first boat. But there was no flag.

"Maybe they just didn't see it," he said. "That's part of the point. It's supposed to be hard to see . . . and it should be faster than the first one. Maybe it went by before they were looking for it."

"Hey, Ronson," Silva said.

"What?"

"I see it."

"Where?!"

Dennis pushed the binoculars down, about the same time chittering laughter erupted in the stands.

"Oh, goddamn!" Ronson spat when he saw his torpedo floating on the surface about forty yards away, its slowly turning propellers pushing it directly back at them like a chastened dog.

"Better luck next time, Mr. Rodriguez!" Silva said with theatrical solemnity.

"I . . . I don't get it. It must've shorted out."

The launch of the third torpedo, the "Mk-3" was the last event of the day, and everyone knew it was supposed to be a somehow more advanced version of the first, so a lot was expected. All preparations were apparently the same as those previous, but as a "hot" torpedo, it was equipped with a fuel source—kerosene—that would send a jet of flame into the air flask as the resultant hot, expanding air and kerosene exhaust gushed into the motor. Theoretically, this would generate exponentially greater pressure, speed—and heat, of course. That was how it worked on the Mk-14 torpedo they'd copied in most ways except the engine. They were experimenting with turbines for the short-lived torpedoes, but like the batteries, they weren't there yet. After the directional and depth performance of the Mk-1, however, Bernie was emboldened to think the Mk-3 was "it," and with yet another signal from Adar, he confidently pulled the lanyard.

The tube *boomped* again and the fish lashed out into the water, leaving a far more energetic trail of steamy froth behind.

"'Ook at her go!" Lawrence cried excitedly. Compared to the first two, the Mk-3 was indeed going like a bat out of hell. Bernie was the first to notice that the wake looked a little . . . wobbly, though, and his fingers clenched his binoculars more tightly. Nearly to the first boat, the torpedo suddenly porpoised, almost leaping out of the water for an instant before diving under the boat and the erratically waving flag.

"Now!" a striker shouted.

"Maybe thirty knots!" Abel cried in response. He'd been looking at his watch and hadn't seen the surprising caper. At perhaps three hundred tails, the torpedo jumped again, significantly off track to the left, and this time it looked like a leaping fish, the sun glinting sharply off its polished body. It fell back in the water with an enormous splash and a crazy corkscrew of foam. Seconds later, a large, steamy bubble exploded on the surface close enough to rock the second boat and nearly toss several of the observers into the bay.

"Wow," Ronson gushed, and Bernie rounded on him.

"I'd say that one went hot, crooked, and abnormal as hell," Dennis quipped, "but between it and the first, it looks like you're circlin' the right tree, Mr. Sandison!"

Bernie spun to face Silva, enraged and embarrassed, but when he didn't see the mocking expression he'd expected, he took a breath.

"He's right," Ronson said, waving toward the standing, cheering spectators. "And everybody knows it but you! Sure, it's not perfect. Mine sure wasn't! But it *did* work . . . mostly. And you'll figure out what didn't." He grinned and pointed at the torpedo mount, smoke still hazing the third tube. "Just think: by the time the Skipper gets back with *Walker*, we can put that back on her—and stick fish in it too!"

CHAPTER 17

The Torpedo Day festivities at an end, all those in charge of the various divisions who'd participated joined Adar and most of the Allied high command at long banquet tables beneath a colorful pavilion rigged considerably back from the old seaplane ramp. The spectators dispersed rapidly as the usual afternoon showers threatened, and guards were posted to keep the curious from disturbing the planned debriefing discussion.

Silva and Lawrence sat near Bernie, but a little to themselves, with Silva suddenly unsure he was supposed to be there. The gathering had a kind of "no enlisted men allowed" air to it, which was very unusual in Baalkpan, but he'd simply followed Mr. Sandison, Ronson, and Abel Cook when they made their way over, and they didn't object. Lawrence had followed him and probably never noticed the odd atmosphere. Risa sat with a group of 'Cat Marine officers and other infantry types. Something was up, Dennis decided. Something besides the debrief, and he'd hang around until he found out what it was or somebody ran him off.

Adar, wearing a grin, stood near the head of the central table, and his body language displayed pleasure as he spoke briefly with Alan Letts, Steve Riggs, Bernie, Ronson, and a late-arriving Ben Mallory. But Silva knew Adar well enough to tell when the dignified Lemurian was distracted by weighty matters. He controlled his blinking well, but his tail betrayed a measure of agitation. Ben's appearance with a couple other guys Dennis didn't know—including an army sergeant in grease-darkened coveralls that made him more comfortable about being there—seemed to be the signal to begin. A few moments later, Alan stood beside Adar.

"Ladies and gentlemen," Alan began, nodding at a small group of ex-pat Impie women in Navy dress who were probably ensigns or lieutenants in his new logistics division. Sitting with them was Alan's wife, Karen, in her surgeon commander uniform. She didn't have her new daughter, Allison Verdia, with her, and Dennis realized he hadn't even seen the little scudder yet.

"We have a lot to go over, some good . . . and some not so much," Letts said, confirming Silva's suspicions. "We'll get right to it. First I want to say how pleased I am at the results of the day's testing, not only from a technical standpoint, but from the obvious good it did for the many spectators to see the results of their labor and sacrifice." He turned to Adar. "Mr. Chairman, would you like to speak to that point before we proceed?"

"Absolutely," Adar said. "I am told that not all the experiments resulted in absolute satisfaction for those who performed them, but with a few small exceptions, that was not abundantly clear to those watching. What *was* clear is that great progress has been made toward developing modern weapons of all types and principles that represent profound advances beyond what has already been achieved." He waved a hand. "If some few of those weapons still require further development, none consider them failures. I emphatically do not, and I bear no doubt they will soon be perfected." He looked directly at Bernie and smiled, blinking reassurance. "Your experimental ordnance division has made great strides, Mr. Saan-dison. I can scarcely believe it. You demonstrated new small arms, naval artillery, and three varieties of torpedoes today! All were successful, or at least succeeded magnificently in demonstrating what few defects remain to be resolved. You have my utmost appreciation and thanks, sir!"

Bernie stood. "Ah, thanks, Mr. Chairman. I appreciate it, and so will my division."

Adar turned to Ben Mallory. "Colonel, I am astounded. Not only are there now eighteen fully operational 'pee-forties' ready for combat in all respects, but you have a sufficient pool of experienced aviators and ground persons to operate and maintain them—wherever they might be employed."

Ben stood and looked around with a mixture of self-consciousness and lingering irritation. Dennis noted that Pam Cross was seated beside the airman, and wondered why his gut seemed to twist.

"Yes, sir. We've got eighteen Warhawks ready to go. The two we bent in training will soon be ready to fly again, one with those Jap floats"—he shook his head—"which gives us a P-Forty floatplane, of all things. The other thrashed its gear and prop, but we've got plenty of propeller blades. The gear was ruined, and instead of replacing it from salvage, we're reconfiguring it as a fixed-gear, two-seat trainer." He paused. "It's probably a miracle, but only three of the twenty-four ships we made airworthy have been totaled. One went down in the jungle north of the city—we still don't know why. Another ground looped and landed on its back. Mack's ship was the only one lost in combat—if you count stepping in a bomb crater when he came in for a landing as a combat loss. As you know, all three of those resulted in fatalities."

Adar nodded solemnly. "I mourn their loss as you do," he said. "They watch us now from the Heavens they so briefly touched in this life!" He gazed at the awning above for a moment amid the murmured agreement before looking back at Ben. "The new planes are very impressive," he said, changing the subject. Ben brightened.

"Yes, sir!" He grinned, justifiably proud. "I like 'em! They're not as versatile as 'Nancys'—they can't carry a bomb load to speak of even with the guns removed, and they can't land on the water—but as dedicated pursuit ships, they're swell! They'll be able to take off and land on a carrier or grass strip in a heartbeat. They're fast and maneuverable, and don't use much gas. Even with the current Blitzer Bugs, they can cut up a Grik zep and strafe the enemy on the ground. Mr. Sandison's working on more powerful weapons to hang on 'em and that'll make 'em even better.

They'll be good recon planes too, when we get some decent, lightweight, pilot-usable transmitters installed."

"Most impressive," Alan echoed dryly, "especially when somebody who probably shouldn't be risking his neck in such a way puts them through their paces."

Ben stiffened. "What's that supposed to mean? The Mosquito Hawks are as safe as we can make 'em. The air-cooled radial has almost nothing to go wrong with it, and pound for pound they're even stronger than 'Nancys.' Don't forget, I practically learned to fly in *our* Peashooters." He glanced around. "Uh, very similar planes from our world," he explained. "Anyway, I'm a lot more familiar with the design, and we've been testing 'em east of Baalkpan for the last two weeks." He looked back at Letts. "Besides, *nobody* flies anything *I'm* afraid to fly, so yeah, I've pushed 'em around a little!" He shrugged. "But not today. For your information, this morning's demonstration was performed by Lieutenant Conrad Diebel, formerly of the Dutch Air Corps, not me." He nodded at the blond man seated nearby. "I was sedately coasting around in one of the P-Forties!"

"Braa-vo, Lieutenant Diebel!" Adar said. "A most exciting display! I presume you are settling in well . . . after all?"

Diebel, wearing an aging but still yellow-violet shiner, stood. "Yes, Mr. Chairman," he said with somewhat rueful irony and a glance at the NCO in coveralls. "I have been . . . disabused of any misconceptions I may have harbored regarding the situation here. I am happy to serve."

"Excellent," Adar said happily. He looked back at Ben. "How many Mosquito Hawks are complete and how soon can we deploy them?"

"We've got six total, and four combat ready. The guys stood two of 'em on their nose, but nobody was hurt. They're really light and landing will take some getting used to, especially since most of the new pilots are out of 'Nancys.' All they've ever landed on is water. Based on performance, I took the liberty of pulling the trigger on production, so they should roll out pretty fast. We really need rubber, though, for tires. We get that"—he paused, considering—"we can have ten a week in two weeks, and twenty a week in a month."

"That's much faster than 'Naan-cee' production," Adar observed. "You do not mean to cut back on that, do you? As you say, 'Naan-cees' are versatile and popular with the Allied Homes—and we have promised many to the Imperials."

"We don't have to cut anything, sir, though I think we should concentrate more on the big 'Clippers' here in Baalkpan. With the Maa-ni-los making them too, we can't *crew* 'Nancys' as fast as we make them. 'Clippers' aren't B-Seventeens, but they're the closest thing to a long-range, heavy bomber we've got. Besides, we need them as transports, to move people around. As for the Mosquito Hawks, now that we've done the heavy lifting development-wise, they're less complicated in many ways than the others and require less than half the materials."

"Indeed?" Adar said, but his grin faded. "Mr. Letts, perhaps it is time to reveal the not-so-good subjects we must discuss, so we may determine what to do about them. Colonel Maallory's rubber is just one of many things at stake."

"Yes, sir," Alan agreed. He looked around the gathering, trying to meet as many eyes as he could, just as he'd seen Captain Reddy do so many times. "We've taken some hits," he admitted at last, "and, as usual, it seems like everything has hit the fan at once. I know it's impossible, but it's enough to make you wonder if all our enemies somehow coordinated it. You all know about *Mizuki Maru* by now, and the threat *Hidoiame* represents? Well, the Skipper and *Walker* will try to deal with her on their way back here." He grimaced. "I wish the Skipper was already here and the hell with the Jap, but right now *Hidoiame*'s like a fox in the henhouse—ah, like a skuggik in the akka aviary. She's got to be stopped." He took a breath. "What you don't know, because we've kept a lid on it until now, is that not only has the First Fleet Expeditionary force slammed into a brick wall in India, but we've got reason to believe things are about to get a lot worse in the west. The Grik are on the move on land and sea. They've finally brought their new fleet up, and Keje says it's a doozy. We have to move everything we can up to Andaman—planes, ships, ordnance, supplies, the works—and we've got to make it snappy. No holding back."

He looked at Adar. "What makes this a little awkward at this particular time are two other things that just came in. The elements of Second Fleet have rendezvoused, and Commodore Jenks has assumed overall command in the east, but reconnaissance confirms that the Doms have occupied at least a part of the Enchanted Isles. It looks like some of the Brit garrison is still holding out, but its relief has taken on even greater urgency, and the situation has become considerably more complicated and potentially more costly. Add to that, we just learned that an attempt has been made on the lives of the New Britain Imperial family, as part of an apparent coup."

Nearly everyone cried out and stood at that announcement. Despite an almost universal attachment to Princess "Becky," all knew how disastrous it could be if the Empire suddenly dropped out of the war. Not because it had large forces in the west yet, but because nearly a third of the Allied fleet and personnel relied on the Empire for logistical support and transport of supplies. Besides, though perhaps not an immediate threat to the western allies, the Doms were a terrible enemy.

Alan held up his hands. "The princess is safe!" he assured everyone, "and in the care of loyal forces, including our own. Mr. Bradford is also safe and, as you know, has considerable influence with her. He should be able to help her cope with the current emergency. Unfortunately, we don't know yet if her mother and Governor-Emperor McDonald survived the attempt. They were attending a session of the Court of Directors when some kind of big-assed bomb went off. The wireless station on New Britain went down at about the same time and most communications are currently via a very confused and busy station on New Scotland. Some traffic is getting through to our ships there, repeated by the new Midway station."

The great Lemurian Home *Salaama-Na*, commanded by "reserve" Admiral and High Chief Sor-Lomaak, had been tasked to establish a wireless and fueling station on "Wake" Island, but when it was found to be even smaller than its "other world" counterpart and entirely without water, Sor-Lomaak proceeded to discover that Midway was bigger than expected and did have water, which was necessary for the establishment of any long-term, secluded outpost.

"Nobody, even Mr. Bradford, knows exactly what's going on," Letts continued. "Needless to say, rescue efforts are underway, but few survivors have been discovered so far."

It took a moment for the shouted questions and roars of outrage to subside, but eventually, Alan continued. "Clearly, we must lend whatever support we can to the princess and we will, but with the situation in the west heating up, our resources are limited. In response to these various emergencies, Chairman Adar and I have asked Commander Herring to assess the situation in his capacity as the new Chief of Strategic Intelligence." He gestured at a thin man still seated to his left. "Commander Herring, if you please?"

Herring stood. He was tall and still gaunt, but his expression was determined. "Most of you don't know me yet," he began. "But after acquainting myself with the situation here and abroad as best I can, I have wholeheartedly embraced the Alliance and its cause. I am honored by the trust that has been invested in me, and I plan to do everything in my power to perform the duties asked of me. In my capacity as CSI, I have proposed a list of things I believe we must and can do immediately, along with other actions I consider crucial to prepare and that, I frankly believe, have been neglected." He paused, frowning in the surprised silence.

"Let me say now that you have all accomplished amazing things before I ever arrived. I recognize and stipulate that, so please don't take anything I say as criticism. The actions I must propose to counter not only the immediate crisis, but also to lay the groundwork for long-term operations are the result of independent and, hopefully, objective study. No one here has ever been trained for strategic thinking, and you have done well within the limits imposed on you. But I believe some rather fundamental changes must be made regarding the future prosecution of the war."

"Sorta puffed up, ain't he?" Silva whispered aside to Lawrence.

Herring continued. "In the short term, as Mr. Letts has said, the most pressing emergency is in the west, and all available assets must be sent to salvage that situation. Hopefully, the circumstances in the Empire will stabilize, but there is nothing we can do here to influence that at present, beyond assurances of support. Even Saan-Kakja is too distant to render immediate material aid—if, indeed, it is required. Consequently, Second Fleet must make do with what it currently has, or what is already in the pipeline for the foreseeable future. Likewise, Captain Reddy is essentially out of the picture for now." He smiled, a little smugly, Silva thought.

"We will, of course, continue to value any . . . suggestions he might make regarding the disposition of our forces, but we are on the spot and must ultimately decide those dispositions for ourselves."

Letts calmed the angry murmurs that arose over that. Captain Reddy was still Supreme Allied Commander, by acclamation, and Silva wasn't the only one who'd noticed the new CSI's tone—and no one had "acclaimed" Herring.

"Hear him out," Letts said. "He's right. The Skipper isn't here, and he *wants* us to think for ourselves!"

Herring nodded at him and continued. "We find ourselves in this current predicament as a result of shortsighted thinking and an acute lack of intelligence regarding not only the strength and disposition of the enemy, nor do we have even the most remote understanding of the situation beyond the world we know. These deficiencies must be remedied. We must push harder to obtain land, aerial, and even seaborne reconnaissance. I know this will be dangerous for those involved for many reasons, but that danger must be balanced against the even greater danger now faced by the Alliance due to less . . . diligent attention to this necessity in the past." There was more uncomfortable murmuring, but Herring pressed on.

"I understand an expedition to meet and treat with . . . certain natives on this island has been planned, and I agree it must go forward without delay. Not only will we learn more about what is out there than has ever been known, but we might even secure more valuable allies with a unique grasp of Grik psychology, not to mention field craft!

"In addition, I recommend that another major expedition be commissioned to explore the world *beyond* the Grik and attempt to measure not only the true extent of their influence, but also discover what possible threats lie past their domain. For this I propose the use of the frigate *Donaghey*, now refitting at Andaman. Her captain, Commander Garrett, has demonstrated uncommon courage and adaptability and the ship itself, as with all dedicated sailing vessels, is not nearly as dependent upon supply—and honestly, offers limited further utility in the combat operations either planned or underway. Commander Garret should take her, and perhaps at least one of the razeed Grik corvettes, or DEs, as her consort and supply ship."

"You're saying Garrett and his crew are expendable?" Ben demanded sharply.

"I'm saying all of us are, in the grand scheme of things. With that in mind, however, and in light of the recent dreadful losses of men possessing . . . special knowledge, I think it's time that such men, and even Lemurians they have trained, be interviewed extensively and as much of their knowledge be collected and recorded as possible before it is lost forever." He looked at Adar. "I know a major effort has long been implemented to copy and distribute the many technical manuals and indeed every book that has survived. But we must go beyond that to capture the *experience* of men who know how to do the things described in the texts."

"Okay," Ben said, still standing, "maybe that even makes some sense. Why don't we encourage everybody to write journals or something?" He paused. "But what do you want to do right now?"

"We must immediately reinforce First Fleet with all air and sea assets at our disposal. As I hear so often, we know nothing of the fleet the Grik and their Japanese allies have constructed. The Alliance has made great strides since last the two forces met. We must presume the enemy has done the same." He looked at Alan. "I suggest considerable thought be given toward how to counter naval forces even more powerful than our own."

"As you may have noticed today, we've *already* given that a lot of thought," Letts said a little stiffly. "And Lieutenant Monk says *Santa Catalina* is about ready for sea." Alan personally believed the newly "protected cruiser" could stand up to anything the Grik could dish out. Besides, Herring's manner was finally starting to rub him a little raw as well.

"Of course."

"So," Ben asked, "by 'all assets,' do you mean all my modern birds too?"

"That is what I recommend. You demonstrated today that the new domestically produced aircraft should soon be sufficient to defend the city from any further air raids. I consider those unlikely at present, based on . . . what little real intelligence we have received from the west. In addition, Mr. Letts assures me that small cargos of rubber are on their way as we speak. They should be sufficient to finish a large number of . . . Mosquito Hawks."

Ben looked at Alan and Adar. "If all my P-Forties are going, I'm going too," he stated forcefully.

Alan shrugged, expression troubled. "I'll update the movement order and start the wheels rolling to increase the planned support."

Silva eased over and whispered in Bernie's ear. "Sounds like the whole damn war's headin' west for now. Any chance I can slip outta my little campin' trip?"

Bernie shook his head. "If I have to stay here, you still have to follow your orders too. The *Skipper's* orders."

"Okay," Dennis agreed, nodding at Herring. "But you keep an eye on that guy. Mr. Letts stood up to him, but I think he's a little brass-blind, if you know what I mean. I ain't famous for my noodle, but I've seen a ambitious politician or two on the stump and in the Navy both."

CHAPTER 18

Eastern reaches of the Fil-pin Sea
Three days out of Respite
March 16, 1944

The honeymoon was over—in every respect. USS *Walker*, DD-163, was steaming at twenty-five knots on all three remaining boilers beneath puffy clouds and a dazzling sun. The sea was mild and there would be little breeze if not for the ship's speed, which kept the temperature bearable, at least above deck. Tabby had reported that it was nearing 130 degrees in the firerooms, and Matt had no idea how the furry cats could stand it. They took frequent breaks, drank a lot of water, and shed a lot, of course. Spanky's allergies wouldn't even allow him to go down there right now.

Matt sat in his chair, trying not to brood. His time with Sandra had been amazing, and his heart still quickened at the thought of her. He hadn't believed it was possible to feel such joy, even now while he tried to hide it, and his memories of the time they'd had were still glowing fresh. But then upon returning to the ship, he'd finally been briefed on all he'd missed. The crew, his officers, *his friends* had all conspired to keep him ignorant of the various developments; the battles in India, the situation in the east, even the attacks on Princess Rebecca and her family. It was still unknown if

Rebecca was an orphan or not. A few survivors had been found in the rubble of the directors' building, but hope was beginning to wane. And all that time, while all those momentous events were unfolding, he'd remained blissfully unaware.

He'd actually ranted when he heard. He felt guilty that he'd been so happy while everything everywhere seemed to be falling apart, and he took it out on Spanky and the Bosun more than anyone. They'd been most responsible for keeping him informed, and they'd consciously decided not to. He trusted the people on the scene, but he was profoundly frustrated that he and his ship were so remote from everything that had occurred, thousands of miles from anywhere they could have been of assistance to anyone. That was bad enough. But by keeping him incommunicado, he hadn't been involved at all! Spanky had assured him that if anything had come up that really needed his input or permission, he would have been told, but that didn't make him feel any better—or better inclined toward the conspirators.

Spanky had been somewhat contrite but defiant that he'd done the right thing. Matt had needed a real "liberty" more than anyone on the ship, he'd argued, particularly under the circumstances. And what could he, or any of them, have really done? *Walker* couldn't go anywhere until her stopgap repairs were complete. She damn sure couldn't tangle with *Hidoiame* until then! She needed the rest at least as much as her skipper. Even now, neither, in his view, was in top shape. *Walker* still needed a real yard and a dry dock. The snipes were back to using "baling wire and gum" to keep her at twenty-five knots!

Chief Gray had listened to the harangue in silence, then finally shrugged.

"So, bust me back to third class," he'd growled defiantly. "Wouldn't be the first time, and maybe I'd have more to do. Boats Bashear's shaping into a good chief bosun, and mostly I just twiddle my thumbs."

Matt rounded on him then and promptly made him the assistant damage control officer. Damage control was the first officer's job, but in addition to his other duties, Norm was so busy teaching navigation to the 'Cat QMs (and anyone else who cared to sit in on the arguably heretical—to some—sessions), that he'd been stretched by teaching and running the essential damage-control drills. If anybody knew every aspect of damage control, Chief Gray did.

Matt felt a little better now, sitting in his chair and sipping Juan's monkey joe, but he couldn't help brooding over the fact that he—and *Walker*—were vast, unsympathetic *oceans* away from anywhere he *wished* they were. The one consolation was that *Walker* was finally racing inexorably closer to one place she *needed* to be, however. Nancys from PatWing 7, newly stationed at Yokohama, had confirmed both *Hidoiame* and her tanker were on the move at last, apparently searching for a new nest, as they'd predicted. They'd been seen by the light of last night's moon and their wildly phosphorescent wakes, steaming at about eight knots south-southwest toward the Korea Strait. Phosphorescent wakes, caused by blooming plankton and other tiny creatures, were not new to Matt's human destroyermen, even if the brilliantly vivid and varying colors on this world were. Lemurians were familiar with the occasional and somewhat regional phenomenon as well, but they'd only recently seen the intensity evoked by the higher speeds and churning screws of modern ships, particularly from the air. The wakes made the enemy easy to spot, and the diminishing, miles-long trails led almost magically to the ships that left them. Such a small, unexpected bonus now gave Matt a huge advantage over *Hidoiame*, at least at night, and he hoped the enemy hadn't recognized it.

He suspected that the murderers would avoid the Fil-pin Lands, knowing by now they had enemies there. That left a possible run across the Yellow Sea, maybe to Tsingtao or somewhere in that vicinity, but Matt doubted it. A run down the coast of China would put them briefly closer to the Fil-pin Lands, but ultimately beyond what they must think was the center of activity for these new enemies of theirs. They couldn't have any idea of the true scope of the Alliance . . . could they?

Hidoiame's tanker was the key. If she limited the Japanese destroyer to eight knots, Matt could drive *Walker* at her best possible, groaning speed, and refuel at Chinakru's Samaar, where he also expected Saan-Kakja to have another Nancy available for him. With his own scout plane, and those provided by the patrol wings on Formosa and in the Fil-pin-Lands, he hoped to catch *Hidoiame* in the vicinity of the Formosa Strait.

"Permission to come on the bridge?" came a very welcome voice behind him. Sandra had never asked permission before, but things were . . . different now.

"Um, sure," said Chief Quartermaster Patrick "Paddy" Rosen, with a quick glance at Captain Reddy. He had the deck and the conn. "I mean, permission granted." The redheaded kid had been S-19's quartermaster and had assumed the chief's spot on *Walker* when Norm became first lieutenant. He was a good navigator, and nearly as good a teacher as Norm.

Matt turned and smiled. Sandra couldn't help but brighten his mood. He raised an eyebrow when he saw Diania had followed her on the bridge and was walking as carefully and fearfully as if there were molten lava between the wooden strakes beneath her feet. The girl was listed as a carpenter's mate, but she was still more Sandra's stewardess than anything. She was learning to fight too. Chack had taught her a lot before he left the ship, and Stites and, increasingly, Gray were teaching her how to shoot. To Matt's amazement, Gray had already suggested that Diania be included in the Captain's Guard, so she could learn the ropes and be prepared to serve in an equivalent capacity for "Mrs. Minister" Sandra Reddy, or "Lady Sandra," as the Imperials called her. Even among Matt's human destroyermen, that title seemed to be gaining steam. He shook his head.

"Sandra," he said. "Miss Diania. Welcome to the bridge. Sandra, you'll retain all the privileges you enjoyed . . . previously," he assured her, "and are always welcome on the bridge except when you're at your battle station. Miss Diania, you may accompany her. You"—he sighed—"may eventually even find yourself on the bridge-watch bill. In the meantime, you're welcome to look around, but please don't touch anything or distract anyone." Matt knew the last warning would be tough for her to avoid. She was a beauty, and Paddy couldn't seem to keep his eyes off her.

"What have you got there, Captain?" Sandra asked, gesturing at the clipboard in his hand.

"Well, the watch bill, for one thing." He flipped the page. "This is another message from Baalkpan, via Maa-ni-la." He scanned down it. "There's some good news on top of the bad. Adar's Torpedo Day bash went off pretty well. Ben didn't crash any of his new pursuit planes into anything, and most of the small arms seemed to work okay. The torpedoes still need work, but they *did* work. Sort of." He grinned. "On that note, *Mahan* still has two salvageable torpedo mounts, and she may even get four eventually. Lots of work still to do on her." He raised his eyebrows and blinked. "I still can't believe they raised the old girl, and we might get her back. She won't look the same, they say, but that doesn't matter as long as she's back in the war!" He chuckled. "Speaking of not looking the same, Irvin's finally settled on what to do with S-Nineteen. He means to keep her gun and bow tubes but gut everything else that makes her a sub. The conversion will take a while, but the increase in buoyancy and freeboard, as well as the extreme decrease in weight, should make her a lot quicker on her feet. No telling how she'll handle—she's liable to roll her guts out—but she ought to be at least as good a torpedo boat as anything we had in the Great War, with a lot longer legs."

"It sounds like *Mahan* and S-Nineteen are counting an awful lot on Bernie's torpedoes," Sandra observed.

"Yeah, but Bernie'll come through," Matt agreed with certainty. Then he frowned. "I'm still not sure what to think of this Herring guy. I agreed with Alan and Adar that it was high time we had some snoops, and we need somebody who knows how to gather and compile intelligence on our enemies." He shrugged. "Lord knows we haven't done a good job at that. We probably already have a lot more information than we know what to do with, or how to apply. We need somebody to analyze it all." He grunted. "He's even already come up with some pretty good ideas. Sending Greg Garrett off exploring in *Donaghey* is brilliant, and I should have thought of that. Apparently even the Grik are starting to go to steam—I don't like the sound of those big ships of theirs!—and *Donaghey*'s days in a battle line are probably done. On the other hand, even though Greg's the perfect choice to lead the expedition, he's too damn good to lose! That kid ought to be an admiral!"

"I know you're close to Greg," Sandra began.

"I'm close to *all* my people," Matt said sternly.

"Of course. But you *are* a little closer to him."

Matt sighed. "Maybe so. He reminds me a little of myself at his age, I guess—not that I'd accomplished nearly as much as he has by then! I just . . . It's an awful big world out there, and we still don't know what might be over the very next hill!"

Sandra looked at him. "Tell me the truth. If you were in his position and got an assignment like his, how would you feel?"

"Ha! Thrilled, I guess."

"There you are. Now, what else about this Commander Herring bothers you?"

"I don't know. I haven't met him, and that's part of it, I guess. Also, if you read Alan between the lines, I get the feeling he thinks Herring already has too much influence with Adar. Even that wouldn't bother me too much if Saan-Kakja hadn't tacked on that she doesn't trust the 'arrogant and rude' Mr. Herring when they retransmitted from Maa-ni-la."

Sandra chuckled. "For us *and* Adar to receive! I do dearly love Saan-Kakja, though you may have created a monster when you helped break her out of her shell!"

"She and Princess Rebecca are two of a kind, only one doesn't have a tail!" Matt agreed. "About the same age, fearless, honest, and very quick to anger . . ." He paused. "God, I hope Governor-Emperor McDonald and his wife, Ruth, are all right! I think Courtney, Sean, and our forces in the New Britain Isles will help keep things together if . . . they're not. But if Princess Rebecca winds up on top, a lot of heads will roll, and she may not be too particular whose they are!"

"Courtney won't let *her* become a monster," Sandra said with conviction. "And don't forget: something else Saan-Kakja and Princess Rebecca have in common is their devotion to *you*."

Matt shifted uncomfortably. "Well, the point is," he said,

skipping Sandra's observation, "that Saan-Kakja thinks Herring's a jerk. Alan doesn't come right out and say it, but he does too." He rubbed his nose, broken in the Battle of Baalkpan. "You know, we've always gotten along with the 'Cats, right from the start. Sure, we had differences—still do—but nothing we weren't both willing to try to overcome. We're more like them now, and they're more like us—but we had a lot in common to start with . . . and it makes me wonder."

"What?"

"Well, we both saw it before the war back home. There were a lot of different navies within the United States Navy that didn't even think the same way. The rivalry, the different *cultures*, of the deck apes and snipes are just the tiniest example. Destroyermen might almost be a different species from submariners, and the battleship boys are something else." He rolled his eyes. "Then you've got the tenders and oilers! It . . . was like different tribes! To make it even more confusing, crews attached to the different fleets for a while were different too. I had to make some big adjustments when I came from the Pacific Fleet to the Asiatic Fleet, and it took me a while. The Pacific Fleet was always more spit and polish, with newer ships and better gear." He shrugged. "Maybe it was even more professional in some ways, but the guys in the Asiatic Fleet did what they could with what they had, and the Philippines felt more like home than home did, to some. They were more laid-back, more tolerant, I guess, and more used to people who didn't look and act like 'us.' I've always believed that's why we hit it off so well with the 'Cats, and I'm not so sure a ship from the Pacific Fleet, even another destroyer, would've had it so easy"—he snorted—"in that respect, at least."

"I think I understand where you're headed," Sandra said thoughtfully. "Herring's not Asiatic Fleet. He's not even a fleet officer. On top of that, he's very recently suffered terrible mistreatment from the Japanese—people who are 'different.' Do you think that's why he rubbed Saan-Kakja the wrong way? Just his attitude?"

"I hope so. Like Letts said, Adar seems to trust him, and Adar's a good judge of character, I think. . . ."

"But?"

"But," Matt agreed, "he's also—understandably—obsessed with exterminating the Grik, and with things heating up in the west, he might lose some of his objectivity." Matt shook his head as if to clear it. "I trust Adar's judgment," he repeated, "but I also trust Saan-Kakja's instincts. She's been stampeded before and knows what it feels like." He smiled at his wife. "I guess we'll see when we get there."

"Cap-i-taan," Minnie said behind them. "Lookout says 'pleezy-sores bearing seero tree seero, relaa-tive! Two t'ousand yaards! Many pleezy-sores!' "

Matt left his chair and stepped out on the starboard bridgewing, raising his binoculars. "Wow," he muttered. "What a pack!" It looked like hundreds of the things were swimming along, blowing on the calm surface of the sea. Their backs rising and falling like whales. He handed the binoculars to Sandra. "I've never seen so many before."

"What are they doing?" Sandra asked, adjusting the glasses. Then she saw. "Why, they're like dolphins!" she exclaimed. "Maybe they're not leaping at our bow, but they do seem to be pacing us from a distance!"

"Better they stay at a distance! They're a lot bigger than dolphins," Paddy said.

"What're daw-fins, if ye please?" Diania asked hesitantly.

"Cap-i-taan," Minnie said. "Lieutenant Campeti requests permission to test the new ordnance again, an' shoot at them devils."

Matt shook his head. "Permission denied. I thought he was happy with what he learned last night against that mountain fish?" The new shells worked much better than they'd expected, almost perfectly tuned to the gun director—as a distant mountain fish discovered to its mortal confusion under the light of a bright, clear moon. The trajectories were good and consistent and the tracers worked—even if the color was a little off. The explosive force was better as well, even though the bursting charge was the same. They were simply better projectiles in all respects than anything they'd had since they ran out of those they'd brought to this world.

"No," Matt confirmed. "If those things keep their distance, we'll leave 'em alone." He took a deep breath. "No sense wasting ammunition we might need very badly soon."

Spanky climbed the skeletal iron stairs to the upper-level catwalk in the aft fireroom. Heat shimmered off the top of the massive, roaring number three boiler. It was absolute hell here in the highest reaches of the fireroom where, contrary to physics, the heat seemed almost to compress itself into a physical, oppressive presence. He wore a bandanna over his mouth and nose to protect him from the 'Cat fuzz that hung in the space like a fog, but it was already soaked with sweat and plastered to his face. His eyes watered, and seemed to float in little pools of salty, caustic acid.

"There you are!" he hollered over the thundering boiler and the blower that forced air into the contained inferno. Tabby shot a grinning, sopping glance at him before returning her attention to a pair of 'Cats wielding a massive wrench.

"Hi, Spaanky," she shouted over her shoulder, intent on the work she was supervising.

"Damn, it's hot!" Spanky said, joining her.

"You get soft running around in cool air topside," she accused.

"Yeah, maybe. It was nice being off the equator for a while."

"We head north soon, right?"

"We already have. We're in the Fil-pin Sea, but we had to stay south of the Carolines until we cleared 'em. Too many uncharted knobs in there to run into in the dark. It should cool off tonight, and we'll be off Samaar tomorrow."

"Gettin' close. We kill them damn Jaaps, we go in dry dock?"

"That's the plan."

Tabby wiped the foamy sweat matting the fur above her eyes and slung it at the boiler. "Thank the Maker. I don't know how long we keep steaming on this bitch."

"Another leak?"

"Not real leak," she assured him. "Just hot foggy round this coupling." She shook her head. "Mr. Letts's gasket stuff is swell, but it seems to be going all at once. Like it gets saturated an' steam just kinda smokes out, see? We ain't had no failures, but we gotta tighten couplings all the time."

"I bet it's the heat," Spanky said, and Tabby nodded.

"Me too. Meantime, I gotta watch these dopes, make sure they don't spin a bolt or nut off the flange. I think we get a big failure then."

"Yeah. Hey, be careful, wilya?"

Tabby sent him another damp, tired smile. "Don't worry. We keep number three goin'—at least till after the fight!"

"Yeah. But *you* be careful! You and the rest of your snipes. If you get cooked down here, who am I gonna replace you with?" He chuckled. "I'll have to come back down here myself!"

"No worry, *Mr*. Spaanky! I keep you safe in cool air!"

Spanky left them with it, tapping gauges as he went. He stood with a water tender for a moment, eyeing the water level in the feedwater line. All the pumps, feedwater, fuel, everything, were starting to gasp, and no wonder. The ship had steamed halfway around the damn world, fought several battles, and then steamed back. He didn't want to think about how many hours of continuous steaming each boiler had racked up. He sighed and cycled through the air lock into the forward engine room.

"Howdy, fellas," he said to the throttlemen, even though half were female and a couple of those were human women. He tried not to notice the way their sweaty T-shirts clung to them.

"We're goin' in the yard when we get to the Philippines, right?" asked Johnny Parks. The kid had been a fireman's apprentice on *Mahan*, and now he was a machinist's mate (engine). He seemed like a good kid, but he was just now catching up with some of the 'Cats.

"Right."

"Good. The lube oil in the reduction gears is getting mighty thin."

"I know, and we can't change it out underway. Should've done it at Respite."

"Yes, sir . . . but we changed it at Scapa Flow twice, coming and going, and, well, we're out."

Spanky scratched his chin under his whiskers. "Yeah.

Right. I saw that in the division report." He shook his head. "The old girl's just about as beat up as she was when *Amagi* sank her. I'm starting to lose track of it all—and now I've got more than just engineering to worry about." He forced a grin and slapped Johnny on the shoulder. "It'll be okay. Plenty of lube oil waiting for us at Manila!"

He moved aft, past the giant turbine that dominated the space and paused by the reduction gear housing. He frowned. He'd never wanted to be exec. As engineering officer he'd had enough problems and responsibilities to deal with within his complicated but limited domain. Now he had to worry about the whole ship—and he still didn't have half the worries the Skipper had. He didn't regret keeping Captain Reddy in the dark about recent developments. What could he have done? But he finally understood why he'd been so mad. There was nothing he could do about the lube-oil shortage or the failing gaskets in the firerooms, but he *needed* to know about them. He suddenly remembered a heated lecture he'd given Tabby once, when she'd torn down a boiler without telling him. He'd told her she'd been wrong not to keep him fully informed because the Captain was basing his plans on what he thought his ship could do. Maybe this was different, and he honestly couldn't think of anything the Skipper could have done if he'd known immediately what was happening, but he and Gray had been wrong not to tell him.

"The ship's a wreck," he admitted aloud to himself, "and the Skipper damn sure needs to know *that* before we tangle with that Jap tin can!"

CHAPTER 19

March 17, 1944
Scapa Flow, New Scotland
Empire of the New Britain Isles

Mrs. Carr quietly brought a pot of tea into the Imperial Library in Government House and set it near the sunken-eyed girl sitting on the leather-padded chair behind the broad, cluttered desk. It was her father's desk, and the disheveled stacks of papers, books, and odd contraptions sprawled across it, just as he'd left them, seemed to represent him in the room. Princess Rebecca Anne McDonald stirred herself to nod slightly in thanks. With a dreadful sigh and what might have been a disapproving glare at Courtney Bradford, Mrs. Carr left the room. Courtney sat across the desk, leaning forward, yearning to enfold the girl in a comforting, supportive embrace, but the young princess had forbidden it and Courtney knew why. Possibly endless tears lurked behind those tortured eyes, and they couldn't be released, not yet, lest they quench the white-hot steel that burned in the girl's soul. He'd said everything he could possibly say, and she knew of the protective support, even love, he felt for her, but things—momentous things—had to be attended to, and she could not let anything interfere with that just yet. Even grief.

Mechanically, Rebecca poured a cup of tea for Courtney

and another for herself; then they continued to wait. The odd, colorful, furry reptile named Petey remained drooped across the back of Rebecca's neck like a fat little stole. He hadn't even stirred except to cut an eye in Mrs. Carr's direction when she came and went. Perhaps he sensed something of his master's mood, because he definitely knew Mrs. Carr was the primary source of food in the house, and normally, he would have begun yapping "Eat! Eat!" at the first sight of her.

There came a soft knock at the door and the Imperial Factor, Sean Bates, stepped into the room, accompanied by the blond-furred Lemurian Lieutenant Ruik-Sor-Raa. Bates's expression was little different from Rebecca's, and Ruik was blinking rapidly in condolence. Beyond the door, before it closed, a glimpse of the hallway showed it well supplied with Imperial and Lemurian Marines.

"Yer highness," Sean began softly, his own eyes red. News had finally come. "I wanted ta say, I *must* say, yer father an' mother . . . they were . . ."

"You will address me as Your Majesty, from this moment on, so there will be no misunderstanding, no possibility that any might doubt my legitimacy or intent!" Rebecca said sharply.

"Of course, Your Majesty . . . Of course," Sean replied, forcing a formal tone. "The coronation'll make it official . . . after the funeral, of course, but there's certainly precedent for a direct transition of Imperial power through inheritance. . . ." He nodded harshly. "An' I advise ye ta seize that power immediately, or everything we—and your parents—so recently accomplished might still be undone. The primacy o' the Governor-Emperor could still be subverted, particularly since . . ." Bates stopped and lowered his eyes.

"Particularly since I am a woman—and not only that! A child!" Rebecca interjected.

"There's the issue o' lawful age," Bates conceded. "An' with today's discovery of both yer father's and mother's remains in the ruins o' the Court o' Directors . . . Even many who support ye will insist on the namin' of a guardian. That cry has already begun."

"Then you will be my guardian!" Rebecca insisted.

"You cannot name me thus, Yer Majesty. Only the courts o' Directors or Proprietors can do so. With the one disbanded an' the other extinct, that leaves only . . ."

"Who?"

"The High Admiral o' the Imperial Navy. In this case, Lord High Admiral James McClain. Jenks's authority ta relieve him came directly from the Governor-Emperor, but he wasn't dismissed the service, or even reduced in grade! McClain is still high admiral."

"Never!" Rebecca cried. "The man is a coward and a military imbecile, and if poor Bigelow's suspicions were correct, a murderer as well! His dying words could only have meant that McClain suggested the traitorous beaters! Now McClain will surely name *himself* as guardian!"

Petey finally stirred and raised his toothy snout from Rebecca's breast. "Never!" he shrieked, approximating Rebecca's indignant tone. "Goddam!"

Realization suddenly dawned, and Courtney bolted to his feet. "At last!" he cried. "We have a true motive for this damnable atrocity! I suspected the insidious fiend all along! No one opposed the treaty reforms more, and he certainly had the opportunity! Now the proof is laid bare at last!"

"Perhaps not *proof* yet, Your Excellency," Ruik tactfully interjected, "but I believe you say . . . the evidence of circumstance? And it does make sense. The attacker we captured conveniently—and rather oddly—died in the Navy hospital before we were able to interrogate him. If the man was murdered, who might have arranged it most easily?" He paused. "As I think on it, to call what the Lord High Admiral did in the east mishandled or incompetent is a weak understatement. Not all were convinced he did mishandle the situation, as far as *he* was concerned." Ruik blinked resentment. "I was there when he was relieved for cause, and he objected, of course. Cap-i-taan Reddy and Commodore Jenks did not believe he was a traitor or that he was in league with the Doms, or they would have hanged him then, I'm sure. Perhaps they were right, but in his disgrace, he could have turned traitor since, I suppose." He blinked consideration. "Or . . . It did strike others with greater understanding of human face moving than I, that even disgraced, the high ahd-mi-raal did not act . . . defeated?"

"Most interestin'," Bates mused; then he looked at Rebecca. "Mr. Bradford's right: the motive's clear. But we ha' nae proof his military blunders were deliberate. His actions showed incompetence, p'raps, but no more than many o' our other commanders ha' shown in this war! He made no bones about his disagreement wi' the strategy either." He glowered. "An' ta be honest, I don't meself believe him in league with the Doms, regardless how his actions er inactions may ha' aided 'em. But this terrible murder . . . I cannot put beyond him. I stand wi' Mr. Bradford on that." He sighed roughly. "An' McClain's neither a coward nor an imbecile, Yer Majesty," he added. "More's the pity."

"But how may we prove it?" Rebecca asked almost desperately. "We must at least give reason for our suspicion. How could he have arranged the murders? It is already known that those who attacked Lieutenant Ruik, Factor Bates, and myself were Dominion zealots."

"Dominion assassins were used." Ruik considered. "That has been confirmed by our own observations, the marshals, and Imperial Intelligence—but the high admiral is chief of Imperial Intelligence. Is he not? Who is better placed to mislead and use such creatures, particularly amid all the confusion after the revolt?" He suddenly stood even more rigid. "I am personally convinced of his guilt," he stated, "and am certain that Cap-i-taan Reddy, Chairman Adar, and Ahd-mi-raal Lelaa-Tal-Cleraan would desire me, and all our forces currently in the vicinity of the New Britain Isles, to offer *you* any assistance you may require for any reason, Your Majesty."

"Your offer goes without saying, Lieutenant," Courtney said with a wave. "But I think you have just connected a most significant dot. Suddenly, means matches step with motive and opportunity. Who better than Imperial Intelligence to leak the plans of our campaign on New Ireland? We now know the enemy anticipated our every move there, and only courage and divine providence prevented a most . . . distracting disaster." Courtney drifted with his thoughts a moment. "I have it! Perhaps the lord high admiral was not in league with the Doms, but he did use them most effectively to distract the Governor-Emperor with domestic battles. This not only weakened our thrust against the Doms—a unifying enemy, if there ever was one—but delayed the implementation of the reforms that the high admiral opposed. Reforms that once made, could not be undone."

He looked around at the others. "I propose that he laid the egg for his plot in this very room, when we discussed the campaigns both to recapture New Ireland and to secure the continental colonies! He and those loyal to him in Imperial Intelligence then hatched the scheme to supply the Doms and rebels with information that would cause a more lengthy, costly campaign on the island, while preserving the Doms in the east as a unifying foe that he could use to consolidate his power once the Governor-Emperor and his wife were out of the way." He looked sadly at Rebecca. "And your own demise, my dear, which was so nearly achieved. What would that have gained him?"

"With both courts an' the entire Imperial family disposed of, the high admiral would step directly into the Governor-Emperor's office!" Bates declared, aghast.

"No wonder he did not seem defeated when he was relieved," Ruik said with sudden certainty. "He *wanted* to be relieved, to be sent back *here*!"

"Well. Then Admiral McClain is *clearly* the most likely culprit. Isn't he?" Courtney asked, a trifle smug.

"Yes, he is, and that does constitute sufficient cause to prevent his guardianship," Rebecca stated icily, "and hopefully get him hanged. In the meantime, *I* am Governor-Empress, by inheritance, and Sean Bates will be my guardian if one is required! We will see to"—her voice cracked—"my parents' funeral and the coronation, at which I shall crush McClain's agenda of stopping the reforms and fulfill my parents' legacy!"

"What will you do, my dear?" Courtney asked, focusing on the girl again.

"This very instant, I command the arrest of Lord High Admiral McClain and his particular associates," Rebecca said darkly. "We must get ahead of this plot. Initially, he will be charged with gross dereliction of duty, and face a martial court to determine whether he should be dismissed the service. That should allow us time to investigate those associates and the Imperial Intelligence Service as a whole. Remember, the 'Honorable' New Britain Company virtually ruled New Ireland, and I sense the hand of its remnants in this. Look more closely for connections there as well." She considered. "We should not even mention our other suspicions just yet, I think. We do not want to frighten unknown conspirators into flight."

"Unknown conspirators. Particular associates. Hmm." Courtney made a face. "As your first act as Governor-Empress, I think you should be careful, my dear, not to arrest people solely because they *know* the admiral. *I* know him, you know. Besides, Captain Reddy and his Americans—human and Lemurian—are quite taken with the Constitution they all swore to defend. It contains various tedious guidelines about having actual *reasons* to arrest anyone, not just important traitors such as the admiral. As the somewhat reluctant representative of the powers growing attached to that Constitution, I should warn you that they take it quite seriously indeed, to the point that their articles of war—based upon what they occasionally refer to as 'Rocks and Shoals'—also reflect those individual protections. I think they will be impressed if your first commands set the precedent that you also value individual liberties."

"Very well," Rebecca said, reflecting that there'd been a time when Bradford's ironic tact would have had her laughing. "Factor Bates, please see that the lord high admiral is arrested on the charge I specified—and do find legitimate reasons to arrest any of his associates who might have knowledge of a conspiracy. I will leave the detective work to you, the marshals, and any member of Imperial Intelligence you believe to be pure in this." She looked at Bradford and bit her lip.

"As to what else I shall do: first, I will bury my parents. After that, I will make the very same address my father meant to give at the Court of Directors." Rebecca's chin rose. "I will affirm the reforms that my father began. All indentures will be rescinded, and women will be *people* in this nation once and for all, with the same freedoms and protections as any man." She glared at Bradford. "And those protections will be very similar and just as universal as those described in the Constitution you mentioned." She paused. "I read it, you see, while I was in Baalkpan. There was a book about government from a dead surgeon's library. Astonishing . . ." She shook her head and continued. "The military alliance between the Empire and the western allies—the Grand Alliance—will be ratified by me, as will the cultural and material trade bargains we reached." Rebecca's voice became granite once more. "And I will proclaim that, as Captain Reddy suggested, the war against the evil Dominion will end only with its complete and unconditional defeat!"

"What of . . . what of the Dom prisoners we took on New Ireland?" Bates asked quietly.

Rebecca rubbed her eyes. "I *want* to kill them. Does that make me as evil as they?" She paused. "I can't do that, and I won't. They must remain confined, and those with sympathies toward them must be confined as well." She glanced sadly at Courtney. "We are not yet completely ready for this American Constitution. We cannot continue with our war even as we guard against our own people." She took a deep breath and released it. "I must order the arrest of all Dominion priests and congregations within the Empire, and those who associate with them shall be carefully questioned as well. Even . . . even the True Faith Catholics on New Ireland require study, I'm sad to say. Many did support the revolt there at first." She looked at Courtney, her eyes suddenly pleading. "Sister Audry has convinced me that the Doms are not Catholic at all, but a hideous perversion that merely wears its cloak to hide their evil." She sighed. "I believe she is right. I hope she is." She shook her head. "Ultimately, it is for their own protection, as most in this land will not believe it, and many may seek to harm them."

Rebecca looked at her hands, laid out flat on the desk. "Mr. Bradford, I . . . I need Sister Audry here! I *know* she is a good and godly woman. My people will come to know that too. If she went among the people of New Ireland, she could *assure* me, assure us all, that they have no connection to the Doms, no evil in their hearts! She could speak to our own clergy, become an ambassador between the faiths... Perhaps she might even speak to the prisoners! Do you think she could show them the wrong they do, teach them how they have been seduced—used—by evil?"

Courtney leaned across the desk and patted a small hand. "You ask a great deal, Your Majesty. Not of Sister Audry, because I think she would be more than willing to come. But you may be asking the impossible of her and of your own people in terms of result. It might even be difficult just to keep her safe, you know." He paused. "But I will ask her with you. She doesn't like me much," he admitted, "but in that, as in all things, she is honest. You can trust her advice regarding the people—and prisoners—on New Ireland." He turned to the others. "Now, gentlemen, if you please, why don't you leave us for a time? Her Majesty and I have sensitive, private matters to discuss."

Bates paused, then nodded. He knew Rebecca would feel constrained around him. He was no longer just her protector, but her factor now as well.

"Aye, Mr. Bradford," he said softly. "Come, Lieutenant Ruik, yers an' Her Majesty's Marines have arrests to make."

Even as the library door closed, Courtney Bradford finally moved around the desk to hold the small girl who, now that they were alone once more, began to tremble beneath the crushing weight of grief and Empire.

A while later, perhaps a long while—Courtney's watch had finally been stilled by the terrible blast—he stepped quietly out on the wide veranda and sat heavily in a chair. He was in a dark humor, and placed what he hoped was a sympathetic decanter of brandy on the small table nearby. Setting a glass beside it, he deliberately, almost masochistically—given his noble efforts in recent months—poured it to the very top. The night was pleasant enough, but his spirits were very low, and he stared at the stars and yearned for his long-lost pipe. Suddenly, to his surprise, a common cat rubbed up against his leg.

Courtney had never been fond of domestic cats—few Australians were—and perhaps the fact they'd been great favorites of his unlamented wife had influenced him as well. But strangely, right then the little creature did provide some small solace. If nothing else, it distracted him just a bit from his grief and worry while he contemplated its desperate attempts to win his affection. Only two cats were known to have been aboard the "passage" ships, yet they'd quite infested the New Britain Isles, and many other places within the Empire that man had touched. They came in all sizes and colors, and it remained difficult for Courtney to believe they all sprang from only two specimens. At the same time, for all their numbers and variety, only two basic types seemed to have endured: those that were utterly feral and those that did not wish to be. The former were a nuisance that had done great harm to the ecology, just as they had in Australia, but the latter could be nearly as annoying. The people of the Empire were not particularly tolerant of any of them, as a rule. There were exceptions.

At the time, a clowder of cats had chosen the space beneath Government House porch for shelter to rear their young. They were endured because they kept the rodents and insects around the house to a minimum, and because Her Majesty was somewhat fond of them. Eternal warfare raged between the cats and Petey, who, though often wounded in battle, kept their numbers at bay. Rebecca scolded Petey for his depredations, but seemed to have a fatalistic tolerance beyond her years for his lamentable but quite understandable behavior.

I wonder, Courtney thought, *if all her hardships and adventures, all the suffering she's seen and endured, has contributed to that. Certainly she's holding up better than I would have imagined.* He took a gulp of brandy. *Better than I am, in some respects. She's as strong as Saan-Kakja and the Lady Sandra, as she calls her, as determined as Captain Reddy—and doubtless her long association with and strange affection for Dennis Silva has helped her as well.* He sighed. *She will ruthlessly move forward to quell this challenge and punish these atrocities in ways she may one day regret.*

The cat, a kitten, really, continued rubbing against him, and seemed to be gauging the possibility of achieving his lap.

Sergeant Koratin suddenly sat in a chair opposite him, and Courtney blinked, stirring from his dark thoughts. "There you are, Sergeant," he said. "I wondered what became of you."

"I have been here," Koratin replied.

"Hmm."

"Sister Audry will come?" Koratin asked.

"I presume so. How did you know?"

"I guessed. She will be needed here, and once the treaties are ratified, which is a certainty now, you will no longer be."

Courtney began to bristle, but Koratin was right. He'd come as an ambassador, but he'd largely become the face of the western allies here. Governor-Empress Rebecca would sort out the current mess, he was sure—one way or another—but she had to be *seen* as doing it herself. It wouldn't do at all for her confused and frightened people to think she was weak or that she was being propped up by foreigners, no matter how popular those foreigners might be. Bates would help, of course, but as Rebecca's prime factor and possible guardian, he'd be expected to. Ultimately, the reorganization and re-creation of the Imperial government must have an Imperial face. Still, Courtney was reluctant to leave the Governor-Empress.

"You are wasted here, Your Excellency," Koratin persisted more softly, "and you have other work to do. The new Governor-Empress will need *soldiers* to advise her now. She will need Sister Audry to counsel her as only she can do, and help her with the . . . spiritual dilemmas. And . . ." Koratin paused, then continued almost regretfully, "she will need such as I, who has trodden the rotten decks of treachery before. I will serve her however she will let me, and I will protect both her and Sister Audry with my life. They will *need* protection."

"I'm sure Her Majesty will have more protection than she can bear," Courtney predicted, "but I do fear for Sister Audry." He peered closely at the former Aryaalan noble.

"She *did* convert you, didn't she? You *have* become a Christian?" he probed.

"Of a sort. I am not sure what kind as yet. There *are* different kinds, it appears."

"Indeed," Courtney agreed with a grimace, "and I'm perhaps the same sort as you." He chuckled. "Somewhat nondenominational, shall we say?" He took another long sip. "I suppose you're right, though. Despite recent . . . events . . . here and the looming confrontation with the bloody Doms, it seems *our* war against the Grik will of necessity focus the western allies' attention more firmly against *them* quite soon. For a time, at least." He took a deep breath and leaned back. "I'm no soldier, but I do feel drawn in that direction. Particularly by these reports that the Grik are growing more dangerously sensible." He scowled. "And our dear Rebecca will need Audry's sweeter voice of restraint and compassion more than yet another angry friend of her father's." Suddenly he started and looked around. "Where did the cat go?"

"Cat?" Koratin was confused.

"Yes . . . Oh! My apologies! There was one of the small ones, a *Felis catus*, standing about. It's gone now." He frowned. "I wonder if that villainous Petey has frightened it away—or worse." He looked thoughtful. "For all I know, the little creature might already be dead!" He looked skeptically at Koratin. "I don't suppose you ever heard of a lecherous Austrian named Erwin Schrödinger?"

Koratin blinked.

"No, of course not. Why should you?" Courtney swallowed more brandy, then leaned forward. "My scientific specialty, beyond geology and industrial engineering, is comparative biology, but my horizons have necessarily expanded of late. I'm no physicist, let that be plain, and I paid only passing attention to the flurry of physical theories that drifted about Europe in the past decade like so much paper snow. Certainly Dr. Einstein and others made interesting observations, but their proposals seemed to require the elimination of every conceivable variable that might affect attempts to *prove* them. As a natural scientist, Heisenberg's uncertainty principles—which, to me, stressed the *impossibil-*

ity of eliminating every variable in any real-world scenario—seemed more relevant to my interests, since variations in climate and habitat are the essential parts of, and not incidental or destructive to, any biological equation."

Courtney admonished Koratin with the brandy glass. "You're doubtless wondering what all this has to do with our missing furry friend, but it was the sudden memory of Schrödinger's unfortunate *cat* that set me thinking about *paradox,* you see!"

"Paara . . ?"

"Of course!" Courtney thumped his chest and stifled a belch, then refilled his glass. "As a mental exercise and not an actual experiment, to be fair—I wouldn't want to slander the bugger—Schrödinger proposed that a cat had been placed in a box with a diabolical device that would execute it at some point. As an offering to Einstein, the device utilized a trigger that would activate it at a presumably predictable moment, based on its atomic degradation. . . ." Koratin's confused blinking distracted him, but Courtney shook his head and plowed on. "As an illustration of paradox, I can't see the point of *that,* because THE . . . point . . ." He paused, blinking himself. "The *ultimate* point was that the cat, once in the box, was both alive and dead!"

"I . . . don't see how that can be," Koratin muttered suspiciously. Courtney's belch finally escaped, and he drank down the rest of his glass before filling it again.

"But it *can* . . . in a sense. It seems to me that an appeal to Heisenberg's uncertainties would add to the drama of such a test, but perhaps he was trying to create a deterministic paradox." He shrugged. "I frankly can't remember. But though I believe determinism, that cause and effect has its place, chance—or uncertainty, if you will—constantly fiddles about with it outside the laboratory. Subjective, *perceptual* paradox involving life and death happens all the time—without imprisoning cats." Courtney rubbed his bushy brow.

"Just today, for example, when the remains of Gerald and Ruth McDonald were recovered, we learned they'd been dead since the bombing—were probably killed instantly, God willing—yet until that word came, they were still alive to us. How many times have you heard of the passing of an old friend years earlier, and realized you'd thought of them as alive and perhaps wondered what they were doing after they were dead and gone, but before you got the word? That person was dead, but alive to *you*. I often think of my son, even now, flying Hurricanes for the RAAF, and he'll always be alive to me, even if somewhere on the world we came from, he's been lost for many years. Conversely, if he lives, he *knows* I'm dead. If he manages to discover how I left Surabaya aboard an ancient, dilapidated destroyer, he'll learn that USS *Walker* was lost somewhere in the Java Sea—along with USS *Mahan*, USS *Pope*, HMS *Exeter*, and HMS *Encounter* on that dreadful, fateful day. Hopefully, there were survivors from the other ships, but there were none, *could never be*, survivors from *Walker* and *Mahan* . . . back there. All of us who remain, the so very few of us, are *dead* on another world—yet we live on here." He took another long swig of brandy and then stared at his shoes. "Or do we?" he almost whispered. He sat up straight, with some difficulty, and smiled. "*That,* my dear Sergeant Koratin, is a paradox."

Koratin stood and gathered the decanter and the glass. "Go home, Your Excellency, back to Baalkpan. Write your book. Put these . . . strange thoughts to use against the Grik."

"I believe I shall," Courtney said distractedly. "Look there, Sergeant! The kitten has returned!" He leaned down and extended his hand. "Come here, little fellow, and I may condescend to pet you!"

CHAPTER 20

March 19, 1944
Second Fleet
120 miles west-northwest of the Enchanted Isles

"Hooked on!" shouted Sergeant Kuaar-Ran-Taak, or "Seepy," as he completed attaching the hoisting cables to the lifting points atop the battered Nancy. "C'mon, you bunch'a dopes!" he insisted loudly to the crew on the lifting boom high above. "Take us up before we sink!"

Orrin Reddy climbed out of his flooding cockpit and joined Seepy up on the wing. The purple, cloud-shadowed sea was relatively calm beneath a mostly white sky. Patches of blue peeked through the high cloud layer here and there, dashing brilliant sunshine, like bright, photo-negative squalls, on the water. It was calmer still in *Maaka-Kakja*'s massive lee that shielded the returning flight from the light wind, but Orrin and Seepy grabbed the lifting cables as the slack came off. Their plane had grown heavy with water in the five minutes or so since it touched down, and both feared it wouldn't take the strain of the lift.

Orrin could have taken his ship into the cavernous, semi-submerged, sea-level hangar bay that could be opened in the side of the ship, but like Tikker, his counterpart in First Fleet, he considered it important that he take every opportunity to test the capabilities of his aircraft, and that included recovery procedures. Besides, this Nancy was so shot up, it would probably never fly again. If the plane collapsed during the lift, they might lose a good engine and one of the priceless .50-caliber Browning machine guns, but other than a few other spare parts, that was all—as long as he and Seepy had a good hold on the cables.

The lift crew's timing was a little off, and the plane jerked up out of a light trough, streaming water from a dozen holes. Orrin held his breath and grasped the cable tighter, but nothing came apart. He began to relax as the plane made its swaying, slowly spinning ascent, and watched the other four planes of his flight—none leaking, thank goodness—position themselves beneath other booms along *Maaka-Kakja*'s starboard side. His mood darkened. There should have been another Nancy maneuvering below, but a flock of "Grikbirds" had jumped them out of the sun and taken one of his planes and its crew before the others could react.

He blamed himself. They'd expected Grikbirds, but *he* hadn't expected them to use such a simple, time-honored tactic. He hadn't expected them to use any real tactics at all. He should have. The damn things were aerial predators, after all, and had probably been attacking prey out of the sun, by instinct, for millions of years! *They're not as fast as a Nancy, thank God*, he thought. *And even if they're smart enough to use them, I don't see them aiming Dom muskets—or any chase weapons—with their feet. But they're natural-born dogfighters*!

Still urinating streams of seawater, the Nancy was brought level with the hangar deck, and Seepy rose with the coiled line that came down with the hooks. "See you in a minute, boss," he said, and scampered down the bobbing, turning wing, uncoiling the line behind him. At the wingtip, just as it started dipping under his weight, he flipped the line through a pigtail and *leaped* across to the hangar deck with the tagline in his hand!

"Show-off!" Orrin shouted after him, but inwardly shuddered. Setting the planes down on the flight deck could be tricky in rough seas or high winds, but it was fairly straightforward. The same went for motoring in through the side of the ship. Bringing a plane inboard on the hangar deck had presented a few problems for the humans helping design the capability. A separate boom system was proposed, but the Lemurians on the project had simply asked, "Why?" They hadn't foreseen any problems. Sometimes, despite their fur, their tails, their expressionless faces—but highly expressive body language—the human destroyermen still forgot just how different they were. No "right" way for getting planes on the hangar deck from the water had ever been established as regulation, because the 'Cats just naturally seemed to know the best way at the time, under the prevailing conditions.

Just about any Lemurian could have done what Seepy did—the jump wasn't really that far—but Seepy had been a wing runner on a Home and made it look easy. Even as he cringed at the sight of the careless leap, Orrin couldn't prevent a touch of resentment and he'd meant it when he called Seepy a show-off. Orrin believed he was just about fearless in an airplane, but there was no way he could have done what Seepy did.

With the tagline secured to a steam windlass, the dripping Nancy was hauled inboard with Orrin still sitting on top. He helped hook new lines from an overhead track to the lifting points, and when the slack was taken up again, he unhooked those from the outside boom. Finally, the plane was lowered down on a three-wheeled cradle truck, and Orrin hopped down to the deck. The entire process had taken less than five minutes. Orrin's plane was the only one brought onto the hangar deck; the others would be deposited on the flight deck above. With no reports of casualties or malfunctions, they'd be prepared for further operations up there. The main reason for this was that the hangar deck resounded with the racket of other ships being uncrated and assembled. Flight ops were about to go into full swing, and soon Orrin's wing would have almost fifty aircraft at his disposal aboard *Maaka-Kakja* alone. Other ships had a scout plane or two, and twenty-odd crated planes remained in the holds of the various transports.

"I am glad to see you are well, Mr. Reddy," came a voice over the noise. Orrin turned and was surprised to see General Shinya, Commander Tex Sheider (*Maaka-Kakja*'s exec), and Commodore Jenks approaching. Orrin had met Jenks only once, when his elements first arrived from Saint Francis and joined Second Fleet. He was easily recognizable, though, in his Imperial uniform and great braided mustaches. He hadn't been aboard when Orrin's flight left that morning. Orrin, Seepy, and all those around came to attention, but didn't salute. Airy as it was, they were "indoors," after all.

"As you were," Tex barked, and everyone relaxed. But Orrin was suddenly very conscious of his sweaty flight suit and wet shoes. It was Commodore Jenks who'd spoken before. . . . Of course, he wasn't commodore anymore, was he?

"Thank you, sir," Orrin said to the Imperial. "And please accept my condolences for . . . what happened at your home. I was honored to meet with the Governor-Emperor and his wife several times. He was a great leader, and she was a gracious lady. I understand you were close to them."

"Indeed. Thank you. I am equally close, I think, to the new Governor-Empress, Rebecca Anne McDonald."

"Jenks is the Empire's new lord high admiral," Tex said.

"Yes, sir, I heard. Congratulations."

"Thank you," Jenks replied dubiously.

"What happened? What did you see?" Shinya asked, a little impatient with the prolonged pleasantries. He knew from their wireless reports that there'd be a fight for the Enchanted Isles and he was anxious to get Orrin's firsthand impressions.

"Just a second." Orrin didn't like the "Jap's" tone. He didn't like the Jap at all, but he knew his cousin Matt did, and Shinya was in charge of all the ground forces. He untied the damp clipboard from his thigh and held it up so they could see a rather crudely drawn map of the Enchanted Isles. He'd never seen what had been the Galápagos on the old world; hadn't even known they existed. He'd been told that like the Hawaiian Islands, they were a lot different here, with many islands blended into a few higher ones, but with no previous reference, he hadn't been confused by the odd configuration.

"As we sent, the Doms have full control of this King

James Island, King Charles, Crossman, Abington, and Brittles." He shrugged. "They've got some forces on all the other little ones too, not that I can imagine why. There didn't look to be anything there to sustain them. Fortunately, the Imperial garrison still holds most of this biggest island," he said, pointing. "This Albermarl. The Doms have landed a lot of troops in the north and on the southeast coast, but the Impies . . ." He looked up. "Excuse me. The Imperial troops have 'em stalled on the west flank of this big mountain—seventeen forty-three—in the north, and hold the pass between eleven fifty-four and twenty-one nineteen. . . ."

"Those mountains have names," Jenks said, but Orrin just shrugged again.

"Yessir, but the only thing I was real concerned with were the elevations." He frowned. "Those guys are way outnumbered. The only thing that's saved them is the terrain, I bet. The good thing is, this Elizabeth Bay on the west coast is clear, except for what looked like a few whopper battleships cruising off the mouth. It doesn't look like they want to try the forts in the bay."

"Those forts mount some of our heaviest guns," Jenks agreed, looking at the map. He straightened. "It would seem, gentlemen, that we have arrived in time after all!"

"I hope so, Comm . . . I mean, Admiral," Orrin said. "But I doubt we got here with much time to spare. If they've been fighting as long as we think, they're bound to be low on ammo. And there's another thing: Grikbirds. The Doms have 'em on King James Island, for sure. That's where they jumped us and we lost a plane. We shot down a few of the bastards ourselves. They surprised us, but we knew how to handle 'em this time. Still, that island is crawling with Doms, and they've got plenty of transports to reinforce their beachheads on Albermarl. It looks like it's getting tight for our guys."

"Is that how your plane was damaged?" Shinya asked. "Scouting the enemy?"

Orrin's face reddened. "No . . . sir. The Doms shot at us, sure, but we stayed high, out of range of musket fire. It was when we dropped those damn leaflets on Elizabethtown to tell 'em help was on the way. We started out high, but most of 'em blew out over the water—so I went low to drop my load, and I bet two hundred guys shot at me."

Tex chuckled. "They've never seen an airplane before. Probably scared the crap out of 'em. They *know* the Empire doesn't have any. At least it didn't the last they heard. Remember, these poor bastards have been cut off for months. They probably thought you were some kind of new Dom terror weapon."

"Well, I hope they can read and they spread the word. The last thing we need is *everybody* shooting at us," Orrin complained. He patted the plane behind him. "I *liked* this one, and it's probably junked! And they could've hit me or Seepy."

Shinya motioned for him to hand over the clipboard, and Orrin—somewhat reluctantly—complied. If Shinya noticed Orrin's attitude, he made no comment. "These elevations are correct?" he asked Jenks.

"Yes, although two of the mountains on Albermarl are active volcanoes: the one on the far northern peninsula, and that larger one in the south. The northern mountain has not been measured since its last eruption."

"But the terrain is accurately depicted?"

"Essentially." Jenks fidgeted. "We have never been able to map the islands from the air, of course, and the coastlines are depicted somewhat vaguely because they change, you see."

"I understand." Shinya studied the map a few moments more, then handed it back to Orrin. "As I see it, we have only one battle to fight here: for Albermarl Island. That will likely involve action on land and sea and in the air—but I see no reason to expend effort and lives retaking these other islands."

Jenks's brow furrowed. "And why is that, sir?"

"Because once we have Albermarl, we can isolate them from each other—and their lines of supply. They will then have no choice but to surrender or die. I was only marginally involved in the fighting for New Ireland, but I have learned enough about the enemy that I don't much care which they choose. Either way, you will have all your Enchanted Isles back eventually, and regardless of losses on Albermarl, the bulk of my army will survive intact and concentrated. The Doms will never evict us, and we will have the nucleus already in place for the forces we will eventually need to conquer the Dominion itself."

"But . . . there are civilians on those islands! Fishermen, miners! Not many, granted, but some!"

Shinya regarded him gravely. "I submit, Lord High Admiral, that if there were once civilians on those islands, there are none there now." He pointed at Orrin. "The enemy has Grikbirds—dragons. Remember, sir, what they feed them to maintain their cooperation."

After a moment of reflective silence, broken only by the racket of the hangar deck, Orrin looked at Jenks. "How come you call them the Enchanted Isles, sir? They're right on the frigging equator, bound to be hot as hell . . . and they *look* like hell itself from the air. I mean, other than their strategic value, I couldn't see anything very damn enchanting about them."

"That is what they were first called, I believe," Jenks answered absently, then looked at Orrin. "And some quite enchanting creatures once dwelt there. Some still remain and are now protected. You see, only there of all the places we have contacted on this world since the passage was there not a single species that was of deliberate danger to man. Even Respite cannot boast that. There were even great, monstrous tortoises of a type somewhat similar to those described in pre-passage journals, though they were larger and more oddly shaped." He sighed. "Ambassador Bradford would understand. He shares my interest in such things. Sadly, the tortoises and other benign creatures were also known to be tasty, and after all this time with the garrison's provisions doubtless running low, I'm sure they have become virtually extinct. Particularly on the islands occupied by the Doms."

"Maybe some have been preserved," Tex suggested encouragingly.

"Possibly. Governor Sir Humphries is a naturalist." Jenks chuckled softly. "As you said, otherwise the place is hell on earth. One would *have* to be a naturalist to request a posting there! You have cheered me a bit, Mr. Reddy."

"Good," Shinya declared. "We have a battle to plan, and I have learned that a positive mood promotes objectivity in regard to such things."

CHAPTER 21

The Battle of Cape Comorin
March 16–20, 1944

Captain Jis-Tikkar, or Tikker, saw the massive fleet spread across the hazy sea off the southwest coast of India, and for a moment he thought he would have to swallow his heart. He'd seen a bigger fleet before, riding as copilot with Colonel Mallory in the old PBY Catalina during the Battle of Baalkpan, but he'd never seen *so many big things* in *any* fleet. Before, there'd been *Amagi*, which was terrifying enough at the time, but now there were five—no, *six*—ships defining themselves against the blurry horizon, that looked just as big as the Japanese battle cruiser. The things were dark, squat, and massive, with four tall funnels each, all belching thick, black coal smoke. They looked like mountain fish that someone had built pyres upon—and they weren't alone. Trailing above and behind the great ships were zeppelins, just as had been reported, and they looked . . . maybe even a little bigger than others he'd seen. Looking back down, Tikker saw more large ships as long as *Walker* but with higher freeboards and two tall masts, steaming in company with the monsters. There were more than twenty of those. The hundreds of Indiaman-style Grik ships flocking along hardly gained his attention.

"Get on the horn," he shouted into the speaking tube to his backseater over the roar of the engine and the slipstream. "Send that the scout reports are correct, but you really need to see these things to believe them!" He paused a moment. "Enemy position is about forty miles west-northwest of First Fleet flag, course one two zero. Speed, about eight knots. I confirm the number at two hundred plus, including, ah, twenty-three heavies, and six *really* heavies! I also confirm at least a dozen airships—they're all bunched up from here. Request instructions!"

He waited a few minutes for a reply while he led the First Naval Air Wing in a gentle circle north, then west, keeping the enemy in sight. "Hey! The zeps are breaking away!" he cried into the tube when he suddenly saw the large tan shapes start to scatter. "They seen us! First and Second Pursuit Squadrons, taallyho the zeps! They gonna be makin' for land or the fleet, I bet!"

The entire 1st Pursuit was armed with a single .50-caliber machine gun each. The 2nd had no mounted guns so far, but the OCs each had several shortened rifles—carbines—loaded with hollow-based bullets filled with the same phosphor compound they were using in the new tracers. They *would* light a zeppelin if they could hit it.

"Taallyho! Taallyho!" Tikker cried as the two squadrons peeled off in pursuit of the airships. The First Naval Air Wing didn't have voice communications yet, but he remembered having it before, in the *Catalina*, and he got caught up in the moment.

"You want me send what I already send two time more, or take down fleet orders?" came a shouted, peevish voice through the tube.

"What's fleet say?" he asked.

"The old-style ships gotta be full o' Griks. We don't want them on shore. We do want idea what ordnance does on *all* ships. Fift Air Wing forming up over *Arracca* now. Fift COFO report to you for taac-tical direction when it arrive!"

"Okay! Send: First Bomb Squadron on me; we go for big monster ships. Second will attack the little monsters, and Third will burn Grik transports! Taallyho!"

The three remaining squadrons of the 1st Naval Air Wing

turned toward the enemy together, at an altitude of five thousand feet. The pursuit ships had already scattered into pairs, going for the zeppelins their squadron commanders sent them after, and Tikker tried to concentrate. Except for the scary, ugly steamers, there wasn't really any shape to the enemy formation, so his guys would have to be careful not to run into each other. Target fixation had been a problem for his pilots before and he worried about that, particularly when the targets were so large—and frightening. Over the next few minutes, he delegated three planes of the First to attack each of the lumbering behemoths ahead. The commander of the 2nd would work out his own assignments, as would the commander of the 3rd Bomb Squadron. As usual, the air frequency turned into a hash of OCs stomping all over each other, but they had a sequence now, so it didn't last long. He wondered if Ahd-mi-raal Keje-Fris-Ar himself was sitting in his own COFO chair, in *Big Sal*'s Flight Ops right now, monitoring the traffic. He doubted it. This would be First Fleet's first "fleet action," and the admiral was doubtless busy with many things.

The two planes that would attack the lead monster ship with him stayed on his wing as the squadron began to ease apart. The closer they got to the dreadful-looking thing, the bigger and more invulnerable it looked. *It's iron,* he told himself with sudden conviction. *The whole thing is iron—or at least covered with it!* The Allies had begun plating sections of the sides of their ships to protect the engines and boilers, but they hadn't done anything like this! He felt his heart drop down in his gut then and he knew—*knew*—their puny firebombs would have little or no effect on such a thing.

"Steady," he said aloud, and pushed the stick forward.

PB-1B Nancys were good all-around practical aircraft. Even without knowing much about seaplanes, Ben Mallory's education and experience had paid off on their first real try, and Nancys had become the workhorses of the Allied air effort. They'd proven themselves many times and were now in combat across the known world. With their center of gravity where it was, redundant wing bracing, and, yes, relatively high drag configuration, they even made tolerable dive-bombers. After much practice at close air support on land, the ships—particularly the very large ones—should be easy targets, if Tikker's pilots remembered to lead them. Sailing ships could do little to avoid the bombs, and Tikker doubted the plodding iron monsters could maneuver very smartly. He wondered in a flash what kind of antiair defenses the things might have.

"Send: We're going in!" he cried.

Maker, that thing is big! he thought as the Nancy steadied its dive, angling just forward of a massive raised structure that seemed to extend most of the length of the ship. Smoke gushed skyward from the four tall funnels, and he thought the flat, wide feathers of the ship's wake had grown a little broader. Maybe it had increased speed? Perhaps the most unsettling thing about the great ship was that despite its size, there was not a living thing moving upon it. All its crew had to be enclosed within. It was as if this huge thing he, his OC, and two other frail planes were hurtling toward was a giant, unfeeling, uncaring—maybe unkillable—machine. His left hand inched toward the low, leather-wrapped lever nestled down to the side of his wicker seat. The closer he got to his target, the surer he was that the iron was bolted onto some kind of framework, at least. But the bolt pattern was almost continuous, so maybe there was solid wood beneath the iron? That had to be it, and the bolts were huge! Big enough to see at— Shutters suddenly rose near the apex at the top of the ship, where the sloping iron of one side joined that of the other, and what looked like dozens of small muzzles appeared briefly before his target was obscured by a monstrous, white cloud!

Large objects, bigger than musket balls, *vrooped* past Tikker's Nancy, and the plane shuddered when one struck the leading edge of his starboard wing. Instinctively he knew it was time, and he pulled up hard on the lever and back on the control stick almost simultaneously. The weight of two two-hundred-pound incendiary bombs dropping away and the backward pressure on the stick caused his plane to rocket skyward, and it dashed through the bitter coal smoke and rising white smoke of . . . whatever shot at him. Moving the stick to the left and pushing hard on the left rudder, his plane practically spun on its axis, and he saw the immediate aftermath of his bomb hits. Both had struck, as had at least two other bombs, and black mushrooms roiled above splashes of greasy orange fire. But as he'd feared, he could see no gaping holes beneath them, vomiting flame. He continued his tight bank, hoping for a better look. Maybe they'd gotten some fire through the open ports at the top? *No. They must have closed them just as we released,* he realized. Still, that may be something . . . The burning fragments of a Nancy were in the water, disappearing aft of the monster as it churned forward, and Tikker knew he'd lost at least one of his planes and two talented young people. Whether it had been shot down or just crashed into the ship didn't matter; its crew was doubtless dead, and they hadn't even hurt the thing! He quickly leveled off and looked around. Another Nancy was off his starboard wing, apparently still trying to match his maneuvers. He sighed with some relief and led his surviving companion back through the black smoke and southward. Only then did he try to gauge the success of his other squadrons.

The attack on the transports had gone well. Fiery columns of gray smoke stood, slanting slightly, against the bright sky. Some of the smaller monster ships were burning as well, a few dead in the water. *They* were vulnerable, at least. Great, falling fires crept down toward the sea in the distance to join other smoldering, sinking heaps. So. His pursuiters had done good work against the zeppelins too, but . . . Burning specks lay upon the water here and there, and he knew he'd lost other planes as well. Turning back to see the big monsters again, he saw them all still steaming relentlessly forward, the fires from the bombs already diminishing. One still smoldered, he thought. Maybe some fire did get into that one, but the rest . . .

"Send to all squadrons: Regroup on me as soon as all ordnance is expended; then fly to *Salissa* to refuel and rearm. Send to CINCWEST and the Fifth Air Wing: Attack successful against Indiamen and smaller iron ships, but ineffective against larger ones. The enemy has dangerous, close-range antiair capability, so watch out. Suggest concentrate on small boys for now, but enemy heavies may be vulnerable when antiair is in use. Propose a combined assault on them using both the First and Third Wings after the current sorties have rearmed."

The air attack that swirled above and around General of the Sea Hisashi Kurokawa's Grand Fleet for the last several days had been . . . interesting, certainly. But the frustration it caused was threatening to send him into one of the almost incapacitating rages he'd guarded against for so long. There'd been reports of the enemy aircraft for a long time, of course, and Kurokawa had appreciated the threat and even taken precautions, but until the first attacks slashed down on him, he secretly hadn't expected much. Now he was, frankly, amazed that the Americans and their pet monkeys had put such capable craft—and in such numbers!—into the air.

Kurokawa's conventional ships—mere transports, as far as he was concerned—built along the age-old East Indiaman lines the Grik had used for centuries, had been savaged during his plodding advance. He'd started with nearly two hundred of them, filled with fifty thousand more of the new Grik he'd been so instrumental in creating. Some had been lost to sea monsters, of course, but more than half had been bombed into sinking torches by the highly effective enemy air. He didn't really care about dead Grik, regardless how elite, but knew General Esshk would be furious. He finally released the ships after nightfall of the first day to make their own way to the coast. There was no port they could reach before daylight, and trying for one would leave them helpless again beneath the sky, so he'd ordered them to run themselves aground on the closest shore so the troops might survive to report to General Niwa, who Kurokawa knew was in the south.

Kurokawa *did* care about the loss of many of his towed zeppelins, armed with Muriname's special bombs, and he'd released them immediately—to make for the concealed aerodromes where Muriname himself had begun hoarding airships after his own arrival two weeks before. Sadly, there had not yet been enough of the special bombs completed for Muriname to bring more than a few at the time, and none had been sent since. Kurokawa had been bringing more himself and there was no way to know how many of the towed zeppelins survived. Hopefully, the enemy had been too focused on destroying the transports to chase fleeing airships, but he had to assume most were destroyed. The "specials" might now lack the punch of numbers he'd hoped for, but maybe there would be enough—and it was still possible he wouldn't need them.

What annoyed Kurokawa most were the losses of cruisers and battleships his fleet had endured—many before it ever came in contact with the enemy! The capital ships of his invincible fleet, ships that had taken almost two years to build, had dropped like flies before ever firing a shot. He'd been faced with the fact that regardless of how well constructed and mighty his navy was, his engines, all of them, were *kuso*. They were simply too crude and inefficient for reliable service—and, of course, when the machinery didn't fail, the Grik engineers did. He had a sprinkling of Japanese engineers in his battleships, but even they were plagued by breakdowns. For once, no suspicion of treachery entered his mind; he felt secure that all his engineers were dedicated to him and the parts of his mission he'd revealed to them, but if the fundamental design of his engines wasn't at fault, then shoddy, crude construction was to blame.

He'd started with fifty *Azuma*-class cruisers and a dozen *ArataAmagi*-class battleships, but he'd lost half his battleships and almost thirty cruisers just getting here! Many of the damaged cruisers would be along eventually or make it home under sail power. His helpless battleships didn't have that capability, however, and he'd been forced to send operational cruisers to take them under tow. Some would be repaired and would rejoin the fleet, but he smoldered. He'd taken consolation in the fact that he still had twenty-three cruisers and six battleships to destroy the enemy. More than enough, he'd thought.

All his ships were lumbering, gawky-looking things, to his sensibilities, but they could all strain to accomplish ten knots and carried heavy batteries. The cruisers were virtual copies of Japan's very first French-built ironclad ram, *Kotetsu/Azuma*. Designed to use sail and steam, and powered by double expansion engines, they'd taken almost as much effort—if not materials—to build as his battleships. He'd hoped their hundred-pounder smoothbores would make short work of the powerful American frigates.

His battleships were his pride and joy, and resembled nothing more than monstrous, eight-hundred-foot, four-stack versions of one of the first ironclad warships that fought in the American Civil War. He couldn't remember which side it was on—it was the one without a turret—but that didn't matter, and the irony was amusing. His own *ArataAmagi* was the flagship, and all the others were essentially identical. *ArataAmagi* had an eighty-foot beam, two engines, and four boiler rooms. She mounted a four-hundred-foot sloping casemate amidships that protected 32 hundred-pounder guns behind three feet of hard, laminated timber and six inches of armor plate. Kurokawa would have preferred more armor, but when he first learned about the enemy aircraft, he'd been forced to add more sloping plates atop the originally flat upper deck, fo'c'sle, and fantail to protect against falling bombs. The ships were already somewhat top-heavy. He was glad he'd taken those precautions now, and they had worked to some degree. The overhead protection he'd added to his battleships kept bombs off exposed wooden decks, and the small, high-angle cannons loaded with grapeshot had accounted for a number of attacking aircraft. But the enemy had recognized the momentary vulnerability their use revealed and had managed to set barely containable fires in the upper casemates of two of his battleships. Much as he hated not being able to fight back, he'd been forced to order that his only air defenses not be used again.

Still, the enemy could have nothing that would pierce his armor or they'd have used it already, and he'd steamed ahead, confident of victory.

Unfortunately, so far, the enemy had not obliged him with a meeting engagement. Their air attacks were almost constant—so he knew he had to be close to their fleet—but it remained tantalizingly out of reach. He had to find it soon or retire to refuel—which would show enemy scouts where his primary coaling depot had been established on the west coast of India! Worse, his cruisers had proven sadly vulnerable to bombs from above, and he was down to nine fire-scorched survivors.

Pacing back and forth in the heavily armored pilothouse of *ArataAmagi*, Kurokawa fumed. As before, with his old beloved *Amagi*, he had all the power in the world but was frustratingly unable to bring it to bear! He considered sending the cruisers away. They were fine ships for what they were designed to do (if one forgave the engines), and at this rate, they would all be destroyed sooner or later. *Bachiatari aircraft!* Nothing had really scratched his battleships, despite countless bombs hurled at them, and they could easily handle the enemy fleet alone—if they could catch it. . . . He stopped pacing and stared ahead through the viewing slits in the armor. *Or threaten something it* has *to protect!*

"Captain Akera," he said, keeping his voice as calm as he could. Akera had been a lowly ensign on *Amagi*, but came highly recommended, and he was loyal. All Kurokawa's battleship commanders were Japanese, as were most of their officers.

"Yes, General of the Sea?" Akera replied nervously.

"We cannot continue like this," Kurokawa said flatly. "We haven't the fuel to chase the enemy forever when we don't even know where he is! Our . . . reports . . ." He glanced around. Even though there were no Grik on the bridge, he was still hesitant to discuss radio or the wireless set and operators that Niwa had been given when Muriname arrived in India. "Our reports indicate that the enemy has established his base of operations at Madras. Do we have the fuel to achieve that port?"

Akera considered. "To steam entirely around Ceylon and that far north . . . we would not make it back to our own coaling station."

"But we could make it to Madras?"

"I believe so . . . but then what would we do?"

Kurokawa ignored the impertinent question and smiled. "There is plenty of coal at Madras," he assured Akera. "It was the primary export there, after all. Looking back, I do wish we had chosen oil to begin with, like the Americans, since the Grik possess such vast reserves of it, but when we refitted *Amagi* at Colombo, coal was all that was available. Now most of our coal reserves are under enemy control! We shall take it back!" He paused, peeking through the viewing slits. "We are not under attack at the moment. Rig the signal staff," he said, using the euphemism for the wireless antennae, "and signal the other battleships—and General Niwa—that the fleet will make for Madras! We will *drag* the American monkeys into battle, if we must, and General Niwa will provide the troops we need to secure the port!"

"Of . . . of course, General of the Sea," Akera said, "but the enemy will see where we are going. They will have time to prepare!"

"Excellent!" Kurokawa barked.

***Aboard USS* Salissa *(CV-1)* "Big Sal"**

"So, what do you think?" asked Ahd-mi-raal Keje-Fris-Ar, CINCWEST, from a simple chair in the large ready room, or pilot's wardroom, aboard *Salissa*. Captain Jis-Tikkar sat across from him, as did nearly two hundred pilots, OCs, and senior support personnel. Sandy Newman and Kathy McCoy were the only humans in the compartment. The ready room was still mostly illuminated by lamplight, but a single, globular, incandescent lightbulb dangled from a chain-reinforced socket in the center of the compartment, its glare harsh. Soon, all *Salissa*'s lights would come from "bulbs"; they were safer and used the electricity the ship produced in abundance. But the light lacked the soft normalcy of lamps.

Tikker was clearly exhausted, and if the "big board" hadn't been there on the long bulkhead to remind him, he wouldn't remember how many sorties he'd flown. Lemurians usually wore as little as they could get away with, but the pilots had taken to wearing their flight suits all the time. Not only did they need them in the air, but it set them apart from "ordinary" People in ways perhaps similar to the old clan structure. Tikker's flight suit was soiled and stained, and crackly with dried, foamy sweat.

"I think they are licked in every respect but the one that matters most," Tikker replied with a toothy yawn. "We have destroyed most of their smaller steamers and all the Indiaamen we could find, but nothing we do seems to faze the iron-clad battleships." He nodded at Sandy, who'd coined the term. "They alone, and six of their smaller steamers, continue on as if they have *won*, and they are no longer groping in the dark for us; they are clearly bound for south Saa-lon."

"They can't find us, and have given up trying," Keje surmised. "They cannot know we are faster than they, at any rate." He considered. "They know we must have forces at Colombo, but do not make for there. They *may* know we have a base at Trin-com-lee, on east Saa-lon—but Colombo would be the closer, more logical objective. To me, this change of theirs can only mean they intend to round Saalon and threaten Maa-draas—or Andamaan!"

"I don't see how they can even *know* about Andaman," Newman objected. "They haven't acted like it, anyway. Elements of their big bombing mission that sank *Humfra-Dar* off Colombo made it all the way to Aryaal and Baalkpan, but none of them even flew over Andaman."

"The sea is vast," Keje said. "We cannot watch it all. They may have sneaked a scout ship past us. As for their failure to bomb Andamaan, that only means they either don't know about our presence there or they don't want us to *know* they know," he groused.

"Growing a bit paranoid?" Kathy asked with a small smile. Keje didn't smile back.

"As CINCWEST, do I have any choice? Perhaps General Aalden and his Second Corps would not be in the predicament they are now if others exercised a touch of paar-aanoiaa now and then!" The statement was the first time he'd openly criticized Alden—even though Alden had already been criticizing himself almost daily. It showed how frustrated Keje was becoming. He glanced around, blinking apology.

"Forgive me," he said. "General Aalden is our greatest field commander. He planned his campaign based on what we know of the Grik. Unfortunately, what we 'know' is not always *right* and has shown a depressing capacity for change of late." He sat straighter in his chair. "General Aalden *will* consolidate his force and rescue Second Corps—and General-Queen Maraan! In the meantime, we must deal with this other threat." He sighed. "I agree that Andamaan is most likely safe. The defenses are well established and many ships are gathered there, preparing to come forward. In addition, the P-Fortys will soon arrive, able to carry a single, but heavier bomb. Maa-draas *must* be the enemy objective. But if those . . . battleships achieve it, they will block General Aalden's line of supply. We *must* stop them."

Kathy looked around the room. "These guys have flown their hearts out and it seems clear there's nothing more they can do. They're beat, Admiral."

There were cries of protest, but Keje nodded. "Agreed. We have lost half a wing of aircraft, at any rate, between us and *Arracca*, and even though the enemy no longer shoots them down, the machines are failing. We will make for Maa-draas immediately. The aircraft based on Saa-lon can defend against any landings there. We will use the time to rest our aircrews and machines, then use them to help General Aalden." He grinned. "Do not forget, my friends: We still have a powerful surface fleet of our own! We have Commodore Ellis and his DDs, in addition to our own, and *Salissa* and *Arracca* have mighty batteries! Perhaps we are not encased in iron, but I will match our stout sides against anything the Grik can build!" There were cheers and stamping feet. "Even if we have no further help by then," Keje continued, "we will offload all aircraft and their necessary support, and clear our carriers for a surface action such as this world has never seen!"

CHAPTER 22

March 20, 1944
***USS* Walker**
Northwest Fil-pin Sea

"Hold on!" shouted Super Bosun Fitzhugh Gray as he grabbed the little anchor crane far forward on *Walker*'s fo'c'sle. The bull-nose and jackstaff disappeared as the knife-sharp bow—just a few paces away—pitched down beneath another gray-green roller. The torrent of seawater would have swept his repair detail away like crumbs on a plate without his warning, and even Gray felt his feet leave the deck as the flood cascaded past, erupting against the splinter shield of the number one gun and booming against the bridge structure beyond. He glanced quickly around at the 'Cats in his detail, making sure he hadn't lost anyone. Like him, they'd been scrambled around a bit, but they were all there. "Hurry the hell up!" he roared, regaining his feet with the help of the cold iron crane.

"We almost done!" cried Pack Rat, pounding a big, cork-like plug into the hole in the deck where the starboard anchor chain vanished below. God knew what happened to the old cover; fell apart and washed away, most likely, but the chain locker was more than half-flooded and the pumps had more than enough to do.

Gray turned around. "How 'bout you?" he asked Jeek, the flight-crew chief for the Special Air Division. Jeek had a new plane now, a day out of Samaar, where they'd taken it aboard and filled *Walker*'s growling bunkers with oil. But with the plane carefully stowed aft, he was part of Gray's damage-control division, and it wasn't like they'd be flying that day!

"This damn hatch cover leak no matter what I do," Jeek said angrily. He was trying to seal the hatch over the forward companionway. "Them gals in chief's quarters just gonna have to live with it. It *ever* not leak?"

"No," Gray admitted. "Just thought we might try somethin' while we was out here. Leave it be." The hatch had always leaked, leaving the deck in the Chief's quarters slick when the sea was high. The swooping, elevator-ride experience of living under the fo'c'sle was unpleasant enough even without the damp, but you got used to it. The only thing was, Diania lived in there now with Tabby, so she could be close to Sandra. She hadn't made a peep about the conditions, but Gray could tell just by looking at her that she'd been miserable ever since the sea kicked up. He could spot that "look" a mile away after all these years. He shook his head, almost angrily. He'd tried. He looked back at Pack Rat, who'd sealed the opening as best he could. "C'mon, Jeek. Damn sure ain't worth losin' nobody over. Let's get out of here."

They waited until after the bow took another plunge, and then scampered aft across the fo'c'sle until they reached the starboard hatch below the bridge. One of Jeek's 'Cats opened the hatch, and they all darted through. They barely had it shut before another surge slammed against it.

"Whew!" said Gray. "We're done, for now. You guys can relax, but hang here until you're relieved." It had been a very wet, busy watch, and they'd spent it plugging leaks all over the forward half of the tired old ship. The worst had been a sprung plate in the forward berthing space, which wasn't that bad in and of itself—except all the females aboard would have damp racks now—but a lot of seams were opening as the ship worked in the heavy seas and the pumps were starting to strain to keep up. The water in the chain locker had been just the latest concern, and they'd handled that quickly enough. "I'll go report to the Skipper," Gray said, turning for the stairs.

Captain Reddy was standing beside his chair when Gray entered the pilothouse. He'd obviously left it so Sandra and Diania would have something to hold on to while the ship pitched. They were the only humans on the bridge, and the rest of the watch was all Lemurian. That didn't bother Gray at all. Just about everyone on *Walker* could stand a bridge watch now, and they'd had plenty of practice in all conditions.

"The old girl oughta ride easier after we get that water out of the chain locker," Gray said, and Matt and the two women turned. Everyone was a little damp—that was the nature of things, and *Walker*'s semiopen pilothouse didn't help—but Gray was utterly drenched and dripping on the wooden strakes.

"Thank you for trying to fix the leak down the forward companionway," Sandra said with a smile. She didn't even look at Diania, but Gray felt his face heat. "I'm sure the ladies quartered there appreciate it."

"Didn't work," Gray objected. "I think the goddamn hatch was designed to leak . . . if you'll excuse my French."

"You're probably right," Matt admitted, "but it was thoughtful to try. The chain locker?"

"Tight, but that's the only thing." Gray hesitated. "Ah, Skipper? Maybe we ought not chase this Jap tin can right away. The ship's tired, real tired, and she needs that drydock pretty bad. We could probably do most of the work at Manila in just a couple of weeks. Just tighten up the hull. We could tear down engineering once we catch the Jap and get back to Baalkpan."

Matt nodded but turned back to face out the windows. From here, the sea looked like jagged, broken gray iron beneath a lighter gray sky. Sandra looked at Matt, and her expression . . . troubled Gray. He was glad she and the Skipper had finally taken the plunge, and their happiness had been an infectious thing for their first few days at sea, but the reports that continued coming in had turned the Skipper anxious and restless, kind of like he'd been when they were racing back to Baalkpan to face *Amagi*, but less focused. That had been a bad time, but now there was a lot more going on, and almost nothing Matt could personally do about most of it. The man was a born leader. Maybe not in a MacArthur sort of way, thank God, but the kind who inspired others to do their best because they knew he was doing his right alongside them. Regardless how worried he was about Keje, Rolak, Pete, Safir Maraan, and all of First Fleet, he wouldn't give orders to Keje because Keje was on the spot and he wasn't, but the situation had to be driving him nuts. Gray was suddenly glad the Skipper hadn't left Sandra at Samaar to take an empty oiler back to Maa-ni-la, like he'd suggested. Sandra had refused, of course, as *Walker*'s medical officer, and Matt hadn't pressed. After all, they'd probably need her if they caught *Hidoiame*—and her just being around was good for the Skipper.

Gray noticed that Diania was still looking at him, a curious expression on her face. He probably hadn't spoken a dozen words to her since that fine breakfast on Respite—but they were shipboard now, damn it! She shouldn't even be here!

"Can't, Boats," Matt finally said, still looking forward. "I wish we did, but we just don't have time to go in the yard. Mr. Palmer was just here with the latest"—he paused—"and things are getting desperate in the west. You know most of it, but now it looks like Keje's going to go up against those Jap-Grik battlewagons in a straight-up fight with his flat tops. What a damn mess! If he loses, not only could it cost us all our carriers in the area, but Pete and the entire expeditionary force will be cut off!

"On the good side, sort of, it looks like Jenks has made it to the Enchanted Isles in time to salvage the situation there, but there's going to be a fight. . . ."

"And all this fighting is too far away for you to do anything about," Sandra said quietly.

"No! . . . Well, yes, damn it, but we've still got that Jap 'can' out there, full of real bad Japs, and we're all there is. We can't help Keje or Jenks or anybody right now, except the people that ship has killed—and still will, if she's not stopped. *This* is our fight, and nobody can do it for us. Our scouts are keeping an eye on her and she's still headed southwest, but if she gets away now, we might never find her."

"Okay," Sandra said, "but just so long as *Hidoiame* hasn't turned into your white whale." One thing she and Matt discovered during their brief honeymoon was that both enjoyed Melville.

Matt snorted, and when he turned to look at Sandra, the intensity that must have been growing in his green eyes was already fading.

"No," he said with a crooked smile. "The only white whale around here is Earl Lanier, and our peg-legged Filipino is more than a match for him." His voice lowered. "This is just a *job*, and my only obsession is you. Maybe I'm a little obsessed with the bigger job of winning the war, but we're not in the big picture right now." He raised his voice again so all could hear. "*Hidoiame*'s just another job for *Walker* and her gallant crew," he said in a light but serious tone, "but she *is* our job!"

Indiaa
General Halik's HQ

General Halik brooded in frustration in the confined space of his bunker. He hated it! He felt like he'd been forced to hide in a hole like vermin, but the enemy aircraft had shown an unerring knack for targeting his command structure when it was exposed aboveground. It seemed the age-old way of moving proudly into battle beneath the streaming banners of the provincial regent were gone forever. The disciplined column of "new" warriors beneath the very banners of the Giver of Life had suffered cruelly as well, and he'd been forced to disperse the suddenly confused "hatchling host" to some degree. *They, at least, could adjust,* he told himself. They'd been designed primarily for defense, after all, and they could do that wherever they were—but he needed his attacking warriors to mass, and whenever they did that, they were vulnerable. The aircraft alone had forced him to turn this excruciatingly long battle into a series of night attacks, and the unexpected tenacity of his trapped opponent and the added confusion of darkness had caused a disturbing number of even his hardened, "improved" warriors to turn prey! He seethed. *Tonight,* he promised himself. *Tonight will turn the tide!*

Runners had come from General Niwa in the south, telling that General of the Sea Kurokawa *had* finally arrived with the Grand Fleet, and Niwa had received more hatchling warriors. Niwa could now use them to block the tongue, leaving him free to attack the enemy with all his might on the other side of the mountains at Madras. Niwa also promised that "much of what has been confusing will soon be clear," and all their enemies in India would be under their power. The dispatch left Halik even more confused in some respects, but it remained implicit that he *had* to gain control of the pass for the victory to be complete.

He stopped his pacing, listening, as his aides accosted an arrival outside. "Let him in," he said, and General Ugla clanked down the steps and parted the roughly woven curtain that kept dust from entering the bunker—and light from escaping at night.

"Lord General!" Ugla cried, preparing to throw himself on his belly.

"Do not!" Halik said sharply, then paused. "Consider it done, General Ugla," he continued more softly. "We have much to discuss."

"Lord General?"

"We must break the enemy tonight," Halik said. "The battle progresses beyond our view." His yellow eyes sharpened. "I do not know how it progresses in every way, and that does . . . concern me, but I believe our part is crucial." He looked keenly at Ugla. "You were in the highlands on Ceylon and you have seen the fighting here from the very front. You have grown immensely, and I would value your comparisons." Ugla was born to be a general, but this campaign had raised an awareness of war in him that Halik still strove to achieve—and others, like First General Esshk—might never be capable of. That disturbed him, but excited him as well.

"My lord," Ugla began, but paused.

"Do not be concerned. I already know what is bad. Our

losses have been crippling, and the battle remains set as it was when it began."

"Then I will add that our warriors that do not lose themselves fight even better now than they did." Ugla said, then snorted. "The bullet weapons are a great disappointment. Unlike the weapons of the enemy, ours do not work when it rains, or even when the air is wet. Many of our steadiest Uul have died relying on them."

"Ours will improve," Halik assured him. "We captured many of the enemy's arms when we took the southern hill."

"As you say, Lord. That will be a great help . . . someday. In the meantime, the enemy has improved as well, even beyond his skill in the highlands on Ceylon." His crest rose. "Our warriors who have not turned prey do not fear the enemy, but the enemy does not fear us either! How can battles end if there is no fear?"

"They end when we kill them all," Halik said softly. "And they *will* fear us soon."

"Your orders, Lord General?"

"Tonight, we attack with everything! All our reserves, even the hatchlings, will move forward. They will follow behind, but they will not allow the attack to falter. They will kill any that come at them, even our own!"

"We will lose so many," Ugla said in what approximated dismay for him.

"Yes. We may lose *all* of the attackers and that is a great tragedy, but it is the defenders that we must leave in possession of the pass!"

"As you command, my lord," Ugla said, bowing. "But . . . what of the enemy that remains in possession of yonder hill?" he asked, gesturing vaguely northwest. "We cannot just leave them there . . . can we?"

"I would desire the warriors who guard them for this push," Halik said thoughtfully. "The enemy on the hill has been sorely hurt and cannot remain strong. Pull everything away for our assault but those on guard to the north." He paused. "They will join us as well—after they swarm over the top of the hill. Any of the enemy that escapes will have nowhere to go but toward us here, and they will be erased at last."

"Very good, Lord General."

North Hill, west of the Rocky Gap
March 20, 1944

Colonel William Flynn had watched the sun go down on the west side of his hill and now stood in the heavy darkness atop the eastern slope, watching the lightning storm of battle pulse against the low clouds above the Rocky Gap. The indomitable General Maraan had held her ground near the mouth of that pass for . . . could it be five days now? He tried to remember, but the exact number wouldn't come. His time on North Hill with the shattered remnants of his division had blurred into what seemed a timeless span of misery.

There was precious little food and almost no water. Some food and ammunition had been air-dropped to the tattered remnants of Flynn's Rangers, the 1st of the 2nd Marines, and the Sularans, by parachutes. Leedom had told him that his flyers were required to wear them now, but the ones designed to carry a 'Cat or human safely to the ground couldn't land a water cask lightly enough to keep it from shattering. Larger, hastily made patchwork parachutes had been tried, but with only slightly better results. Enough food and water had arrived to keep the division alive, but only just, and fewer and fewer flights could be made because General-Queen Protector Safir Maraan's much larger, equally trapped force required the greater effort. It was a terrible equation. A dwindling Air Corps had to choose between bombs to protect the isolated troops or supplies to sustain them—both of which were in equal demand—and it still had to guard against the occasional but dangerous zeppelin raid. The situation couldn't go on much longer like this.

There had been growing assurances that it wouldn't have to. Communications had finally completely failed the day before, but Flynn knew General Alden was making progress in his drive to relieve II Corps. If he reestablished the supply line, some of the pressure might fall away from General Maraan, and more air could be diverted to Flynn. There was even talk of support from First Fleet air, which would become available for some reason in a few days. The trouble was, none of that really mattered anymore to the survivors trapped on North Hill. Things had suddenly begun happening fast, and time was running out. Flynn could *feel* it.

Captain Saachic approached him in the near-perfect darkness lit only by the distant battle. "Col-nol," he said quietly, "our scouts confirm it: The enemy has pulled everything out but the six or eight thousands that still block us from the north. The rest?" Saachic shrugged. "Maybe they join the attack in the Gap?"

"What about the ones that didn't leave?"

"I think they are coming, Col-nol," Saachic said grimly. "All of them. Why else remain?"

"I bet you're right, Captain," Flynn said, and sighed. Then he chuckled grimly. "Well, we can't stop 'em if they all come at once. Between what we had left and the small-arms ammunition the Air Corps dropped us, we might've had a chance—if they could've given us some artillery ammo. We're completely out of exploding case, roundshot, and mortar bombs—and we've got maybe three rounds of canister left per gun." He looked southeast, toward the battle raging in the Gap. "And we damn sure can't run away from 'em." He almost laughed. "It always comes down to just three choices, doesn't it? All that leaves us is to try to beat 'em to the punch. Attack downhill, concentrating everything we've got right at their gut, and blow through 'em like bowling pins!"

"Sir . . ." Saachic hesitated. "I think we can do that," he said cautiously. "We might even scatter them . . . but most will chase us as they recover—and I think most *will* recover. These are not the same Grik we used to fight, and even if they were, the sight of fleeing prey . . . Our infantry cannot outrun them." Lemurians as a species were amazingly strong and agile. They could even move pretty quickly when they had to and had decent endurance. Unlike humans, however, and particularly unlike Grik, they just weren't built for sprinting.

"I know that, Saachic," Flynn calmly agreed. "But I guess that's not really the point, is it? Meanies *can* outrun 'em, and it'll be your job to get as many out as you can." Flynn interrupted Saachic's dark thoughts with a slap on the shoulder. "Hey," he said, suddenly grinning beneath the mustache that pulsed fire red under the cloud-reflected flashes. "This one's *really* gonna make us famous!"

Saachic forced a grin. "Of course. There is that," he said, then paused. "Assuming we do break through and escape our pursuers, where will we go?"

"Does it really matter?" Flynn asked. "Away, first. Anywhere but here. You can figure out *where* when you can take a breath." He scratched his chin. He really hadn't had time to give it any thought and doubted he'd be around to do so later. "North, I guess," he finally suggested, "then try to find a way east through the mountains. I bet your meanies could do it almost anywhere, but you'll have to get the wounded through in the ambulances—if they make it. Maybe you can rig travois?" He shook his head. "One thing at a time."

Over the next hour, while the distant battle flared and pulsed, the eleven hundred or so effectives under Flynn's command struggled to move every gun remaining on the hill to the northern slope. The maze of fallen trees made it extremely difficult, and several guns had to be disassembled and shifted over obstacles by hand, which caused many injuries in the darkness, but they didn't dare make a light. If the Grik realized what they were doing, they would doubtless attack immediately, and the disorganized defenders wouldn't have a chance. Finally, most of the guns were in position, placed nearly hub to hub, and those too badly damaged for the role they would soon play were spiked and their spokes were shattered.

Every able-bodied Ranger, Marine, and Sularan took his or her place behind the guns, rifled muskets loaded with the loose buck and ball they all still used in desperate situations. Most carried more loaded muskets, inherited from fallen comrades, slung diagonally across their backs. Many of the Marines carried similarly loaded muskets as well. Some would retain their precious breechloaders and serve as guards for the wounded loaded on the various caissons, carts, and other vehicles they'd converted or cobbled into ambulances and hitched to the few surviving paalkas. They were too low on ammunition for the new weapons for them to be of further use, so the rest of the 1st of the 2nd's rifles lined the bottoms of the vehicles beneath the wounded. It was important they not be captured.

Saachic's Maa-ni-lo cavalry waited behind the guns and infantry, carrying two and sometimes three riders each. The extra riders and all the unexpected activity in the dark made the irascible me-naaks nervous, but at least they weren't hungry; there'd been plenty of Grik for them to feast upon. The animals were incredibly tough, naturally armored with thick cases like a rhino pig, so even Grik crossbow bolts didn't bother them much from a distance, but there were fewer than two hundred of them left alive.

"They're getting ready," Bekiaa-Sab-At said, closing her telescope as Flynn joined her. Her head was still wrapped in a bloody bandage beneath her helmet where she'd taken a blow from the flat of a Grik sword. "I see little glowing dots. They are lighting their matchlocks."

Mark Leedom stood beside her in the gloom, much taller than the Lemurian captain of Rangers and Marines. He still had Flynn's '03 Springfield and it was slung on his shoulder, bayonet fixed. "I guess this is it?" he asked nervously.

Flynn chuckled. "I swear, Leedom. I'd be scared to death to fly around in one of those kites like you do. Relax. Folks have been fightin' on their own two feet since there have been folks—of any kind. It's a cinch."

Leedom chuckled back. "Yeah, well, you know? I've learned to prefer to stay *above* such things."

"Just stay close to Bekiaa here and you'll do fine." He nodded in the darkness. "Let's go."

There were no drums, no whistles. There was no audible command at all beyond Flynn's soft words. As he stepped forward, the troops around him did the same, and each company down the line moved off the company beside it. The guns crept forward as well, with pairs of cannoneers on each wheel straining against the weight. Spokes creaked and small stones crunched beneath the iron tires. Prolong ropes trailed behind, held by the rest of the gun's crews, ready to slow them as they reached the gradual slope. Flynn looked around him. He couldn't see much in the dark, but what he could see in the brief, dull, distant flashes made him proud. He didn't have much of a division left, but he was thrilled by the discipline, professionalism, and determination he felt around him. These 'Cats, his *troops*, had been through hell, and every one of them had to know what lay before them that night, yet there was no complaint. Even the wounded stifled their cries as the ambulances began to move behind the lines, painfully jolting the occupants. The paalkas lowed sadly, but it was a sound the enemy would be used to. Around the ambulances, now lost to view, Saachic's cavalry would be moving.

God above, Flynn thought, focusing as hard as he could on the prayer. *Even if this is it—you know, the End—thank you, Sir, for the opportunity to die with such fine folks!*

Almost silently, the collection of shattered regiments swept down the slope as if they'd drilled alongside each other many times. At the bottom, as the ground leveled out, the cannoneers on the wheels of their pieces were joined by others, to preserve their strength. Each gun would fire its three shots as fast as possible, and to hell with the sponge—or any other safety measure—before its crew disabled it and joined the charge. On they moved, farther and longer than Flynn ever dreamed they would make it without discovery. No Grik horn had sounded yet, but time had to be running out. The enemy had been about five hundred yards away to start—beyond effective canister range—but they'd closed that distance to two hundred now, maybe one fifty, he estimated. It was impossible to be sure. *Closer is better,* he thought anxiously. *It takes them half a minute or more to get rolling after the horns*—Jesus! *I think I can see their match cherries without a glass!*

A deep, thrumming roar exploded in front of them with an almost physical force. Maybe it was an illusion, but it seemed impossibly close.

"Drummers!" Flynn immediately roared.

Drums thundered up and down the line, plied by younglings too young or small to carry a musket. Flynn had ordered that they jump on the ambulances when their job was done, but the blinking he'd seen when he gave that command made him doubt that many would. The cannons were already loaded; their vent pricks thrust into the charges to keep them in place during the advance. The drums had been the signal for the gunners to pull the pricks and prime their pieces.

"Division Artillery!" Bekiaa roared grandly. "At my command . . . Fire!"

Flynn clenched his eyes shut and opened his mouth—as he hoped everyone had done—and felt the rippling concussions pound his chest and ears and squeeze his eyeballs into their sockets. Thousands of pieces of canister moaned and whistled, but the sound was quickly replaced by a mounting shriek of terror and agony, and the staccato wooden, metallic, fleshy drumming of high-velocity metal slashing into an army.

"Muskets!" Flynn bellowed, echoed by the cries of the regimental and company commanders. "Present! Fire!"

A scorching volley seared out, the long jets of flame from crackling muskets finally showing Flynn the enemy—less than fifty paces away! *My God!* he thought. *They're right there!*

"Independent, fire at will!" he roared, raising his own musket and shooting into the ragged mass of wailing, writhing Grik. The canister and musket volleys had been delivered so close and so suddenly that they'd hacked a gaping, gory hole in the center of the Grik line. Shredded grass fluttered down like red-green snow, and a haze of downy fur competed with the billowing smoke. The guns barked again, jolting back across the level ground in the knee-high grass, flashing like smoke-shrouded strobes, their muzzles slamming down before tipping up again, the breeches clanking hard against elevation screws.

Some Grik were already shooting back, shockingly fast after such a devastating surprise. Large balls *verped* past Flynn amid the swish of crossbow bolts, but judging by the flashes, a lot of Grik were still shooting wild, maybe blinded by the cannon fire. Flynn heard a metallic *clung*, and a 'Cat beside him pitched to the ground, a huge hole in the front of his helmet. He jerked his eyes away and concentrated on reloading his musket. With a skin-crawling swiftness that would never have been tolerated under other circumstances, some of the guns were already belching their *third* round of canister. Flynn looked just in time to see a gun 'Cat ram a charge down a smoking tube—and be shredded by the premature discharge caused by lingering embers. The rammer staff—and much of the 'Cat—added themselves to the projectiles the gun coughed at the Grik.

For the next several minutes while the remaining guns chewed the Grik before them into bleeding meat and shattered bone, the fight remained a fairly one-sided slaughter. The Grik *were* fighting back, but right then, where the weight of the blow had fallen, there was little they could do.

"Charge!" Flynn finally yelled, his voice cracking. Enough of the drummers had ignored his orders that the scratch division went forward accompanied by a mighty rumble. Muskets flared directly in toothy faces, and Rangers and Sularans crashed into the reeling Grik on the right, while Rangers and Marines drove left in a screaming, sweeping turn. A company of cavalry led by Captain Saachic dashed forward, down the middle, firing buckshot-loaded carbines and swinging their long, heavy swords, splashing themselves with blood as thickly as if they were crossing a stream. Nobody needed Flynn's orders now; the fight was joined and they were stuck all the way in. The objective: Make a lane for the cavalry and the ambulances. That was it.

For the first time in a quarter century, William Flynn became nothing but an infantryman again. Incorporating much of what he'd learned from General Alden and Tamatsu Shinya and what he remembered from his own long-ago service, he'd basically written the new drill manual. He'd spent months teaching on the drill grounds at Baalkpan and later Andaman Island, demonstrating, remembering, adding, and writing it all down. *Flynn's Tactics* had become the approved textbook for officer candidates throughout the Alliance.

Oddly, none of that meant anything at the moment as the muscle memory of battle, so long forgotten, came back as effortlessly as breath. He rammed his projectile, but just as he withdrew the iron rod, he was forced to lunge at one Grik with the bayonet as he stabbed another in the eye with the tapered, threaded end of his rammer. Backing away, he slammed the sticky, bloody rod back in its groove and lunged forward again, driving the long, triangular bayonet into a shadowy throat. Hot blood spurted at him and he spat the salty, raw-meat taste from his tongue. Grik were piling forward now, over the corpses and mewling bodies, trying to use their spears and small shields to batter the Gap closed.

The first ambulance plowed through, bouncing and grinding across the fallen. Fusillades of fire from the Marines atop the ambulances armed with Allin-Silva breechloaders punched through the puny shields and, usually, several enemies at once. The heavy bullets of the .50–80s were hard to stop, and the rapid-fire muzzle flashes cast plenty of light on the killing. Flynn stabbed again, twisted, withdrew, then drove the butt of his weapon down on the long nose bridge/forehead of a Grik that attacked from behind. Trotting alongside the converted caisson for a moment, he stabbed at charging shapes with his bayonet while trying to place a new cap on the nipple of his rifle.

The noise was tremendous, even with the guns now silent. 'Cats trilled defiant cries, muskets fired on both sides, and the Grik shrieked or snarled their rage. The combination created an incredible surge of sound that subdued even the Grik horns that continued to blare. For an instant, he wondered again what had ever come of the idea to use the horns they'd captured against the enemy. They would help right then, he reflected, to confuse the Grik response to the breakout. Such a tool could likely only be used once, however, and even if he had them then, he probably wouldn't have used them. This fight was the biggest test his Rangers would ever face, most likely, but regardless how momentous to him and his comrades, the outcome here would have little effect on the war. He continued stabbing.

Leedom was down right in front of him, on his hands and knees. His helmet was gone and his head was bloody. Flynn didn't even wonder how the kid had gotten so far ahead of him; he just jerked him to his feet.

"Where's your—MY—weapon!" Flynn demanded. Leedom blinked, eyes unfocused.

"Here!" cried Bekiaa, running up behind them and scooping the Springfield off the ground.

"How'd you get back *there*?" Flynn asked.

"Got in a fight. There's a big one, you know."

Flynn barked a laugh, then looked back. For the moment, the Rangers and Marines were holding the Grik away, and the ambulances, screened by meanies, were surging through the bloody gash in the Grik horde. The sight gave him a thrill—until he looked north. The Grik were throwing warriors into the fight ahead of them, deepening the line they'd have to cut through. He calculated the odds for an instant, then shook his head. It was just too much. "Where's Saachic?"

"Here, Col-nol," the 'Cat yelled down at him, his meanie almost sliding to a stop on something slick in the grass. "I'm sorry," he said miserably. "They react too fast! We'll never get the wagons through, sir."

"No shit," Flynn agreed, thinking fast. "But *you* can still cut through if you do it quick!"

"Col-nol!"

"Shut up! Call all your troopers here now. Bekiaa! Get over there and tell them to direct the ambulances to gather here as well. We'll never get them into anything organized, but we can throw 'em over, fort up, wreck the breechloaders!"

Saachic began blowing the three shrill recall notes on his whistle, over and over, and other whistles dully repeated them over the tumult.

"Is this loaded?" Bekiaa asked Leedom, raising the Springfield. The flyer still seemed stunned, blood leaking from his forehead and down each side of his nose, but he nodded.

"Yeah. I just used the sticker . . . not very well." Bekiaa was already gone.

No longer quite like ants, perhaps, the Grik horde began to encircle its prey, even as that prey fought to consolidate itself, to fend off the gnashing jaws that prepared to close on it. Quickly, the remaining ambulances joined the hasty laager, but not all of them made it. Out of ammunition, paalkas killed, Marines and wounded fought to the last and died in little clots. Captain Bekiaa's chore complete, she raced back toward where she'd left Colonel Flynn, but spun when a crossbow bolt slammed into her side. She tried to continue on through the sharp, searing agony that made her left arm and leg almost useless, but a Grik musket ball sent her helmet flying and she dropped like a stone. She couldn't know it, but the shot that ended the battle for her was one of the last ones fired by the Grik. A mist had moved in. Slow match fizzled, and fouling-caked priming pans turned into slimy black soup bowls. The allied caplocks would still shoot, but the ammunition was almost gone. The bayonet, spear, and sword had replaced most of the firing as the roar of battle turned even more primal. Bekiaa never felt the hands that lifted her from the high, bloody grass. She would never even know whose they'd been.

"You guys better go!" Colonel William Flynn roared over his shoulder, Baalkpan Armory rifled musket in his hands, bayonet fixed. His helmet was gone and his thinning red hair was sweat-glued to his scalp. The eyes were sunken with exhaustion but bright with excitement. Lieutenant Mark Leedom knew that was how he would always remember the man.

"We can't hold 'em much longer," Flynn continued as the Grik surged relentlessly closer, "and they're getting thicker over there." He tossed his head northward, then nodded at Bekiaa's still, bloody form. "You gotta get her out of here!"

Leedom's eyes filled with red tears as he looked helplessly back at Flynn, the unconscious, bandage-wrapped 'Cat held close at his side on top of one of the scary-looking me-naaks. "But . . . God damn it, Colonel, I ought to stay. Give her to one of the other fellas! I don't even know how to . . . to control this damn thing!" Every single paalka was dead now, and fewer than 150 meanies remained, their riders doubled, even tripled up with wounded. Leedom watched with suddenly wide eyes while NCOs grimly strode among the meanies, cutting away the muzzles that protected the riders from their terrible jaws. "What the hell?"

"Don't worry," Captain Saachic said, his voice dull with sadness and exhaustion. "You don't have to control him. He'll follow the rest of us. Just hang on."

"But . . . what if he tries to eat me?"

"He won't. He'll snatch something to munch on along the way." Saachic shrugged. "If he *does* try to eat you though, shoot him a couple of times in the side of the head with your pistol. He'll leave you alone after that."

Leedom blinked, then looked back at Flynn. "But . . . why me?"

Flynn actually laughed. "Hell, boy. We'd all be dead already if it weren't for your planes. We need you. The *war* needs you. I'm just an old pig-boat chief who took up a rifle. Nothin' special about me." He pointed at Bekiaa. "*She*'s special, and so are you." He paused. "And so are my Rangers. Don't let 'em forget us!" He looked around. "Remind 'em there was Marines here too! And Sularans, by God!" A ragged, gasping cheer built around them. "Besides, we ain't finished yet. We'll form a square and bust one more hole for the meanies!"

"What then?" Leedom demanded.

Flynn shrugged. "We'll kill Grik until we can't kill anymore. Who knows?" He pointed at Bekiaa. "She and Garrett did it at the Sand Spit, and Captain Reddy did it at Aryaal! Maybe we've got a little farther to go, but there's more of us!" He grinned. "If you get through to General Maraan, tell her to come get us. Hear?"

Leedom nodded woodenly. "I will, Colonel. I'll tell her that and more." Everyone knew there would be nothing left to "get." This wasn't Aryaal—or the Sand Spit.

Flynn looked at Saachic. "Remember, when you toot your whistle, everything we've got will surge ahead of you and make a hole. Keep going and don't slow down for anything, or it'll all be for nothing."

"We could have broken out . . . like this—just leaving you bchind—from the hill!" Saachic blurted accusingly.

Flynn nodded, but gestured at the overturned ambulances. "Yeah, and I probably should've made you do it . . . but I had to try." He looked back at Leedom. "You've got my Springfield. Tell Bekiaa she can use it . . . till I want it back." Suddenly, he shifted back and forth on his feet. "Hey! You know, my muscles are kinda sore—but my joints ain't hurtin' anymore!" With that, he turned back to face the thickening mob of Grik.

A long, harsh whistle blast shrilled above the sound of battle.

CHAPTER 23

Enchanted Isles
March 22, 1944

Lord High Admiral Harvey Jenks entered Elizabeth Bay in the predawn darkness aboard his old *Achilles*, commanded by his former first lieutenant—now Captain—Grimsley. USS *Mertz* and USS *Tindal* followed him in. Elizabeth Bay, located on the southwest coast of Albermarl Island, was the largest anchorage in all the Enchanted Isles, and Elizabethtown, nestled on the north side of the bay between two great, looming peaks, was the capital of the far-flung outpost. As they approached the batteries guarding the harbor, all three frigates, or DDs, fired the green recognition rockets the leaflets dropped by the aviators told the defenders to expect, but a measure of tension lingered. The defenders had fired on the planes, after all, and they'd had no contact with other Imperial forces for months. They might even be suspicious that three ships had so easily evaded the Dom blockade. As for that, it had not been too difficult. The Doms were dedicated sailors, and the steamers had only to wait until they could pass to windward—but that might not be clear to the defenders. Jenks had added a greeting to Governor Sir Thomas Humphries in the leaflets, with a personal reference the man should understand

and appreciate, but that was no guarantee. Sir Thomas might be dead.

Besides, a lot had been going on that night, and even now the northern sky pulsed with sharp, distant lights. The mountains of Albermarl blocked much of the show, but it looked as if one of the mountains itself had come to life. That happened sometimes, but Jenks knew that wasn't the case now. At that moment, the bulk of Second Fleet was pummeling the Dom encampment and positions on the northern part of the island, and soon three thousand Lemurian troops and roughly the same number of Imperial Marines, all led by the enigmatic General Shinya, would launch what promised to be the largest amphibious assault of the war in the east—so far. Most of the visible flashes likely came from the mighty guns of the Second Fleet flagship, *Maaka-Kakja,* herself.

It was likely the defenders were unnerved by the distant spectacle, not knowing what it was, but there was no way Jenks could have warned them about it. Some of the leaflets might have fallen into enemy hands and the Allied invasion had to be a surprise.

The forts answered the signal with rockets of their own—instead of roundshot from their formidable guns—and Jenks's tension ebbed a notch. Cannon suddenly lit the sea to the southwest, opening what should be a fairly one-sided mauling of the Dom blockade, and Jenks ordered several troop transports that had been hanging back to join the three DDs. Soon, the entire squadron passed beneath the quiet guns into the confines of the bay, and saw the greatfish oil lamps of Elizabethtown glowing dimly off *Achilles*' larboard bow. Another rocket arced, sputtering into the sky from the surface of the water just ahead.

"Picket boat," Grimsley suggested, and Jenks nodded in the darkness.

"I shouldn't wonder. Ring 'steerageway only,' and send 'reduce speed' to all ships. Stand by to heave to—we shall see what the picket has to say."

"Very good, sir."

Jenks hurried down from *Achilles*' flying bridge amidships, between the two great paddle boxes, and moved forward while Grimsley repeated his orders. Gun's crews stood ready around their squat, heavy weapons, and the men brought their forefingers to their brows as he passed. Reaching the fo'c'sle, he found the Lemurian Marine captain Blas-Ma-Ar with several of her contingent who'd joined *Achilles* from *Maaka-Kakja*. One of *Walker*'s Lemurian gunner's mates was also there—Stumpy, he was called, because of some misfortune that had significantly shortened his tail. Jenks had kind of temporarily inherited him after the fierce running fight south of Saint Francis. Someone had to remain with him as a technical liaison, and Stumpy had volunteered. The 'Cat liked Jenks, and with all the Imperial back-stabbing that had been going on, he also considered himself "on loan" as one of Jenks's personal guards. Currently, Stumpy was poised by the American searchlight mounted at the bow. The light was powered by electrical generators spun by steam from *Achilles*' own boiler. It wasn't as large as the lights on *Walker*, but Jenks remained amazed by the ingenious device.

"Ahd-mi-raal," Blas greeted Jenks with a salute.

"Captain Blas. You are ready?"

"Of course, sur." Blas and her mixed regiment of Lemurian and Imperial Marines, apportioned between the three DDs, would go ashore immediately, with Jenks to organize the landing and deployment of the Marines on the transports.

"Very well," Jenks said, and turned to the short-tailed 'Cat near the light. "Do not blind them, Mr. . . . Stumpy," he cautioned. "Cast the beam above them, if you can."

"Ay, sur," Stumpy replied, and twisted a large switch.

A solid beam of light stabbed into the dark, humid air, the peripheral glow revealing a small cutter off the starboard bow. Men could be seen scrambling about excitedly on her deck, clearly startled by the blinding light.

"Ahoy the cutter!" cried Jenks through a speaking trumpet. "I am Lord High Admiral Jenks—perhaps better remembered here as Commodore. I command the Allied fleet here to relieve the Enchanted Isles at last! I beg to meet with Governor Sir Thomas Humphries!"

"Aye! Aye!" came a tinny voice in response. "Which we

were sent ta meet ye—but could ye stysh that infernal light!"

"You may secure your searchlight, Mr. Stumpy," Jenks said, then raised the trumpet to his lips again as the searing beam faded. "Make a light of your own," he instructed the men on the cutter, "and we will follow you in. Be quick about it; there is no time to lose!"

Achilles, *Mertz*, and *Tindal* moved alongside the government docks, where their lines were secured by excited, willing hands. There was some confusion and considerable shouting back and forth between *Tindal*, *Mertz,* and the shore, since the two screw steamers didn't need the long boom bumpers that Imperial side-wheelers required—and, of course, there was considerable surprise when Lemurian Marines began streaming ashore and demanding cooperation and assembly areas from stunned locals who'd never seen a Lemurian before. The 'Cats were accustomed to Imperials, and humans in general, so it was no big deal to them, and Jenks was relieved and impressed by the way they deflected a potentially tense time by simply and professionally carrying out their assigned tasks with occasional reassuring shouts of "Don't worry about it, fellas. We're on your side!" The mixture of well-fed, fresh-uniformed Imperial Marines helped, no doubt, but the long-suffering garrison of the Enchanted Isles was surprisingly willing to take them at their word and any fear that Elizabethtown was being invaded by "creatures" was short-lived.

"Admiral Jenks! Admiral Jenks!" came the excited shout of a thin man dressed in bedraggled civilian clothes, pressing his way through the disembarking troops with a small, wide-eyed escort of equally thin and somewhat shabby garrison regulars. "Sir Humphries's factor for Admiral Harvey Jenks!"

"Here I am, sir," Jenks said, striding down with Captain Blas, Stumpy, and some other officers in tow. Stumpy wore a Navy khaki kilt and T-shirt and still carried the '03 Springfield he'd had since Saint Francis. Blas wore her blue Marine kilt and the new camouflage battle dress with the tie-dyed tunic and painted rhino-pig armor. Her black cartridge box and bright Baalkpan Arsenal musket were ready for business.

The civilian looked at her, his dark eyes stilled by wonder before fixing on Jenks. "Lord High Admiral!" he said, and bowed, removing the large tricorn from his head. "Your . . . astonishingly delivered message was received with great relief, sir, but I frankly confess a personal unpreparedness for the appearance of the allies you mentioned! I thank God for them, and no mistake, but they are not the only surprise. There would also seem to be a battle in the north. . . ."

"Indeed. Where is Sir Humphries?" Jenks demanded.

"He awaits you yonder"—the man pointed—"beyond the press. He craves that you enlighten him further about your plans."

"Take me to him, and I shall do so at once."

"Of course." There was just enough light upon the dockyards to see the factor's expression change. "A word first, sir. The governor is . . . not the man he was. None of us are, I fear—our resources and resilience have nearly reached the bitter end. But Sir Humphries has suffered even more than most, for many reasons."

Governor Sir Thomas Humphries had been a cheerful, corpulent man, devoted to his studies of the natural world, when last he and Harvey Jenks met. He'd been an effective governor of this tenuous outpost—in his spare time, he'd often joked—but in reality, there hadn't been much for him to do, and the Enchanted Isles had been the perfect posting for a man of his interests. Seeing him now, Jenks realized Sir Humphries had changed as much as anything else he'd ever known before he met the Americans, before the war began. Where once Humphries would have been fascinated by the appearance of the Lemurians, now his eyes darted fretfully back and forth in the gloom. He was no longer overweight or cheerful either, and seemed to wear his former self like a baggy suit.

"Damn me, Jenks, it *is* you conducting this circus!" the diminished man managed, gazing about. "Thank God you're here! Too late for so many, I'm afraid—my poor tortoises!—but here you are at last. The princess?"

"Safe, Sir Humphries." It occurred to Jenks that the last the governor would have heard of him was his expedition to seek the lost princess, and there was no way he could know of all that transpired since. Some few ships had escaped the Enchanted Isles to report that the Doms were coming, but apparently no word had made it back until the leaflets were dropped. Well, this wasn't the time to catch him up on everything.

"Thank heavens the dear child is safe," Humphries continued. "I met her once, you know? I believe she was two or three. Couldn't possibly remember me . . ." His voice trailed off; then he spoke with more energy. "I've read of these ape folk, of course, in the Founders' logs. You've found them again, have you? However did you train them as troops?" He paused, scrutinizing Blas. "And females! Extraordinary!"

"Sir Humphries, I cannot even begin to tell you all that has occurred these last months in the time we have, but these"—he nodded at Blas and Stumpy—"are not ape folk; they are Mi-Anaaka, or Lemurians, and firm allies of the Empire against the bloody Doms. And honestly, sir, if anyone has been training troops, theirs have been training ours!"

"Extraordinary!" Humphries repeated. "Are there tortoises in their lands? There are none left here, you see, except for a very few I could not bear to see eaten. But the Doms have all the other islands, and the tortoises and other creatures that lived on them were different, unique!" His expression became desolate. "All gone, most likely."

"A great tragedy, Sir Humphries," Jenks said, "but we must look to the present for now." The transports were coming alongside the dock. "You have noticed the battle in the north? Our troops are landing there as we speak under the command of a most able officer, but we must land more forces here to march to his relief as quickly as we can. The enemy will have turned to face him and may yet retain the advantage of numbers. If we strike quickly across the frontier you have maintained, we should catch the enemy in the rear, perhaps even while he is redeploying."

"What remains of our garrison is in no condition for an attack," the factor said doubtfully.

"I expected that," Jenks agreed, "but if you shift all you

have to face the enemy beachhead in the east, surely it can no longer threaten the city here. We will destroy it at our leisure. Once the sun is up, our aircraft—"

"Aircraft? You mean the flying machines that brought your note?" Humphries asked, seizing upon the unfamiliar word.

"Yes. A gift from our allies. They will bomb the enemy in the east and prevent resupply. Soon the Doms there will be in worse straits than you were."

"Extraordinary," Humphries muttered. His sunken eyes grew earnest. "Your . . . Lemooans. They will not eat any tortoises they stumble across? Perhaps a few others have survived?"

"You have my word, Sir Humphries," Jenks said gently.

"Sir," Blas said to Jenks, motioning at the transports. "Colonel Blair will soon be ashore."

"Of course. You have duties. Good hunting, Captain, and God bless."

"Thank you, sir, and may the Maker be with you." Saluting the governor, Blas backed away, then darted through the jumble of forming companies.

"Extraordinary," Humphries repeated again, watching Blas depart. "Such a polite little thing."

Jenks smiled. "I assure you, sir, the enemy will not think so."

Nancys started landing in Elizabeth Bay by early afternoon. Most of these were damaged to some degree, by ground fire or Grikbirds, but some were just low on fuel or out of ordnance. They gathered around a tender to be refueled and rearmed or hoisted out of the water for repairs. The citizens of Elizabethtown lined the shore, watching the strange machines come and go, as fascinated by the Nancys as they were the people who flew them. Supplies were landed on the dock to be distributed among the people. Guards stood around the bales and crates, but hungry as the people had to be, there was no rush, no misbehavior. The island had been relieved and there would be food. They could wait a little longer. The wind carried the sound of the great battle in the north, but the same wind swept the thunder of the closer battle in the east completely away. The only evidence of the fighting there was the quick return of aircraft that flew in that direction, and the steady trickle of wounded that wound back down the high-pass road.

"Doc'Selass," daughter of CINCWEST Keje-Fris-Ar, flew down from the fighting in the north to tend the wounded in the city and take charge of the local hospital. There was the usual resistance by Imperial doctors, but when Jenks commanded that Selass, as personal physician to the Imperial family, be obeyed in all things medical, indignant obstructionism turned to skeptical observation—and soon enthusiastic cooperation. Human and Lemurian physiologies were strikingly similar, but Selass had grown quite familiar with the differences as well. She was far more qualified than any local physician, particularly when dealing with battle injuries, and when the curative powers of the Lemurian polta paste were explained—and confirmed by Selass's Imperial assistants—her former rivals became willing students and helpers.

At nightfall, Jenks trotted up the steps of Government House with Admiral Lelaa-Tal-Cleraan and Orrin Reddy in tow. Lelaa matched Jenks's energetic steps, even though her massive ship had been in the thick of the fight since before dawn. *Maaka-Kakja*'s great guns and aircraft had pounded the surprised and horrified Doms in ways they'd never imagined. *Maaka-Kakja* had taken a few light hits herself, mostly by heavy roundshot dropped by Grikbirds—but new countermeasures rendered Grikbirds less of a threat to well-protected ships and aircraft than they'd been before.

Orrin was dragging a bit. He'd flown many sorties that day—before flying Lelaa here. He couldn't stop yawning. Jenks had never even approached the front as the battle raged. Forming and sending troops forward had required all his efforts and he was just as tired as Orrin, but nervous energy kept him going.

Sir Humphries's factor met the trio at the top of the stairs and led them inside to a sitting room where the governor sat hunched in a chair, a large brandy at his elbow. The garrison commander was seated beside him, his white tunic with red facings was stained and rumpled. Jenks glanced around. Frankly, he'd expected a larger reception. He bowed to the governor, and the garrison commander stood. The factor edged around the room to stand behind Sir Humphries, who remained seated, staring at the once-lush carpet at his feet.

"Sir," Jenks began, looking at the sitting man. "May I present Admiral Lelaa-Tal-Cleraan, commander of the Naval element of Second Fleet?"

"How charming," Humphries said softly. "Another Lemooan female! And a Naval officer, damn me!"

"And this is Orrin Reddy, Commander of Flight Operations. It was his aircraft you saw today—and that the enemy have learned to fear so much."

"Indeed?" Humphries asked, a spark igniting behind rheumy eyes. "Flying machines might be of great use in locating tortoises!"

The garrison commander cleared his throat uncomfortably. "I am Colonel Alexander, and am most pleased to meet you all. As you may have gathered, the situation here had grown quite dire. Another mere week would have seen the end of us." He cast a quick glance at the governor. "Many have suffered, in a variety of ways."

Jenks looked at the man. "Then you will appreciate the honor it gives me to announce that Albermarl Island is secure and your suffering is over. General Shinya and Colonel Blair have pushed the remnants of the northern invasion force against the base of that smoldering hill on the northernmost point. It cannot escape and has no choice but to surrender or die."

"The Doms'll send ships! More men!" Sir Humphries barked desperately.

"No, sir," Jenks gently assured. "Our air power has sunk or burned the bulk of the enemy fleet at Norwich Bay on King James Island. He has nothing left there to send."

"But . . . what of the murderers to the east, just across the isle, that threaten us here in Elizabethtown?"

"We pounded 'em all day from the air, while the garrison"—Orrin nodded at Alexander—"kept 'em pinned on the beach with nowhere to go. It was like shootin' fish in a barrel, poor bastards. They're in the same boat as those up north: quit or croak."

"They might slip men across under cover of darkness!" Humphries insisted.

"They could, a few," Orrin agreed, "but then they'd be stuck too. If I was them, I'd try to pull my people *out* in the dark." He paused. "But that'll be tough. We control the strait between the islands, with DDs and searchlights—"

"DDs?"

"Frigates," Jenks said. "Mr. Reddy is right. In a few days, there will not be a free—or live—Dom on Albermarl, and more of *our* troops and ships will be coming all the time. Soon, this island will fairly shudder beneath the weight of the force we will build to invade the Dominion itself and destroy the murderous threat it poses forever!"

"Extraordinary!" Humphries said with a trace of his old cheer at last. He peered intently at Orrin. "You are a . . . rider . . . of flying machines?"

"Yes, sir."

"You have flown over this isle? And King James Island, perhaps?"

"Ah . . . yes, sir." Orrin decided not to mention he'd been shot at the first time.

"Amazing! To see the world as a bird—or those horrible Dom dragons see it . . . I can only imagine." He took a gulp of brandy, suddenly excited. "Did you happen to see any tortoises at all?"

CHAPTER 24

March 25, 1944
Rocky Gap

General-Queen Protector Safir Maraan, her silver-washed armor dented and tarnished, her black cloak torn and stained, stood in her command tent, staring down at the map before her. She wasn't really looking at it anymore; the image was intimately familiar, and besides, she could hardly see through the kaleidoscope of amber tears colored by the guttering lanterns. Colonel Billy Flynn had saved her tail in the Saa-lon highlands and had since become an excellent friend. Now he was dead, along with nearly all the Marines, Rangers, and Sularans that had been with him—and there'd been nothing at all she could do. She'd been stuck here in this useless Rocky Gap for more than a week now, her own troops dying in front and behind while supplies and munitions dwindled. She looked into the east, through the open tent flap, where the Sacred Sun would rise above the high crags and bathe the gap with light, and said a silent prayer for Flynn and his lost command.

Somewhat selfishly, she thought, she also said a prayer of thanks that her beloved Chack-Sab-At was safe in Maa-ni-la, working up his new elite force instead of in this bone-grinding pit. She feared she might have lost him too if he'd been here—perhaps with Billy Flynn. The 2nd Marines had been Chack's, after all.

"Maker preserve him. Preserve us all," she murmured at the first graying streaks in the eastern sky.

A knock came against the tent pole, discreetly beside the flap. "They are here, my gener-aal," said a low voice. It was almost unnaturally quiet outside, Safir realized. Ammunition was low, but the Grik were not short. They were shifting their forces, she knew, but she hadn't expected the silence.

"I am coming," Safir replied. She took a breath and stepped outside.

Colonel Enaak, commander of the 5th Maa-ni-la Cavalry, stiffened to attention at the sight of her. Another trooper, one she knew well, fought against his exhaustion to stand straighter at his side.

"Cap-i-taan Saachic, reporting as ordered, Gener-aal."

Without a word, Safir moved forward and embraced the trembling Maa-ni-lo, the tears finally spilling down and wetting the blue-black fur on her face. "Thank the Maker you are safe! When Colonel Enaak told me you made it through, I could hardly believe it. Come. Sit inside, and tell me what you saw. Orderly!" she said louder, "bring refreshment!"

"At once, my gener-aal!"

"Col-nol Flynn, all those we left behind, must be lost," Saachic said miserably after a long gulp of seep-laced water. Safir had offered him a stool instead of a cushion because she didn't want him to drift off to sleep. The small torture of the stool struck her as less cruel than waking him after his ultimate crash would be. "We were surrounded; no way out. Col-nol Flynn had a plan, but it didn't work. He tried to save everyone. . . ." Saachic was rambling, and Safir tried to focus his thoughts.

"*How* did you get out?"

"Ahh . . . most of the Grik pulled away to reinforce some movement against you—" Safir looked meaningfully at Enaak. Now they knew where the sudden influx opposite their lines came from. The scouts had seen no approaching column. "And we tried to break through those that remained," Saachic continued. "It might have worked—

should have worked against the Grik we fought before, but these are not the same."

Safir and Enaak nodded. They'd noticed that as well. Somehow, the Grik were finally becoming soldiers. Not all of them had . . . transformed, but enough had done so to keep them bottled up here, and their defense—a concept they'd all thought utterly alien to the Grik—was only growing *stronger*.

"The breakout stalled," Saachic murmured. "The col-nol ordered what remained of my cavalry to make a run for it, carrying as many others as we could. His final effort . . . the sacrifice of all who remained, was . . ." He paused, glancing at Safir. Aryaalans and B'mbaadans were not followers of the prophet Siska-Ta. "It was a tale for the Sacred Scrolls," he finished, almost defiantly.

Safir nodded. "I'm sure it was," she assured him. "But having broken out, how did you make it here?"

"Eighty of our beasts, most wounded to some degree, survived until we reached the mountains north of here with the morning. Most carried two or three persons and there were almost two hundreds of us." He stopped a moment, shaking his head and blinking uncertainty.

"Two hundreds?" Safir asked. Saachic had entered 2nd Corps' lines with five riders. "Did you meet more Grik?"

"There were no Grik, but we could not find a pass. It was then that we met . . . other riders."

Enaak stood. "Other riders! *What* other riders?" he demanded.

"I . . . I do not know, Col-nol Enaak," Saachic replied. "I confess I was not entirely myself." He held up his left arm. "I took a wound and there had been no time to dress it. A fever was upon me. You may ask others who were there, but the riders were *hu-maans*—some were, at any rate." His blinking turned to confusion. "I think there were others; not human, but not like us. They rode upon creatures I have not seen; like me-naaks, but with . . . horns? Their mounts and ours did not like each other." Saachic's tail swished in consternation. "I am sorry. I cannot recall much more about them."

"Perhaps you can," Safir prodded. "You say you 'met' them. What did they do? What did they say? How many were they, and why were they there?"

Saachic appeared to concentrate. "I think they were of like numbers to us. There *was* one, a large hu-maan with a great face mane who spoke a kind of rough English." Saachic grew more animated as memory returned. "I think I asked him if he was Amer-i-caan—someone did—and he laughed." He shook his head. "I remember nothing more but events and impressions. I believe they had been watching our battle; they knew of it, at least. They must be from a land beyond Grik control, but they clearly know much of this one because it was they who showed us the high, winding pass that brought us through to General Aalden."

"General Aalden?" Safir exclaimed. There'd been no direct communications with Maa-draas for two days, not since the comm 'Cats and their aerials had been driven from the heights. Some notes had been dropped by planes, and she knew Aalden was trying to reach them—but she also knew the Grik fleet was coming and a major offensive was grinding at Aalden and Rolak from the south.

"Yes," Saachic said. "That is why only six of us broke through to you. The rest remained with the relief force." He looked at Safir with a small smile when he realized she must have thought his six were the only survivors. "Lieutenant Commander Leedom is well, and will resume command of the remaining air forces in Indiaa. Your cousin-to-be, Cap-i-taan Bekiaa-Sab-At, also survived, though she is sorely wounded. I . . . I am sorry I did not mention that immediately."

Safir closed her eyes for a moment in thanks. Not *all* lost, at least. She didn't know Bekiaa well, but she was practically family. More important, Chack loves her, and she is an exceptional officer.

"So. What will Generaal Aalden do?"

"He intends to force his way through to you today, come what may. Any help you can provide would be appreciated, but the most important message he charged me to give is that you *must* hold here, whatever the cost. The enemy cannot gain this gap. He fears Madraas may be lost when the Grik fleet arrives."

"Maker!" breathed Colonel Enaak. "But what, then, would be the point in remaining here?"

"General Aalden believes that if we are forced out of Maa-draas, we must consolidate here and around that lake to the south. The mountains will provide a barrier to the west, and the lake will allow us to continue to operate aircraft. They are our only defense against Grik zeppelins. Also, though it will doubtless be watched and perhaps even fortified, the river that flows from the lake to the sea is somewhat navigable—but much too shallow for the Grik battleships. Whatever happens, we must assume a position with secure internal lines."

"It has come to this?" Safir murmured. "A hasty defense on foreign soil? Like Colonel Flynn's stand on North Hill writ large?"

"General Aalden anticipated your concern," Saachic said. "He bade me assure you that this entire 'mess' is his fault alone, but we *will* get out of it. The Grik may have caught us with our kilts down—"

"A most colorful and appropriate metaphor," Enaak interrupted.

"—but our own forces," Saachic continued, "new weapons, better aircraft, heavier ships all gather at Andamaan even now. And soon we will do the same to the Grik."

"Very well," Safir said grimly, standing and putting a hand on Saachic's shoulder. She nodded at a large cushion in the tent. "Sleep now, Cap-i-taan Saachic. You have done . . . well." She blinked irony at the insufficiency of the word. "I will speak to your companions about these other riders you met."

Tears suddenly gushed down Captain Saachic's face. The dam he'd held in place by will alone had broken. "He died for us. Col-nol Flynn, the Marines, Rangers, Sularans . . . they all died so I could sit here in comfort . . . and spill tears like a youngling!" He sounded disgusted with himself.

"They died for you," Safir agreed softly. "They died for all of us, so you could bring us your words—and the warriors *you* saved. If not for their actions and yours, we would know nothing of what we face beyond this hateful gap, of General Aalden's plans, or of these enigmatic strangers." Safir gently stroked the filthy, blood-crusted fur on Saachic's cheek. "They will be remembered for what they did, and so will you."

CHAPTER 25

March 25, 1944
***USS* Walker**
South China Sea
1142

The world was a cold, metallic, liquid gray, much as it had been for days, and the rough, disorganized swells still bared their jagged, windswept teeth. Most of the Lemurians on USS *Walker* moved slowly, with considerable determination, and even some of the old hands weren't feeling too hot. They'd followed the slow-moving, raging storm as it thundered northwest across the Fil-pin Lands (old Luzon), until it veered north across Formosa on its way up the China coast and into the Yellow Sea. It had been a wild, bitter thing, not quite a Strakka, but certainly a respectable typhoon. Matt was no meteorologist, but the weather of this world still confused him. This should have been the tail end of the rainy season on swell-hidden Formosa, he thought, but it was too early in the year for typhoons. The experienced 'Cats on *Walker* weren't surprised by the weather—even if the skinny, vigorously bucking ship gave them a hard time. Maybe *Walker* needed a Sky Priest "sailing master" of her own, at least as a weather weenie.

The worst had passed, leaving the old, groaning, complaining ship bounding reluctantly through the Luzon Strait. They'd deliberately made that passage in early daylight, with keen lookouts on the alert. The spray of little islands, north and south, had given Matt and Spanky the creeps. They still couldn't get a proper fix on their position, but when the lookout high in the crow's nest confirmed Formosa to the northeast, they knew they were in the clear. Matt never saw the island from the bridge, but it was just as well. If he had, in these seas, it would mean they were way too close.

Spanky clanked up the stairs aft and came on the bridge just a few moments before the bell at the base of the foremast was struck, indicating the afternoon watch change. Other men and 'Cats had already begun appearing, relieving those who'd been standing the morning watch. Spanky looked at the quartermaster's log, then lurched toward the captain's chair as the ship's bow took a sudden plunge.

"I'm ready to relieve you, sir," Spanky said a little anxiously. Matt had been standing far too many watches, in his view, or just hanging around the bridge too much, even when off duty. The news from everywhere had them all uptight, but Matt was letting his own impatience and frustration show a bit more than usual. The Skipper's mood put everyone on edge, and Spanky knew Sandra was worried about her new husband. It was obvious he wanted to be where the action was, and Spanky sympathized. Particularly when their own mission was looking more and more like a wild goose chase. *Hidoiame* might be just a few miles away—or a thousand by now. Nothing had been able to fly for a week, and they had no recent reports of sightings. Of course, there was no way they could launch *Walker*'s own new Nancy either. The storm was leaving them at last, but they might as well have been groping in the dark with their hands tied behind them.

Matt yawned hugely. "Am I ever ready to be relieved!" he said, making Spanky smile. "How are things in engineering?" he asked, knowing Spanky would have checked personally before he reported for duty.

Spanky's smile faded. "They're keepin' her together, but a week of heavy seas, as beat up as she was to start with, has kind of roughed her up. Tabby really wants to secure number four boiler, and it's like a sauna down there. Loose steam all over the place." He shook his head. "I never seen anything like it. Letts's gasket is swell stuff, and there haven't been any failures, but, well, if they were water lines, I'd say they were weeping. As it is, the couplings just seem to smoke, see? No jets, no gushers. Nothing has blown, but . . ." He shook his head. "It gives me the heebie-jeebies. The guys tighten 'em up and they quit for a while—but directly they start smokin' again. It's like the gaskets are too tough to blow, but as the creosote stuff in 'em starts breakin' down, they get kind of permeable."

"There hasn't been anything like this reported on our other ships, has there?"

"No, sir, but we keep higher pressure, and we been doin' it a *long* time. Maybe some of the industrial power plants have been running longer, but they're in the open air and lose a lot of pressure at the piston packing. Hell, you know? I've never *asked* if they've ever had a failure. Maybe it happens all the time and they take it in stride—just cool her down and change the damn gasket!"

Matt tried a grin on for size. "If that's so, it's still better gasket material than we've ever had. At least it warns you when it's time to replace it! Not many gaskets would have held up to as much steaming as we've done over the past few months."

Spanky brightened. "I guess you're right."

Matt looked at him. There was something else; he could tell. "What's eating you besides that?"

Spanky grunted, angry at himself. "Just those stupid rivets I signed off on. We're starting to get water in the fuel bunkers, more than usual. That means loose rivets—or loose seams caused by loose rivets. Either way, it's the damn rivets."

"The ship's been working hard," Matt suggested.

"Sure, but it's already about as bad as it was when we hightailed it out of Surabaya. It's like the old gal's face-lift fell in record time."

Matt nodded grimly. "We've done a lot of fighting, Spanky, and taken a lot of hits. We did a lot of fighting after Surabaya, if you'll recall. We'll have her in the yard soon, one way or another. She'll hold up."

Spanky managed another grin. "Damn straight! Now why don't you go get some sleep, Skipper?"

Matt yawned again. "I think I will, just on my little cot in the chart house." He stood. "I stand relieved," he said formally. "Commander McFarlane has the deck."

Half an hour later, Sandra made her way up the stairs. She usually made an appearance after the midday casualties reported to the wardroom. There were always a few, especially when the sea was up. Cuts and scrapes mostly, but sometimes broken fingers and worse that the crew hadn't reported to her mates. She had sick-berth attendants now to check on those confined to their racks.

Spanky happened to be looking aft to check if they were making smoke when he saw her. Her long hair was damp and escaping its ponytail, and her smile when she saw Spanky was radiant. *What a dame,* he thought. The contrast between the pretty woman and the rusty iron and roiling sea that filled the rest of his view was striking. After everything they'd been through, Sandra had been as much a rock for all the destroyermen as she'd been for the Skipper. Spanky had seen her as scared, stubborn, mad, or otherworldly calm as anybody in a fight—but he'd never seen her whine or really carry on much at all about the hand they'd been dealt. She'd made the most of things and saved countless lives. *She may have saved all of us, in a way,* Spanky thought, *by keepin' the Skipper steady.* Now that she'd finally gotten her guy, he was happy for both of them.

Spanky nodded at the chart-house hatch, and Sandra hesitated. If Matt was asleep, she didn't want to wake him. Her mission to the bridge was to order him to get some rest, after all. Spanky waved her in with a grin, and she nodded. Opening the hatch on the side of the chart house, she stepped inside. The hatch squeaked and the sound 'Cat stationed inside started to stand, but she motioned him back down. Matt was lying on a rumpled cot, his feet hanging off the end. His head rolled from side to side with the pitching of the ship, and he was fast asleep. Again, she was amazed by what he could sleep through—what all the old destroyermen could tune out. The hatch had been noisy, its hinges rusty, and her steps were loud, to her, as she moved to the chair beside the cot. The active pinging of the sonar sounded like a china-bell heartbeat in the earphones of the sound 'Cat, and the blower and cumulative machinery of the ship vibrated in the bulkheads, deck, and even the cot. Over all was the wild motion of the old destroyer, the booming sea against her plates, and the whistle of the wind around the rotten hatch seal. None of it bothered the tired man on the cot, but if the sounds changed, or there was an instant of silence, of all things, he could come instantly awake. She smiled and adjusted the damp pillow to still her husband's head. He started to snore.

For a brief time, there in the pitching chart house, sitting by Matt's sleeping side, Sandra felt a sense of happy normalcy. In the dim light of the porthole and sonar equipment, with a musty-smelling 'Cat sitting beside her in a compartment that stank of old sweat and mildew, she forgot their difficult task and greater responsibility. For a little while, Sandra was just a wife with a wifely concern for her exhausted husband, and Matt Reddy was just a man, taking a nap.

She jumped in her seat when the general quarters alarm gargled its insistent cry, and when she looked back at Matt, she saw his smiling green eyes.

"Good day, m'dear," he said. "Help me with my shoes, wilya?"

"Of course, Matthew."

"What have we got?" Matt demanded before Minnie could announce him.

"Smoke, Skipper," Spanky replied. "Sorry to bug you, but the lookout in the crow's nest is pretty sure he seen smoke due north in the Formosa Strait." Spanky scratched an ear. "Kid must have freaky-good eyes to spot gray smoke against all that gray out there, but I believe him." He looked thoughtful. "I guess it could be one of our guys, but I don't think so."

"Me either," Matt agreed. "All our steamers are supposed to have cleared the area." He looked at Spanky with a predatory grin. "I think we've caught our Japs, Mr. McFarlane."

Spanky nodded. "Looks like. Or they've caught *us*."

Matt didn't reply. He looked at the diminutive talker.

"Ask the lookout if he could determine anything about range, course, and speed."

"Ay, ay, Cap-i-taan," Minnie said in her small voice. She spoke into her microphone. "Nothing yet, Skipper. Jus' smoke bearing tree fi oh. A blue-gray smear at angle to horizon."

Matt rubbed his forehead above his eyes. "Very well. Let's go have a look, Mr. McFarlane."

"Aye, aye, sir. Helm, make your course three two zero. If they're steaming southeast, we'll have to meet 'em. Lee helm," he said to the 'Cat on the engine-room telegraph. "All ahead two-thirds."

"Making my course three two zero," replied Chief Quartermaster Paddy Rosen.

"All ahead two-thirds," announced the 'Cat as the engine room pointer advanced from Standard to match his Two-thirds, and the old destroyer reluctantly surged against the sharply corrugated swells. Once, standard would have signified twenty knots, but it meant closer to fifteen now. Less, in these seas. Two-thirds *would* take *Walker* churning through the rough waves at a touch over twenty. Matt looked at his watch. "You still have the deck, Spanky. I'll be back in half an hour. Call me when we get a positive ID, or if anything breaks."

"Aye, aye, Skipper. Uh, you gonna get some more rest?"

Matt shook his head. "No, I think the surgeon and I will take a walk around the ship." He looked at Sandra. "If you like?"

"Sure."

"Okay," said Spanky, "but use the damn hand ropes!" he warned. "The old gal's still hoppin' around like a ca—" He caught himself and looked around. "Like a rabbit on hot asphalt!"

The whole crew was still at general quarters, and Matt wanted to see them there. He couldn't roam the ship as often as he liked, but he always tried to see his people at times like this. Everyone knew they'd seen *something*, and there wasn't much doubt among the crew that it was the murderous Japanese. They'd all seen a lot of action now, but only about half the ship's complement had faced a "modern" enemy, either aboard *Walker* or *Mahan*. *Amagi* had been infinitely larger and more powerful than their present quarry, but they had essentially mousetrapped the great battle cruiser. A lot went wrong and a lot went amazingly right, but they'd still sunk her almost by accident. Few retained any illusions that their upcoming fight would be a cakewalk. Even the newest hands no longer believed *Walker* was invincible. She'd taken too much damage from relatively primitive enemies to think that way anymore. And if anyone forgot how fragile she really was, she reminded them herself with her groans and rattles, her deep, painful shudders, and the running rust sores the long voyage had given her.

Matt knew enough about *Hidoiame* to fear her; he'd seen earlier versions of her Kagero class. He was pretty sure they'd fought some on their run out of Surabaya. They'd been faster and more heavily armed than *Walker* even then. He knew from what the crazy cook had told Okada that this specimen had only two twin five-inch mounts instead of three; one forward and one aft, but an augmented battery of 25 mm guns like the two mounts *Walker* had taken from *Amagi* had been added. Apparently, surface actions had grown less common in that other war, and clusters of twenty-fives were better against aircraft. Enough of those things could shred his ship by themselves, despite what Spanky or the Bosun thought of the weapons individually. Campeti had grown to like them—and if he liked them, they were bad news.

We'll have to keep our distance, Matt thought as he and Sandra descended the companionway and went forward to the wardroom.

"Boats!" he exclaimed when he saw Chief Gray sitting on a chair beside a clearly miserable Diania. He'd wondered where the Super Bosun was. Gray looked up, probably horrified he'd been caught like this. One hand was holding a bucket, the other tentatively patting the sick girl's back. Diania's face was in the bucket, her trembling hands holding wet, dark hair out of the way.

"Oh, you poor dear!" Sandra exclaimed, rushing forward. She looked at her pharmacist's mates. "I thought she was doing better!"

"She was," one said, but then gestured around. Diania wasn't the only human female puking in the wardroom. "I guess it come and go," the 'Cat said with a slightly superior air. Sandra was annoyed. All the 'Cats had been just as sick the first time they rode *Walker* in a storm. She knelt in front of Diania.

"Are you all right?" *What a stupid question.*

"Aye'm," came a muffled croak from within the bucket. "I'll be back tae me duties soon enu . . ." The bucket thundered.

"Boats," Matt said softly, "you're damage-control officer. You need to be . . . You've got other duties."

"Aye, sir," Gray grumbled. "An' I was doin' 'em too, when I came through here an' seen this. I ain't never seen so many broads . . . blowin' tubes, as it were, all at once. It was . . . terrible! I had to do somethin' to stop the leaks."

Sandra snapped her fingers at a PM. "You! Relieve Mr. Gray this instant! He *does* have other duties, and right now, this is yours!"

Gratefully, Gray surrendered the bucket, but paused, electrocuted, when Diania grabbed his hand.

"Thankee," she mumbled, her red-rimmed eyes peering up at him. "Ye're not sich a beast as ye make out. I'll nae fergit!"

Gray retrieved his scalded hand.

"I'll, uh, get on down to, ah . . . make sure . . ."

Matt shooed him off. When Sandra was sure Diania and the others were receiving proper care, they got the coffee they'd come for and headed aft.

"Chief Gray seems almost *scared* of Diania," Sandra said as they neared the airlock to the forward fireroom. She'd rarely been in there before.

"Can you blame him?" Matt asked. "He was married once, you know, and it didn't go well. They had a kid, but he was probably lost on *Oklahoma*, last we heard. At Pearl." Matt frowned. "All Gray's ever had out of . . . obligated relationships is pain. He never even shacked up with a Filipino gal. I'm sure he's visited his share of . . . professional ladies over the years, some just as young as Diania, but that's not what she is, and he doesn't know how to handle it.

He *won't* take advantage, but with her stalking him like the hunting dame her name sounds like—" He snorted. "I'd be scared too. He's old enough to be her grandpa!"

"You really think she's stalking him?" Sandra asked, amused.

"Don't you?"

"Maybe. I know she admires him. I also know age shouldn't matter, not here—certainly not with them. Consider their respective backgrounds; both somewhat monastic, and Diania never expected the opportunity for an 'obligated' relationship of any sort, other than practical slavery." Sandra smiled. "Diania's an adult, over twenty, I'm sure, even if she doesn't know exactly. Mr. Gray obviously cares for her. I think they'd be good for each other."

They cycled through into the forward fireroom and passed between the large bunkers that filled the space where the number one boiler used to be.

"'Ten-shun!!" cried a Lemurian snipe.

Matt quickly called, "As you were!" before he could disrupt anything. "Lieutenant," he greeted Tabby when she appeared before him.

"Skipper," she said. "We fixin' to get them damn Japs?"

"I hope so. Any serious problems?" Matt knew better than to ask if there were any problems at all. There were plenty of nuisance issues he already knew about, and Tabby would dutifully recite each one if she thought that's what he wanted.

"Nothing new not already in report," Tabby said. "I'll keep screws turnin' as long as you keep holes outta my spaces!"

Matt chuckled. "I'll do my best."

"Uh," Tabby paused. "Spanky have the deck?"

"He does."

"He on aft deckhouse when we fight? On auxiliary conn?"

"That's right."

"You . . . you tell him I ask he be careful?"

"I sure will, Lieutenant," Matt said. "Carry on."

"Yes, indeed," Sandra said cheerfully as they moved aft. "And Mr. Gray is worried about *his* stalker!"

"Damn it," Matt muttered. "Nothing I can do about it, but this is exactly the sort of thing that proves that women—females of any sort—just don't belong on warships!"

"Of *course* we don't," Sandra soothed with a grin. Matt rolled his eyes.

The sea remained just as vigorous when they came on deck through the forward hatch of the aft deckhouse. Everywhere they'd been, they'd stopped a moment and asked a question or passed an encouraging word. The 25 mm mounts were manned by wet 'Cats and men. The ship always took a lot of water across the deck here. Matt waved at the crews when they stood from behind the shelter of the steel tubs. Jeek and Chief Gunner's Mate Paul Stites met them at the galley beneath the amidships deckhouse.

"I was looking for you, Chief Jeek," Matt said, blowing misted seawater off his lips.

"Cap-i-taan?"

"If that is *Hidoiame* up ahead, we'll likely have to have the 'Nancy' over the side."

Jeek nodded sadly. "We just got her too."

"I know, and I hate it. But the last thing we need is a burning plane on deck."

"Ay, ay, sur."

Matt turned to Stites. "What have you got?"

"Uh, yes, sir. Two things. First, Mr. Campeti has arrested Lanier."

"*Arrested?* My God, what's he done now?"

"Well, most of the mess attendants and such are shell handlers and on gun's crews when we go to battle stations . . ."

"So?"

"Lanier wouldn't turn half a dozen of 'em loose until they stowed his damn Coke machine. He's done it before, and the fellas are always late to their stations, but Campeti's sick of Gunnery always bein' the last to report—and him and Lanier got into it. Lanier said his machine was more important than any damn gun, and when Campeti said it was a useless piece of . . ." Stites glanced at Sandra. "Anyway, Lanier took a swing."

"A swing?"

"Yes, sir. I saw it myself. Course, it was kinda slow and Mr. Campeti dodged it fine—but there was a lot of weight behind that punch and Lanier sorta capsized."

"Was he hurt?"

"No, sir, but he landed on Juan, uh, Mr. Marcos, and snapped off that wood leg of his. That's why there's a problem."

"Okay."

"Well, the fellas'll need fed before we go into action"—Matt always insisted on that, and Stites continued—"and since Juan's in dry dock, he can't run the galley—"

"So Campeti can't clap Lanier in irons like he deserves," Matt finished.

"Yes, sir—I mean, no, sir."

"I see."

In an odd way, Matt was actually enjoying this. Once again, he might soon be responsible for all their lives, but this . . . complaint harked back to a simpler time, before the war here, before the Squall, before the war back home. Even before the tardy, frantic, prewar readiness exercises when many of his duties involved just riding herd on a shipload of rambunctious . . . boys. He had to stifle a nostalgic smile. He stepped closer to the galley window where he was sure Earl Lanier had been listening.

"Is this true, Lanier?" he shouted over the sea and the roaring galley furnace inside. Lanier appeared.

"Not completely, sir, though *some* folks might'a seen it that way."

"Very well. I'll deal with you at mast. Consider yourself confined to your duty station—the galley—until further notice."

"Aye, aye, sir." Lanier sulked.

Matt looked back at Stites. "What else?"

"Sir?"

"You said there were *two* things?"

"Oh! Mr. Campeti asks if we want any of the black-powder shells in the ready lockers or the lineup, you know, in case the new ones give us fits."

"Does he expect any fits?"

"No, sir, he hopes not."

"Then no. The older shells'll put us in range of those things." Matt gestured back at the 25 mm guns. "That's no good."

"No, sir."

"Anything else?"

"No, sir."

Matt looked at his watch again. He'd been gone a little over twenty minutes. If Spanky had decided the target was an illusion, someone would have found him and told him. If it was doing anything threatening, he'd have been called back to the bridge. All the same, whatever it was, it ought to be in sight by now.

"Carry on, Stites, Jeek. I'll be on the bridge if any more . . . domestic hostilities erupt. And since we're liable to be in action before long, the punishment for such acts will increase exponentially. Is that clear?"

CHAPTER 26

March 25, 1944
Battle of Madras 1216

Admiral Keje-Fris-Ar leaned against the bridgewing rail of his beloved *Salissa*, staring through his Imperial telescope. Commodore Jim Ellis was leading the battle line with his DDs, under full steam and with all sails set. The crisp morning breeze out of the northwest was giving the graceful frigates an extra two or three knots and they seemed to fly across the purple agate sea toward the looming, smoking behemoths on the horizon.

Keje wasn't happy sending Ellis and his Des-Div 4 against the Grik battleships. He feared even its powerful guns might prove ineffective against the enemy's sloping iron sides. He'd heard how Marines sometimes used angled shields to turn musket fire, and suspected the Jaap Grik had designed their mighty ships with similar principles in mind. Jim was right, however. They wouldn't know until they tried. All the bombs they'd used had been mere incendiaries with little explosive force. The thirty-two-pounders mounted on most of Jim's ships would give the enemy the first real battering they'd taken. *Salissa* and *Arracca* were more heavily armed—*Salissa*, in particular, with her captured Jaap guns—but much as he hated to admit it, Jim was right about something else as well: *Salissa* and *Arracca* were more valuable than every other ship in First Fleet combined, and they shouldn't be risked unless absolutely necessary, or there was some chance they might inflict more damage than they received. Besides, if Jim failed, only *Salissa*, *Arracca*, and the few DDs Jim had left to screen them would remain to defend all the helpless transports, oilers, tenders, and their priceless crews when they made their break. Reinforcements *were* on the way, but none could possibly arrive in time to make a difference. Ben Mallory's P-40s were supposed to arrive at Andaman that day, but to be of any use here, they'd have to land and refuel on Saa-lon. Grass strips had been located and laid out, but there were no facilities, fuel, or ordnance in place yet. Keje sank lower against the railing. No, First Fleet would have to fight with what it had.

He glanced down at *Salissa*'s flight deck as the last of her Nancys lofted into the sky. There would be one last airstrike before Ellis made his attack, and the pursuit squadrons still carried incendiaries. There was always the chance they could get them through the antiair cannon ports if the enemy opened them. All the planes still carried hand-dropped mortar bombs, but those relied on fierce but relatively light antipersonnel fragmentation and hadn't been effective at all against the armored ships. Somebody had come up with the bright idea of having the bomb squadrons' OCs light fuses on the much heavier naval exploding case shot before dropping it on the enemy. Keje shuddered. The fuses were like little signal rocket motors and would flare fiercely—and possibly disastrously. There was a chance someone might drop one of the improvised bombs down an enemy stack, or a near miss detonating alongside might open seams below the waterline. It wasn't much to hope for. There were better bombs on the way, but for now, they had to make do.

Keje sighed and nodded at Captain Atlaan-Fas. "Get on the TBS yourself. Send to Commodore Ellis on *Dowden*: Attack the enemy at your discretion, and may the Maker above be with you all."

USS Dowden

"What a sight!" cried Lieutenant Niaal-Ras-Kavaat, Jim's exec, while the 1st and 5th Naval Air Wings swirled around the monstrous Grik battlewagons like a swarm of stingers above a herd of rhino pigs. Incendiary bombs spewed rivulets of flame across the ships and the sea, keeping the antiair cannons from firing, if nothing else, and white puffs, like big cotton balls, blossomed around the ships as case shot exploded. Heavy geysers erupted in the air when the bombs hit the water.

"What a sight," Jim agreed, watching through his binoculars. A form of hell was being unleashed on the oncoming monsters, but as far as he could tell, the six dreadnaughts—suddenly, he *had* to call them dreadnaughts—just shouldered it all aside and kept on coming. One of the ironclad frigates that remained with the enemy fleet suddenly jetted fire from every port and silently disintegrated under a muddy gray pall. It was long moments before the dull crack of the detonation reached them, but it was drowned by cheering. Jim was tempted to silence the crew. The destruction of the smaller ship meant nothing. Instead, he let them enjoy the moment. He didn't know what size guns those monsters carried, but they were probably bigger than his—and longer ranged. His crew would get a wake-up soon enough.

He looked aft. Trailing behind *Dowden* were USS *Haakar-Faask*, USS *Naga*, USS *Bowles*, USS *Felts*, USS *Saak-Fas*, USS *Davis*, USS *Ramic-Sa-Ar*, and USS *Clark*. All were newer than *Dowden* and carried thirty-two-pounders to her twenty-fours, but *Dowden* was his ship, and would fire the first shots. Suddenly, Jim chuckled.

"What?" Niaal asked, blinking.

"Oh, nothing," Jim said, then shrugged. "There's six of them—eight, counting those frigate things they have left—and nine of us. Hell, this is the first time we've ever had 'em outnumbered!"

Niaal chuckled uneasily. "Yeah . . . but maybe we should've brought the whole division. I'd feel better if we outnumbered them a little more."

Jim shook his head, pointing to windward where three

more "destroyers" paced them. "They can come up quick enough if it looks like we're doing any good. No sense wasting good ships and crews if we can't scratch the bastards!" Niaal nodded, but wasn't sure he agreed. More ships would disperse the enemy fire between more targets . . . wouldn't they?

"Besides," Jim continued, "if they knock us out, I can't leave Keje naked. *Scott*'s the only new DD he's got back there." He forced a grin. "Hoist the battle flag, Mr. Niaal!"

Niaal repeated Jim's command. Moments later, the oversize Stars and Stripes ran up the halyard and broke to leeward. As the man and 'Cat watched, every trailing ship hoisted its own big flag, and Jim felt a stirring in his chest.

Niaal strode to the cluster of speaking tubes by the helm. Rather ironically, and unlike the Imperials who'd adopted an elevated flying bridge amidships, "American" frigates still retained their primary conning station on the quarterdeck, aft. Maybe it wasn't as practical, but it was more traditional and the helm was better protected behind the heavy bulwarks on either side. The auxiliary conn was aft as well, but belowdecks and tied into the same speaking tubes. "Range?" Niaal cried into the tube that ultimately snaked up the main mast to the fire-control platform in the maintop.

"Six, fi, double oh," came the tinny reply.

Dowden may be older, but like her consorts, and most of the warships in First Fleet, she'd recently been fitted with some relatively simple but fundamental improvements. She had a crude VHF radio telephone, a "TBS" (Talk Between Ships) that, though limited to line of sight, allowed her comm officer to speak directly to his counterparts on other ships. It would come in really handy when they had transmitters small enough for aircraft. More important at the moment, Des-Div 4 also had rudimentary fire control. The guns had to be shifted manually from side to side for windage adjustments, but they could be elevated to fire broadsides—true salvos—at relatively precise ranges determined by the gunnery officer. This was accomplished with new electric primers and a gimbaled switch that would complete the firing circuit when the ship was on an even keel. The new rig wasn't as good as a gyro, of course, but it was better than nothing. In practice, they could now put nearly every round in a ship-size target at fifteen hundred yards—even with smoothbores.

None of these improvements had made it to Second Fleet yet, due to the distances involved. *There are probably some politics involved as well,* Jim thought grimly. On one level, he understood. The Grik were still perceived as the immediate threat by most, including Adar, and though he supported the Imperial Alliance, he, like most Lemurians, considered the Doms as primarily an Imperial problem. What made that attitude gall Jim was the fact that there were Lemurian—American—ships, crews, and troops in the east, and they shouldn't bc deprived of better equipment simply because some thought their fight was less important. Or maybe in this instance, politics had a place. The Empire was still racked by security issues, and it had been drummed into everyone that, crude as it was, the new fire-control apparatus must never fall into enemy hands. The Japanese would probably come up with something similar for the Grik, if they hadn't already. (*We're about to find out,* Jim thought.) But it should remain a major advantage over the Doms for a long time to come—if nobody squealed. Jim shook his head and concentrated on the business at hand.

"Forty-five hundreds," Niaal repeated the latest estimate.

"Very well. Sound general quarters."

"Generaal quarters! Generaal quarters!" Niaal shouted at the 'Cat standing beside the alarm bell. "Clear for action!" The heavy bell began to ring and drums thundered in the waist. Jim clasped his hands behind his back and fixed a calm expression on his face. This would be his first real surface action since the Battle of Baalkpan. He hoped it wouldn't be his last. More important, though, he hoped he wouldn't screw it up.

The Grik dreadnaughts churned inexorably closer, their massive, sloping sides rearing high out of the sea. Des-Div 4 had the advantage of the wind, speed, and position, angling to cross the enemy's projected course. Its first salvos should take the lead Grik ship dead on the bow in succession, and Jim wondered why Kurokawa—*It has to be Kurokawa over there,* he thought—would so obligingly let him "cross his T." Was the maniacal Jap really so supremely confident? Jim felt a chill.

"Three thousands!" Niaal reported. Three huge clouds of smoke blossomed at the forward casemate of the oncoming ship.

"Kind of ambitious," Jim muttered. A few hundred yards short, widely spaced geysers erupted into the sky. They looked like the splashes of the eight-inch cruiser guns that had dogged *Walker* so long ago.

"Jeez!" Niaal whispered. "Kind of *daamn big*! Those must be hundred-pounders, maybe bigger!"

"They'll never hit us from this range. Grik gunnery has always been crap," Jim reassured him. Reassured himself. "Keep track of the time between shots."

"Maybe they don't hit us from here, but we gotta get closer," Niaal reminded. "Quartermaster! You timing the shots?"

"Ay, sir."

"All ships will concentrate fire on that devil up front," Jim ordered, even as the enemy line began to assume an echelon formation, the dreadnaughts behind starting to ease to the side and increase speed. Soon all the enemy ships would be approaching parallel to one another. Jim suspected they would make a coordinated turn to starboard, exposing their port broadsides when Des-Div 4 entered what the enemy considered his own best range. Niaal saw it too.

"You sure you want to concentrate on just that one?"

"Yeah. If we can't hurt one of them with everything we've got, there's no hope against them all, and we might as well break off. Send it."

"Ay, sur."

Time passed as the fleets drew nearer one another, and the tension rose proportionately.

"Two t'ousands!" came the shout through the voice tube.

"Stand by! We'll commence firing at fifteen hundred. The gunnery officer will give the command."

Three more massive puffs of smoke obscured the target before the wind swept them away.

"Eight minutes, twenty seconds!" cried the quartermaster.

"Very well."

Two great splashes erupted fairly close astern, and one mighty shot moaned by overhead, snapping a single backstay before it plunged into the sea a hundred yards to port.

"Starboard baat-tery, match elevations for fifteen hundreds!" the gunnery officer commanded.

"Elevations matched!" came the replies of the midshipmen, each in charge of a pair of guns.

"Stand clear!"

"All clear!"

Moments later, with only the brief clanging of a bell in the maintop as warning, all twelve of *Dowden*'s twenty-four-pounders in the starboard broadside vomited smoke and fire with a precision only *Walker*'s guns had ever shown in combat. The smoke drifted downrange, toward the target, but quickly dissipated as Jim watched the impressively tight cluster of roundshot rise and rise, then plummet toward the target.

ArataAmagi

ArataAmagi rattled and shuddered like a tin roof under an impossibly dense onslaught of giant hailstones. Her forward armor was not as sloped as elsewhere on the ship and was therefore the thickest, but shards of shattered iron, from armor and shot, sleeted in through the viewports, killing the helmsman and two others in the pilothouse. Even Kurokawa felt a sting as a sliver of iron clipped his ear.

"Take the helm, fool!" he screamed at Captain Akera, who seemed stunned by the sound and density of the pummeling *ArataAmagi* just received. Jerking his head as if clearing his senses, he lunged for the spoked, wooden wheel. "Secure all battle shutters but the three directly in front of the helm!" Akera shouted. "Report all damage!" he added into the ship-wide speaking tube.

"One of the forward guns has shattered," came an immediate, coughing reply. They already knew that the gun deck filled with smoke whenever they fired any of the main battery, and the ventilation was poor. "Its crew is dead. Other gun's crews were wounded by fragments that ranged the length of the gun deck!"

"Any other damage?" Akera asked.

"None I can see, Captain," came the voice. "Perhaps a little buckling in the timbers backing the armor."

"Very well," Akera said. "Pull in the guns and secure the gunport shutters!"

"Belay that!" Kurokawa screamed. "We must continue firing!"

"General of the Sea," Akera pleaded. "We must wait until the enemy is closer and we can unmask our entire broadside! Clearly they have devised a fire-control system of some sort. I doubt a quarter of their shots could have missed us. Leaving the forward ports open only invites more damage we have little hope of answering!"

Kurokawa opened his mouth, but before he could speak, *ArataAmagi* shuddered again under another cacophonous hammering that seemed even heavier than the first. Even through the thick deck beneath their feet they heard the bloodcurdling shrieks of Grik that time.

"A shot came *through* the starboard bow port that time!" came the excited, coughing cry of the Japanese gunnery officer. "It killed several, and pierced the forward smoke-box uptake! We have exhaust gas on the gun deck!"

Akera looked at Kurokawa.

"Very well!" Kurokawa seethed. "We will close the shutters and endure this insulting barrage as long as we must to come to grips with the enemy!"

Akera repeated his earlier order, then looked through the slits just in time to see the third ship in the distant line stream white smoke. He ducked down as more hammer blows pounded his ship and more shattered iron sprayed into the pilothouse, tearing jagged holes in the bulkhead aft. Kurokawa was the only one who hadn't ducked, and he was miraculously spared. The first ship fired again, and after that, the beating became continuous.

USS Dowden

"She's taking a beating, all right," Niaal said, staring through his telescope. "Her frontal armor looks all dented up—and I think it's bolted on in layers. We may have knocked a few plates loose, or maybe shattered them!"

"Hmm," was all Jim said. He was pleased with his division's gunnery; fewer than half the shots fired had missed their mark and they still only had smoothbores, but it wasn't good enough. At this rate, they'd eventually batter in the forward casemate of that one ship. They might even destroy her. But she no longer led her sisters; the other five had joined her in a parallel advance. When they turned—soon, most likely—they'd present their undamaged sides and all the guns behind them.

"Get on the TBS to Admiral Keje," he ordered, the thunder of *Haakar-Faask*'s guns just astern nearly drowning his words. "Tell him we're doing damage, but the enemy is about to turn on us and it won't be one-sided anymore. We could get smeared pretty fast. We have to decide right now whether to break off or go all in. Either way, we're gonna get hurt. If we break off, we lose Madras. All in, we could lose the fleet *and* Madras." He shook his head. "Keje has to call this one."

USNRS* Salissa *(CV-1)

Keje nodded, blinking, when he heard Jim's message. From his elevated post high on *Salissa*'s bridge, he could see it all. The first Grik dreadnaught *was* taking a beating, but none of the enemy had been firing back for a while. The deadly accurate fire of Des-Div 4 must have gotten through forward and spooked them. They were still coming, though, and must think they had the advantage. They probably did—against Des-Div 4. Keje felt sure he could overwhelm the enemy with *all* his ships. His had the advantage of speed and maneuverability. But once they got in close, the fire control that had been working so well would be of little use—or would it? If his ships could coordinate their windage adjustments as well as their elevation, concentrate on small areas of the enemy armor, much like they'd been doing, they might punch through. . . . *Salissa* had 50 thirty-two-pounder smoothbores, and *Arracca* carried an equal number of fifty-pounders; probably more guns each than the enemy, but their likely hundred-pounders would outrange them and pack a heavier punch. Of course, *Salissa,* at least, wasn't constrained to going toe to toe. She had some modern weapons as well. . . .

On a pivot mount forward, under the leading edge of the flight deck, she had a breeched section of one of *Amagi*'s ten-inch guns that could fire *Amagi*'s own shells. The two hundred-pound projectiles had been modified for muzzle-loading use, with a reduced-diameter bearing band and a heavy copper skirt to expand into the rifling. But even at the lower velocity the new gun could achieve, he knew the heavy shells would be devastating, and the gun's crew could put the big bullets on a target the size of a felucca at fifteen hundred tails. *Salissa* also carried two of *Amagi*'s 5.5-inch guns, with Japanese ammunition, on her superstructure. These were long-range weapons, more powerful than *Walker*'s four-inch-fifties, with high-explosive, armor-piercing shells. He knew something about steel now, and there was no way those Grik monstrosities could match *Amagi*'s armor, no matter how thick their plates were laid on. He made his decision.

"Send to my dear Cap-i-taan Tassana-Ay-Arracca that she and *Arracca* must remain with the transports and oilers. I will yield to no arguments." He paused. "Do ask her to keep a pursuit CAP above us all to guard against Grik zeppelins, though. *Salissa* and the remainder of Des-Div 4 will join the action against the enemy! The ship will be cleared for surface action, and all planes of the First Air Wing but that of COFO Cap-i-taan Jis-Tikkar will proceed to Maa-draas!"

***USS* Dowden**

"They're turning!" Niaal excitedly echoed the cry from the lookout. The gunnery officer in the maintop was continuously updating range, course, and speed estimates. Jim could already see the aspect change of the enemy battle line through his binoculars. He had no idea how accurate the enemy fire would be at nine hundred yards, but he suspected his division would take *some* hits—and they'd be bad. The question became, Should he have his ships continue to concentrate on a single enemy, and maybe punch through somewhere? Their own fire would be accurate enough at this range that it would be hard to miss. On the other hand, if they spread their fire among all the ships, they were less likely to do serious damage to any—but they might disrupt the enemy's gunnery and cause them to rush their imperfect aim. The second alternative might be safer, but the first was more likely to achieve something. He sighed. *This* one was *his* call. He decided on a compromise.

"*Dowden*, *Haakar-Faask*, *Naga*, *Bowles*, and *Felts* will continue firing on the first target—the Grik flagship, most likely," Jim ordered. "All others will target their opposite numbers in the line of battle. Maybe we can wreck the one while keeping the others shook up." Niaal repeated the order to fire control and the comm shack.

"Range eight, fi', oh! Bearing, tree tree seero! Speed . . . they still turning, but I make it eight knots!" came the report from aloft.

"Match elevations at eight hundred, and fire when ready!" Jim replied.

"Stand by . . . Stand clear!"

"Clear!" chorused the midshipmen, and the salvo bell rattled for a long moment as the ship steadied. Then, with a thunderous jarring that shook the ship, all twelve starboard guns spat fire and heavy shot. An instant later, *Haakar-Faask* was enveloped in smoke as her guns thundered. Then *Bowles*, *Naga*, and *Felts* all seemed to fire at once. Even while the mighty spheres were still in flight, the rest of the division opened up on their respective targets.

ArataAmagi

Kurokawa was thrown to the deck of his pilothouse when perhaps fifty heavy shot struck his massive ship with an unprecedented, ear-splitting fury. Somewhere aft, deep, it seemed, he heard a terrible crashing and a chorus of shrieks.

"Fire back, you fools!" he roared. "Destroy those ships at once!"

Akera staggered back to the wheel, catching it as it spun, and leaned over the ship-wide tube. "Commence firing!" he cried. "Commence firing!"

"Not all the guns yet bear!" came the tinny reply, "and we took two roundshot through the open shutters—not to mention some serious dents that time! The timber backing has splintered in many places I can see from here!"

"All the more reason to return fire at once!" Akera almost screamed, glancing quickly at the compass binnacle in front of the wheel. He spun the wheel again. "Fire as they bear!"

Kurokawa had regained his feet, and his eyes smoldered. "Have the special comm division contact General Muriname at his aerodrome! I had hoped we wouldn't have to use him—it will be costly—but we are taking damage, and the enemy capital ships do not seem inclined to engage. Tell Muriname it is time for his ships to come up! He knows what to do."

***USS* Dowden**

"That *had* to leave some bumps," Ellis muttered, staring through his glasses. The target had almost disappeared behind the blizzard of battering, shattering shot that churned the sea around it with splinters of iron. All his division used iron shot now that enough sources had been found to provide it. With so much copper needed for mixing the bronzelike metal for the big guns, and alloying brass cartridges for the new breechloaders and the "old" modern weapons they had, iron had actually become more disposable. Shot-grade iron was crude, high-phosphor, brittle stuff that could be cast quickly—but the process also made nearly perfect spheres that could be pushed at high relative velocities. Velocity was key to smoothbore accuracy. Without the spin provided by rifling, the shot *would* eventually hook, but the faster it was going, the farther it went before the hook became apparent. Shot-grade iron also hit nearly as hard as copper, but instead of deforming, it sometimes exploded like a ball of glass. That could be handy against wooden ships and enemy flesh. Maybe it *wasn't* so good against armored targets, though. . . .

Jim gazed back down the enemy line. All the Grik dreadnaughts had been hit, and the sunlight revealed suddenly mottled, dented armor that had shone smooth just moments before. Dented, but apparently not broken. He frowned. There'd been a few return shots, but none of his ships had reported any damage. *How long can that last?* he asked himself anxiously. He heard the gunnery officer shout, "No change, no change! Same elevation!" Cries of "Ready!" reached his ears. "All guns report ready," Niaal yelled in the tube.

"Stand clear!"

"All clear!"

Jim looked back at the target. A mere instant before *Dowden*'s salvo bell began to ring, he saw the side of the dreadnaught vanish behind its own massive, stuttering pall of smoke. The entire Grik battle line and the ships of DesDiv 4 fired almost simultaneously, but the projectiles that passed one another on opposite trajectories didn't care. The Allied shot flew faster, but the Grik shot was heavier and retained its lower velocity better—and still had more than twice the energy when it hit naked wood.

It was Jim's turn to tumble to the quarterdeck when two one-hundred-pound balls crashed through his beloved *Dowden* amid massive near-miss plumes of white seawater that stood high in giant columns around her. The splashes rocked the ship and left her deluged when they collapsed.

"Damage report!" Niaal bellowed, even as Jim quickly jumped to his feet and studied the results of their own fire. The spray around the target was clearing, revealing a sloping iron side that had begun to resemble the surface of the moon.

"She still looks as invincible as ever!" commented Niaal's lieutenant.

"Maybe," Jim replied. "But all those dents are going to start raising hell inside her."

"Commodore!" Niaal cried. "We're taking water forward. The balls punched straight through both sides of the ship, and one came out at the port waterline! Damage control is trying to plug the hole, but it is very large."

"Worst case?"

"It won't sink us. If it comes to that, we can seal the compartment and the pumps will handle the seepage. But it will slow us down."

"What of the other ships?"

"*Naga* and *Bowles* report damage. *Naga*'s is much like ours, but *Bowles* lost her mizzenmast and her engine. I recommend you order her to retire under sail."

"No," Jim said firmly. "She stays in the fight until she falls too far behind. *Then* she can retire!"

"Stand clear!"

"All clear!"

Dowden spat iron once more, and Jim followed the *shoosh!* of the shot. *Haakar-Faask* fired, and her smoke passed in front of him, so he couldn't see their own broadside strike, but did see *Haakar-Faask*'s hit. Was it his imagination, or did he see plates spin away from the enemy and fall into the sea? Something flashed bright at the periphery of his view, and he redirected his glasses toward the rear of the enemy line. The rearmost Grik dreadnaught had just . . . blown up! There was no way to know what caused it; only *Clark* had been targeting it. Maybe it was a super lucky shot—or even an accident on the Grik's gun deck? Whatever the cause, he would take it, and the crew of *Dowden* cheered and pranced exuberantly as tons of debris splashed into the sea.

"Commodore!" Niaal pointed aft. *Haakar-Faask* was heeling hard over on her port beam, making a radical starboard turn. Debris was still flying from a massive wound at her stern. Perhaps worse, USS *Davis*, just aft of *Haakar-Faask*, looked like she'd just been the target of a gigantic shotgun blast. Her masts and cordage practically sprayed away from her amid a cloud of bright splinters, and steam gushed from her innards. By the extent of the damage and volume of splashes, two Grik dreadnaughts must have targeted her at once, some of the shot pattern catching *Haakar-Faask* too.

"Jesus!" Jim muttered. "She's done for! What's *Haakar-Faask*'s status?"

"She just report!" Niaal said. Like many 'Cats, his normally good English slipped under stress. "She lose helm control, but still have auxiliary conn. She back in line soon!"

"Stand clear!"

"All clear!"

BaBOOM! SHHHHHH!

Dowden heaved, and Jim felt like somebody hit him in the face with a baseball bat. It didn't hurt, not really, but his thoughts were scattered. *They always say you see stars,* he thought, *but* purple *stars?* 'Cats scurried around him and he heard shouts and screams, but for a while—maybe a long while—he didn't feel like he was really *there*. "Hey!" he finally said, realizing Niaal was holding him up—*For how long?* The deck around was scattered with shredded corpses and great, jagged splinters. Jim looked down to see a huge gap that had opened not far away, as if an enemy shot had torn his ship from beam to beam. "What the hell?" he murmured, noticing his mouth wasn't moving exactly right. Hot blood started getting in his suddenly watery eyes.

"We hit bad," Niaal said, blinking concern.

"How bad?"

"I still waiting on report from the carpenter, but we take maybe six hits that time. Prob'ly bad enough!"

Wet, grimy, coughing 'Cats scampered up on deck from below, followed by a gush of gray-black smoke and the first tongues of flame. Jim Ellis quickly came to his senses and realized Niaal might not have all of his. He grabbed the 'Cat and shook him.

"Get all the ready charges over the side right damn now!" he said. He felt like he was mumbling, and his words sounded weird. "Flood the magazine!"

"Maag-a-zine already flood!" shouted the blood-streaked gunnery officer. "Shot punch right through. Another knock hole in fuel bunker. We sink or burn, but not blow up!"

"I already order ready charges over," Niaal assured him. "Boilers are secure, an' we venting steam."

"But . . . if we can't move, we'll be sitting ducks!" Jim managed. He looked at the gunnery officer. "And why aren't you at your post?"

The 'Cat shrugged and pointed up and forward. The mainmast was gone. All that stood amidships was the shot-perforated, steam-gushing stack.

"My post *gone,* Commodore. I fall out, land on longboat cover in the waist! Lucky!"

"But . . . well, we *are* sittin' ducks," Jim said. Longer

tongues of flame flailed from below, while 'Cats shoveled sand down the companionway from barrels that stood nearby. The ship was nearly dead in the water, her flooding carcass moving only slightly under the foremast sails.

"You gotta sit, Commodore," Niaal said. "You bleeding—an' I think you jaw is broke." The Lemurian was easing Jim aft, toward the skylight above the great cabin/wardroom. He cried for the surgeon—*Again,* Jim thought. The carpenter appeared, also soaked and grimy. Jim saw him, but darkness was creeping in around his field of view. He felt the hard, raised sill around the skylight under his butt and heard an excited, grim exchange, but the words didn't make any sense.

"*Haakar-Faask* is coming alongside to take us off, Commodore," Niaal said, breaking through the gathering haze with a gentle shake. "We're going to lose the ship, sir. Nothing we can do. *Clark* and *Felts* are taking the survivors off *Davis* now. She's goin' down fast."

"Dammit!" Jim managed to shout. "Then they'll be sitting ducks too!"

The gunnery officer looked at Niaal. The commodore *had* missed a lot.

"Sure, but . . ." Niaal nodded northwest. Jim slowly followed his gaze. The Grik line, the five dreadnaughts and two armored frigates that remained, were already past Jim's shattered, almost-stationary division, steaming west-northwest. "Ahd-mi-raal Keje's bringin' up *Big Sal*, Commodore, an' them Griks think they got a *bigger* duck just sittin'. She gonna sit on their damn heads, I figger." He looked at Jim with a new flurry of concerned blinks. "Sur, we got the fire under control—most of the bunkers underwater now—but *Dowden*'s gonna sink. Surgeon's dead, an' we gotta get you over to *Haakar-Faask*! Sur? Commodore!"

CHAPTER 27

***USS* Walker**
South China Sea
1240

There was no question about it; that was *Hidoiame* and her tanker up ahead—unless there was more than one Kagero-class destroyer and accompanying oiler loose in these seas. *I don't even want to think about that,* Matt told himself. Both ships were clearly visible to the crow's-nest lookout when *Walker* climbed atop the taller swells. All the lookouts had been studying the silhouette drawings they'd been given, and the keen-eyed watcher in the uncomfortable steel bucket high on the foremast was positive.

"I guess she hasn't got radar after all," Matt mumbled. "That, or maybe Okada knocked it out." He'd been worried about radar. No Japanese ships had it when they'd met before, but it existed. The cruiser USS *Boise* had it—and took it with her when she was damaged and ordered out of the area, leaving no other radar in the entire Asiatic Fleet either. Aircraft had been the only way to spot distant argets—and only the Japanese had aircraft by then. Here, these Japanese had no aircraft, but those at Matt's disposal couldn't fly in this weather. Time had passed "back home," however, and who knew what kind of ugly surprises *Hidoiame* concealed?

"What makes you so sure, Skipper?"

"No reaction yet. With radar, they might've just avoided us."

"I don't think so, Skipper," Gray said. "Radar can't be much good in this sea, and now we've spotted 'em, that tanker damn sure can't avoid us."

Matt nodded. "I guess you're right. Then the question now is, Do they see *us* yet, radar or not, and if they do, are they just trying to sucker us in?"

It was raining again, and the pilothouse windows were practically opaque. Matt walked out on the bridgewing and looked through his binoculars until the spray clouded them as well. He caught only glimpses of the enemy and quickly stepped back under cover. A damp towel was draped over the back of his chair, and he used it again to wipe the binoculars and dry his face. His hat and clothes were soaked. *At least I can get out of it,* he thought. *The guys on deck at their battle stations or on the fire-control platform are probably miserable.*

"Their lookouts'll *have* to see us soon."

"Range, fifteen-t'ousands!" Minnie cried. "They *do* see us! Lookout says the Jaap tin caan is turning this way!"

Matt gestured for her to hand him the microphone headset. "Mr. Campeti, this is the captain speaking."

"This is Campeti."

Normally, Matt might have just stood on the bridgewing and shouted his question up at the man, but with the rain and wind . . .

"Those Jap five-incher's have about the same range our new ammo's supposed to have, right?"

"Yes, sir, but they got advantages and disadvantages."

"Advantages?"

"They throw a heavier shell, high explosive—and their gun's crews'll stay dry in those enclosed mounts."

"That's it?"

"Well, chances are, they've got better fire control. Otherwise, we've got the edge in rate of fire and maybe fire correction."

"Why?"

"Those five-incher's are *bag* guns. They gotta ram the projectile, then the powder bag, and they have to change elevation to do it. They're fast, don't get me wrong—we've *seen* 'em—but we should get off four or five more rounds per minute than they can—until the ready lockers run dry. It'll even up when we have to start passing ammo from below by hand."

Matt considered. "Okay, Sonny. How close do you want 'em?"

"We *should* be in range now, but with this sea . . . I'd feel more confident at ten thousand, and that would still keep us out of range of their twenty-fives. Course, we're already technically in range of their five-inchers."

Matt nodded, though Campeti couldn't see it. He had a hunch that the Japanese captain would be frugal with his ammunition. According to Okada's cook, *Hidoiame* had seen action before she crossed over, and then she'd used ammunition on *Mizuki Maru* and the other ships she'd murdered. Her bunkers might be full for now, with that tanker she had along, but her magazines could be seriously depleted. *Walker* could always get more ammunition.

"Range is fourteen thousand and closing, Skipper. Target has increased speed." Campeti shouted.

"What's the range to the tanker?" Matt asked.

"Ah, about fourteen. I think she's turning away."

"Can you hit her?"

There was a brief pause. "I . . . think so. She's bigger than the tin can—not a *lot* bigger. She ain't no fleet oiler, but she's slow."

"Very well. Target the tanker with every gun that will bear!"

"Aye, aye, Skipper—but what about the can? She's really pourin' on the coal now!"

"The tanker, Sonny!"

"Aye, Captain."

Matt handed the headset back to Minnie.

"Why the tanker, Skipper?" Spanky asked. "We get the can, we'll have the tanker on a plate."

"Something I guess I have to try," Matt said. "There'll be a smaller crew on the tanker, and maybe not all those men are murderers." He shrugged. "Let's just say I owe General Shinya one."

"One what?"

"A chance we never really gave the ordinary seamen on

Amagi, Spanky: a chance to do the right thing." An ironic smile appeared on his face. "Those're Japs over there, Mr. McFarlane, but you do realize that's not why we've been chasing them, don't you? That's all over—or it should be for us. We're here because they're murderers with a very deadly weapon and they have to be stopped. I'm going to give them an option, a single chance; then I mean to start taking all the options they *think* they have away!" He smiled fondly at his friend. "Now take your station aft, at the auxiliary conn. I have the deck and the conn."

"Aye, aye, sir. I stand relieved. The captain has the deck and the conn!" Spanky announced, and with a quick, curious nod at Matt, he bolted aft, down the ladder.

Matt went to the heavy Bakelite telephone mounted on the aft bulkhead that connected the bridge to the comm shack. "Mr. Palmer, this is the captain speaking. I want you to send a voice-radio message. Start with the frequency Okada used to contact the Japanese ships. Message contents: This is the cruiser USS *Walker*." (Matt knew the Japanese had often mistaken the very similar silhouettes of four-stack destroyers with the bigger four-stack light cruisers like the old *Marblehead*. Maybe that would help.) "Our old war does not exist here, and this ship is no longer at war with the Empire of Japan. Yours is a criminal ship, however, with criminal officers who murdered helpless prisoners of war and civilian . . . natives. That's not *war* on any world. You have become pirates, and your leaders must be held accountable for their crimes. Surrender your ships now and you'll get a fair trial. Those of you innocent of the crimes I described will be honorably treated and allowed to emigrate to a land governed by honorable Japanese! Refuse, and you'll be destroyed. This offer will not be repeated, nor are the terms negotiable. You have one minute to reply."

The seconds ticked by, the only sounds from the straining ship and the sea.

"Lookout reports Jaap destroyer open fire!" Minnie cried.

"That's the option I kind of figured they'd take," Matt said resignedly. "Time to show them they don't have any."

"Twin waterspouts, four hundred tai— yards off port bow!" Minnie reported. They were invisible from the pilothouse.

Matt looked at Sandra. She'd eased away from him, toward the chart table, as if trying to remain unnoticed. "Your station is in the wardroom, I believe," he said gently. She slashed a nod, but took a step closer.

"We'll lick them, won't we?" she asked. She couldn't help it.

Matt nodded confidently. "They're newer, bigger, quicker, and their guns are heavier, but we can put just as much iron on target." The bridge watch growled agreement. "Besides"—he grinned and patted his chair—"we're the *good* guys, and we've got *Walker*. We can't lose."

Sandra smiled, but the expression was brittle. "Be . . . careful," she mouthed, but visibly cursed herself. *There I go again,* she thought. *What a stupid thing to say!* She firmed up. "So long, Captain Reddy. I'll see you after the fight!" Without another word, she left the bridge.

"Hoist the battle flag," Matt ordered. "All ahead full! Come right ten degrees! Have Mr. Palmer transmit to all stations that we are engaging the enemy at thirteen twenty-one hours. Mr. Kutas, provide him with our current position, if you please."

"Aye, aye, Captain," Norm replied.

Matt looked through the water-smeared windows. He thought he could just see a small, dark, blurry shape far away on the heaving sea. "Inform Mr. Campeti to commence firing the main battery—at the tanker!"

Spanky was soaking wet, but he had to admit he had an amazing view. The ship had never gone into action, nor had he been on the auxiliary conn atop the aft deckhouse with the sea running quite this high. *Everything* was moving, and he could see it all. The sea was roiling, shifting, every second, and a light rain swirled in all directions, whipped and tattered by the wind. Helmeted heads bobbed and moved all over the ship, in the gun tubs of the twenty-fives, along the deck below as Jeek's division prepped the Nancy to go over the side, and up on the amidships gun platform. Some of the helmets were gray and others polished bronze, but they all had the same distinctive doughboy shape. The slightest wisps of smoke darted from the tops of three funnels and almost instantly vanished. Farther forward, he saw the large battle flag, a replica of the ruined flag that flew over *Walker* at the Battle of Baalkpan, with her major actions embroidered on the stripes, lurch up the foremast halyard and stand out to leeward.

The greatest motion of all seemed to come from *Walker* herself, though Spanky knew that was an illusion. He was almost as far aft on the old ship as you could get, and the stern swooped up and down like an elevator gone amok as she pitched. Sometimes the stern rose so high that the screws flailed at the sea and then dropped so low he thought the waves would swallow him up. Even on the upswing, he never personally saw the target, and again he was struck by the miracle of modern naval gunnery. He knew as much about the mechanical fire-control computer as Campeti did—it was just a complicated machine, after all. Sonny was better with ballistics and trajectories and all the math and stuff, but intellectually Spanky understood how the gun director would be nearly as efficient now as when the sea was at rest. In his gut, however, he couldn't imagine how they could even hit the *sea* on purpose right now.

The worst illusion—he hoped it was one—was the way the hull itself seemed to twist and squirm in the foam that gushed alongside. He knew *Walker* was working hard, but she couldn't be doing all that. *Could she?* He looked to his right. Chief Quartermaster Paddy Rosen had joined him; Norm was on the bridge. Norman Kutas might be first lieutenant now, but he'd been at *Walker*'s helm through almost every fight. That's where he belonged. Back here, Spanky had a good backup crew. *Walker*'s bench got deeper all the time, but he, Paddy, and several 'Cats were just hanging around (and hanging on) for now. He took the sodden tobacco pouch from his pocket and crammed a handful of the yellowish leaves in his mouth, then tried to look confident—and hoped to God they wouldn't be needed to conn the ship. The brand-new Nancy splashed into the sea alongside, landing awkwardly, upside down. The starboard propeller guard brushed it aside, and it swirled away aft. A single waterspout suddenly jetted skyward a good distance to port.

"You guys better move!" cried Pack Rat. The Lemurian gunner's mate was gun captain on number four, right behind the aft conn, and the muzzle of the Japanese 4.7-incher was cranked around almost even with the signals station on the forward port side of the platform. The gun was near the maximum elevation of *Walker*'s other guns, but the muzzle blast would be intense.

"Let's go!" Spanky ordered his companions, and they hurried starboard aft.

"Pointers matched! On target!" Pack Rat shouted to his talker.

"Fire!" the talker yelled back. The 'Cat on the left seat stabbed down on the foot trigger, and nothing happened at once. Then, for an instant, *Walker* was level enough for the gyro to complete the firing circuit, and guns one, two, and four roared.

"Up two hundred, right ten degrees!" Sonny Campeti shouted. The new tracers were more orange than red, but he could see them—two had actually passed uncomfortably close to his left—and they converged beautifully. He'd even seen the reasonably tight group of splashes through his binoculars. The rain was tapering off, but *Walker* still didn't have a range finder. Her old one had been a piece of junk *before* it was shot to pieces, and nothing had been built to replace it. Campeti was very good at estimating ranges, however, almost as good at Greg Garrett. *That kid's an artist,* Campeti thought. "Match pointers!" he yelled.

Three salvos had arced away toward the distant tanker when Palmer rang the bridge. "Captain speaking," Matt said when the phone was handed to him.

"Skipper!" came Ed Palmer's excited voice. "I got Japs jabbering like mad, and somebody with a little English is begging us to stop shooting!" The ship shook as another three-gun salvo flashed. Splashes rose near *Walker* again, but off to starboard this time.

"Well who the hell is it? The tin can is shooting at us, and we haven't even started on her yet. Must be the tanker."

"I think so, Captain. I can barely understand—"

The horizon flashed pinkish red through the wet windows, and a yellow-white glare ensued. There were cheers on the bridge and Matt even heard yelling from the number one gun down on the fo'c'sle. Stites's voice was particularly clear.

"Ah . . ." said Palmer. "The hollering just quit."

"Guess it *was* the tanker," Matt said simply. "Thanks for the report, Mr. Palmer. Carry on." He handed the phone back. "Have Mr. Campeti target the enemy destroyer," he told Minnie, and stepped out on the port bridgewing. *Hidoiame* was clear in his binoculars now, steaming almost directly at them. *She's a strange-looking duck,* he thought. Her bow curved up and forward like a clipper ship, and her superstructure was high and blocky. So far, only her forward two guns would bear, and they were enclosed within a large, odd-looking turret on her fo'c'sle. As he watched, the two guns flashed.

"Captain, it's Palmer again!"

Matt stepped back inside and took the phone.

"Skipper? I . . . I got the Jap destroyer captain on the horn. He's asking to talk to you!"

Matt blinked. "Pipe it up," he said. A big splash erupted close alongside, and there was a crash aft as a fifty-pound shell skated off a wave top and hit the forward funnel sideways, nearly shearing it in two. Another splash exploded close to starboard, and shell fragments whined and peppered the hull. Three guns boomed, following closely on the salvo alarm, and hot orange streaks converged on the enemy destroyer. They exploded short, sending a wall of spray and white smoke gushing over the distant ship.

"Up fifty!" came Campeti's excited roar. "Load! Three rounds, rapid salvo fire!"

Walker was in a gunfight for her life, and Matt was about to talk to the bad guy.

"This is Captain Reddy of USS *Walker* speaking," he said calmly into the mouthpiece. "Do you wish to reconsider my offer?"

"I am Captain Kurita, of his Imperial Japanese Majesty's ship *Hidoiame*," crackled the harsh, heavily accented reply. It always surprised Matt how many Japanese naval officers spoke some English. Then again, they'd had to for a long time. . . . "Surrender," Kurita spat the word, "will not happen. True warriors of the Emperor gladly prefer death to such dishonor. Besides, as you have made clear, there is no . . . incentive for myself and certain others of my crew to do so, in any case," the Japanese captain continued. "What we did was considered a necessary expedient at the time. We might not have done it had we known then. . . . Regardless, there will be no surrender. You are no *cruiser*," Kurita accused. "Your ship is a relic, an antique! You should beg *me* to spare *you*!"

Two very near misses straddled *Walker,* and Matt nearly lost his footing when the deck heaved. "Range nine t'ousands," Minnie reported. "The enemy begins to turn to starboard!" *Walker* bucked as another salvo lashed out. Matt glanced down at the fo'c'sle and saw Stites directing the deadly dance of the crew of the number one gun. A shell handler snatched the empty brass casing with gloved hands and another slammed a long, heavy, shiny shell into the smoking breech Stites held open.

"Not a chance in hell," Matt barked, "and you have no choice. Your tanker is afire and you have nowhere to replenish. Everywhere you *think* you might do so is well protected. Even if we don't sink your murdering ass, you're about to be stuck, out of ammo, out of fuel, and out of luck—wallowing helplessly until you end up on some strange shore and tear your guts out on a reef!" He laughed fiercely. His blood was up. "And if any of your people get ashore, they'll be lucky to survive long enough for something to eat them. You have *no place* to go!"

Kurita was no longer listening. He'd broken the connection, and Matt slammed the instrument in its cradle on the bulkhead.

The fight became a drawn-out duel, both ships sprinting and turning to spoil the other's aim, while closing in an ever-tightening embrace. At six thousand yards, 25 mm occasionally tested the range and sometimes clattered against steel. The sea remained heavy, the wind strong, and in the distance, the burning tanker cast an eerie glow on wet gray paint and dull whitecaps. Now that *Hidoiame*'s aft turret would bear, both ships started landing heavy blows on one another like lightweight boxers in a slugfest without any rules. *Hidoiame* had better speed and firepower—four guns to only three on *Walker* that would ever bear at once—but the old destroyer's better, more experienced gunnery was starting to eat her up. Fires burned all over *Hidoiame*, and a lot of her 25 mm batteries had been shot away. The aft funnel was gone and smoke coursed from a spectacular hole low in the large bridge structure. Other hits had been observed along her hull.

Matt also had no illusions about what his ship could take, and not only did he have a lot more practice at . . . bizarre surface actions than his opponent, but he'd been baptized by fires much heavier than *Hidoiame* could dish out. He'd learned his ship like his own hand, and he controlled that hand like a surgeon.

Walker was taking a beating of her own, however, mostly from that aft turret on *Hidoiame*. The forward turret hadn't landed many hits. Maybe it was damaged. Still, *Walker* was trailing an oil slick from near-miss buckled plates, and high-explosive shells had made a shambles of her starboard 25 mm mount. A heavy hit amidships had cut off the guns on the platform above the deckhouse from the gun director. They were in local control now, but still getting occasional hits. A blow behind the deckhouse would have taken out the number two torpedo mount if it had still been there. As it was, it buckled the deck and nearly blew the aft funnel off the ship. The fireroom beneath it started losing pressure. Another hit shredded the chief's quarters and sent the number one gun's crew sprawling before Stites rounded them up and pushed the half-stunned 'Cats back to their posts. *That one came awful close to the wardroom,* Matt thought anxiously. Gray was down there now, somewhere in the bow, trying to stop the flooding.

Cheers and stamping feet rocked *Walker* when *Hidoiame*'s forward turret erupted like a fireworks show spraying from a volcano. Matt knew the turret was designed to blow *up*, not *out*, so there might be little internal damage, but the turret was down for the count—and *Hidoiame* suddenly turned away and started making smoke!

"We've got her!" Matt breathed.

"Target course is t'ree two seero!" Minnie cried, then paused, listening to reports. "Flooding in forward fireroom! Tabby says it coming from forward—she think the bulkhead's sprung! She shoring up now. Super Bosun says we taking lots of water forward!"

"What're we gonna do, Skipper?" Kutas asked. "They're running."

"Chase 'em!" Matt growled. "Make your course three zero zero. We'll give the number three gun on the starboard side a chance."

Norm nodded. He'd known the answer before he asked. "Making my course three zero zero," he confirmed. The salvo warning rang, but the guns waited while the ship changed course. When she steadied up on the new heading, the bell rang again and the guns flashed.

Chief Gray swung the heavy maul against a wooden wedge, trying to force a shoring timber against a sprung hull plate low in the forward crew's berthing space. Damage from the hit above, in the chief's quarters, had radiated outward, and he hoped—he prayed—it ended at this plate. The gap was right at the waterline, and the sea sprayed in around the seam with varying pressure, like blood from a terrible wound, as the bow rose and fell.

"Hold it!" Gray shouted through clenched teeth. "Hold that brace steady, goddammit!"

"We trying!" the damage-control 'Cats chorused. He knew they were. Other 'Cats darted around him, unhooking racks and tearing them out of the way, and the space was a hell of hammering, yelling, groaning noise; acid sweat that burned the eyes; and a heaving tide of water that flowed across the deck with the motion of the ship. All this was punctuated by the steady salvos of *Walker*'s guns, and the explosions of enemy projectiles striking the sea nearby. Shell handlers, mostly Lemurian, but a couple of men, kept up a supply relay through the confusion, bearing shells from the forward magazine, up the companionway, through the wardroom, and up to the number one gun. Gray took a huge, rancid breath and swung the maul with all his might. The gap nearly closed—but a rivet head shot across the compartment and grazed a 'Cat's forearm, raising a fuzz of fur like a dandelion.

"Jeezus!" the Lemurian yelped and crossed himself.

Gray just stared for a moment, then shook his head. He looked back at the repair and saw the flow had dwindled to a gentle surge. "Here," he said, handing the maul to a big 'Cat shipfitter. "Try to finish it up. But for God's sake, be careful you don't knock it *out*! Goddamn rivets! Spanky was right."

Tabasco stuck his head down the companionway. "Tabby need help! Water coming in the forward fireroom! You not hear call?"

"No, I 'not hear call'!" Gray shouted. The intercom speaker was sliding across the deck. Something had knocked it off the bulkhead. He called three Lemurians by their Navy names: "Dusty, Sleepy, Poot: Go help Tabby. I'm gonna run up and check on the repairs above, then head aft. I'll be there in a minute."

He ran up the companionway stairs, breathing hard despite his better condition. He *was* a touch over sixty, after all, and you didn't run a lot on a ship. . . . The chief's quarters had become a maze of twisted bulkheads and supports, dangling cables and conduits, and scattered personal belongings. Besides the dashing shell handlers, a few 'Cats were working there, electrician's mates, he thought, but there wasn't much else to do right now. The sea was visible through a gaping hole in the port side and there was no flooding—but water splashed in when the sea slapped against the bow. There was fresh air, however, and he paused a moment to take a breath. The wardroom curtain fluttered behind him, and he stepped through.

The first thing he saw was Sandra. She was standing beside the wardroom table with the light rigged low so she could see to sew. Sick-berth attendants and corps 'Cats were holding a large mound of flesh on the table while she worked. Earl Lanier had taken one in the gut again, and a large flap of his oversize belly had been laid open. Yellow fat and blood glistened. Wounded 'Cats were on the deck, lying on rack mattresses. Some were covered with bloody bandages, and others were just covered up. SBAs were moving a steady flow out of the wardroom—either to their racks or just out of the way. The ammunition relay did their best not to step on anyone, but they were exhausted and their passage caused an occasional cry.

"What're you lookin' at?" Earl demanded, surprising Gray. The cook was not only conscious, but was watching Sandra sew. He took a large gulp of seep from a brown bottle.

"Just admirin' your armor belt, Earl. A battleship's got nothin' on you. I bet your belly would stop a torpedo."

"Why don't you get out there and fight, damn you!" Earl roared. "I'm a wounded hee-ro. You let those Jap bastards sink my Coke machine, you'll be eatin' scum weenies for the rest of your damn life!"

Machinist's Mate Johnny Parks stirred from his mattress on the deck. He had a heavy bandage on his head and Gray noticed Diania was there, trying to hold the injured man down. She still looked terrible—and beautiful, he thought—and seemed to have gotten control of her stomach at last. Most of the SBA women had, he realized. Combat tended to focus one's attention, he reflected.

"I'm with you, SB," Johnny said. "I can't listen to that fat bastard's bellyachin' anymore." He grinned. "Not that he ain't got a helluva belly ache!"

"You stay put!" Sandra ordered Parks. "Your skull may be fractured! Do you want your brains to fall out?"

Johnny laid back down. "I guess not. Gimme some cotton for my ears, at least."

"No. You can't sleep right now, and with all the seep you've had, you might drift off."

"No chance o' that, with that elephant's ass carryin' on so."

"Why, you . . ."

"Hush!" Sandra ordered, and Lanier looked at her with bleary, almost-drunken eyes.

"Well . . . you want I should keep the lug awake or not?" Lanier complained.

Gray lurched through the crowded compartment, headed aft. Sandra stopped him. "How is it going?" she asked. "Is Matthew all right?"

Gray patted her arm. "Damned if I know."

Hidoiame was difficult to see through her smokescreen, but she *was* visible, and Campeti continued punishing her with the numbers one, three, and four guns even as she slowly drew away. She was faster than *Walker,* and Matt wouldn't strain his engines more than necessary in these seas and with the damage his ship had taken. Not yet. The enemy was still well within range. But so was *Walker*. Matt's crew cheered again when there was a bright yellow flash and white smoke burst out of the distant black cloud. One of their guns had hit a boiler, no question about it. If that didn't finish *Hidoiame*, it had to slow her down.

"By God! I think we *do* have her, Skipper!" the scarred, battle-hardened, First Lieutenant Norman Kutas shouted jubilantly. They were the last words he ever spoke.

A massive geyser erupted just to port, the spray reaching as high as the fire-control platform. A mere instant later, a 5-inch, 51-pound "common" projectile impacted *Walker*'s fo'c'sle at the very base of the bridge structure, and 4.1 pounds of Type 0 high explosive detonated. The force of the blast and shrapnel it created surged through the thin steel into officers' country and slaughtered the wounded that had been placed there, every one. More high-velocity fragments slashed in all directions, perforating the hull and sweeping up through the radio room. Signals Lieutenant Ed Palmer's chair saved his life, but he was dashed against the aft bulkhead like a rag doll. Everyone else in the compartment was killed instantly. Heavier fragments of the shell itself punched through the pilothouse deck, launching blizzards of strake splinters. A hot shard of ragged steel hit Norm Kutas under the jaw—and didn't stop until it snatched the steel helmet off the top of his head. Norm fell to the deck without a sound—but there was plenty of screaming on the bridge.

For an instant, Matt thought he was the only person in the pilothouse to escape injury. He was stunned by the concussion, but the only thing he felt had been a terrible jolt in his feet and legs. There was no fire, thank God, but the air was full of brown smoke and drifting fur. Norm was down, he realized, and he took a step toward the vacant wheel. He felt the pain then. Something was wrong with his leg, and there was a hot poker in his lower abdomen. "Uhn," he said through gritted teeth, and pressed his hand against his side. Suddenly, Minnie was up, and so were a few others. Minnie lunged for the bright brass wheel, straddling Norm's still form.

"The helm don't answer, Skipper!" Minnie cried when the wheel spun freely and the ship didn't turn.

"Inform Mr. McFarlane he has the conn," Matt managed. "I'm on my way there now." He tried to turn, but had to grab his suddenly warped chair to keep from falling.

"Skipper?" Minnie cried. For the first time she saw the blood streak down Matt's trouser leg and saw how much there was. She dashed for her headset dangling from the aft bulkhead. "Mr. McFarlane, you have the conn!" she cried. "Caap'n's orders. Corps 'Cats to the bridge, on the double!"

Sandra's worst nightmare had come true. Again. Once more, her love, *her husband,* was laid bleeding before her, and she didn't know if she could save him. Before, he'd been on a bloody canvas cot on the beach at Aryaal. Now he was on the green-linoleum wardroom table in the middle of a battle on a heavy sea. She had better equipment and help this time, but as she cut Matt's sopping trousers away, she began to suspect this wound was much, much worse.

"How bad is it? Gray demanded. He'd raced to the bridge immediately after the explosion and carried the captain down himself. He wasn't injured, but he wore just as much blood.

"I don't know yet!" Sandra shouted in frustration. "Something went in his leg and there's a lot of bleeding. It may have cut the femoral artery! The way he's holding his lower abdomen, though, I'm afraid whatever it was didn't stop in his leg!"

Matt was still conscious, but his face was pale. "Feels like something burning in my belly," he confirmed; then he grabbed Gray's sleeve. "Go, Boats," he said. "Tell Spanky . . . get those murderous bastards! We can't let them escape!"

"Skipper . . ."

"Go! That's an order."

With an anguished glance at Sandra, Gray bolted aft.

"No, goddammit!" Spanky stated firmly. His face was black and his beard was singed, and he looked as determined as Gray had ever seen him. A fire around the aft deckhouse was just coming under control as hoses played on the flames.

"Japs hit a gas can for the 'Nancys' with a wild twenty-five, I guess," he explained, seeing Gray's stares. "You musta' passed Boats Bashear coming aft. He damn near burned to death rollin' all the depth charges before they blew the ass completely off the ship! I think he got hit by something too." He shook his head. "We're done here, Boats,"—he gestured at the column of smoke on the horizon, aft now—"and so are they. We *got* 'em, don't you see? The *Skipper* already got 'em. Even if they don't sink, and my guess is they will, they got no fuel and damn little ammo left. They *are no longer* a threat!" He stopped and hawked out the hard-used tobacco he'd been chewing.

"I'm exec. I'm in charge. It's my decision," he said. "I won't waste another man or 'Cat like Bashear"— he jerked his head at Pack Rat—"him, or even you, to stomp a roach just 'cuz it's still got one leg twitchin'. More important, I won't risk this ship, what's left of her, and I damn sure won't risk the Skipper." He crossed his arms. "We still got a lot bigger war to win, and he's the one." He turned to Paddy Rosen. "Reduce speed to one-third—or however she rides easiest. We'll see. Our surgeon has some delicate work ahead of her, and so do our damage-control parties. Make your course one seven zero. We're bound for Manila."

"One seven zero to Manila, aye," Rosen replied, his expression carefully neutral.

Gray let out a breath he must have been holding. "I had to pass the order, Spanky," he said softly. "I . . . I'm glad you see it this way. The Skipper's . . ."

"I know," Spanky interrupted. "He's special." He scratched his bearded chin. "Hell, we're all pretty scarce fellas. Now get back forward and find out what kind of blood the Skipper needs. That Jap can is finished. Let's make sure *Walker* and Captain Reddy aren't."

Gray nodded. "What about the crew of that tanker? There might be survivors in boats."

Spanky took another chew. "The hell with them. *Our* survivors got priority, and if gettin' 'em to Manila soonest would save just one of ours, I'd leave a hundred o' theirs behind any day."

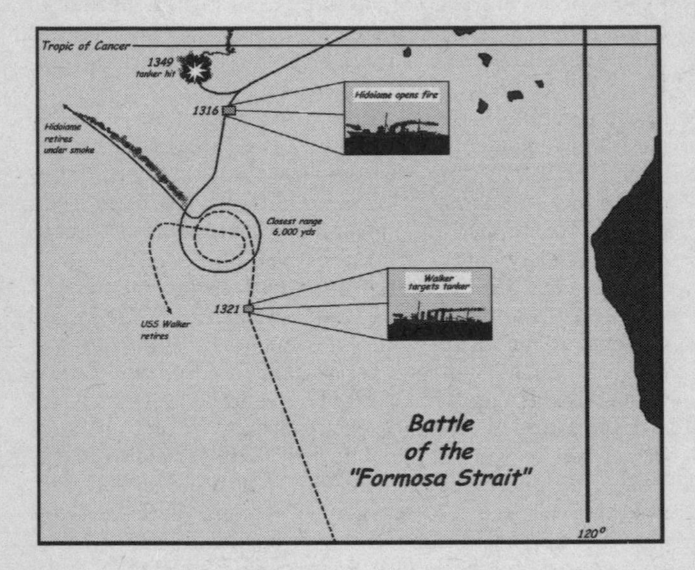
Tropic of Cancer
1349
tanker hit
Hidoiame opens fire
1316
Hidoiame
retires
under smoke
Closest range
6,000 yds
Walker
targets tanker
1321
USS Walker
retires
Battle
of the
"Formosa Strait"
120°

CHAPTER 28

Battle of Madras 1322
USNRS* Salissa *(CV-1)

Admiral Keje-Fris-Ar studied the oncoming monsters, their dark smoke standing high to leeward. Beyond the approaching columns of smoke was a more distant, grayer pall that marked what remained of Des-Div 4. He couldn't grieve for them now, not yet. He had to concentrate. He realized furiously that ultimately, he'd made the same mistake as General Aalden: he'd split his force in the face of an underestimated foe. But his had been the greater failure because he'd had even less cause for confidence. His flyers had been telling him about the Grik ships all along, but he really had believed he still held the qualitative edge. Well, maybe he did in many ways, but not in a slugfest like Des-Div 4 had just endured. He would send no more frigates—DDs—against the enemy, but he must take *Salissa* into battle after all. She alone might still retain one qualitative—ironic—edge over Kurokawa's malignant creations . . . the very weapons Kurokawa had once commanded. Keje knew the risk; his ship was not only indispensible to him, but also to the entire Alliance. Still, he had to try. If the enemy could not be stopped, all the troops on Saa-lon and Indiaa would be on their own, for a time, at least, and there was no telling how long they could hold without support.

"Range?" Keje called. The enemy had reassumed a column approach, and Keje's telescope showed him that the line had rearranged itself. The lead ship had almost no damage forward.

"Fifty-two hundreds!"

"Very well," Keje said. "The secondary baat-tery may commence firing!"

Salissa's fifty muzzle-loading smoothbores were still considered her main battery. The big gun forward was simply "gun number one." The secondaries were the 5.5-inchers, and they alone were tied into a salvaged Japanese gun director. Like *Walker*, *Salissa* also had a salvaged alarm bell for a salvo buzzer. It rang.

Captain Jis-Tikkar orbited high above the battle in his hard-used Nancy, leading the airworthy remnant of *Arracca*'s pursuit squadrons. He had only ten planes left. None had taken any fire on their bomb runs against the Grik, but two had been damaged by their own mortar-bomb fragments and he sent them to Madras. Two more had developed serious engine trouble, their overworked motors finally giving up, and he'd directed them to set down as close to what remained of Des-Div 4 as they could. He shuddered. The terrible sea was always full of monsters, but battles seemed to attract them somehow, like cannon fire drew rain from a heavy sky. The destroyermen had to be very busy, he knew. He understood that only one ship in Commodore Ellis's battle line had escaped damage—but the three DDs that had remained to windward were racing in to help. . . . He told his OC to ask *someone* to pick up the *Arracca* flyers.

Below him now, the battle had reached a terrible climax. Five Grik battleships and a lone remaining armored frigate were plodding toward *Salissa*—as she steamed directly at them. The sight of the massive ships, the columns of smoke, the long, white wakes against the purple sea, was stirring but horrible. *Salissa* was a little larger than her foes, but as mighty as he knew her wooden sides to be, they *were* only wood—and she was all alone.

Two tall geysers erupted just in front of the lead Grik ship, and Tikker knew *Salissa*'s 5.5-inchers had opened up. That was one consolation, he thought; the Grik would have to get *much* closer to *Salissa* than they had to the DDs to seriously damage her—and she had those 5.5-inchers and that massive gun forward. If she could find a range where she could dish it out without taking too much . . .

"Cap-i-taan!" came an excited cry through his voice tube. "I just receive from *Arracca* COFO. He lead our other planes to Maa-draas—"

"Yeah? So?"

"He say Grik zeps, twenty plus, head this way! He . . . he can't do nothin'! The pursuit ships already down, and his bomb planes . . ."

"I know," Tikker said. "They've got nothing to shoot with, and they'll be low on fuel!" He paused, considering, looking down. *Salissa*'s guns had scored a telling blow on the lead Grik ship. Smoke gushed out of the foremost part of the casemate, and the ship was heeling out of line. A stutter of broadside guns flared, but their shot fell short of *Salissa*. He took his left foot off the rudder pedal and caressed the .50-caliber Browning machine gun mounted in the Nancy's nose with his toes. The 1st Pursuit had more machine guns, but besides being out of gas, they'd used most of their ammunition on strafing runs against the Grik behemoths. They didn't have armor-piercing (AP) rounds, and their bullets had achieved nothing he could see. Only one other plane in this squadron had such a weapon. The rest had muskets loaded with incendiary tracers, but the Grik zeps had teeth now too. He sighed. "Confirm that Ahd-miraal Keje got the word, then send to all planes: We will intercept enemy airships!"

***USNRS* Salissa**

Salissa's fifth salvo slashed into the crippled Grik battleship, and black smoke and steam jetted high in the sky above its two center funnels. Fire spurted from the tortured forward casemate where the wheelhouse likely was, and smoke started pouring out the gun ports spaced down the side of the ship. Abruptly, it lost speed and wallowed to a stop. *We have punched through their armor!* Keje realized with a thrill—but the next fresh Grik battleship was now steaming past the derelict and growing relentlessly closer. Three guns situated in the forward casemate fired one after the other, and Keje was sure he *saw* the monstrous roundshot rise out of the smoke on surprisingly high trajectories! Moments later, two of them struck *Salissa*.

The massive ship barely flinched. One ball glanced off the starboard bow below the leading edge of the flight deck, just beneath the number one gun, and the splash drenched its crew. That strike did no more than leave a long, deep dent in one of the thickest parts of *Salissa*'s hull. The other shot landed on the flight deck, however, plunging down through the relatively thin timbers and crashing through the hangar deck as well. Even as Captain Atlaan-Fas called for reports from the damage-control parties, the salvo bell rang and the 5.5s barked again.

"Have number one commence firing!" Keje ordered.

"The range is still long," Atlaan warned, "and we have not many shells for the great gun!"

"We have enough for this fight, and it is more accurate than theirs," Keje said, "which they are already hitting *us* with! Besides, if they hit it, we will not be able to use it at all! It is fairly exposed."

Atlaan nodded. "Of course." He spoke into the fire-control tube. "The number one gun will commence firing!"

Shortly after, *Salissa* flinched again as the powerful gun sent its two-hundred-pound shell shrieking toward the enemy. It landed short, but it threw up a geyser that dwarfed any other so far that day. Keje stepped back out on the bridgewing for an unobstructed view of the enemy. A haze of smoke and mist still hung where the shell had fallen, and the target had turned slightly to port. One of its stacks was gone, perhaps a victim of the 5.5-inchers. The ships behind it—except for the derelict, now burning fiercely—were also beginning to turn, moving into a line abreast once more, just as they had against Des-Div 4.

"I think this fight will soon grow more lively," Atlaan observed with a nervous flick of his tail. "They turn a thousand tails farther out, but they are clearly *in* range to hit, at least occasionally, and once the turn is complete, they will have many more guns to try it with."

Keje paced behind him, his mind racing. He had learned a great deal about his new role in this war and thought he had done reasonably well commanding the carriers of First Fleet. That was only part of his greater responsibility as CINCWEST, however, and in that position he knew he had performed . . . poorly. The looming disaster on land and the mauling of Des-Div 4 was sufficient evidence of that. As much as General Aalden blamed himself for the mess ashore, Keje knew he bore the greater responsibility and deserved the greater blame. He just didn't have the strategic wits and flexibility to control such a large, diverse campaign—and he'd been taken as much by surprise as any other by the sudden improvements and flexibility of the enemy. Somehow he should have foreseen . . . There *had* been signs, as early as Saa-lon. He hadn't ignored them, but he hadn't taken sufficient precautions either. This was all *his* fault! *Maker above, but I wish Captain Reddy was here!*

Now the enemy was turning west, forming its new line of battle while also shaping a course toward Madras. His few options had just been further limited.

"Ahd-mi-raal, what are your orders?" Atlaan asked almost desperately. The number one gun roared again, and Keje shook himself. Now was not the time for self-pity. He must be decisive, and he had to get it right. Huge waterspouts straddled his ship, but none hit that time.

"I do not think they can pierce our sides at this range," Keje said at last, then gestured out at the flight deck. "But their plunging fire can do great harm. We *could* turn and present our own broadside, but then the great gun may no longer bear." Even shortened, the massive number one was so long and heavy that its traverse was limited to barely seventy degrees in the space it occupied. "Besides," he concluded grimly, "as the distance narrows, *Salissa* cannot survive trading broadsides with four of those armored monsters for long, and this ship *must* be preserved, whatever happens here today. We will keep our distance; let our long-range guns do their work!" He paused, considering how best to accomplish that.

"Slow to two-thirds," he ordered. "We will let the enemy get ahead of us, then pursue. If he continues on toward Maadraas, so much the better; we can work our way up from behind, destroying his ships as we advance!"

Atlaan blinked hopefully and gave the order.

Keje's gaze was drawn to the west by a peripheral flare of light. Perhaps ten miles away, toward the hazy dark coast of Indiaa, Captain Tikker and his pursuit ships had intercepted the enemy zeppelins. One had crumpled and was falling toward the sea, trailing a smear of flame and black smoke. With a start, Keje realized that two smaller smoke trails were already tumbling to the sea. The salvo bell rang and the 5.5-inchers roared.

"What is happening to our planes?" he demanded of Lieutenant Newman, who hurried into the pilothouse.

"Yess!" Tikker shouted as his smoky tracers ignited the hydrogen they'd released from the Grik airship before him and it began to fall within a quickly growing ball of fire. He banked right and pulled back on the stick, lining up another target. Suddenly, he saw one of his planes almost stagger in midair, then pitch downward trailing a thin stream of smoke.

"Tell them not to get too close!" he shouted to his OC. "They have weapons, some sort of small cannons, remember?" *Another* Nancy was tumbling down!

"I tell them," the OC cried back, tinny, scared. "But I already getting reports these zeps got more little cannons than usual!"

"What? They *can't* carry more cannons if they have their usual bomb load!" His crude sights aligned on his target and he pulled the lever that would depress the trigger on his gun. The plane shook violently while tracers arced into another zeppelin. Something hit his starboard wing as he blew by, beneath an airship he hadn't had an angle on. He looked out at the wing and saw a frightening number of holes. Another gun from the same source fired at him, but must have missed aft. "Daamn! They *do* have more guns, and they're pretty good with them!" He looked back at his target and saw it drooping, but then at least *four* small guns, all in the forward gondola, fired at him at once!

"Sheet!" He chirped. A number of half-inch holes appeared in his ship, and something stung his neck. With the detonation of its guns, however, his target literally exploded in flames, falling in burning chunks toward the sea. *They must have lit their own gas,* he thought, feeling his neck with his fingers. They came away bloody. He took a moment to make sure his engine sounded okay and all the controls still worked.

"You still back there?" he asked.

"Yes." The OC's voice sounded shaken.

"They gotta have at least *eight* little—like, swivel guns—on those things. Maybe more!" he shouted. "Send it!" If each of those guns was loaded with a double handful of half-inch balls, they could throw a lot of metal at his planes that had to get close—and fly steady for a moment—just to fire a single shot. He was through the Grik formation, and he banked left to make another run. "Maker!" he breathed. The sky was filled with fire and long trails of smoke. Zeppelins were falling, engulfed in flames, but at least one more of *his* planes was spiraling down toward the sea.

"Cap-i-taan! I only get four rogers, an' two o' them say they hit bad! The other ship with maa-sheen gun losing oil pressure. He gonna try to make it to Maa-draas!"

Tikker was stunned. In just a few short minutes, he was down to only three planes, and there were probably a dozen Grik zeps still headed for Second Fleet! *No,* he realized, *they're heading for* Salissa*!* "Tell what's left to keep their distance—don't bore in! Try to snipe them around the edges!"

"Ay! But . . . what we do?"

Tikker blinked a shrug. "We *have* to bore in. The gun's in the nose, remember? I'm going to try something different, though."

He pulled up, climbing above the enemy, then pushed the stick forward. *They* can't *have guns on* top *of those things . . . can they?* He hadn't seen any place for one before, and it was assumed the Grik dirigibles probably leaked at least a little gas all the time. Setting off something that spat a lot of fire up top like that would have to be pretty dumb. A zeppelin appeared in his sights, and he hosed it hard. Even as flames belched from the seam he'd torn, he pulled up slightly and fired at the next in line. Black smoke and rising, burning fragments of fabric engulfed the plane as he eased left. If the second target went up like the first, he didn't want to fly through the fireball! He broke out of the smoke and barely missed colliding with another zeppelin just off the port wingtip. He blew by so fast and so suddenly that the enemy never had time to fire at him. He looked up as he darted under the airship—and saw something strange.

He was behind and below the formation now, and he slammed the Nancy into a tight, banking turn to bring it back around. Rising from aft of one of the trailing machines, he started to pull the firing lever . . . but waited a moment. He couldn't see any guns on the aft "bomb" gondola, and he wanted a better look at what he'd seen. Drawing closer, he noticed that the gondola had no floor, at least not a complete one. There was a large rectangular hole in the bottom—and nestled inside, protruding down a bit, was what looked like a really *big* bomb!

"Maker!" he mumbled. But that didn't make any sense! The zeps already had a lot of new weight forward—the guns. Calculations had determined about what the zeps ought to be able to carry, and the added guns had to eat into that. So how could they carry something *else* that big, unless . . . Maybe they had fewer crew than usual forward. Maybe they weren't carrying much fuel. . . . And maybe the bomb wasn't as heavy as it looked. *No more time.* With his sight in the vicinity of the bomb, he pulled the firing lever. Tracers arced in, and the zeppelin exploded with a force that tossed Tikker's Nancy away like a youngling's paper toy in a Strakka wind.

ArataAmagi

"No!" Roared General of the Sea Hisashi Kurokawa as *ArataAmagi* heaved from another mighty impact—and explosion!—aft. There was only one explanation. The miserable apes and their Americans had mounted one of *Amagi*'s main guns—*his guns!*—on their stupid, pretentious aircraft carrier! In addition to what the weapon was doing to *ArataAmagi*, he could hardly bear the horrible, unfair irony. He'd thought he'd already won. The unarmored enemy ship, the last obstacle to his fleet's conquest of Madras, had seemed to be holding back, letting them pass. That was acceptable. She was not his goal—and she would be destroyed soon enough. . . . He'd expected continuing fire, but also assumed the lone ship had realized how mismatched she was and had essentially given up. He'd been wrong.

After *ArataAmagi*'s earlier pounding, he'd moved her to the rear of the battle line to protect her from what he'd already recognized must be *Amagi*'s salvaged secondaries. The ships that replaced her in the van had taken the brunt of the battering then. He'd already lost two of his precious battleships: *Lugk* (with its vile Grik name) had, ridiculously, just blown up, and *Satsuma* was a smoldering, sinking wreck far astern. Now his precious *ArataAmagi* was being slain—and he was *in* her!

A young Japanese lieutenant—Kurokawa couldn't remember his name at present, and didn't care—was reciting a litany of damage reports.

"All three aft guns are out of action, as well as seven broadside guns, mostly aft, but on both decks! The steering engine is damaged, and repair parties cannot reach it for the flooding in the compartment. Boilers seven and eight are wrecked, and there is water in the aft fireroom—and there are fires in the coal bunkers on either side! Casualties are—"

"The only casualties I care about are those affecting the operation of this ship!" Kurokawa roared. "What do I care for dead Grik!"

"Sir," the lieutenant persisted, "some of *our* people—"

"Shut up!" Kurokawa forced himself to breathe the

smoky air, willing the calm he'd cultured so long to soothe him. "Captain Akera, is there no way to stop this turn, to put some distance between us and that . . . thing that pursues?"

"No, Admiral," Akera said. His eyes were fearful, but his voice was flat.

Kurokawa didn't notice. "Then instruct our remaining cruiser to close on the port side to take me off. I must transfer my flag to *Kongo*."

"But . . . what of the rest of us?"

Kurokawa's dark eyes narrowed. "You will continue to fight your ship, fool! She *is* your ship, and you have failed her! Failed *me*! Consider yourself fortunate that you retain an opportunity to redeem yourself in your ancestors' eyes—and mine! Order the remaining guns in the starboard battery—all guns to fire as they bear! When you are beam on to the enemy, you will stop the engine and fight that ship as long as you are able, do you understand?"

"I . . . I understand."

Hisashi Kurokawa stared at the man a moment longer while the great ship writhed beneath his feet. Finally, he nodded, and strode out of the wheelhouse.

The young lieutenant looked at Akera, eyes wide. "What will we do, Captain?"

"What he told us to," Akera snarled back. "What else is there?"

The OC was screaming while Tikker fought with the stick and rudder pedals to bring his tattered plane under control. He finally succeeded, but he'd lost altitude, and the nine remaining airships had gained considerable distance. He looked down. Just a few miles away, *Salissa* seemed to be *chasing* the Grik battleships! Splashes rose around her, but the trailing Grik battleship in the slightly staggered line was on fire aft, and reeling to starboard! The sole remaining armored frigate was steaming toward her, but he couldn't tell what it meant to do. Maybe it would try to take the bigger ship in tow? The battleship was beam-on to *Salissa* now, considerably less than a mile from her, when its guns flashed and gushed white smoke, sending more great splashes rising around Tikker's Home. He was sure some must have hit.

"Send to *Salissa*!" he shouted. "These Grik got some kind of huge bomb, I don't know how, and . . . I don't think we can stop them!" He pushed on the throttle, but it was already at its stop. He tried to force it even farther, but knew it was no use. He was gaining on the trailing zeppelins, but figured he might get two or three at most before they dropped their bombs. He glanced down in the nose of the plane and horror clenched his heart. He didn't have enough ammunition left for two or three! He'd be lucky to get one! He pounded his leg with his fist; then a chilling calm flowed through him. He *could* get two—if he fired very carefully at one—and then flew his plane into the other.

USNRS Salissa

Salissa was horribly jolted that time by a succession of heavy hammer blows, and Keje's heart was torn by the chorus of screams that arose above the bedlam. The range was such that the enemy shot no longer plunged as steeply, and a long section of the flight deck beside the bridge structure had splintered and peeled away. Exhaust gas swirled in the pilothouse from a capricious eddy that carried it up and forward from a pair of punctured funnels. One 5.5-inch gun had taken a direct hit and was knocked askew on its battlement platform. Its crew was either dead or crawling on the deck, wounded and helpless. The crew of the other gun wasn't much better off. Fragments of the shot or pieces of the first gun had scythed them away from their own weapon. Most of the windows in the pilothouse had been shattered by a blow that fell on the platform above, and broken glass crunched beneath the sandals of the bridge watch as they shook themselves out, returned to their posts, or raced off on errands.

"Damage report!" shouted Captain Atlaan, lurching forward to peer through the empty window frames. He was bleeding in several places, cut by glass. Keje joined him, miraculously untouched. Before them, the Grik battleship seemed hove to, almost still, silent for the moment while the smoke of her guns and fires drifted downwind. They *had* to get past that thing so they could continue their pursuit of the others! For the first time, Keje noticed one of the armored frigates—the last, he thought—was churning away from the stricken ship under full sail, her stack billowing black smoke.

"What's the status on the great gun?" Atlaan asked anxiously.

"Preparing to fire!" answered his talker. "They were . . . delayed in their loading by some strikes around them! They have splinter casualties, two serious, and request assistance!"

"Corps 'Cats and replacements to the number one gun!" Atlaan commanded. Keje looked at him. *Salissa* was still *his* ship, *his* Home, but Atlaan had become her captain of necessity. An Ahd-mi-raal had to worry about far more than the operation of a single ship, and as CINCWEST, Keje had been almost overwhelmed. Atlaan was earning his post well, he thought.

"Ahd-mi-raal!" cried a signal 'Cat, "*Scott* is coming up!"

"She was ordered to remain back!"

"Nevertheless, Cap-i-taan Cablaas-Rag-Lan is steaming to join us. He says in case we need assistance."

Keje blinked irritably. He didn't want to contemplate the possibility, but they might just need it. "Very well, but by the Heavens, tell *Scott* to stay behind us! I will deal with her cap-i-taan later!" He turned to face forward. Judging by the time that had passed, *Salissa* could expect another enemy salvo at any minute. He hoped she would survive it. The Grik battleship across their path was getting close! Suddenly, without warning, the number one gun fired and its huge smoke cloud swept back toward the bridge. The wind took it quickly, and Keje actually saw the massive projectile, like a black dot, rise into the sky. The line looked good. He almost lost it when it reached the top of its trajectory, but there it was! Nosing down, down—a large brown-black explosion shrouded in a mighty waterspout convulsed the Grik ship just forward of amidships. Smoke jetted from the forward funnel, then the funnel itself tumbled into the air on a cushion of scalding steam. Some of the Grik guns fired almost simultaneously with the hit, but they only churned the sea a few hundred yards from the ship.

"She is rolling!" Atlaan guessed loudly. "We have gutted her!" Cheers swept *Salissa* as the enemy did indeed begin listing radically toward them. Keje tried to imagine the monstrous, glorious hole the great gun must have blasted in the ship, probably just below the waterline. The effect must have been much like the terrible torpedoes Captain Reddy so craved. Tons of seawater would be filling the ship, heeling it ever farther onto its shattered beam. Guns would be breaking loose and crashing across the canting decks and he thought he could almost hear the frantic shrieks of the likely thousands of panicked Grik inside their ironclad tomb. Another boiler went, and the opposite casemate, just coming into view, vomited iron plates, shattered timbers, and gouts of steam.

Keje grinned, his sharp teeth bright against his dark fur, and embraced Atlaan beside him. "Three down, and just three to go! *Perhaps* we do have a chance to save Maa-draas!"

"Ahd-mi-raal, Cap-i-taan Atlaan!" the talker almost screamed. The signal 'Cat hadn't even taken time to run to the bridge. "The Grik zeps! They are almost upon us—and Cap i taan Tikker says they carry some new, giant bomb! He cannot stop them! His OC sends that he thinks they will ram—but it will make no difference!"

The report followed them even as Keje and Atlaan rushed out on the bridgewing. "*Arracca* also reports zeps closing on her and her charges!"

"*These* are here already!" Atlaan gasped. The tight gaggle of airships was directly above *Salissa*, about eight thousand feet up. One Nancy was descending at a steep angle—probably trying to keep airspeed with a dead engine, Keje guessed. Behind them, a single, last Nancy was climbing hard, trying to catch them. "Send to COFO Jis-Tikkar to break off! There is nothing he can do now but waste himself—and he is liable to bring one of those things down on top of us!" Keje shouted back to the talker. "Get everything at Maa-draas that will fly in the air! *Arracca* has only her reserve squadron to defend the rest of the fleet!"

"They have not dropped their bombs yet," Atlaan observed suddenly. "Shouldn't they have dropped them by now?"

It was hard to tell, but Keje was sure the zeppelins had crossed well beyond the optimum release point, and no bombs had fallen. "I believe they should have," he agreed guardedly. He realized he'd been steeling himself for something like what he'd seen happen to *Humfra-Dar*. He squinted his eyes. "I am no aviator, but surely if they drop now, they will miss far astern. Could they have decided to go after *Arracca* or Des-Div Four instead?" That made no sense. The battered DDs still lay in the enemy's path, but *Arracca* was north, with most of the rest of the fleet they'd pulled out of Madras as a precaution, and apparently already targeted.

"Look! Oh, look!" Atlaan shouted. "The Grik formation fragments! It splits apart!"

Keje snatched the Imperial spyglass to his eye. Atlaan was right! The Grik gaggle was splitting up, turning in all directions—and bombs, big ones, like Jis-Tikkar said, were falling now. A single large bomb dropped from one, three, seven of the zeppelins—but the last two never had a chance to release theirs because they suddenly blew up.

"P-Forties!" Keje shrieked with glee as four of the amazing aircraft bored in for the kill. He'd never seen a P-40 before, but he'd heard about them, of course, and he'd known they were coming . . . but he hadn't really expected them! Now he understood why the Grik had hesitated—then panicked. They must have seen the planes boring in! "Oh, by the Heavens, are they not wonderful?" he chortled as three more airships erupted in flames, then two more, before the sleek, dark shapes hurtled past the aerial conflagration and turned toward the final two survivors.

Lieutenant Newman appeared, grinning hugely. "Colonel Ben Mallory's respects, Admiral, and he's sorry it took him so long to get here!"

"I wasn't expecting him at all!" Keje laughed. "I *knew* he was expected at Andaman today. . . ."

"He was afraid to blow in case the Jap-Griks might be listening. He refueled six of his ships at Andaman and came straight on," Newman said. "Two had to turn back with engine trouble, though. They were cutting out. Plugs probably fouled. Ben says he hopes to God those grass strips on Ceylon are ready for him, and somebody can get gas, ordnance, food, and booze—in that order—there in a hurry!"

"He should be able to land there," Keje said more soberly, "but it may take a few days to supply him. We had to pull our ships out of Trin-con-lee in the face of those"—he gestured at the battleships forward—"and the supplies are crossing the highlands from Colombo." Keje blinked sudden eagerness. "Did he bring any bombs of his own?"

Newman shook his head. "They had to leave them for extra fuel. All they've got is a half load of ammo and empty auxiliary tanks. Ben says his plane has some AP and he'll give that a try, but he *really* needs to get on the ground."

"Ahd-mi-raal!" Atlaan blurted. He was gazing through his own glass.

"Yes?"

"The . . . the bombs that fell from the enemy! They are still falling—back toward *us*!"

"What?" Keje looked. The bombs *were* very large, he thought again—and getting larger! *How can that be?* His glass fixed on one of the objects that seemed to be falling *diagonally* from east to west now, perhaps a mile off *Salissa*'s starboard beam. "It is a long, white cylinder with a blunt nose and extra-large fins on its tail," he muttered, "and. . . are those little *wings*?!" The glass shook in his hand. "Send to Col-nol Maallory at once! Ignore the Grik battleships! Destroy the zeppelins making for the remainder of the fleet at any cost—*any* cost!"

"What do you see?" Atlaan demanded, trying to look for himself.

"Those bombs are also little aircraft! They are controlled, probably by a Grik lying inside on his belly!"

"Then perhaps they are not bombs! With a pilot—"

"Of *course* they are bombs!" Keje roared, as much to convince himself as Atlaan of the horrifying madness of the scheme. "They have no engine! They *will* hit us—or the water. Which do you think they were brought here to try?"

"Ahead flank!" Atlaan bellowed, dashing into the pilothouse. "Right full rudder! Sound the collision alarm!"

Almost calmly now, Keje refocused on the flying bomb he'd been watching and saw it turn toward his ship. He wasn't prepared when a much closer one, descending through *Salissa*'s own smoke, plunged down through the forward flight deck and exploded.

CHAPTER 29

South of the Rocky Gap
India

"So, here we are," General Pete Alden said softly, unnecessarily, gazing out over the long, narrow, forest-crowded lake. The water was dappled by the last rays of the sun, sinking beyond the mountains to the west, and great, wide trees hung low over the shallows. Angrily squawking duck-shape lizard birds wheeled and darted in rough formations, trying to find undisturbed moorings while weary planes jockeyed toward the open shorelines, their tired engines echoing across the water. Compounding the aggravation of the lizard birds, hundreds of now-free-roaming dino-cows dominated a lot of the shady shallows they preferred, capering and bugling happily in the superabundance of water they apparently craved and had been denied by their former wranglers. Musketry still rattled in the distance, punctuated by the heavy rumble of artillery and mortars.

"Yes, here we are," observed General-Queen Protector Safir Maraan with sharp irony. She had discarded her black cloak at some point in the fighting that brought them here, and her silver armor was dented and dark. She sounded utterly spent, but she was growing impatient with Pete's self-recriminations. "We are here, *alive*, because you bravely and brilliantly saved us from the trap you sent us to," she said bluntly. "A trap that General Rolak might have warned us against, but didn't. A trap Colonel Flynn and I *should* have recognized because it was not dissimilar to one the enemy tried on us before. The Grik grow more . . . adaptable . . . than we had thought, were willing to believe, they were able." Her tail swished irritation at herself. "Now we know. Henceforth, we must design our battles as if we were fighting against ourselves, not thoughtless animals." She shrugged. "The majority of them may still be such, but those who design their battles are not!"

Pete Alden reluctantly nodded. "I guess. Rolak's Corps has fully replaced yours, and nothing'll get past him as long as he has enough ammunition." He stopped, as if unwilling to admit he'd done something right. "We carted a *lot* of ammunition out of Madras before . . ." He shrugged. "We've got a fair amount of fuel too, since we didn't have to worry about hauling water." Nobody would drink lake water without boiling it first, but there was plenty of it. "We've got a good perimeter here, from the Gap down to the river that runs out of this lake," he continued, "and we rounded up a lot of those dino-cows the Grik were staging in the jungle, so we won't starve for a while. Eventually, ammunition and fuel *are* going to be a problem." He rubbed his neck, then nodded at the lake. "I guess it might've been kind of pretty here once, without all the floating junk."

All of Leedom's remaining Nancys, battered and dingy, either floated alongside a long "dock" of fallen trees, or choked one of the gravelly beaches they'd been dragged up on to keep them from sinking. Other planes, most from *Salissa*, had been coming in periodically from Madras, fleeing the approaching Grik. *Arracca* was overcrowded, and after what happened to *Big Sal*, her planes had nowhere else to go. Some looked okay, but most showed hard use. One of the latter was trying to touch down now, its overworked engine wheezing and smoking, the control surfaces in rags.

"That will be Captain Jis-Tikkar," said Safir. "We have comm again at last, and he sent that he was on his way here." Her large eyes cut toward Pete. "He is the last."

"Orderly!" Pete shouted. "My compliments to Captain

Tikker, and get his ass over here as soon as he steps out of that heap. Make sure you get some water in him—or anything else he wants to drink."

"*Big Sal*? Pete asked when Tikker saluted him.

"Afloat and underway," Tikker replied. "Somehow."

Pete had heard that, but it was nice to have it confirmed. *Salissa*'s comm was out, but Keje—thank God Keje was safe!—had reported via *Scott* that his ship was out of danger but was incapable of flight ops of any sort and couldn't even defend herself. She had taken two direct hits from the crazy Grik gliding bombs, and all her upper works forward of the bridge had burned. There was also serious damage amidships on the starboard side.

"I could see her burning all the way to Maa-draas," Tikker reported, "but once the rest of the fleet joined her, they brought the fires under control. The entire fleet now retires to Andamaan, except for *Scott,* a gaas-o-leen tanker, and a few other DDs that will make a run to Trin-con-lee to offload whatever they can for Colonel Maallory's planes and aircrews."

"They're staying?"

"I do not know, Gen-er-aal."

"Well . . . but otherwise, we're on our own?"

Tikker shook his head, blinking denial. "I cannot say, sir. All is still very confused. Three Grik baattle-ships are in Maa-draas, bombarding the empty city"—he snorted and blinked—"and if that were all there was, I think Ahd-miraal Keje would remain aboard *Arracca*. A broader combat air patrol could ensure against more Grik zeps getting close enough to use their gliding bombs—but reports from a picket ship off south Saa-lon say more Grik baattle-ships are on the way. Perhaps they were sent later, or were delayed by breakdowns. . . . Regardless, since the only weapon we had to usefully combat them was *Salissa* . . ."

"Yeah," Pete said. "No sense risking the fleet if we can't even dent the bastards. But that brings us back to Ben Mallory. His P-Forties could make short work of them with proper bombs. They brought something to Andaman they thought would work—"

"Yes, sir, but they cannot, could not, bring them *here*. The range was too far to bring the bombs *and* the fuel necessary to make the trip."

"Maybe a 'Clipper' . . ."

"That is one discussion we monitored between Ahd-mi-raal Keje and Colonel Maallory," Tikker said.

"Rest assured, Gen-er-aal Aalden," Safir Maraan told Pete, "Cap-i-taan Jis-Tikkar is correct. Nearly every message we have monitored or received involves relieving this force. It has become *the* priority of the western war effort. All we have to do is hold out until help arrives, as it surely will."

Pete smiled at her. She made it sound so easy, but he knew she had no such illusions. She did have faith, though; that was plain. Faith that help *would* come and they *would* hold. Pete remembered his earlier mood with embarrassment. Clearly General-Queen Protector Safir Maraan still had faith in *him* in spite of everything, and he determined then that he would die before he disappointed her.

"We'll hold," he said, his voice firm. He gestured out at the lake. "Tikker, you and Leedom have the biggest air wing in the world right now. Even after you strip the wrecks, you'll have more planes than a carrier, I'll bet. We brought some fuel out of Madras, and we've got incendiaries. Maybe the battleships shrug 'em off, but they kill the hell out of Grik in the open. The guys are digging in like fiends. We'll see how the Grik adapt to trench warfare." He grinned. "Which I never was a big fan of, by the way. We'll let 'em get used to it and see how they like it; then, out of the blue, we'll knock the shit out of 'em!"

Grik Madras

"We have achieved a great victory!" General of the Sea Hisashi Kurokawa loudly proclaimed as he met generals Niwa, Halik, and Muriname in the heavily guarded field north of Madras. The sky was utterly black and only the fires of the burning city hinted at the huge bulk of the black-painted airship that had brought the other leaders, besides Niwa, to him there. He knew it must have been a harrowing flight, because even Muriname's personal craft, heavily armed as it was, required only a spark to roast them all alive as they plummeted to the earth. Kurokawa felt a chill. *He* would never ride one of the terrifying things. There were already reports that many of the enemy aircraft had escaped to a lake west of there. Surely some of them would be on the prowl?

The two Japanese generals saluted him, followed a moment later by Halik, who mimicked the gesture. "Come, my friends," Kurokawa boomed, still for the benefit of the many onlookers. "I have a large tent, captured from the enemy, that we may relax within while we discuss our ultimate reconquest of my regency!"

Halik and Niwa looked at each other. *Kurokawa*'s regency? It occurred to both of them then that N'galsh was nowhere to be seen, nor had Niwa seen the vice regent since Muriname arrived in the south. Niwa didn't know Muriname well. The scrawny former NAP 1/c seemed older than his years and was already losing his hair. Niwa barely recognized him. Together, they moved toward the tent. Once inside, Kurokawa's temper took a profound turn. Never did he raise his voice to a level that might be overheard by the guards some distance away, but Niwa recognized an old, almost fanatical intensity.

"Why, General Halik, was the enemy not destroyed in the pass? With the numbers at your disposal and the new warriors you were sent, it should have been simple enough!" Kurokawa demanded.

"The enemy is not a stone that one may overturn at will," Halik replied evenly. His words were carefully enunciated to be clearly understood, and Kurokawa almost recoiled in surprise. Halik had been "just another elevated Grik" when Kurokawa saw him last. He'd been talented, certainly, and clearly had great potential, but that potential had not yet been realized. "His discipline is better than all our warriors but the hatchling host, and his tactics more flexible. They have better weapons—I understand you have seen the examples we captured?—and he uses them well." Halik continued, his crest rising. "Ultimately, we could not force the Gap because our air power was taken from us—and we had not enough artillery when we needed it most."

Niwa was proud of his Grik friend. Never had an underling stood so straight and spoken so forcefully to Kurokawa before. He hoped it wouldn't cost Halik his life. He prepared for Kurokawa's explosion. Instead, to his amazement, the general of the sea merely stared. Eventually, he nodded.

"You make sense, General Halik. The enemy has better weapons than even I believed possible," he admitted. He glared at Muriname. "As the travails of my own Grand Fleet can attest. I suppose you did well, under the circumstances. You did not take the pass from the enemy, but you denied him the open plain beyond where I fear his flexibility would have been far more difficult to counter—and where he might have interrupted your only secure line of supply." He fumed, looking around. "We have no other as yet, and will not until we control the sea and sky!" He glared at Muriname again.

"In all honesty, my Grand Fleet was savaged," he confessed. "We have more ships on the way, but nothing faster than theirs, so the matter of supply and reinforcement remains. If the new bombs had been used sooner, I would not have lost so many ships—including my own flagship!" The rage threatened to spill over again, and Muriname shifted uncomfortably.

"General of the Sea," Muriname said, "I ordered the attack as soon as I received word—and it did succeed in the likely destruction of one of their carriers. . . ."

"For the loss of nearly every airship under your command!" Kurokawa snapped. "And you would not even know what they accomplished if I had not seen it myself! All that attacked were lost!" A troubling thought resurfaced in Kurokawa's mind. He'd been too distant to see what did it, but *something* destroyed the last of Muriname's airships before they could finish the big enemy carrier, and something else wiped out the second force with equal ease. *Or could it have been the same thing that destroyed both?* he wondered.

"More airships are on the way," Muriname soothed. "But they remain at a disadvantage in speed and maneuverability—not to mention other inherent risks." He straightened and looked strangely at Kurokawa. "Ultimately, they are all we have for now. We must make do, and devise better tactics for their use."

Kurokawa nodded thoughtfully, oddly quick to halt his attack against Muriname, Niwa thought. *What is that look? Is there something better than dirigibles taking shape at the Japanese enclave on Zanzibar?* Suddenly, Niwa was sure of it. *But why keep it secret?* Then it was clear. *For the same reason they kept communications secret—from the Grik.* He remembered Kurokawa's ways well enough to know the madman doubtless still plotted and schemed.

Finally, Kurokawa turned to Niwa. "I have missed you, General, more than you know. You have accomplished much and made me proud."

For a moment, Niwa could only stand in shock. "Uh, thank you, General of the Sea," he managed at last.

Kurokawa smiled for an instant, then a frown creased his face as quickly as if a switch had been thrown. "Your exemplary actions to this point leave me particularly surprised that you did not seize the opportunity to destroy the forces that retreated from Madras. They were strung out, drawing supplies, helpless. Now they have established a strong defensive position that cannot be ignored."

"I . . ." Niwa stalled. How could he describe how difficult it was to launch any kind of coordinated attack through that dense jungle south of the road the enemy took? He *had* attacked, and the fighting had been fierce—it was still going on—but most of the enemy had reached its new defensive perimeter. He simply hadn't been able to bring sufficient force to bear at any one place to scatter the column. "I have no acceptable excuse, General of the Sea," Niwa finally replied. "I tried, but was not successful." He glanced at the others. The same could be said of all of them.

Amazingly, Kurokawa's expression softened. "Never mind," he said. "You and General Halik will have a chance to redeem yourselves. You have the enemy surrounded now, do you not? It should be a simple matter to coordinate your forces now and utterly destroy these . . . refugees. I leave the planning and execution to the two of you." He held up a hand. "I *will* require some thousands of your warriors to assist in the refitting of my ships. Also, some of the local civilian population, including many artificers, that fled the enemy are with you, General Niwa? I need them back. See that they are sent here immediately."

"Of course, General of the Sea."

"Very well. Then if you have no further questions, I shall leave you to your task." He turned to Muriname. "You remain a while longer before you fly away. I have other things to discuss with you."

Niwa turned to leave, but noticed Halik hadn't moved.

"You refer to your regency, General of the Sea, but what of Regent-Consort Tsalka and his vice regent, N'galsh?" Halik asked.

Kurokawa swiveled his head and rested his eyes on the Grik general. An odd smile twisted his lips. "Lord Regent Tsalka was given the traitor's death," he said bluntly, watching Halik's crest flatten with horror and disbelief. "Vice Regent N'galsh died leading the airship attack against the enemy fleet, and I will have to replace him. But by the express wish of the Celestial Mother herself, *I* am Regent-Consort of Ceylon and All India now, by conquest!" Kurokawa paused, and actually giggled. "Perhaps not Consort," he said, "but Lord Regent? Oh yes! I have reconquered the bulk of the lost regency; Ceylon will come in time. This land is mine, by promise of the Giver of Life!"

Niwa's head spun. *N'galsh lead an attack? Impossible! Kurokawa, a Grik noble? The man is* utterly *mad.*

"Does First General Esshk support that?" Halik demanded, and Kurokawa's face reddened.

"Why on earth would that matter?" he roared, forgetting himself at last. "It is the will of the Celestial Mother, supported by the Chooser. And as Lord Regent, I am no longer bound by the whims of such as General Esshk!" Kurokawa's smile twisted further. "This land belongs to *me* now, as do all the warriors upon it. As do *you*, General Halik!"

CHAPTER 30

Baalkpan, Borno

The mood was grim in Adar's Great Hall. It wasn't an open meeting, and with a few exceptions, only the high command and senior Allied representatives were present for this first consultation. But there were too many for the privacy of the War Room. Adar sat rigidly on the stiff cushion he preferred, while frantic jabbering filled the lamp-lit chamber. He tried to calm himself by staring at a charred tapestry on the far wall, reminding himself that things had been much worse before. The tapestry was one of the few that had survived the destruction of the previous hall presided over by the great Nakja-Mur. Rising, angry voices brought him back to the present.

"General Alden and three corps—nearly forty thousand troops—are all alone out there!" Alan Letts shouted. "Surrounded and cut off! We have to get him some relief! Figure out a way to resupply, reinforce—"

"I doubt he has nearly that many troops *now*, Mr. Letts. He has lost! We should concentrate on getting his remaining troops *out*!" Commander Herring shouted in return. He paused in the silence that ensued. "I agree about relief, however. General Alden should be relieved of his command at once!"

"Under *these* circumstances? Are you insane?" Alan

yelled, stunned. "And pull out? You *are* insane! We must have India, to keep it from the enemy, if for no other reason. Ceylon can't hold without it nor can Andaman, eventually. After all the blood we've spilled, you'd have us right back where we started!"

"I guess it's a damn good thing you ain't in charge, *Mr*. Herring." Dennis Silva rumbled. He was one of the exceptions, and he'd just "come along" with Bernie again. Now he towered beside Letts, his mighty arms crossed. "Or is that what you're anglin' for, *Mr*. Herring?"

"Don't be absurd!" Herring snapped. "And just who the devil are you to make such an accusation?"

Silva leaned forward. "You might just be *amazed* how 'absurd' I can work myself up into bein'," he said in a tone too many people recognized. Herring took a step back, but Sister Audry—another exception—reached up and put a restraining hand on Silva's bicep.

"You might indeed be amazed, Commander Herring," Sister Audry said, just as angry, but controlled. "Very briefly. Pray do not bait the beast. You are new here, so perhaps you do not understand. General Alden and his command are *family* to most of us here. In some cases, quite literally. God alone knows how many cousins our Lord Adar himself has in the field! General Alden has faced the Grik many times before, and you have never done so. It is easy for you to decry his 'incompetence' while safely away from the fight!" She glared around. "It would seem General Alden made some mistakes, but so did Admiral Keje—so did everyone! The enemy is changing somehow, and most dramatically." She looked back at Herring. "But once those mistakes were made, can you think of anyone else who could have salvaged anything of the situation, as it appears General Alden has done? Could *you*?"

Adar began to realize that perhaps things had never been this bad after all. Before, they'd always been united, and now he saw . . . factions . . . developing. Far too many of his own people seemed to support Herring's proposition. He reached over and struck the bronze pipe gong insistently. "Gentlemen! My dear Sister Audry!" he said into the dissolving roar. "My people, my friends," he continued more quietly. "As you know, the situation is this: The government of the Empire of the New Britain Isles remains in disarray after the cowardly assassination of the Governor-Emperor and his mate. Our dear Princess Rebecca Anne McDonald, whom many of you know so well, has ascended to the throne with the aid of loyal elements and our ambassador, Mr. Braad-furd. I am hopeful that stability there will soon be restored." He blinked determination. "I said the new Governor-Empress is ours, and I meant it. She has won greater love from Baalkpan, Saan-Kakja, and doubtless the Amer-i-caan clan than *I* ever will. She and Saan-Kakja are as sisters. If nothing else, her ascension will likely garner even greater support from Maa-ni-la than had been forthcoming thus far.

"Otherwise, in the east, Second Fleet has succeeded in driving the Dominion from Aal-ber-maarl, the most important of the Enchanted Isles, thereby securing a forward base for eventual operations against the evil Dominion itself." He sighed. "That is the good news, such as it is.

"In the west, Generaal Aalden has encountered a more vigorous and much more advanced and cunning Grik force than we have ever seen. He was unprepared for this, as anyone would be, and his campaign is faced with stalemate."

"Disaster, you mean!" someone shouted in Lemurian.

"*Not* disaster!" Adar retorted. "He has quickly—and I must say, masterfully—consolidated his continental force into what he calls a 'satisfactory' defensive posture. He needs supplies to maintain it, of course, and with the reverse suffered by First Fleet, those will be difficult to deliver for a time. We still hold all of Saa-lon, and should be able to keep it. The enemy has no means of delivering troops there at present except across the low-tide crossing, and it is well defended. Saa-lon will become our forward supply base for the Expeditionary Force. We *will* sustain it until it can be relieved!"

He stared hard at Herring. "And as long as I am chairman of the Grand Alliance, there will be no more talk of retreat, or relinquishing *one single tail* of territory we have conquered from the enemy! Most of you know there is no negotiation with the Grik, and with every backward step we take, the Grik will try to take two steps forward. We grow stronger each day, but so does the enemy. We must not—*will not*—abandon our gains. As the hu-maans put it, this war is for all the marbles, and always has been. If we retreat now, where will we stop? There will be no second Battle of Baalkpan!"

"How can we supply Gen-er-aal Aalden, or even Saalon? The fleet is destroyed!" blared a former Aryaalan noble, and Adar wondered again how the creature—and others like him with little interest beyond themselves—had been acclaimed as representative for anyone.

"The fleet is *not* destroyed!" Letts countered. "Sure, we got licked," he admitted, "and we lost some ships. A good chunk of Commodore Ellis's DDs were lost or damaged. But Jim's alive and sorting things out at Andaman—still working with a busted jaw!" Letts looked hard at the Aryaalan. "Other than that, we came off pretty light, considering what they threw at us. Ironclads, zeppelins, suicider Grik! Damn!"

"What of *Salissa* and the Ahd-mi-raal?" Adar asked softly, still concerned for his younglinghood friend. "They also reached Andamaan?"

"Yes, sir. I got the word on the way here." He paused. "Keje's okay," he said to the anxious faces. "Singed his fur a little, I hear. It was touch-and-go for *Big Sal* for a while, though. Most of her boilers were blown out by some kind of hit amidships, and she was burning bad. If those Grik battleships hadn't been so focused on Madras, she'd be a goner. As it was, the rest of the fleet helped put out her fires, and she got a lot of her boilers relit. She averaged ten knots to Andaman, even with a hole in her guts near the waterline hangar. She won't be carrying planes for a while," he admitted. "Nearly her whole flight and hangar decks were gutted by the fire. If Keje hadn't turned her downwind when he did, she probably would've burned to the waterline. Damn good damage control."

"Will she have to come here for the dry dock?" Bernie asked.

"Hopefully not," Alan replied.

"But what of the rest of the fleet?" the obstinate Aryaalan asked.

"Colonel Mallory tore up the zeps that were headed for it. *Arracca* didn't get a scratch. One of those crazy suiciders got one of the new fleet oilers, but that was it. The rest of the fleet got out before those damn Grik battleships could cut 'em off. Captain Tikker and some other 'Nancys' were up and down; saw the whole thing. He said the battleships didn't act like they much cared about anything but steaming into Madras and blasting hell out of everything." Alan smiled. "Of course, our people were already out of there. Either on the ships or back at Alden's perimeter."

"So . . . if Alden's backed up against the mountains, with no sea access, how *are* we gonna supply him?" Silva blurted uncomfortably.

"By air, mostly," Adar said firmly, "any way we can. And there might *still* be sea access," he added cryptically. "In the meantime, the 'Clipper' program will get whatever resources it needs to double—triple—production of long-range aircraft. Col-nol Maallory is on Saa-lon, and will coordinate the air supply—and air offensive! Generaal Aalden may be isolated, but we will continue killing Grik!"

There was stomping and cheering, but it was subdued. Adar blinked at Sister Audry. He'd discussed his next subject with her and Alan, as well as with Saan-Kakja, Ambassador Forester, and Courtney Bradford, over wireless. There was currently no communication with *Walker* and Captain Reddy; nothing since her announcement that she'd engaged the Japanese destroyer. Only a few people were aware of that, and he wasn't going to bring it up now. He didn't even want to *think* about what a disaster *Walker*'s loss could prove to be. Captain Reddy was too important to the Alliance, and *Walker* was disproportionately important to its people. He tapped the gong again lightly, then stood.

"We have faced desperate times before, but always we prevailed. I think we did so, in greater part, because of our unity. After a long succession of victories, we have been dealt a setback. Was this not to be expected? I hate the Grik more than anyone, but I have learned to . . . respect their capabilities like I never did before." He nodded at Herring. "This is in large part due to the efforts of Commander Herring and his studies of the prisoners. With his . . . different focus, he has made discoveries that might have eluded even our eminent Courtney Braad-furd. He prepares other projects, other missions, to learn even more. These are things we need to do—should have been doing already—but our focus was narrower, of necessity. I believe, with his experience and training, he brings a greater grasp of the big picture, as Cap-i-taan Reddy would say, to the table than perhaps even Cap-i-taan Reddy has been able to do—despite his own long-ago recognition of the need."

Incongruously, he blinked annoyance at Herring.

"Commander Herring has established himself as a valuable asset, and his Office of Straa-teegic Intelligence must be confirmed. But as much as he has learned on our behalf, he has much to learn about *us*. With respect, Mr. Herring, I propose that your perceptions are colored by your admittedly dreadful experiences. You were forced to surrender to the Jaaps and they treated you very badly—yet you survived. You must come to grips with the fact that there is no surrender to the Grik, and no possibility of survival if they are victorious. You consider the misery you suffered to be as bad as any being can inflict on another, but you must grasp the fact that the Grik are even worse than the Jaaps!" Adar paused while a long-ago vision flashed before his mind's eye. "Much worse," he whispered. He glared back at the man. "*I* will decide who requires relief and who gets relieved, Mr. Herring."

There was murmuring over that, but the shouting was not renewed. Adar sighed and took a deep breath with his eyes closed. He opened them. "I was made high chief of Baalkpan by acclamation, then again chairman of our growing Alliance by the same process." He blinked apology. "So, ultimately, it is I who have failed, not Gener-aal Aalden or Ahd-mi-raal Keje-Fris-Ar! I bear the greater responsibility." He shook his head at the rising denial.

"It is true. Too long I have remained disassociated, content to allow others who know more of war than I to set the policy of the war, define its goals, select the stratagems. That must end—I must end it. I am to blame for the situation our family"—he bowed his head to Audry—"faces in Indiaa, because up until this moment, it is I who have neglected my duties. I put it to you now—representatives of all the Western Allies are here, at least—to reaffirm my acclamation or cast me out."

He held up a hand to still the surprised roar that began. "But only bear this in mind," he cautioned. "If I am sustained, there will be no more bickering, no jockeying for precedence among the various Homes. Those Homes will retain their identity as in the past, but they must follow the example of the Amer-i-caan clan; independent but a loyal part of the whole—dedicated to the whole. We will move forward as one people to defeat the twin scourges that threaten us in the west *and* the east, and I will be chairman in deed as well as name. I will decide the priorities of this war, with your able counsel, and I will make the final stra-tee-gic decisions!"

He paused in the near silence that followed his words. "Think carefully, my people, before you decide. What I ask has never been done, not here. And remember this condition: if I am sustained, it will be with a mandate to win the war—and it will last until the bitter end!"

"We cannot acclaim such a thing!" shouted the Sularan representative. "We are too few!"

"I have communicated with Saan-Kakja of the Fil-pin Lands, and she pledges her support, as does the Governor-Empress of the New Britain Isles."

"But that is different! They enjoy hereditary rights, much like the Queen of B'mbaado!"

"Who at this moment is fighting for her life—and yours—in Indiaa! Have you so little support from your people?"

"Have you such great support from *yours*?" the Sularan countered.

"We will see, I suppose," Adar murmured. "They might cast me out. A sufficient number of the various representatives might do so as well—or your Home can always leave the union that I propose. But until that time, as long as I am chairman, I will pursue the war as I see fit, until absolute victory is achieved! If I fail, it will because I did something wrong. Not because I did nothing!"

CHAPTER 31

La Plaza Sagrada del Templo de los Papas
The Holy Dominion
April 3, 1944

The sultry night was utterly black and almost as utterly silent. Occasional steps echoed off the stone pavement of the plaza, accompanied by ghostly, hovering lamps that marked their course. Otherwise the vast expanse was virtually abandoned for once. It was a time for fasting and prayer throughout the Dominion, and there would be no boisterous crowds, shouting vendors, or garishly clad revelers celebrating ancient gods—now officially "servant saints" to the One God—for several days to come.

Kari-Faask had gathered that much, but it was difficult to summon any real interest. Perhaps she would be left in peace for a short time. Her spirit hadn't shattered entirely, but it had been laid very low at last, and she couldn't rouse herself to care about much of anything anymore. No one had pestered her the day that Fred and Don Hernan came to her, but she'd been so depressed by Fred's attitude and transformation that she hardly noticed—and the torment resumed afresh the following day when a different festival commenced. She rarely snarled at the gawkers that gathered around her cage or poked at her with sticks that vendors had started selling for the purpose, and she stopped trying to keep herself fit on the meager slop they fed her. She'd grown too weak and lethargic to do much at all but lie in the vermin-infested, rotting straw within the iron-barred cube that no one bothered to clean anymore. The cage had become her whole world. In a few days, the plaza would fill again as yet another bloody festival began, and she almost hoped, at long last, they'd take her from the cage and drag her to the high top of the central, black-stained temple and end her misery. Even if she'd had the strength, she no longer had the will to resist. The spectacles she'd seen performed there filled her with horror—but the horror would be brief and then she would be free.

"Kari!" came an urgent, imaginary whisper from the gloom. "Kari!" the voice repeated, and she stirred. *It can't be,* she thought. *I am going mad. That sounded like . . . Fred . . . but that is impossible. He has already gone insane, absorbed by the evil of this terrible land. Tortured into accepting the vile faith of our captors, he has entered the service of the demon Don Hernan himself!* The shock and betrayal she felt that one time he visited her had torn her soul. Fred Reynolds had become her closest friend—and he had thrown her away.

"Kari, damn it! We don't have much time! Wake up! Snap out of it! We have to get out of here!" The lock clattered like a bell against the iron hasp.

"It is open, Lieutenant," came another oddly familiar voice, "but I don't know if we can get her out if she does not aid us. Perhaps she is too far gone, after all."

"No!" the first voice insisted. It *was* Fred! Kari struggled to rise from the filth.

"Are you really here?" she croaked. "Is it really you? Who"—she coughed—"who is that with you?"

"We have met before, ah, Ensign Kari-Faask," a man replied. "I told you once that you have friends, and you do. So does Mr. Reynolds. It has taken much longer to arrange this escape than we had hoped, but the time has come—and we *must* hurry!"

"Escape?" Kari asked, amazed.

"Yeah. C'mon, Kari. We gotta go! There're horses waiting outside the wall that borders the plaza."

"Horses?"

"Yeah, ah, like paalkas—sorta. They had 'em in the Empire. Remember?"

Kari started moving toward the cage door, but paused. "You were converted! Turned! You became the tool of Don Hernan!"

A black, strangely haunted chuckle sounded in the gloom. "Yeah, that's what that sick bastard thought. I ought to be an actor! Won't he be surprised? Listen, honey. I'll tell you all about it later, but we have to blow this joint!"

Honey?

Suddenly, Kari could no longer resist. Nothing made sense, but Fred was here. He would sort everything out. She collapsed.

"Damn." She heard the strange, familiar voice again as she slipped toward the darkness. "She's passed out. We'll have to carry her."

"That shouldn't be hard," Fred said bitterly. "*Look* at her! Those *bastards*!"

"You are weak yourself," observed the voice. "Can you manage?"

"I'll carry her on my head, if I have to," Fred swore, "but just who are these folks that are waiting for us?"

"Never fear," the voice replied cryptically. "They will never harm her. *You,* they might kill, but never *her*."

Kari heard nothing more as her thoughts swirled away.

Baalkpan
April 3, 1944

The Saanga River Ferry north of Baalkpan was one of the most advanced outposts of civilization short of the very first Allied oil fields farther upriver. It was relatively new, and used primarily to transport hunters, workers, and light cargo upstream or across the river to the wild and still vaguely explored frontier. It was *on* the frontier in many respects, and was the only work of Lemurians or men visible on the landing hacked from the dense jungle around it. A broad, well-patrolled avenue connected it to the curing yards, processing plants, and other industries that supported the city and expanding shipyard, but those were several miles distant, and the illusion of utmost isolation prevailed.

The landing was unusually crowded today, however, as the Corps of Discovery and Diplomacy—or, as Silva irreverently called it, the Codd— prepared to set out at last. Lemurians heaved crates of supplies to the ferry from carts drawn by paalkas that squeaked nervously at the unfamiliar smells the foreign beasts didn't know. Lawrence directed his fellow Sa'aarans—and the few "tame" Grik attached to his contingent. The Sa'aarans would serve as scouts and pickets and were combat loaded and dressed in their camouflage battle dress. The half-dozen Grik would be unarmed porters. They seemed slavishly devoted to their new masters, but they were still Grik. It was impossible to be comfortable around them, and they had sufficient natural weapons to defend themselves. Their presence on the trip was an experiment and even they seemed to realize they had something to prove. In any event, for now, everyone worked together to get the expedition underway.

"For the record," Dennis Silva muttered to Ensign Abel Cook, as he threw a crate of ammunition for his massive new cartridge-converted Doom Stomper on his shoulder, "I think we should've called off this jaunt, at least for now."

Cook looked at him. "Chairman Adar remains insistent. And besides . . . why?"

Dennis shrugged, and the crate on his shoulder rustled metallically. "'Cause you can't go without me, and with the mess in the west, a fella of my . . . powers . . . why, such as me, oughta be there, savin' General Aalden's ass."

Cook chuckled. "I thought you said you were out of the battle-winning business and would now allow others a share of fame. Besides, *Walker* will be here soon for her refit, and you should be back in time to join her when it's complete. That was the plan, as I remember."

Silva frowned. "Yeah, but who knows if that's *still* the plan. Plans are highly overrated, if you ask me. Besides"—he lowered his voice—"why's ever'body so mum about

Walker, anyway? The scuttlebutt is she got into it with that *Hoodoo-y-yamy* an' popped her bubble. Couldn't report it herself 'cause she took some hits and lost her comm gear, but a Fil-pin DD met up with her an' passed the word she was headin' in to Manilly with some new holes—an' some wounded."

Cook shook his head. "That's more than I have heard," he said with a trace of concern, "and I have learned to respect this scuttlebutt phenomenon."

Silva nodded seriously, then stiffened, looking down the road to Baalkpan. Another cart was approaching in the distance. But closer, a tall form was walking toward them. "Why, if it ain't Gunny Horn!" he hooted as the black-bearded China Marine approached.

Horn grinned strangely as he neared, backpack and weapons slung, apparently effortlessly, over his still somewhat skinny shoulder. He'd clearly piled a lot of weight back on, but he had a way to go to match Silva's powerful form.

"Been looking for you, you diabolical squid," Horn said menacingly.

"An' I been here, easy to find," Silva challenged. Lawrence and Brassey had joined Silva, and Lawrence bristled at the hint of hostility. *Who is this man?* Ensign Cook was also alarmed. He was already nervous, as the expedition's titular leader, and they hadn't even started out yet. Now it looked like his two biggest men were about to have at each other.

Horn stopped in front of Dennis and laid his burden on the ground. "Not as easy to find as you should have been."

Silva shrugged. "Hey, I'm a busy man! Mr. Sandison's had me jumpin' up and down an' flappin' my arms over in Ordnance, and Mr. Letts has had me figgerin' up ever'thing we might ever need to pull this stunt. Then, once in a while, Mr. Cook needs me for somethin!"

Noticing Cook for the first time, Horn saluted the boy. "Good morning, sir!"

"Good morning, ah, Gunnery Sergeant Horn," Cook replied.

Silva snapped his fingers. "That's right, you two already met." He looked at the old Lemurian sergeant Moe, who'd also stepped closer. "Been trompin' around out in the brush, learnin' the primordial ropes of thc neighborhood. Hey! See any super lizards?"

Moe shook his head. "No super lizards," he said. "We kill some rhino pigs, though."

"Hmm. So Gunny Horn here really don't know what he's getting himself into then," Silva said. He looked at the man. "Maybe you oughta stay here, learn how to be a Marine on this world and kill Griks. You could take up knittin' or croquet."

"In honest, *you* don't know what you get in to, Si'va," Moe quipped, then shrugged. "Me neither. *I* rather stay here."

"I've been cooped up in one place too long," Horn grumbled. "I'd like to stretch my legs. From what I hear, there'll be plenty of Grik to kill when we get back."

There was still a palpable tension between the two men. Finally, Silva revealed his gap-tooth grin. "Well? You still got it, Gunny?"

Horn grinned back and fished his dog tags from around his neck. "Japs would've taken it if I had it in a suitable, jewel-encrusted gold setting." The tags slid down the chain, and Horn displayed a human tooth.

"Ha!" Silva barked.

"Is that . . . yours?" Cook asked, amazed.

"Yep. Gunny Horn . . . extracted it for me one night in Shanghai!"

"Saved your useless life!"

"I misremember the details," Silva grudged. "Last time I ever went ashore with Dean Laney, though, I'll tell you that!"

"Laney," Horn spat. "Of all the *really* useless bastards to show up here—"

"So . . . you two are *friends*?" Cook ventured hesitantly, wondering what on earth had required Horn to—apparently—knock Silva's tooth out to (evidently) save his life.

"Hell no!" Dennis said, indignant. "He's a Marine!" He looked seriously at Horn. "But I won't never worry about my back in a fight with him around." He reached over and ruffled Lawrence's crest.

"Sto' that!" Lawrence yelped.

"'Specially with ol' Larry along," he placated his Grik-like friend. "Won't be much for me to do but see the sights, er"—he laughed at Horn's expression—"what was it? Chase butterflies!"

"Chasing butterflies is against the rules." Horn grinned back.

"Except along Soochow Creek," Silva agreed, mock serious, and both men exploded in laughter.

Utterly mystified, and wondering if he ever would—or wanted to—hear the tale Silva and Horn shared, Cook glanced at the cart that should be bringing the last of their supplies. "Oh no!" he breathed when he saw the cart's lone passenger hop down. Nurse Lieutenant Pam Cross wore a light, linenlike smock and trousers of the nearly universal tie-dyed camouflage adopted from the Sa'aarans. She reached up and grabbed a medical pack and a Blitzer Bug submachine gun off the cart and carried them over to the suddenly speechless group.

"What're you dopes gawkin' at?" she demanded.

"Why . . . you, I s'pose," Silva said evenly. "Just weren't expectin' you to show up here, all dressed up like you thought you was goin' with us."

"This outfit needs a doc," Pam said simply, defiantly. "I'm it." She handed Cook a sheet of rough paper. "Adar's orders."

"Bullshit," Silva said more harshly. "We're headed off to make contact with them Injun jungle lizards—which might be hostile as hell—through some of the scariest country we know of on this screwed-up world! This ain't no trip fer—"

"For what?" Pam demanded. She gestured at some of the female Lemurian troops loading gear on the ferry. "For dames? I don't think you can really stand there an' say that, you big jerk. The dame famine's over."

"Wull . . . what about Colonel Mallory? Ain't you two a item? What'll he say?"

"He left," Pam said harshly, "just like you have a dozen times. He doesn't own me," she snapped ironically, and Silva winced. "Nobody can tell me what I can or can't do anymore, except a superior officer—an' I damn sure outrank *you*. Adar said I could go, an' so did Mr. Letts. We ain't short o' doctors anymore neither."

"You outrank *me*, Lieutenant," Abel Cook observed as neutrally as possible.

Pam shook her head. "I'm medical officer. You command the expedition."

Without thinking about it, Cook looked at Silva. He might be in command, but everyone, including Adar, knew who was in *charge*. After a long moment, Silva shrugged, his one eye narrowed to a slit. "Suit yerself, doll," he grunted, and turned to carry his ammo crate to the ferry. "Let's get this circus on the road," he growled over his shoulder.

Maa-ni-la
April 3, 1944

"By the Heavens above," Saan-Kakja murmured in sick sorrow as USS *Walker* (DD-163) crept closer to the Navy dock at the Advanced Training Center on Maara-vella. "How often can that poor ship sustain such damage and survive?" she pleaded.

Chack-Sab-At stood beside her, summoned from some training exercises his special Marines had been undergoing. He didn't trust himself to speak. Isak Rueben was there as well, with the floating dry dock *Walker*'s escorting frigate had summoned, and Ambassador Lord Forester had accompanied Saan-Kakja from Maa-ni-la. Also present were General Ansik-Talaa of the new Fil-pin Scouts, Colonel Dusaa of the coastal artillery, and quite a few troops and medical personnel who'd rushed down from the hospital and barracks in the booming military town.

Walker was low by the head and had a decided list to port. Gaping holes yawned wide just behind her tall, dingy, half-submerged number, and on the fo'c'sle just forward of the bridge. The bridge structure itself looked warped and disheveled, and the canvas on the rail around the fire-control platform was shredded. Water streamed from within the ship in solid torrents and splashed alongside, and more water ran from temporary hoses attached to auxiliary pumps and coursed along the deck. The forward funnel looked like a ruptured pipe, and the aft funnel was even worse. Smoke streamed only from number two, so the boilers in the aft fireroom had to be cold. The main blower behind the bridge still rumbled, but with an exhausted, hurting gasp. The whole ship looked diseased with rust.

Yet *Walker* still lived, and her torn battle flag streamed to leeward on the stiff breeze off the nearby mountains. 'Cats in whites stood on the leaning fo'c'sle with lines in their hands, contrasting sharply with the rust, smoke stains, and faded gray paint. The number one gun—all the ship's guns, Saan-Kakja now saw—were clean and trained fore and aft, and men and Lemurians were on the bridgewing, amidships deckhouse, and fire-blackened aft deckhouse. It was from there, Chack finally told her, that the ship was being conned.

Isak Rueben took the pipe from his mouth and exhaled a stream of rank smoke that smelled like burning leaves and ammonia. He coughed.

"Just as long as her crew can take it, an' as often as we got the stuff—an' the gumption—to patch her back up, Yer Excellentness," he said with uncharacteristic forcefulness. Saan-Kakja looked at the odd, scrawny man and saw tears on his cheeks.

"You are right, of course," she agreed firmly, but deep down she still wondered.

The tired old ship was finally secured to the dock, and corps 'Cats streamed up the gangplank as quickly as it was rigged. Soon, *Walker*'s wounded started coming ashore, helped along or carried on stretchers. Earl Lanier's stretcher required extra, somewhat sullen bearers, and he waved imperiously as the space alongside the battered ship continued to fill. "Boats" Bashear was still swaddled in bandages, but he strode down the gangway unassisted. There was a sudden commotion aboard *Walker* as Chief Gray's distinctive, comforting bellow gathered a side party, and amid a twitter of pipes, another stretcher came down the gangplank with Sandra and Diania anxiously pacing it and Juan Marcos clomping along behind on a crutch that replaced his wooden leg. Saan-Kakja and her party had been staying out of the way, but now they moved forward. Sandra saw them coming, and for just an instant, Saan-Kakja caught the slightest hint of the anguish that lay behind Sandra's eyes. Rushing forward, the High Chief of all the Fil-pin Lands wrapped her arms around the taller woman and held her in a tight embrace.

"He's going to be all right," Sandra managed through the tears of relief and appreciation that began to flow. She sounded like she was trying to convince herself as much as those gathering around, but she repeated herself with more certainty. "He's going to be all right."

Saan-Kakja looked down at the unconscious man on the stretcher, the man who meant so much to them all—not just because they needed him, but because they loved him.

"I have no doubt," Saan-Kakja agreed, her mesmerizing, gold and black eyes beginning to fill. "Let us get him to the hospital, and then you must rest and refresh yourself!"

Matt was dreaming, sort of. He was awash in seep, and the differently refined version of the analgesic, germ-fighting paste that had been used to treat his wounds had left him almost comatose in appearance, but somewhat aware as well. Seep was a popular intoxicant in reasonable doses, but they'd learned it performed much like morphine when used in large amounts. Like the paste, seep also apparently had some antibacterial properties, because it killed off a lot of the good bacteria in one's innards as well as the bad, and often left heavily dosed patients with a bad case of the "screamers." He hated that. He also hated the sick, unreal, helpless feeling it gave him.

He felt himself being carried out of the wardroom and heard the Bosun's pipes. He knew he was being brought ashore and *Walker* was safe at last. He even heard the voices of Sandra and his friends as they gathered round, and he was pleased, in a kind of disassociated way. But then, for a while, he . . . left.

"You've got an awful strange setup around here, Matthew," Orrin Reddy told him, staring out at the sea. Somehow, Matt was back on New Ireland, and he'd been walking along the rocky, secluded northern coast under the warm sunshine where he'd taken a quick trip to visit his cousin.

Orrin! Of all people to find in this goofed-up world! Orrin and a flight of *Maaka-Kakja*'s Nancys had been helping scour the island of any remaining Grikbirds after the fearsome battles that snatched it back from Dominion control. He'd been conked on the head and wasn't flying, but he would remain there as long as any of his pilots did.

"It *is* strange," Matt agreed, "in a lot of ways." He grinned. "But not much stranger than finding you here." Orrin chuckled. He looked good, considering what he'd been through. Matt had been amazed to hear the kid had shown up on this world, and still marveled at the coincidence of it. Orrin had been his favorite cousin, more like the little brother he never had, and they'd been close before his uncle and aunt took Orrin and his five brothers and sisters off to California. That had been in . . . 'thirty-two? Right before Matt entered the Naval Academy. He'd heard Orrin joined the Army Air Corps in 'forty-one and hoped to be assigned to the Philippines, where he and Matt would be close. Orrin even arrived in the Philippines while Matt was still there, but they never had a chance to get together. Either Matt had been on maneuvers or Orrin had been busy with training and readiness exercises. Then, just a few weeks later, the Japanese bombed Pearl Harbor and the Philippines, and *Walker* was ordered south to Java.

"Honestly," Matt continued, "when I had time to think about it, I figured you'd been killed fighting the Japs. So many planes were lost so quickly, I knew the odds weren't in your favor. The slaughter of the Air Corps was *why* the Navy had to leave the Philippines. We were sitting ducks."

Orrin nodded with a frown. "I know. And I nearly *was* killed more times than I care to think about."

Matt said nothing to that. The same was true for all of them now. "In retrospect," he said instead, "I shouldn't have been *that* amazed you made it here. On the scale of amazing things I've seen or learned over the past couple of years, that doesn't really even make the chart. But I'm glad to see you."

They talked of many things that day. There was a lot of reminiscing, and they both considered what a tough war it must have been for the Reddy clan back home. They talked about the situation on this world, as Matt knew it, and Matt noticed how the war here was increasingly becoming Orrin's war, as much as anyone's. Then they talked about the old war, as Orrin knew it.

Matt was appalled by the treatment Orrin and other POWs had suffered at the hands of the Japanese, and equally horrified by the atrocities inflicted on the Filipinos, whom the Japanese supposedly invaded to liberate. He'd never really liked the Philippines when he was stationed there—hadn't much liked *Walker* back then, or the Asiatic Fleet in general, but he'd hated being run off. And then to hear what the Japanese had done after they left . . .

"Our Jap guards crowed a lot about their successes," Orrin explained, "which were depressingly frequent at first," he admitted. "Then they started to clam up and things got worse for us, if that's possible. Things started to go sour for them after the Coral Sea and Midway, and Guadalcanal. They didn't crow about those, and most of what we heard about them was smuggled in by Filipinos to boost our morale." He grinned. "But the first really good news we got was that Jimmy Doolittle had bombed Tokyo itself!" He looked seriously at Matt. "That was right after we heard the Asiatic Fleet had ceased to exist. I hated to hear that."

He kicked a black rock, and his grin returned. "Anyway, Doolittle's stunt wasn't much more than a poke in the eye, see? But it caused the Japs to take forces from their advancing fleets to beef up the defenses around the home islands, so the strategic effect was all out of proportion to the tactical one. Besides, it drove the Japs absolutely, fanatically nuts, and gave us a shot in the arm when we heard." His face turned grim. "In spite of the increased beatings and sometimes ridiculously petty mistreatments." Orrin had told Matt that the front line Japanese pilots and troops were first-class fighting men, but the prison guards acted like capricious, sadistic children with deadly weapons.

Matt wasn't surprised by Doolittle's stunt. Doolittle had been a national hero long before the war, and Orrin, in particular, had practically worshipped the man when he and Matt were kids together. The son of a sailor, Matt had rooted for the Navy in the air races, but he still admired Doolittle immensely.

"You know, I wonder," Matt said absently, "if we could figure out a way and a reason to pull a stunt like Doolittle's here." He slapped his cousin on the back. "I think I'm going to keep that in my back pocket. I don't believe— You said they made him a general? I don't think General Doolittle would mind!"

Matt woke up in a white-painted, plank-wall room. A light breeze stirred the green curtains in the window, and at first he had no idea where he was. Then he remembered. *Why on earth did they put green curtains in here?* he asked himself. Yuck. *They must've thought it was regulation or something.* He sighed. His mouth was dry and he began to realize he hurt all over. His eyes were full of gummy goo and he wondered if he could get somebody's attention. He heard an abrupt snort beside him and turned his head to see Isak Rueben sleeping in a chair beside the hard bed he was lying on. Isak's head was tilted back, his mouth open, and Matt realized he'd been making those snorting sounds for some time.

"Chief Rueben," he managed to say. "Wake up, Chief."

Isak raised his head and blinked, then looked at Matt. He jumped to his feet, knocking the chair over with a loud crash. "Why, Cap'n Reddy! You've woke up at last! I'll . . . I'll run fetch somebody!" He darted from the room like a minnow.

"Not exactly the face I'd hoped to wake up beside," Matt murmured grumpily.

"Which face is that?" came Sandra's soft voice, almost beside his ear. He turned his head toward her and looked into her eyes.

"Yours is better," he said, and smacked his dry lips. Sandra was fully dressed but lying beside him on the skinny bed, with maybe a foot of it to herself. He wondered how long she'd been there.

"Chief Rueben had the duty," she answered his unasked question, "but when I came to check on you, he was asleep and I didn't want to wake him."

"My ship?" he asked, and she nodded. "He helped Spanky get her in the floating dry dock." She grinned. "And argued with Tabby like they were married the whole time." Sandra screwed her face up and tried to re-create Isak's weird voice. "You may be a engineerin' loo-tinnit now, Tabby, but I recollect when you was pilin' brontasarry turds on top o' each other! This is *my* . . . GD dry dock!"

Matt tried to laugh, but winced. Sandra rose and felt his forehead with the back of her hand, then stood. "I'll get you some water," she said.

"I'd rather you stay here."

A commotion in the hallway preceded Chief Gray's arrival with a pitcher and a cup. Others were behind him, trying to pass, but Gray kept them back with his elbows. He paused in the doorway. "Visitors?" he growled.

Sandra shook her head. "Not yet. Saan-Kakja and the ambassador first. Maybe others later." She motioned Gray forward with the pitcher.

Gray looked over his shoulder. "You heard the lady, you buncha savages! The Skipper requires further repose!" The crowd eased back down the hall, and Gray handed over the pitcher triumphantly.

"You too, Fitzhugh."

As taken aback by Sandra's use of his first name as by the dismissal, Gray backed out of the room.

Sandra turned back to Matt and poured water in the cup, then held it to his lips. "Slowly," she said. "Just a few sips." Matt obeyed, then looked at her. "Just us, just now, how bad is it?" he asked. His memory was returning, and he'd localized most of the pain to his right thigh and lower abdomen. Sandra took a breath.

"I nearly lost you," she whispered. "Again."

"Comes with the territory."

"I know," she said, soft but harsh. "That doesn't mean I have to like it." She looked at him. "A fragment of steel—Spanky saw it later and is convinced it was a piece of a rivet. He blames himself." She rolled her eyes. "Anyway, it went deep in your thigh and clipped the femoral artery. That was actually the worst of it, but we couldn't *find* the fragment! It just kept going up—and we were afraid it got into your intestines. That's why you're split from just above the knee past your belt line. It actually did get past your pelvis, but stopped short of anything . . . else. Thank God. You'll be very sore for a while!"

"Huh," Matt said and looked under the sheet at the long, bandaged area. "Did you go ahead and take out my appendix while you had the hood up?"

"This is *not* funny," Sandra snapped.

"No, it's not," Matt agreed. "Sorry. But it might have been a good idea. . . ."

"I was busy! That fight killed some good men and Lemurians, and hurt a lot more. Carl Bashear was badly burned, and Ed Palmer had a broken collarbone and arm, and internal bleeding—"

"And we lost Norm Kutas," Matt said, remembering. "Damn."

"We lost Norm," Sandra confirmed, "and nine Lemurians. It could have been much worse. Probably should have been. We were lucky."

"Well. At least we got that Jap destroyer," Matt said quietly. "That's one less thing to worry about."

Sandra hesitated, and his eyes narrowed. "We *did* get her, didn't we?"

"Spanky is almost certain we did," Sandra admitted.

"Almost?"

Sandra's eyes flared. "Yes, almost! She was badly hit, she has no fuel or any way to get it, and even if she didn't sink, she has nowhere to go! Ultimately, we *did* get her, whether we saw her sink or not, and your ship and your crew—not to mention you—needed immediate attention! Mr. McFarlane made the right call, and you need to tell him so! Between that and the faulty rivets, he thinks he let you down, and we—everybody—need Spanky at the top of his game right now."

Matt was nodding. "You're right," he said.

"What?"

"I said, 'You're right'!"

A tentative smile touched Sandra's lips. "Well. Of course I am." She paused. "Saan-Kakja and Lord Forester will be back here soon, I'm sure. They met you when you came ashore, but I doubt you remember." Her expression changed. "There have been a lot of developments, and no doubt they'll want to hear your views. In the meantime, do you feel like eating anything?"

Saan-Kakja, Ambassador Forester, Chack, and Spanky arrived while Matt was eating a soft, colorless goo he couldn't recognize, but which tasted something like tapioca pudding without the "fish eggs," as he called them. After a short visit, they described the current situation in the east and west, and Matt had trouble finishing his meal. He was glad to see that the ambassador and Saan-Kakja seemed to like each other. That was going to be important.

"What are your plans, Your Excellency?" Matt asked Saan-Kakja.

"We must send everything we can to Generaal Aalden immediately!" she said. "His position is precarious, and the war in the east is stable for now."

Matt was shaking his head.

"You do not agree?"

"With respect, I think you should stick to the plan. High Admiral Jenks has done well, but if you interrupt his supply line now, it'll take many more months to amass the combat power he needs to take the war to the Doms, and we have to keep them off balance. The Grik are the greatest short-term threat, but the Doms will catch up if we give them too much time." He looked at Forester. "I'm sure you would agree."

Forester nodded reluctantly. "The situation in the Empire remains unstable, though the Governor-Empress has made great strides." He looked at Saan-Kakja. "Your continued support and clear dedication to the war in the east will further strengthen her position. Like you, I yearn to aid your General Alden in this time of trial, but I would actually rather send Imperial troops to do it than give anyone in my country the mistaken impression that your resolve there is weakening."

Saan-Kakja was blinking hesitant agreement. "Perhaps. I *would* like to see more Imperial troops in the war against the Grik, and I do not want to even seem to be wavering in my support for my sister, Rebeccaa." She jerked a nod. "It will be as you say, Mr. Ambaas-a-dor. The Fil-pin Lands will continue to concentrate our efforts in the east—but in exchange, I do want more Imperiaal troops brought here, and then committed in the west."

"Very well," Forester said. "I'm sure the Governor-Empress will happily agree. We are in this war together, and the more of it we fight together, the stronger I think we will be."

"But . . . What about Generaal Aalden?" Chack asked. "He must be reinforced."

"He will be," Matt said. "You can count on it. First Fleet took a beating, but it wasn't wrecked—and I'll bet the guys and gals on Andaman and in Baalkpan have already figured out a few surprises to counter the latest Grik stunts. I've got a few ideas myself." He looked thoughtful, and shifted the pillows that kept him propped up. Sandra saw his difficulty and helped. He smiled at her. "What's the status of the regiment you're raising here?" he asked Chack.

"It is not ready for combat. The new weapons are only now being issued, and the troops must grow familiar with them." He shrugged. "So must I."

"And Risa's regiment in Baalkpan?"

"Much further along," Chack confessed. "She has had them longer and has had the weapons from the start. The arsenal here is catching up but . . ." He blinked annoyance.

"But you think you can have your troops ready for action before *Walker* is ready for sea again?"

Chack would have winced if his face had the muscles for it. He'd seen *Walker*'s damage.

"Yes Cap-i-taan. Will we go to Indiaa and aid . . . Generaal Aalden?"

Matt knew Chack's greatest concern was for his beloved Safir Maraan, but he would never say so in this context. He bit his lip. "Maybe . . . but maybe not." He shrugged and pain shot up from his wound, and he shook his head sheepishly. "I've been keeping something in my back pocket for some time now. Maybe this is the time to take it out and have a look at it." He looked at Chack. "It doesn't involve going to India, but if we can pull it off, it should definitely help the expeditionary force that's in a jam there." He paused a moment, looking at the expectant faces. "As a matter of fact," he said with growing conviction, "if we play our cards right, I think the stunt taking shape in my head might just leave the Grik with their ugly necks stuck out just far enough for us to cut their damn throats!"

EPILOGUE

The South of Africa

Lieutenant Toryu Miyata was much recovered from his grueling ordeal. He still mourned his lost friends, but he'd been close enough to death himself, from exposure, that their loss had dimmed, and become somehow remote. Since his rescue, however, and during his gradual recuperation, he'd grown to realize that he'd stumbled into perhaps the most bizarre situation yet encountered on this strange world.

He hadn't seen it himself, but someone once told him about an odd book they'd read before the war about a place called Shangri-La. Somehow, he thought he remembered that the tale was set in China or Tibet, or some such place, but he'd honestly begun to wonder if he hadn't actually found it here on what had to be the south coast of Africa, despite the chill. He hadn't spent any time out of doors yet, or really even out of the room he'd been recuperating in, but there were windows, and he spent a lot of time staring out at the strange city. Never in his life had he seen such an . . . extraordinary combination of peoples—and not all of them were human!—yet they commingled and appeared to get along as well amid the bustle, as any similar number might in Tokyo!

And the architecture! He knew of nothing to compare it

to. He was young, and before the Navy he'd never traveled before, but the substantial buildings he saw from his window combined what he considered ancient traditional, eastern design with what he supposed was some kind of equally ancient western construction—and something else completely different—in an amazingly complementary fashion that he wouldn't have thought possible. The result was a harmony of wood and stone, columns and high pagodas that had clearly been blending together long enough that it seemed somehow right. Curved, ornate roofs predominated, covered with tile or copper, but the columns that supported them flowed as well, sometimes tapering toward the center, with admirable stonework at the top and bottom.

Bright colors abounded beneath the often-overcast sky, and teeming throngs surged in the open markets in equally garish costumes. Stunningly bizarre animals, the like of which he'd never seen among the Grik, pulled long trains of carts loaded with goods or passengers. Several times he saw columns of troops dressed in a warmer, more practical, but also more ornate version of what some of his comrades had termed the Grik Roman-style military garb, march past his window, the crowd parting before them. Just as among the civilian populace, all manner of beings were in their ranks. It was outlandish and amazing and disconcerting all at once.

His nurse—a female human!—appeared normal enough, and was clearly of Asian descent, though he had no idea what other blood she carried. She was nice, attentive, and even beautiful, he thought, but he didn't understand a word she said. It was all so confusing. His nurse was Asian, but his "rescuers" spoke English—and he would have sworn one of them had a German accent! He didn't think he was a prisoner—no one seemed to guard him—but what was he? Probably not exactly a guest. He believed he was recovered enough that he might be ready to explore, but hesitated to push his bounds without talking to someone first, and as far as he could tell, except for the nurse, he'd been forgotten.

He was alone at the moment, and heavy, booted footsteps sounded in the corridor beyond his chamber. He tensed, expecting visitors at last, and stood from his chair. He wished he could meet his benefactors in his uniform, but its remnants had been destroyed, he was sure, and he tried to affect a stoic expression while dressed only in the ankle-length woolen robe he'd been given.

Two men appeared in the broad doorway, accompanied by what looked exactly like one of the Lemurian allies of the Americans! All regarded him intently for a moment before stepping inside. He remained standing, stiffly at attention.

"You look better," said a tall, bearded man in accented English. He wore a battered dark blue, or maybe black, hat with a scuffed leather brim with an embroidered cockade Toryu didn't recognize. He also wore an equally battered dark blue jacket, but his white shirt, trousers, and heavy boots were clearly much newer. Toryu thought he recognized the German who'd found him. The man spoke to the others in what sounded like the same language the nurse used, then turned to face him again. "I am Becher Lange," the man said, and shrugged. "My kapitan calls me kapitan leutnant now, but I was only a fireman in SMS *Amerika* when she staggered into this world, so it makes no difference to me what the old man calls me. You and I have met, though you may not remember. Call me Becher." He extended a hand, and Toryu saw a bright metal oval on his wrist, held by a leather band. He also noted how matter-of-factly he spoke of how he got here, obviously fully expecting Toryu to know what he meant.

"Thank you, sir," Toryu replied, he hoped properly, in his imperfect English. Awkwardly, he shook the hand. He'd never done that before. "You and your companion doubtless saved my life, for which I am grateful, but the news I carry is of great importance to you, I assure you."

"*Ja*. That is what you said."

Toryu blinked. He had no memory of what he'd said to the man.

"I will introduce these others," Becher said, "and you will tell them your news."

Toryu bowed. "Of course." Never did it occur to him that talking to any enemy of the Grik might be treason. He knew almost nothing about his current situation, but he'd somehow managed to escape the Grik—and that madman Kurokawa. He was dead to them, and if he didn't help these people, they would all be dead, eventually.

The other human with Becher was introduced as General Marcus Kim—and what kind of name was that?—who represented the military high command of this . . . Republic of Real People, Becher called it. The Lemurian was "Inquisitor Kon-Choon." The term "inquisitor" made Toryu nervous, until it was explained that he was actually a high-level intelligence officer. That made sense.

"What do you know of us here?" Becher translated for Kim.

"Personally, nothing, sir. The Grik may know more, but I do not think so." There was further discussion in the strange tongue, and Toryu caught the word "Ghaarrichk'k." Apparently, that was the local name for the implacable, barbarous creatures he'd escaped. This was quickly confirmed.

"We know of the Ghaarrichk'k, the Grik, here," Becher confirmed. "We maintain a frontier against them, and patrolling it is how I found you." He paused. "We know of them, and know they will not talk. All contact with them has been hostile. Beyond that, we know little. Are they numerous? How vast is their territory? *Can* we talk to them?"

"You can talk to them," Toryu admitted, frowning. "In fact, I was sent here to speak with you on their behalf." He shook his head. "They want an alliance with you—against other people like us." He waved his hand to include the Lemurian. "All of us."

"What kind of alliance? What are their terms?" Becher asked for the Inquisitor.

"A military alliance, sir, and the terms are simple: Join or die."

"That is a . . . bold ultimatum to make against people they do not know," Becher growled. "Can they make good on their threat?"

"That is their way," Toryu stated simply. "Sir, I know nothing of your land, its population, resources, or military capability." He pointed at the window. "All I know is what I have seen through that, so I cannot say if they can conquer you or not. I will tell you everything I know, however. I was sent here with a message, a message I have delivered. Having escaped them, I will not return, so it is in my interest to counsel you as best I can." He paused. "The Grik are without number, and their empire stretches from just north of here to India, at least along the coasts. You do know the shape of the world?"

"*Ja*," Becher said, and Toryu nodded. Whatever the others were, Becher was a sailor, and obviously a relatively recent arrival.

"They had conquered their way as far as the East Indies before they were thrown back by those other people I mentioned," Toryu continued, "but I fear that is only a temporary setback, since their numbers are almost infinitely greater than their enemies." He looked Becher in the eye. "They are involved in the biggest war they have ever known, but whether they can conquer you or not, they will eventually try. And if they succeed . . . they do not take prisoners, but for food."

Becher spoke animatedly with the others for several long moments before turning back. "Why, then, do I feel that joining them is not what you recommend?"

"Because they will surely destroy you then," Toryu answered softly, "starting with your souls. I hate them, you see. I hate them for what they are and what they do—and because they have already destroyed the souls of my people they hold in their power."

"Who are your people?" Becher asked, also softly, and Toryu stiffened.

"I came to this world aboard the Japanese Imperial Navy battle cruiser *Amagi* almost two years ago. At that time, we were allied with Germany and Italy against virtually the rest of the world, but most especially the British and Americans."

"The Japs have joined the kaiser? And the Italians?" Becher laughed. "When last I knew, you both were leaning the other way . . . and America came in against us?"

Toryu looked at him strangely. "Ah . . . no. We did not join the kaiser. We fought against him—with the Americans, before I was born. . . . Sir, if you would: when did you come to this world?"

"Nineteen fourteen," Becher said, frowning. "Nearly

thirty years ago now. My ship, SMS *Amerika*—that is ironic!—was taken from the passenger service and commissioned as an armed merchant cruiser. We captured the crews of nine British ships—that is why there are so many Britishers here with us!—and scuttled their ships." His expression grew faraway. "Never did war prisoners enjoy such luxury! *Amerika* was a gorgeous thing!" Almost forcibly, he returned to the present. "She was badly damaged in battle with the *Morrie*, we called her. The *Mauritania*! She was armed too! What a fight! She *was* faster, of course, with her damned turbines, but so big, we could not miss her! Both of us were damaged, and we broke off the fight in the storm. But you might tell me! Did we sink the *Morrie*? I actually hope we did not"—he grinned—"but sometimes I hope we did! We were old rivals before the war for the Blue Riband!"

Toryu was confused. "I . . . I do not think so. There was a *Mauritania* carrying British troops to Singapore in 1942, but she might have been a newer ship with the same name."

"Well, but what of the war? You Japs—with battle cruisers no less!—have joined us?"

Toryu's face heated. "We did *not* join you! Your kaiser was defeated! Our war, besides our conquest of Asia, began little more than two years ago, and the Imperial Japanese Navy, the most powerful in the world, was in the process of destroying the combined fleets of the Americans and British! Only your submarines were of any use!" He stopped, realizing he'd given offense, but Becher's expression only looked . . . odd again.

"The kaiser defeated? Impossible!" he muttered. Then he said something that stunned Toryu Miyata to the bone. "Yet another, different world again, then." He saw Toryu's expression and grunted. "You are surprised? Let me try to explain to you, quickly, of our land and our peoples, and you may understand. You may also then pass a . . . better-informed counsel."

The Lemurian jabbered suddenly, then, and Becher listened before turning back to Toryu.

"In fact, if you feel able, Inquisitor Choon believes you should meet immediately with the kaiser—*our* kaiser, or cae-saar, as they say, at the War Palace. The maps there are the best."

"I am able," Toryu assured him, a little taken aback but determined. "After all, there is little time to lose."

They supplied him with boots and a cloak and led him down the corridor to a side entrance facing the cobblestone street, and he stepped outside for the first time in . . . three weeks? Four? He jerked back when he came almost face-to-face with a huge, drooling, camel-like face that regarded him with disinterest before it swung away—on the end of a long, gray-furred neck, almost as long as a giraffe's, but not nearly so upright. Becher laughed.

"He likes you! Sometimes those will bite!" He gestured to a long car, like a Pullman, hitched behind the beast and another like it. "We have steam cars," Becher announced proudly. "We have been busy in our thirty years! But we do not bring them into the city." He waved around. So many strange creatures! "They unnerve the animals—and the people!"

On either side of the Pullman car sat three guards in their Romanesque costumes, mounted on ordinary horses. One of them waved.

"There you are! Good to see you up and about!" The man paused at Toryu's confused expression. "Blimey! I'm the other bloke what found you! Saved you, I did!" The man, also wearing a gray-streaked beard, tossed his chin at Becher. "You didn't think that dastardly Hun'd give a toss if you lived or died?" He was grinning. "I'm Leftenant Doocy Meek, if you care to know!"

"I am appreciative, sir," Toryu managed as he was hurried into the car.

"Doocy is a funny man," Becher said gruffly, pulling Toryu into a seat beside him. "We all take our turns riding the frontier—anyone beneath the rank of centurion," he added, by way of further explanation. "We, most of us from *Amerika*, are still considered part of the foreign centuries, but we also guard the War Palace and all access to it!"

Toryu started to ask how that could be, when the car shuddered and began to move. After that, his questions about the city came in rapid fire.

This amazingly exotic capital city of the Republic of Real People, or Volksrepublik, as Becher called it, was named Aalek-saan-draa, and the mixture of architecture and cultures that created it began to make some sense to Toryu as Becher answered his questions, and he saw the evidence with his own eyes.

He finally knew, *knew*, that whatever had happened to his *Amagi*—and the Americans—in the Java Sea was not unique. Many peoples had found themselves in this place over the millennia. The southern cape of Afri-kaa formed a bottleneck of sorts, between the land and the not-so-distant ice of Antarctica. The storms that plagued the same passage on Toryu's world were even more intense here, and the seas more mountainous. And it was *cold*, if not always on land, then forever at sea. In a way, it was only logical, he decided, that so many people, so many ships throughout the centuries, trying to round the bitter cape, perhaps even unaware of the change they'd endured, should wind up here. They would be exhausted, their ships almost destroyed, but where they would be lost upon some other shore, here they found welcome . . . and a home.

The oldest inhabitants were Lemurians, who'd wound up there after their ancient exodus to escape the Grik. These were later joined by Chinese explorers, Ptolemaic Egyptians, black Africans, and even Romans (from the tenth century!) who established what had become the republic. That didn't add up. Toryu knew little of history, but there seemed to be a number of . . . different . . . histories represented here. Histories even his limited knowledge told him were not quite right.

He shook his head as his mind flailed in this whirlpool of new, contradictory information, and he wondered briefly why no such place existed elsewhere that he'd been. Then he bitterly remembered the Grik. Any lost explorers, traders, or even small fleets that arrived off *their* shores were only prey to be conquered and devoured. But why did the Americans and their Lemurian allies not have other . . . friends as well? Were their outposts too remote and scattered? Was there no choke point in their seas? Becher told him that the castaways most often came from the west, in "modern times." Examples of those had been Boers, British, Dutch, and Portuguese. Did that mean the . . . force that took them was more prevalent in the Atlantic? Was it even the same? It was all so confusing! He suddenly felt strangely relieved to learn that *Amerika*'s arrival was the most recent, by far, so, though not unheard of, the phenomenon was rare.

The enmity of their old war suppressed, her German crew and mixed allied prisoners had been working together for thirty years to improve republic technology to a level similar to what Toryu knew of the Alliance. Becher didn't mention aircraft or steamships, which they obviously had the technology to make, but as the car wound through the streets, drawing nearer to the sea, Toryu saw with his own eyes what looked like good artillery. He also inspected the small arms of the escort riding alongside. They were bolt action, probably large-bore single shots, evidenced by the lack of any floor plate in front of the triggerguard. Decent weapons, then. He wondered what else they had, but didn't press. Despite what they'd already told him, they had no real reason to trust him yet. He'd admitted the rest of his people were in league with the Grik, after all.

"What is that?" he suddenly cried, pointing at a . . . person? Working alongside others of its kind in what increasingly resembled a seaport district. "I mean . . . those?" The creatures were as tall as humans, but with fur and tails—and their faces were more human than . . . Becher followed his gaze, and frowned.

"They are . . . how should I say . . . half-bloods, yes?"

"Half-bloods?"

"Crossbreeds, hybrids. Made long ago when only the Chinese and Mi-Anaaka—that is the name for the Lemurians, as you call them—lived in this place."

Toryu shuddered in spite of himself.

Becher noticed. "You do not like that? Well, neither does anyone else. Interbreeding is strictly verboten—forbidden—in the republic. No one, not humans, not Mi-Anaaka, not even the half-bloods themselves are happy such things once occurred. They cannot blame themselves for what they are, and neither does anyone else—now. They are their own species and intent on remaining so. Such things no longer happen; it is the law, but . . . women have always been in short supply. Not often are they on the ships that come. We brought a few, and there were African women. Some others came, and there have always been a few, but never enough, even now." Becher sighed. "Mi-Anaaka remain the most populous citizens by far.

"We and those who came before have built a good country here, a country to be proud of, but it has not been easy, as you can imagine! There are so many views and so many threats! This is a republic, as I have said, but there is an . . . authoritarian ruler whose word is absolute, and most often just. You must learn the history of this country, but, in short, there was war here for many generations between the humans, Mi-Anaaka, and the half-bloods. It took the Romans to end that—and tension still simmers! Add to that the Grik! Our society is, of necessity, integrated, but very disciplined. We have a tradition of welcoming new arrivals because of low population levels. You would think things would have equalized by now, but women do remain in short supply. This is a harsh land at times, and though we avoid major clashes with the Grik on the frontier, those clashes do occur. There is also the weather, and many predatory monsters encroach on our lands, perhaps driven by the Grik, that can't be hunted to their source across the Grik frontiers! And there have been other violent encounters at this geographic bottleneck. Some of the occasional arrivals are NOT friendly." He paused. "This is . . . a bad land for women. A bad *world*. And though we are not now at war, we must always remain prepared. With the news you bring, I hope we are prepared enough." He stopped, peering southwest.

"Ah! There it is," he said with some humor. "The War Palace!"

Toryu was still digesting what Becher had said, but when he looked toward the harbor, he was even more stunned. He'd seen the garish ways rickshaws and taxis were sometimes decorated, particularly when *Amagi* visited the Philippines once, before the war, but what had been done to SMS *Amerika* was beyond even that, and on a massive scale.

The ship's elegant lines remained essentially the same as when she arrived, with her straight up-and-down bow and two tall, slender funnels. Toryu later learned the once-great luxury liner was 670 feet long, 74 feet wide, and displaced more than 22,000 tons. She boasted twin screws and two triple-expansion engines that once drove her through the sea at close to 20 knots, and was still fitted to carry 2,500 passengers in reasonable-to-palatial style. All that was likely still true, but the ship's upper works were now decorated just at sweepingly as the buildings in the city. Her riveted hull was a riot of colors, painted with everything from what looked like eagles to dragons. Colorful awnings fluttered over her broad decks, and a truly wild variety of flags and banners streamed to leeward of her high, thin foremast.

"Can she still move?" Toryu wondered aloud, seeing black smoke wisping above the aft funnel.

"*Ja*, if she must," Becher said with an awkward chuckle. "She is the War Palace, after all. The point is that she can move the kaiser and his staff to other places. We have several port cities, almost as large as this, up the southwest coast." He paused. "Is it *practical* to move her?" He shrugged. "Steam is maintained to power her electrics and her pumps, and her engines are tested twice a year. But she has not been out of the water for over thirty years. There is no dry dock large enough to accommodate her. Whether it is *advisable* to move her is another thing. Her bottom plates have become thin, I think."

The strange beasts pulling the car grumbled to a stop, and the party stepped out onto a dock and onto a long pier that seemed almost permanently attached to the ship. Doocy climbed down from his horse and joined them.

"The anchorage remains well protected," he said, pointing at some low mountains to the southeast. "That's why we keep her here." There were other ships in the harbor too, sailing schooners mostly, but there were also what looked like iron monitors with low freeboards, tall funnels, and big guns snugged to the pier leading to the big ship. "Those are for harbor defense," Doocy added, noting Toryu's gaze. "They cannot survive in the heavy seas beyond—but they serve their function. The schooners trade with our other ports and other places as well, but no sailing ship can hope to round the cape from the east."

"Even if they could, they would find nothing but Grik along the eastern shore," Toryu warned.

"Aye. But perhaps there are others beyond?" Doocy pressed, and Toryu wondered what all he may have said while he was delirious, if Doocy already knew.

"There are," he confirmed simply as they strode along the pier. He'd already determined to be completely honest with these people. He had no more reason to trust them than they did him—yet—but they'd saved him and they weren't Grik. That's all that really mattered for now.

They came at last to *Amerika*'s garish side and were met by more Romanesque guards, who saluted his companions in the modern way. He didn't know what he'd expected—a fist to the breastplate? Maybe German traditions prevailed aboard the ship? He was led inside, down several ornate corridors, up a grand staircase, and finally into what had to have once been the first-class dining salon. It was a very large compartment, and, unlike the exterior of the ship, its passenger-era elegance had not been tampered with—with the exception of a raised "throne," for lack of a better term, built of matching woods and adorned with similar carvings to those decorating the entire chamber. Upon the throne sat a Lemurian, a Mi-Anaaka, dressed in silklike robes of embroidered blue that matched the curtains and valances over the windows, but of a higher, more ornate quality.

Beside the throne stood a tall, thin man of at least eighty, Toryu guessed, wearing a black-blue coat with twin rows of shiny buttons. He wore a wide, white, waxed mustache, but the only hair on his weathered scalp was a thin white wisp. A dark hat similar to Becher's was clutched against his side by an arm.

Toryu's companions saluted, and Toryu saluted and jerked a bow. As fascinating as he found the pair, however, his eyes immediately swept to the carefully painted map that dominated the entire wall behind the throne. The detail was astonishing in certain places, almost as if he were viewing the world from the distant sky above. The borders of the republic were clearly marked, encompassing all of southern Africa behind a diagonal frontier that extended some distance up the west coast. Beyond that line, the detail was much less defined, but the coastlines bordering the Atlantic Ocean had been rendered with confidence, even if they didn't quite match his own memory. Somehow he knew that confidence must have been a result of exploration, because all the coasts east of the cape, coasts *he* knew, were less exact.

"Ahh! You admire our atlas, eh?" asked the old man in a surprisingly firm, lightly accented English. Toryu was startled for an instant, but the man had apparently once commanded a passenger liner, after all. "We wandered the Atlantic and charted some of the . . . ah . . . differences, before we came to this place," he said. "That was quite an adventurous time," he reflected with a frown. "And there are some . . . interesting, and often unpleasant, places beyond our little refuge! Perhaps you can add to our knowledge of points east?" He paused, glancing at the Lemurian. "Excuse me. May I present His Most Excellent Highness, the Emperor Nig-Taak. You may call him Kaiser, Cae-saar, Tszaar—whatever. He does not mind." He smiled toothlessly. "I am Kapitan Adlar Von Melhausen, commander of this ship and keeper of the War Palace, by the kaiser's grace. You have already met General Marcus Kim and Inquisitor Choon, as well as your rescuers, Misters Lange and Meek!"

Toryu bowed again. "I am honored, sir. I am Lieutenant Toryu Miyata, formerly Junior Navigating Officer of His Imperial Japanese Majesty's Ship *Amagi*. Please let me express my appreciation for my rescue and the hospitality that has been shown me."

"You are welcome, of course," said the kaiser in a soft, strangely accented voice, speaking for the first time. "As Mr. Lange was instructed to inform you, many people have found refuge with us in the past." He waved a hand. "It is an unsympathetic world beyond our land. It can be harsh even here." He peered closely at Miyata with intense, almost purple-brown eyes. "I understand you bring word that further . . . unpleasantness threatens to descend upon us."

"Yes, your . . ." he paused. "Yes, Your Majesty. I was *ordered* to come to you with an offer of a sort of alliance with the, ah, Ghaarrichk'k, as they call themselves, against other people in the east, similar to those who abide here. People both human and Mi-Anaaka, who threaten the Grik for the first time in their history. I stress again that I was commanded to do this, though, in honesty, I cannot recommend it, and I humbly ask you for asylum."

Nig-Taak leaned back on his throne. "Indeed? Well, fear not. You shall have asylum. But what do the Grik think they can do to us if we do not accept their offer to join their war against others of our kind?"

"They think they will annihilate you," Toryu answered softly. Nig-Taak laughed.

"Do they, now? They have had long enough to try in the past—we have guarded against each other for over three hundred years! How can they now do—while threatened elsewhere!—what they have never dared attempt in the past?"

"With respect, Lord, they do not like this land; it can be too cold for them. They have never considered it a worthy place to conquer. As for daring . . . My lord, you must believe me! If you do not join them, they *will* come—unless they are more sorely pressed elsewhere than they are at present."

"Let them come!" Von Melhausen snapped. "We can meet them anywhere they strike with fifteen, perhaps twenty thousand, disciplined troops!"

Toryu paled. "Kapitan, Your Majesty, I beg you to hear! I will not counsel you to agree to their demands, but you must know I watched them assemble perhaps half a *million* warriors for an *oversea* campaign! That force was hurled back, but it pales to insignificance compared to what they now prepare! They have built a thousand ships in only the past year, and they have learned much from their enemies—and, yes, those of my people who aid them. They have artillery, aircraft . . . and just imagine what they could bring against you this close to their major population centers! I am sure your troops are excellent, but it is not that they have not dared to come against you. They have not *cared* to!" He paused.

"Maybe they will not come immediately. The Alliance against them has grown amazingly and assembled powerful forces of its own, qualitatively better than the Grik." He shook his head. "But, honestly, I fear they are taunting a giant in the dark! They cannot truly know what they face! I have *seen* their multitudes, how quickly they can breed if they desire. I have seen the scope of their preparations, and it is not a . . . natural thing. Even now their population nears the maximum they can even feed! I fear they will destroy the Alliance in time, and even if they wait until then to come, they will bring more warriors than they will *want* to survive!"

Toryu heard Doocy gasp and saw Von Melhausen pale. Nig-Taak did not appear to react beyond a rapid blinking. Toryu knew almost nothing of Lemurians, and had no idea what it meant.

"I cannot believe it!" Von Melhausen snorted when he gathered himself. "And why *should* we believe it, my kaiser?" He gestured at Toryu. "This man just wanders in out of the wilderness with this wild tale . . ."

"*I* believe it, Kap-i-taan," Nig-Taak said resignedly. "All at once, it is perfectly clear. We always wondered, but now it makes flawless sense! Do you not see? They never attacked us here in force because they did not *want* our land, but now they cannot afford a threat to their rear! That is the source of this offer! Then, whether we help them or not, they will merely use us to stabilize their numbers once more!"

He turned back to Toryu. "You say we must not help them and I agree. They are monsters and enemies of my race since before the beginning of time, but . . . what else can we do?"

To Toryu, it was suddenly obvious. "They will likely think I have perished, with all the others with me. We were sent at a poor time of year. Suspecting my envoy did not survive, they might send another. If it arrives, perhaps under the direction of a more . . . committed ambassador, you must stall them and prepare."

"Prepare for what?" Von Melhausen asked grudgingly, almost hopelessly, as the enormity and probable veracity of Toryu's revelation sank in.

"To fight them!" Toryu insisted. "Build more weapons,

grow your armies, and somehow contact your *natural* allies! The ones who fight them already!"

"We still have the transmitter aboard here, though it is never used," mused Becher. Then he shrugged at Miyata. "It is a dangerous world, and we never know what we might attract! We do listen. . . ." He paused. "We might send them a message!"

"That you must *not* do!" Toryu warned. "Though he never told the Grik, my former commander, Captain Kurokawa—he styles himself General of the Sea now—has retained communication devices. He will probably hear any message you send, and warn his masters!"

"Then how can we contact these natural allies you speak of?" Nig-Taak asked, frustrated.

Toryu looked at him. "Your Highness, you must go and meet them."

"How?" Doocy demanded. "As we've told you, no sailing vessel nor the few seagoing steamers we have can round the cape. They are just too small to survive those seas!"

Toryu gazed almost helplessly around. There was only one answer, and it was obvious to him.

"What?" challenged Von Melhausen. "You cannot mean . . . ! But *Amerika*'s hull has grown as thin as an egg! I could knock a hole in it with a hammer in the shaft alleys!"

"But an egg is still very strong," Kaiser Nig-Taak reminded quietly. "And I am sure you will avoid any hostile hammers."

"It will take months to prepare," Von Melhausen objected, his mind already shifting to embrace the inevitable. "Some repairs are essential. This ship has not been to sea for twenty years—and neither have I!"

"Then begin your repairs at once, *mein* Kap-i-taan," Nig-Taak advised. "You do not have *unlimited* months. One or two, you may have, if God permits."

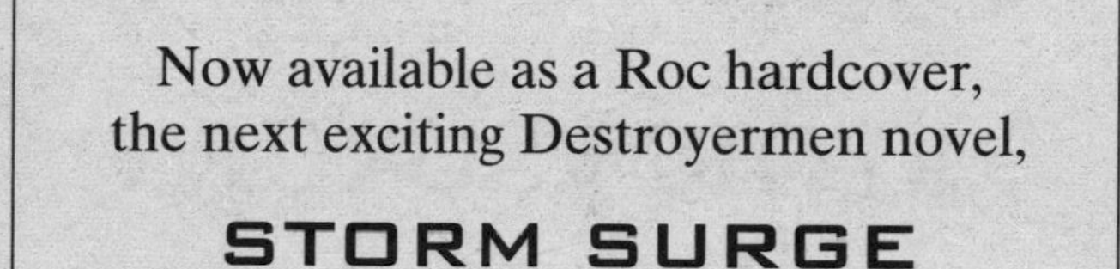
Now available as a Roc hardcover,
the next exciting Destroyermen novel,
STORM SURGE

New in hardcover from
national bestselling author

Taylor Anderson

STORM SURGE

Destroyermen

In the Pacific, still healing from wounds inflicted by Hidoiame, Matt Reddy and the USS *Walker* begin to plan a bold raid against the very heart of the Grik Empire. But time is running out, and the Allied forces in the west must launch an unprecedented campaign to destroy the mighty Grik. All other plans go on hold when the attempt proves more difficult—and more heartbreakingly costly—than anyone imagined.

Meanwhile, the Alliance is on the offensive everywhere, but their enemies have a few surprises—new weaponry, new tactics, and a new alliance with powerful and deadly forces...

Also in the series:

Iron Gray Sea • *Firestorm* • *Rising Tides*
Distant Thunders • *Maelstorm* • *Crusade* • *Into the Storm*

Available wherever books are sold or at
penguin.com

facebook.com/acerocbooks

R0159